Centerville Library.
Washington-Centerville Public Library
Centerville, Ohio
DISCARD

W9-BAZ-327

THE WHITE MOUNTAIN

DAVID WINGROVE is the Hugo Award-winning co-author (with Brian Aldiss) of *Trillion Year Spree: The History of Science Fiction*. He is also the co-author of the first three MYST books – novelizations of one of the world's bestselling computer games. He lives in north London with his wife and four daughters.

Centerville Library
Washington-Centerville Public Library
Centerville, Ohio

CHUNG KUO

THE WHITE MOUNTAIN

CHUNG KUO

BOOK 8

DAVID WINGROVE

CORVUS

SF

First published in Great Britain in 1991 by New English Library.

This revised and updated edition published in special edition hardback, trade paperback, and e-book in Great Britain in 2014 by Corvus, an imprint of Atlantic Books Ltd.

Copyright © David Wingrove, 1991, 2014

The moral right of David Wingrove to be identified as the author of this work has been asserted by him in accordance with the Copyright, Designs and Patents Act of 1988.

All rights reserved. No part of this publication may be reproduced, stored in a retrieval system, or transmitted in any form or by any means, electronic, mechanical, photocopying, recording, or otherwise, without the prior permission of both the copyright owner and the above publisher of this book.

This novel is entirely a work of fiction. The names, characters and incidents portrayed in it are the work of the author's imagination. Any resemblance to actual persons, living or dead, events or localities, is entirely coincidental.

10 9 8 7 6 5 4 3 2 1

A CIP catalogue record for this book is available from the British Library.

Hardback ISBN: 978 0 85789 823 4
Trade paperback ISBN: 978 0 85789 824 1
E-book ISBN: 978 0 85789 825 8

Printed in Great Britain.

Corvus
An imprint of Atlantic Books Ltd
Ormond House
26–27 Boswell Street
London
WC1N 3JZ

www.corvus-books.co.uk

CONTENTS

For Mark and Ben, the new generation

THE WHITE MOUNTAIN

Book Eight

The way never acts yet nothing is left undone.
Should lords and princes be able to hold fast to it,
The myriad creatures will be transformed of their
    own accord.
After they are transformed, should desire raise its head,
I shall press it down with the weight of the nameless
    uncarved block.
The nameless uncarved block
Is but freedom from desire,
And if I cease to desire and remain still,
The empire will be at peace of its own accord.

—Lao Tzu, *Tao Te Ching*, Book One, XXXVII
    (Sixth Century BC)

INTRODUCTION

Chung Kuo. The words mean 'Middle Kingdom' and since 221 BC, when the First Emperor, Ch'in Shih Huang Ti, unified the seven Warring States, it is what the 'black-haired people', the Han, or Chinese, have called their great country. The middle Kingdom – for them it was the whole world; a world bounded by great mountain chains to the north and west, by the sea to east and south. Beyond was only desert and barbarism. So it was for two thousand years.

By the turn of the twenty-second century, however, Chung Kuo had come to mean much more. For more than a century, the Empire of the Han had encompassed the world, the Earth's bloated population of forty billion contained in vast, hive-like cities that spanned whole continents. The Council of Seven – Han lords, *T'ang*, each more powerful than the greatest of the ancient emperors – ruled Chung Kuo with an iron authority, their boast that they had ended Change and stopped the Great Wheel turning. But Change was coming.

It had begun twelve years before, when a new generation of powerful young merchants – Dispersionists, formed mainly of *Hung Mao*, or Westerners – had challenged the authority of the Seven, demanding an end to the Edict of Technological Control, the cornerstone of Han stability, and a return to the Western ideal of unfettered progress. In the spate of assassination and counter-assassination that followed, something had to give, and the destruction of Dispersionist starship, *The New Hope*, signalled the beginning of the 'War-that-wasn't-a-War', an incestuous power struggle fought within the City's levels. The Seven won that War, but at a price they could ill afford. Suddenly they were weak – weaker than they had been in their entire history. The new T'ang were young and inexperienced. Worse than that, they were divided against themselves.

But the War was only the first small sign of greater disturbances to come, for down in the lowest levels of the City, in the lawless regions 'below the Net' and in the overcrowded decks just above, new currents of unrest have awoken. In the years since the War, *Ko Ming* – revolutionary – groups have proliferated, and none more powerful or deadly than the *Ping Tiao*, or Levellers. The War was no longer a struggle for power, but for survival...

PART SIXTEEN   **THE SHATTERED LAND**

Autumn 2207

Chapter 67

THE TIGER'S MOUTH

Ebert looked about him, then turned back to Mu Chua, smiling.

'You've done well, Mu Chua. I'd hardly have recognized the place. They'll be here any time now, so remember, these are important business contacts and I want to impress them. Are the new girls dressed as I asked?'

Mu Chua nodded.

'Good. Well, keep them until after my entrance. These things must be done correctly, neh? One must whet their appetites before giving them the main course.'

'Of course, General. And may I say again how grateful I am that you honour my humble house. It is not every day that we play host to the nobility.'

Ebert nodded. 'Yes... but more is at stake than that, Mother Chua. If these *ch'un tzu* like what they see then it is more than likely you will receive an invitation.'

'An invitation?'

'Yes. To a *chao tai hui* – an entertainment – at one of the First Level mansions. This afternoon, I am told, there is to be a gathering of young princes. And they will need... how shall I put it?... special services.'

Mu Chua lowered her head. 'Whatever they wish. My girls are the very best. They are *shen nu*... god girls.'

Again Ebert nodded, but this time he seemed distracted. After a moment he looked back at Mu Chua. 'Did the wine from my father's cellar arrive?'

'It did, Excellency.'

'Good. Then you will ensure that our guests drink that and nothing else. They are to have nothing but the best.'

'Of course, General.'

'I want no deceptions, understand me, Mu Chua. Carry this off for me and I will reward you handsomely. Ten thousand *yuan* for you alone. And a thousand apiece for each of your girls. That's on top of your standard fees and expenses.'

Mu Chua lowered her head. 'You are too generous, Excellency...'

Ebert laughed. 'Maybe. But you have been good to me over the years, Mother Chua. And when this proposition was put before me, my first thought was of you and your excellent house. "Who better," I said to myself, "than Mu Chua at entertaining guests."' He smiled broadly at her, for once almost likeable. 'I am certain you will not let me down.'

Mu Chua lowered her head. 'Your guests will be transported...'

He laughed. 'Indeed...'

After Ebert had gone, she stood there a moment, almost in a trance at the thought of the ten thousand *yuan* he had promised. Together with what she would milk from this morning's entertainment, it would be enough. Enough, at last, to get out of here. To pay off her contacts in the Above and climb the levels.

Yes. She had arranged it all already. And now, at last, she could get away. Away from Whiskers Lu and the dreadful seediness of this place. Could find somewhere up-level and open up some small, discreet, cosy little house. Something very different, with its own select clientele and its own strict rules.

She felt a little shiver of anticipation pass through her then stirred herself, making the last few arrangements before the two men came, getting the girls to set out the wine and lay a table with the specially prepared sweetmeats.

She had no idea what Ebert was up to, but it was clear that he set a great deal of importance on this meeting. Only two days ago his man had turned up out of the blue and handed her twenty-five thousand *yuan* to have the house redecorated. It had meant losing custom for a day, but she had still come out of it ahead. Now it seemed likely that she would gain much more.

Even so, her suspicions of Hans Ebert remained. If he was up to something it was almost certain to be no good. But was that her concern? If she could make enough this one last time she could forget Ebert and his kind. This was her pass out. After today she need never compromise again. It would be as it was, before the death of her protector, Feng Chung.

The thought made her smile; made her spirits rise. Well, as this was the last time, she would make it special. Would make it something that even Hans Ebert would remember.

She busied herself, arranging things to perfection, then called in the four girls who were to greet their guests. Young girls, as Ebert had specified; none of them older than thirteen.

She looked at herself in the mirror, brushing a speck of powder from her cheek, then turned, hearing the bell sound out in the reception room. They were here.

She went out, kneeling before the two men, touching her forehead against her knees. Behind her, the four young girls did the same, standing at the same time that she stood. It was a calculated effect, and she saw how much it pleased the men.

Ebert had briefed her fully beforehand, providing her with everything she needed to know about them, from their business dealings down to their sexual preferences. Even so, she was still surprised by the contrast the two men made.

Hsiang K'ai Fan was a big, flabby-chested man, almost effeminate in his manner. Treble-chinned and slack-jowled, his eyes seemed to stare out of a landscape of flesh, yet his movements were dainty and his dress sense exquisite. His lavender silks followed the fashion of the Minor Families – a fashion that was wholly and deliberately out of step with what was being worn elsewhere in the Above – with long, wide sleeves and a flowing gown that hid his booted feet. Heavily perfumed, he was nonetheless restrained in his use of jewellery, the richest item of his apparel being the broad, red velvet ta lian, or girdle pouch, that he wore about his enormous waist, the two clasps of which were studded with rubies and emeralds in the shape of two butterflies. His nails were excessively long, in the manner of the Families; the ivory-handled fan he held moved slowly in the air as he looked about him.

An Liang-chou, on the other hand, was a tiny, rat-like man, stringily built and astonishingly ugly even by the standard of some of the clients Mu Chua had entertained over the years. Flat-faced and beady-eyed, he was as nervy as Hsiang was languid, his movements jerky, awkward. Meeting his eyes, Mu Chua smiled tightly, trying to keep the aversion she felt from showing. Rumour had it that he fucked all six of his daughters – even the youngest, who was only six. Looking at him, it was not hard to imagine. She had seen at once how his eyes had lit up at the sight of her girls. How a dark, lascivious light had come to them: the kind of look a predatory insect gives its victim before it pounces.

Unlike Hsiang, An Liang-chou seemed to have no taste at all when it came to dress. His gaudily coloured *pau* hung loose on him, as if he had stolen it from another. Like Hsiang he was heavily perfumed, but it was an unpleasantly sickly scent, more sour than sweet, as if mixed with his own sweat. She saw how his hand – the fingers thickly crusted with jewelled rings – went to his short ceremonial dagger; how his lips moved wetly as he considered which girl he would have first.

'My lords... you are welcome to my humble house,' she said, lowering her head again. 'Would you care for something to drink?'

Hsiang seemed about to answer, but before he could do so An Liang-chou moved past her and, after pawing two of the girls, chose the third. Gripping her upper arm tightly, he dragged her roughly after him, through the beaded curtain and into the rooms beyond.

Mu Chua watched him go then turned back to Hsiang, smiling, all politeness.

'Would the Lord Hsiang like refreshments?'

Hsiang smiled graciously and let himself be led through. But in the doorway to the Room of Heaven he stopped and turned to look at her.

'Why, this is excellent, Mu Chua. The General was not wrong when he said you were a woman of taste. I would not have thought such a place could have existed outside First Level.'

She bowed low, immensely pleased by his praise. 'Ours is but a humble house, Excellency.'

'However,' he said, moving on, into the room, 'I had hoped for... well, let us not prevaricate, eh?... for *special* pleasures.'

She saw how he looked at her and knew at once that she had misjudged him totally. His silken manners masked a nature far more repugnant than An Liang-chou's.

'Special pleasures, Excellency?'

He turned then sat in the huge, silk-cushioned chair she had bought specially to accommodate his bulk, the fan moving slowly, languidly in his hand.

He looked back at her, his tiny eyes cold, calculating amidst the flesh of his face. 'Yes,' he said smoothly. 'They say you can buy anything in the Net. Anything at all.'

She felt herself go cold. Ebert had said nothing about this. From what he'd said, Hsiang's pleasures were no more unnatural than the next man's. But this...

She waved the girls away then slid the door across and turned back, facing him, reminding herself that this was her passage out, the last time she would have to deal with his kind.

'What is it you would like?' she asked, keeping her voice steady. 'We cater for all tastes here, my lord.'

He smiled, a broad gap opening in the flesh of his lower face, showing teeth that seemed somehow too small to fill the space. His voice was silken, like the voice of a young woman.

'My needs are simple, Mu Chua. Very simple. And the General promised me that you would meet them.'

She knelt, bowing her head. 'Of course, Excellency. But tell me, what *exactly* is it that you want?'

He clicked the fan shut then leaned forward slightly, beckoning her across.

She rose, moving closer then knelt, her face only a hand's width from his knees. He leaned close, whispering, a hint of aniseed on his breath.

'I have been told that there is a close connection between sex and death. That the finest pleasure of all is to fuck a woman at the moment of her death. I have been told that the death throes of a woman bring on an orgasm so intense...'

She looked up at him, horrified, but he was looking past her, his eyes lit with an intense pleasure, as if he could see the thing he was describing. She let him spell it out, barely listening to him now, then sat back on her heels, a small shiver passing through her.

'You want to kill one of my girls, is that it, Lord Hsiang? You wish to slit her throat while you are making love to her?'

He looked back at her, nodding. 'I will pay well.'

'Pay well...' She looked down. It was not the first time she had had such a request. Even in the old days there had been some like Hsiang who linked their pleasure to the pain of others, but even under Whiskers Lu there had been limits to what she would allow. She had never had one of her girls die while with a client, intentionally or otherwise, and it was on her tongue to tell this bastard, Prince or no, to go fuck himself. Only...

She shuddered then looked up at him again, seeing how eagerly he awaited her answer. To say no was to condemn herself at best to staying here, at worst to incurring the anger of Hans Ebert. And who knew what he would do to her if she spoiled things for him now? But to say yes was to comply with the murder of one of her girls. It would be as if she herself had held the knife and drawn it across the flesh.

'What you ask...' she began, then hesitated.

'Yes?'

She stood then turned away, moving towards the door before turning back to face him again. 'You must let me think, Lord Hsiang. My girls...'

'Of course,' he said, as if he understood. 'It must be a special girl.'

His laughter chilled her blood. It was as if what he was discussing were a commonplace. As for the girl herself... In all her years she had tried to keep it in her mind that what her clients bought was not the girl but the services of the girl, as one bought the services of an accountant or a broker. But men like Hsiang made no such distinction. To them the girl was but a thing; to be used and discarded as they wished.

But how to say no? What possible excuse could she give that would placate Hsiang K'ai Fan? Her mind raced, turning back upon itself time and again, trying to find a way out, some way of resolving this impossible dilemma. Then she relaxed, knowing, at last, what to do.

She smiled and moved closer, taking Hsiang's hands gently and raising him from his chair.

'Come,' she said, kissing his swollen neck, her right hand moving down his bloated flank, caressing him. 'You wanted special pleasures, Hsiang K'ai Fan, and special pleasures you will have. Good wine, fine music, the very best of foods...'

'And after?' He stared at her, expectantly.

Mu Chua smiled, letting her hand rest briefly on the hard shape at his groin, caressing it through the silk. 'After, we shall do as you wish.'

★

Charles Lever's son, Michael, sat at his desk, facing Kim across the vastness of his office.

'Well? Have you seen enough?'

Kim looked about him. Huge tapestries filled the walls to the left and right of him: broad panoramas of the Rockies and the great American plains, while on the end wall, beyond Lever's big oak desk and the leather-backed swivel chair, was a bank of screens eight deep and twenty wide. In the centre of the plushly carpeted room, on a big, low table, under glass, was a 3-D map of the east coast of City North America, ImmVac's installations marked in blue. Kim moved closer, peering down through the glass.

'There's an awful lot to see.'

Lever laughed. 'That's true. But I think you've seen most of the more interesting parts.'

Kim nodded. They had spent the day looking over ImmVac's installations, but they had still seen only a small fraction of Old Man Lever's vast commercial empire. More than ever, Kim had been conscious of the sheer scale of the world into which he had come. Down there, in the Clay, it was not possible to imagine the vastness of what existed *a wartha* – up Above. At times he found himself overawed by it all, wishing for somewhere smaller, darker, cosier in which to hide. But that feeling never lasted long. It was, he recognized, residual; part of the darker self he had shrugged off. No, this was his world now. The world of vast, continent-spanning Cities and huge Corporations battling for their share of Chung Kuo's markets.

He looked up. Lever was searching in one of the drawers of his desk. A moment later he straightened, clutching a bulky folder. Closing the drawer with his knee, he came round, thumping the file down beside Kim.

'Here. This might interest you.'

Kim watched as Lever crossed the room and locked the big double doors with an old-fashioned key.

'You like old things, don't you?'

Lever turned, smiling. 'I've never thought about it really. We've always done things this way. Handwritten research files, proper keys, wooden desks. I guess it makes us... different from the other North American Companies. Besides, it makes good sense. Computers are untrustworthy, easily accessed and subject to viruses. Likewise doorlocks and recognition units. But a good, old-fashioned key can't be beaten. In an age of guile, people are reluctant to use force – to break down a door or force open a drawer. The people who'd be most interested in our product have grown too used to sitting at their own desks to commit their crimes. To take the risk of entering one of our facilities would be beyond most of them.' He laughed. 'Besides, it's my father's policy to keep them happy with a constant flow of disinformation. Failed research, blind alleys, minor spin-offs of more important research programmes – that kind of thing. They tap into it and think they've got their finger on the pulse.'

Kim grinned. 'And they never learn?'

Lever shook his head, amused. 'Not yet they haven't.'

Kim looked down at the file. 'And this?'

'Open it and see. Take it across to my desk if you want.'

Kim flipped back the cover and looked, then turned his head sharply, staring at Lever. 'Where did you get this?'

'You've seen it before?'

Kim looked down at it again. 'I have... of course I have, but not in this form. Who...?' Then he recognized the handwriting. The same handwriting that had been on the copy of the cancelled SimFic contract he had been given by Li Yuan. 'Soren Berdichev...'

Lever was looking at him strangely now. 'You knew?'

Kim gave a small, shuddering breath. 'Six years ago. When I was on the Project.'

'You met Berdichev there?'

'He bought my contract. For his Company, SimFic.'

'Ah... Of course. Then you knew he'd written the File?'

Kim laughed strangely. 'You think *Berdichev* wrote this?'

'Who else?'

Kim looked away. 'So. He claimed it for his own.'

Lever shook his head. 'Are you trying to tell me he stole it from someone?'

In a small voice, Kim began to recite the opening of the File: the story of the pre-Socratic Greeks and the establishment of the Aristotelian Yes/No mode of thought. Lever stared back at him with mounting surprise.

'Shall I continue?'

Lever laughed. 'So you do know it. But how? Who showed it to you?'

Kim handed it back. 'I know because I wrote it.'

Lever looked down at the folder then back at Kim, giving a small laugh of disbelief. 'No,' he said quietly. 'You were only a boy.'

Kim was watching Lever closely. 'It was something I put together from some old computer records I unearthed. I thought Berdichev had had it destroyed. I never knew he'd kept a copy.'

'And you knew nothing about the dissemination?'

'The dissemination?'

'You mean, you *really* didn't know?' Lever shook his head, astonished. 'This here is the original, but there are a thousand more copies back in Europe, each one of them like this, handwritten. Now we're going to do the same over here – to disseminate them amongst those sympathetic to the cause.'

'The cause?'

'The Sons of Benjamin Franklin. Oh, we'd heard rumours about the File and its contents some time back, but until recently we'd never seen it. Now, however...' He laughed then shook his head again in amazement. 'Well, it's like a fever in our blood. But you understand that, don't you, Kim? After all, you *wrote* the bloody thing!'

Kim nodded, but inside he felt numbed. He had never imagined...

'Here, look...' Lever led Kim over to one of the tapestries. 'I commissioned this a year ago, before I'd seen the file. We put it together from what we knew about the past. It shows how things were before the City.'

Kim looked at it then shook his head. 'It's wrong.'

'Wrong?'

'Yes, all the details are wrong. Look.' He touched one of the animals on the rocks in the foreground. 'This is a lion. But it's an African lion. There never were any lions of this kind in America. And those wagons, crossing the plains, they would have been drawn by horses. The petrol engine was a much later development. And these tents here – they're Mongol in style. Red Indian tents were different. And then there are these pagodas...'

'But in the File it says...'

'Oh, it's not that these things didn't exist, it's just that they didn't exist at the same time or in the same place. Besides, there were Cities even then – here on the east coast.'

'Cities... but I thought...'

'You thought the Han invented Cities? No. Cities have been in Man's blood since the dawn of civilization. Why, Security Central at Bremen is nothing more than a copy of the great zigurrat at Ur, built more than five thousand years ago.'

Lever had gone very still. He was watching Kim closely, a strange intensity in his eyes. After a moment he shook his head, giving a soft laugh.

'You really *did* write it, didn't you?'

Kim nodded then turned back to the tapestry. 'And this...' He bent down, indicating the lettering at the foot of the picture. 'This is wrong, too.'

Lever leaned forward, staring at the lettering. 'How do you mean?'

'AD. It doesn't mean what's written here. That was another of Tsao Ch'un's lies. He was never related to the Emperor Tsao He, or to any of them. So all of this business about the Ancestral Dynasties is complete nonsense. Likewise BC. It doesn't mean "Before the Crane". In fact, Tsao He, the "Crane", supposedly the founder of the Han dynasty and ancestor of all subsequent dynasties, never even existed. In reality, Liu Chi-tzu, otherwise known as P'ing ti, was Emperor at the time – and he was twelfth of the great Han dynasty emperors. So, you see, the Han adapted parts of their own history almost as radically as they changed that of the West. They had to – to make sense of things and keep it all consistent.'

'So what do they really mean?'

'"AD"... That stands for *Anno Domini*. It's Latin – *Ta Ts'in* – for "The Year of our Lord".'

'Our Lord?'

'Jesus Christ. You know, the founder of Christianity.'

'Ah...' But Lever looked confused. 'And BC? Is that Latin, too?'

Kim shook his head. 'That's "Before Christ".'

Lever laughed. 'But that doesn't make sense. Why the mixture of languages? And why in the gods' names would the Han adopt a Christian dating for their calendar?'

Kim smiled. When one thought about it, it didn't make a great deal of sense, but that was how it was – how it had been for more than a hundred years before Tsao Ch'un had arrived on the scene. It was the *Ko Ming* – the Communists – who had adopted the Western calendar, and Tsao Ch'un, in rewriting the history of Chung Kuo, had found it easiest to keep the old measure. After all, it provided his historians with a genuine sense of continuity, especially after he had hit upon the idea of claiming that it dated from the first *real* Han dynasty, ruled, of course, by his ancestor, Tsao He, 'the Crane'.

'Besides...' Lever added, 'I don't understand the importance of this Christ figure. I know you talk of all these wars fought in his name, but if he was so important why didn't the Han incorporate him into their scheme of things?'

Kim looked down, taking a long breath. So... they had read it but they had not understood. In truth, their reading of the File was, in its way, every bit as distorted as Tsao Ch'un's retelling of the world. Like the tapestry, they would put the past together as they wanted it, not as it really was.

He met Lever's eyes. 'You forget. I didn't invent what's in the File. That's how it was. And Christ...' he sighed. 'Christ was important to the West, in a way he wasn't to the Han. To the Han he was merely an irritation. Like the insects, they didn't want him in their City, so they built a kind of Net to keep him out.'

Lever shivered. 'It's like that term they use for us – T'*e an tsan* – "innocent Westerners". All the time they seek to denigrate us. To deny us what's rightfully ours.'

'Maybe...' But Kim was thinking about Li Yuan's gifts. He, at least, had been given back what was his.

Ebert strode into the House of the Ninth Ecstasy, smiling broadly, then stopped, looking about him. Why was there no one here to greet him? What in the gods' names was the woman up to?

He called out, trying to keep the anger from his voice – 'Mu Chua! Mu Chua, where are you?' – then crossed the room, pushing through the beaded curtain.

His eyes met a scene of total chaos. There was blood everywhere. Wine glasses had been smashed underfoot, trays of sweetmeats overturned and ground into the carpet. On the far side of the room a girl lay face down, as if drunk or sleeping.

He whirled about, drawing his knife, hearing sudden shrieking from the rooms off to his left. A moment later a man burst into the room. It was Hsiang K'ai Fan.

Hsiang looked very different from when Ebert had last seen him. His normally placid face was bright – almost incandescent – with excitement; his eyes popping out from the surrounding fat. His clothes, normally so immaculate, were dishevelled, the lavender silks ripped and spattered with blood. He held his ceremonial dagger out before him, the blade slick, shining wetly in the light, while, as if in some obscene parody of the blade, his penis poked out from between the folds of the silk, stiff and wet with blood.

'Lord Hsiang...' Ebert began, astonished by this transformation. 'What has been happening here?'

Hsiang laughed: a strange, quite chilling cackle. 'Oh, it's been wonderful, Hans... simply wonderful! I've had such fun. Such glorious fun!'

Ebert swallowed, not sure what to make of Hsiang's 'fun', but quite sure that it spelt nothing but trouble for himself.

'Where's An Liang-chou? He's all right, isn't he?'

Hsiang grinned insanely, lowering the dagger. His eyes were unnaturally bright, the pupils tightly contracted. He was breathing strangely, his flabby chest rising and falling erratically. 'An's fine. Fucking little girls, as usual. But Hans... your woman... she was magnificent. You should have seen the way she died. Oh, the orgasm I had. It was just as they said it would be. Immense it was. I couldn't stop coming. And then...'

Ebert shuddered. 'You *what*?' He took a step forward. 'What are you saying? Mu Chua is *dead*?'

Hsiang nodded, his excitement almost feverish now, his penis twitching as he spoke. 'Yes, and then I thought... why not do it again? And again...? After all, as she said, I could settle with Whiskers Lu when I was done.'

Ebert stood there, shaking his head. 'Gods...' He felt his fingers tighten about his dagger then slowly relaxed his hand. If he killed Hsiang it would all be undone. No, he had to make the best of things. To make his peace with Whiskers Lu and get Hsiang and An out of here as quickly as possible. Before anyone else found out about this.

'How many have you killed?'

Hsiang laughed. 'I'm not sure. A dozen. Fifteen. Maybe more...'

'Gods...'

Ebert stepped forward, taking the knife from Hsiang. 'Come on,' he said, worried by the look of fierce bemusement in Hsiang's face. 'Fun's over. Let's get An and go home.'

Hsiang nodded vaguely then bowed his head, letting himself be led through.

Towards the back of the house things seemed almost normal. But as Ebert came to the Room of Heaven he slowed, seeing the great streaks of blood smeared down the doorframes, and guessed what lay within.

He pushed Hsiang aside then went into the room. A girl lay to one side, dead, her face bloody, her abdomen ripped open, the guts exposed, while on the far side of the room lay Mu Chua, naked, face up, on the huge bed, her throat slit from ear to ear. Her flesh was ashen, as if bleached, the sheets beneath her dark with her blood.

He stood there, looking down at her a moment, then shook his head. Whiskers Lu would go mad when he heard about this. Mu Chua's house had been a key part of his empire, bringing him a constant flow of new contacts from the Above. Now, with Mu Chua dead, who would come?

Ebert took a deep breath. Yes, and Lu Ming-shao would blame him – for making the introduction. For not checking up on Hsiang before he let him go berserk down here. *If he had known...*

He twirled about, his anger bubbling over. 'Fuck you, Hsiang! Do you know what you've done?'

Hsiang K'ai Fan stared back at him, astonished. 'I b-beg your pardon?'

'This!' Ebert threw his arm out, indicating the body on the bed, then grabbed Hsiang's arm and dragged him across the room. 'What the fuck made you want to do it, eh? Now we've a bloody war on our hands! Or will have, unless you placate the man.'

Hsiang shook his head, bewildered. 'What man?'

'Lu Ming-shao. Whiskers Lu. He's the big Triad boss around these parts. He owned this place. And now you've gone and butchered his Madam. He'll go berserk when he finds out. He'll hire assassins to track you down and kill you.'

He saw how Hsiang swallowed at that, how his eyes went wide with fear, and felt like laughing. But, no, he could use this. Yes, maybe things weren't quite so bad after all. Maybe he could turn this to his advantage.

'Yes, he'll rip your throat out for this, unless...'

Hsiang pushed his head forward anxiously. 'Unless...?'

Ebert looked about him, considering. 'This was one of his main sources of income. Not just from prostitution but from other things too – drugs, illicit trading, blackmail. It must have been worth, oh, fifteen, twenty million *yuan* a year to him. And now it's worth nothing. Not since you ripped the throat out of it.'

'I didn't know...' Hsiang shook his head, his hands trembling. His words came quickly now, tumbling from his lips. 'I'll pay him off. Whatever it costs. My family is rich. Very rich. You know that, Hans. You could see this Whiskers Lu, couldn't you? You could tell him that. Please, Hans. Tell him I'll pay him what he asks.'

Ebert nodded slowly, narrowing his eyes. 'Maybe. But you must do something for me, too.'

Hsiang nodded eagerly. 'Anything, Hans. You only have to name it.'

He stared at Hsiang contemptuously. 'Just this. I want you to throw your party this afternoon – your *chao tai hui* – just as if nothing happened here. You understand? Whatever you or An did or saw here must be forgotten. Must never, in any circumstances, be mentioned. It must be as if it never was. Because if news of this gets out there will be recriminations. Quite awful recriminations. Understand?'

Hsiang nodded, a look of pure relief crossing his face.

'And Hsiang. This afternoon... don't worry about the girls. I'll provide them. You just make sure your friends are there.'

Hsiang looked down, chastened, the madness gone from him. 'Yes... As you say.'

'Good. Then find your friend and be gone from here. Take my sedan if you must, but go. I'll be in touch.'

Hsiang turned, making to go, but Ebert called him back one last time. 'And, Hsiang...'

Hsiang stopped and turned, one hand resting against the bloodstained upright of the door. 'Yes?'

'Do this again and I'll kill you, understand?'

Hsiang's eyes flickered once in the huge expanse of flesh that was his face then he lowered his head and backed away.

Ebert watched him go then turned, looking down at Mu Chua again. It was a shame. She had been useful – very useful – over the years. But what was gone was gone. Dealing with Whiskers Lu was the problem now. That and rearranging things for the party later.

It had all seemed so easy when he'd spoken to DeVore earlier, but Hsiang had done his best to spoil things for him. Where, at this late stage, would he find another fifteen girls – special girls of the quality Mu Chua would have given him?

Ebert sighed, then, seeing the funny side of it, began to laugh, remembering the sight of Hsiang standing there, his penis poking out stiffly, for all the world like a miniature of his rat-like friend, An Liang-chou, staring out from beneath the fat of Hsiang's stomach.

Well, they would get theirs. They and all their friends. But he would make certain this time. He would inject the girls he sent to entertain them.

He smiled. Yes, and then he'd watch, as one by one they went down. Princes and cousins and all; every last one of them victims of the disease DeVore had bought from his friend, Curval.

How clever, he thought, to catch them that way. For who would think that that was what it was. He laughed. Syphilis... it had not been heard of in the Above for more than a century. No, and when they did find out it would be too late. Much too late. By then the sickness would have spread throughout the great tree of the Families, infecting root and branch, drying up the sap. And then the tree would fall, like the rotten, stinking thing it was.

He shivered then put his hand down, brushing the hair back from the dead woman's brow, frowning.

'Yes. But why did you do it, Mother? Why in hell's name did you let him do it to you? It can't have been the money...'

Ebert took his hand away then shook his head. He would never understand – never in ten thousand years. To lie there while another cut your throat and fucked you. It made no sense. And yet...

He laughed sourly. That was exactly what his kind had done for the last one hundred and fifty years. Ever since the time of Tsao Ch'un. But now all that had changed. From now on things would be different.

He turned and looked across. Three of Mu Chua's girls were standing in the doorway, wide-eyed, huddled together, looking in at him.

'Call Lu Ming-shao,' he said, going across, holding the eldest by the arm. 'Tell him to come at once, but say nothing more. Tell him Hans Ebert wants to talk to him. About a business matter.'

He let her go then turned, facing the other two, putting his arms about their shoulders. 'Now, my girls. Things seem uncertain, I know, but I've a special task for you, and if you do it well...'

*

Hsiang Wang leaned his vast bulk towards the kneeling messenger and let out a great huff of annoyance.

'What do you mean, my brother's ill? He was perfectly well this morning. What's happened to him?'

The messenger kept his head low, offering the handwritten note. 'He asks you to accept his apologies, Excellency, and sends you this note.'

Hsiang Wang snatched the note and unfolded it. For a moment he grew still, reading it, then threw it aside, making a small, agitated movement of his head, cursing beneath his breath.

'He says all has been arranged, Excellency,' the messenger continued, made uncomfortable by the proximity of Hsiang Wang's huge, trunk-like legs. 'The last of the girls – the special ones – were hired this morning.'

The messenger knew from experience what a foul temper Hsiang K'ai Fan's brother had and expected at any moment to be on the receiving end of it, but for once Hsiang Wang bridled in his anger. Perhaps it was the fact that his guests were only a few *ch'i* away, listening beyond the wafer-thin wall, or perhaps it was something else: the realization that, with his elder brother absent, he could play host alone. Whatever, it seemed to calm him and, with a curt gesture of dismissal, he turned away, walking back towards the great double doors that led through to the Hall of the Four Willows.

Hsiang Wang paused in the doorway, taking in the scene. From where he stood, five broad, grass-covered terraces led down, like crescent moons, to the great willow-leaf-shaped pool and the four ancient trees from which the hall derived its name. There were more than a hundred males from the Minor Families here this afternoon, young and old alike. Most of the Twenty-Nine were represented, each of the great clans distinguishable by the markings on the silk gowns the princes wore, but most were from the five great European Families of Hsiang and An, Pei, Yin and Chun. Girls went amongst them, smiling and laughing, stopping to talk or rest a gentle hand upon an arm or about a waist. The party had yet to begin and for the moment contact was restrained, polite. The sound of *erhu* and *k'un ti* – bow and bamboo flute – drifted softly in the air, mixing with the scents of honeysuckle and plum blossom.

Low tables were scattered about the terraces. The young princes

surrounded these, lounging on padded couches, talking or playing *Chou*. On
every side tall shrubs and plants and lacquered screens – each decorated with
scenes of forests and mountains, spring pastures and moonlit rivers – broke
up the stark geometry of the hall, giving it the look of a woodland glade.

Hsiang Wang smiled, pleased by the effect, then clapped his hands. At
once doors opened to either side of him and servants spilled out down the
terraces, bearing trays of wine and meats and other delicacies. Leaving the
smile on his lips, he went down, moving across to his right, joining the
group of young men gathered about Chun Wu-chi.

Chun Wu-chi was Head of the Chun Family; the only Head to honour
the Hsiang clan with his presence this afternoon. He was a big man in his
seventies, long-faced and bald, his pate polished like an ancient ivory carv-
ing, his sparse white beard braided into two thin plaits. Coming close to
him, Hsiang Wang knelt, in *san k'ou*, placing his forehead to the ground
three times before straightening up again.

'You are most welcome here, Highness.'

Chun Wu-chi smiled. 'I thank you for your greeting, Hsiang Wang, but
where is your elder brother? I was looking forward to seeing him again.'

'Forgive me, Highness,' Hsiang said, lowering his head, 'but K'ai
Fan has been taken ill. He sends his deep regards and humbly begs your
forgiveness.'

Chun looked about him, searching the eyes of his close advisors to see
whether this could be some kind of slight, then, reassured by what he saw,
he looked back at Hsiang Wang, smiling, putting one bejewelled hand out
towards him.

'I am sorry your brother is ill, Wang. Please send him my best wishes and
my most sincere hope for his swift recovery.'

Hsiang Wang bowed low. 'I will do so, Highness. My Family is most
honoured by your concern.'

Chun gave the smallest nod then looked away, his eyes searching the
lower terraces. 'There are many new girls here today, Hsiang Wang. Are
there any with... *special* talents?'

Hsiang Wang smiled inwardly. He had heard of Chun Wu-chi's appetites.
Indeed, they were legendary. When he had been younger, it was said, he had
had a hundred women, one after the other, for a bet. It had taken him three
days, so the story went, and afterwards he had slept for fifty hours, only

to wake keen to begin all over. Now, in his seventies, his fire had waned. Voyeurism had taken the place of more active pursuits.

'There is one girl, Highness...' he said, remembering what K'ai Fan had said. 'I have been told that she can manage the most extraordinary feats.'

'Really?' Chun Wu-chi's eyes lit up.

Hsiang Wang smiled. 'Let me bring her, Highness.' He looked about him at the younger men. 'In the meantime, if the ch'un tzu would like to entertain themselves?'

On cue the lights overhead dimmed, the music grew more lively. From vents overhead subtle, sweet-scented hallucinogens wafted into the air.

As he made his way down to the pool, he saw how quickly some of the men, eager not to waste a moment, had drawn girls down on to the couches next to them, while one – a prince of the Pei family – had one girl massaging his neck and shoulders while another knelt between his legs.

Hsiang Wang laughed softly. There would be more outrageous sights than that before the day was done. Many more. He slowed, looking about him, then saw the girl and lifted his hand, summoning her.

She came across and stopped, bowing before him. A dainty little thing, her hair cut in swallow bangs. She looked up at him, revealing her perfect features, her delicate rosebud lips. 'Yes, Excellency?'

He reached in his pocket and took out the thousand-yuan chip he had stashed there earlier, handing it to her. 'You know what to do?'

She nodded, a smile coming to her lips.

'Good... then go and introduce yourself. I'll have the servants bring the beast.'

He watched her go, glad that he had gone through all this with his brother two days before.

Sick. What a time for K'ai Fan to fall sick! Surely he knew how important this occasion was for the Family? Hsiang Wang shuddered then threw off his irritation. It could not be helped, he supposed. And if he could please Old Chun, who knew what advantages he might win for himself?

He hurried back in time to see the servants bring the beast. The Ox-man stood there passively, its three-toed hands at its sides, looking about it nervously, its almost-human eyes filled with anxiety. Seeing it, some of the younger princes laughed among themselves and leaned close to exchange words. Hsiang Wang smiled and moved closer, standing at Chun's shoulder.

At once another girl approached and knelt at Chun's side, her flank against his leg, one hand resting gently on his knee.

Chun looked down briefly, smiling, then looked back, studying the girl and the beast, one hand tugging at his beard, an expression of interest on his long, heavily lined face.

Hsiang raised his hand. At once the servants came forward, tearing the fine silks from the Ox-man's back, tugging down its velvet trousers. Then they stood back. For a moment it stood there, bewildered, trembling, its big, dark-haired body exposed. Then, with a low, cow-like moan, it turned its great head, as if looking to escape.

At once the girl moved closer, putting one hand up to its chest, calming it, whispering words of reassurance. Again it lowed, but now it was looking down, its eyes on the girl.

From the couches to either side of Chun Wu-chi came laughter. Laughter and a low, excited whisper.

Slowly she began to stroke the beast, long, sensual strokes that began high up in the beast's furred chest and ended low down, between its heavily muscled legs. It was not long before it was aroused, its huge member poking up stiffly into the air, glistening, long and wet and pinky-red in the half-light – a lance of quivering, living matter.

As the girl slipped her gown from her shoulders, there was a low murmur of approval. Now she stood there, naked, holding the beast's huge phallus in one hand, while with the other she continued to stroke its chest.

Its lowing now had a strange, inhuman urgency to it. It turned its head from side to side, as if in pain, its whole body trembling, as if at any moment it might lose control. One hand lifted, moving towards the girl, then withdrew.

Then, with a small, teasing smile at Chun Wu-chi, the girl lowered her head and took the beast deep into her mouth.

There was a gasp from all round. Hsiang, watching, saw how the girl he had assigned to Chun was working the old man, burrowed beneath his skirts, doing to him exactly what the other was doing to the Ox-man. He smiled. From the look of pained pleasure on the old man's face, Chun Wu-chi would not forget this evening quickly.

★

It was just after nine and in the great Hall of Celestial Destinies at Nantes spaceport a huge crowd milled about. The eight-twenty rocket from Boston had come in ten minutes back and the final security clearances were being made before its passengers were passed through into the hall.

Lehmann stood at the base of the statue in the centre of the hall, waiting. DeVore had contacted him an hour and a half back to say he would be on the eight-twenty. He had sounded angry and irritable, but when Lehmann had pressed him about the trip, he had seemed enthusiastic. It was something else, then, that had soured his mood – something that had happened back here, in his absence – and there was only one thing that could have done that: the failure of the assassination attempt on Tolonen.

Was that why DeVore had asked him to meet him here? To try again? It made sense, certainly, for despite all their 'precautions' the last thing Security *really* expected was a new attempt so shortly after the last.

He turned, looking up at the giant bronze figures. He knew that the composition was a lie, part of the Great Lie the Han had built along with their City; even so, there was an underlying truth to it, for the Han *had* triumphed over the *Ta Ts'in*. Kan Ying *had* bowed before Pan Chao. Or at least, their descendants had. But for how much longer would the dream of Rome be denied?

For himself, it was unimportant. Han or *Hung Mao*, it did not matter who ruled the great circle of Chung Kuo. Even so, in the great struggle that was to come, his ends would be served.

Whoever triumphed, the world would be no longer as it was. Much that he hated would, of necessity, be destroyed, and in that process of destruction – of purification – a new spirit would be unleashed. New and yet quite ancient. Savage and yet pure, like an eagle circling in the cold, clear air above the mountains.

He looked away. A new beginning, that was what the world needed. A new beginning, free of all this.

Lehmann looked about him, studying those making their way past him, appalled by the emptiness he saw in every face. Here they were, all the half-men and half-women and all their little halflings, hurrying about their empty, meaningless lives. On their brief, sense-dulled journey to the Oven Man's door.

And then?

He shivered, oppressed suddenly by the crush, by the awful perfumed stench of those about him. This now – this brief moment of time before it began – was a kind of tiger's mouth; that moment before one surrounded one's opponent's stone, robbing it of breath. It was a time of closing options. Of fast and desperate plays.

There was a murmuring throughout the hall as the announcement boards at either end showed that the passengers from the eight-twenty Boston rocket were coming through. Lehmann was about to go across when he noticed two men making their way through the crowd, their faces set, their whole manner subtly different.

Security? No. For a start they were Han. Moreover, there was something fluid, almost rounded about their movements; something one never found in the more rigorously and classically trained Security élite. No. These were more likely Triad men. Assassins. But who were they after? Who else was on DeVore's flight? Some Company head? Or was this a gang matter?

He followed them surreptitiously, interested; wanting to observe their methods.

The gate at the far end of the hall was open now and passengers were spilling out. Looking past the men, he saw DeVore, his neat, tidy figure making its way swiftly but calmly through the press. The men were exactly halfway between him and DeVore, some ten or fifteen ch'i in front of him, when he realized his mistake.

'Howard!'

DeVore looked up, alerted, and saw at once what was happening. The two assassins were making directly for him now, less than two body lengths away, their blades out, slashing at anyone who got in their way, intent on reaching their quarry. Beyond them Lehmann was pushing his way through the crowd, yelling at people to get out of his way, but it would be several seconds before he could come to DeVore's aid.

DeVore moved forward sharply, bringing the case he was carrying up into the face of the first man as he came out of the crowd in front of him. Hampered by a woman at his side, the assassin could only jerk his head back, away. At once DeVore kicked out, making him stagger back. But even as he did, the second assassin was upon him, his notched knife swinging through the air at DeVore's head.

The speed at which DeVore turned surprised the man. One hand countered the knife blow at the wrist while the other punched to the ribs. The assassin went down with a sharp cry.

DeVore turned, facing the first assassin, feinting once, twice with his fists before he twisted and kicked. The assassin moved back expertly, but before he could counter, he sank to his knees, Lehmann's knife embedded in his back.

There was shouting and screaming from all sides of them now.

'Come away,' Lehmann said quietly, taking DeVore's arm. 'Before Security come!' But DeVore shrugged him off, going over to the second man.

The would-be assassin lay there, helpless, clutching his side, gasping with pain. DeVore had shattered his ribcage, puncturing his lung. He crouched close, over the man, one hand at his throat.

'Who sent you?'

The man pushed his face up at DeVore's and spat.

DeVore wiped the bloodstained phlegm from his cheek and reached across to pick up the assassin's blade. Then, as the man's eyes widened, he slit open his shirt and searched his torso for markings.

DeVore turned, looking up at Lehmann, a fierce anger in his face. 'He's not Triad and he's not Security, so who the fuck...?'

The third man came from nowhere.

DeVore had no time to react. It was only accident that saved him. As Lehmann turned, he moved between DeVore and the man, glancing against the assassin's knife arm. The knife, which would have entered DeVore's heart, was nudged to one side, piercing DeVore between neck and shoulder.

The assassin jerked the serrated knife out savagely from DeVore's flesh, but before he could strike again, Lehmann had lashed out, punching his nose up into his skull. The man fell and lay still.

DeVore sank to his knees, holding one hand over the wound, a look of astonishment on his bloodless face. This time Lehmann didn't ask. With a single blow he finished off the second man, then turned and did the same to the third. Then, lifting DeVore on to his shoulder, ignoring the shouts of protest from all about him, he began to carry him towards the exit and the safety of the transit, praying that their man in Security could hold his fellows off a minute longer.

As for DeVore's question, he had his answer now, for that last man had been a *Hung Mao*, a face they'd seen often in the past: one of several who had always been there in the background at their meetings with the *Ping Tiao*. A guard. One of the ones who had defected to the *Yu*.

So it was Mach, Jan Mach, who'd tried to have them killed.

CHUNG KUO

Chapter 68

WILLOW-PLUM SICKNESS

On the open, windswept hillside the small group gathered about the grave. Across the valley, cloud shadow drew a moving line that descended, crossing the water, then came swiftly up the slope towards them.

Ben watched the shadow sweep towards him, and felt the sudden chill as the sun passed behind the cloud.

So it is, he thought. *As swift as that it comes.*

The wooden casket lay on thick silken cords beside the open grave. Ben stood there, facing the casket across the darkness of the hole, his feet only inches from the drop.

Earth. Dark earth. It had rained and tiny beads of moisture clung to the stems of grass overhanging the grave. In the sunlight they seemed strange, incongruous.

It was still unreal. Or not yet real. He felt no grief as yet, no strong feeling for what he had lost, only a vacancy, a sense of his own inattentiveness. As if he had missed something...

They were all in black, even Li Yuan. Blackness for death. The old Western way of things. His mother stood beside the casket, her face veiled, grieving heavily. Beside him stood his sister, and next to her Li Yuan's Chancellor, Nan Ho.

A cold wind gusted from the south across the hilltop, blowing his hair into his eyes. A sea breeze, heavy with brine. He combed strands back into place with his fingers, then left his hand there, the fingers buried in his fine, thick hair, his palm pressed firmly against his forehead.

He felt like an actor, the 'boy in black' at the graveside. An impostor. Neither loving nor dutiful. Cuckoo in the nest. Too distanced from things to be his father's son, his brother's brother.

Had he ever even said he loved him?

Two of Li Yuan's men came and lifted the casket on its cords.

Ben moved back as they lowered the casket into the earth. A cassette of death, slotting into the hillside.

And no rewind... no playback. Hal Shepherd existed only in the memories of others now. And when they in their turn died? Was it all simply a long process of forgetting? Of blinded eyes and decaying images? Maybe... but it didn't have to be.

The earth fell. He closed his eyes and could see it falling, covering the pale wood of the casket. Could hear the sound of the earth tumbling against the wood. A hollow, empty sound.

He opened his eyes. The hole was a shallow depression of uneven darkness. The T'ang's men had ceased shovelling.

He felt the urge to bend down and touch the cold, dark earth. To crush it between his fingers and feel its gritty texture, its cool, inanimate substance. Instead, he watched as Li Yuan stepped forward and pressed the young tree into the pile of earth, firming it down, then moving back to let the servants finish their task.

No words. No graven stones. This was his father's wish. Only a tree. A young oak.

Ben shivered, his thoughts drawn elsewhere. What was the darkness like on the other side of being? Was it only a nothingness? Only blank, empty darkness?

They walked back along the path, down to the cottage by the bay, Li Yuan holding his mother's arm, consoling her, Nan Ho walking beside his sister. Ben came last, alone, several paces behind.

His father's death. Expected so long, it had nonetheless come like a blow of evil fate to his mother. He had heard her crying in the night: a sound that could not be described, only heard and remembered. A wordless noise, connected to the grieving animal deep within the human – a sound drawn from the great and ancient darkness of our racial being.

An awful, desolate sound. Once heard it could never be forgotten.

He turned and looked back. There was no sign of the grave, the fledgling tree. Banks of iron-grey cloud were massed above the hillside. In a while it would rain.

He turned and looked down the slope at the cottage and the bay beyond, seeing it all anew. Where was its paradigm? Where the designer of all this? The shaping force?

Death had unlocked these questions, forcing his face relentlessly against the glass.

He sighed, then walked on, making his slow way down.

Li Yuan stood in the centre of Ben's room, looking about him. Ben was hunched over his desk, working, making notations in a huge, loose-leafed book, the pages of which were covered in strange diagrams.

It was not what Li Yuan had expected. The room was cluttered and untidy, totally lacking, it seemed, in any organizational principle. Things were piled here, there and everywhere, as if discarded and forgotten, while one whole wall was taken up by numerous half-completed pencil sketches depicting parts of the human anatomy.

He looked back at Ben, seeing how tense he was, crouched over the big, square-paged book, and felt a ripple of unease pass through him. It did not seem right, somehow, to be working on the day of his father's funeral. Li Yuan moved closer, looking over Ben's shoulder at the diagram he was working on, seeing only a disorganized mess of lines and shapes and coded instructions, set down in a dozen brilliant colours on the underlying grid, like the scribblings of a child.

'What is that?'

Ben finished what he was doing, then turned, looking up at the young T'ang.

'It's a rough.'

'A rough?' Li Yuan laughed. 'A rough of what?'

'No... that's what I call it. All of these are instructions. The dark lines – those in brown, orange and red, mainly, are instructions to the muscles. The small circles in blue, black and mauve – those are chemical input instructions; the nature of the chemical and the dosage marked within the circle. The rectangular blocks are just that – blocks. They indicate when no input of any kind is passing through that particular node.'

'Nodes?' Li Yuan was thoroughly confused by this time.

Ben smiled. 'Pai pi. You know, the old artificial reality experiments. I've been working on them these last fifteen months. I call them Shells. This here is an input instruction diagram. As I said, a rough. These eighty-one horizontal lines represent the input points, and these forty vertical lines represent the dimension of time – twenty to a second.'

Li Yuan frowned. 'I still don't understand. Inputs into what?'

'Into the recipient's body. Come. I'll show you. Downstairs.'

They went down, into the basement workrooms. There, at one end of the long, low-ceilinged room, almost hidden by the clutter of other machinery, was the Shell. It was a big, elaborately decorated casket; like something one might use for an imperial lying-in-state, the lid lacquered a midnight black.

Ben stood beside it, looking back at Li Yuan. 'The recipient climbs in here and is wired up – the wires being attached to eighty-one special input points both in the brain and at important nerve-centres throughout the body. That done, the casket is sealed, effectively cutting the recipient off from all external stimuli. That absence of stimuli is an unnatural state for the human body: if denied sensory input for too long the mind begins to hallucinate. Using this well-documented receptivity of the sensory apparatus to false stimuli, we can provide the mind with a complete alternative experience.'

Li Yuan stared at the apparatus a moment longer, then looked back at Ben. 'How complete?'

Ben was watching him, as a hawk watches a rabbit. An intense, predatory stare.

'As complete as the real thing. If the art is good enough.'

'The art... I see.' Li Yuan frowned. It seemed such a strange thing to want to do. To create an art that mimicked life so closely. An art that supplanted life. He reached out and touched the skeletal frame that hung to one side, noting the studded inputs about head and chest and groin. Eighty-one inputs in all. 'But why?'

Ben stared at him as if he didn't understand the question, then handed him a book similar to the one he had been working on in his room. 'These, as I said, are the roughs. They form the diagrammatic outline of an event-sequence – a story. Eventually those lines and squiggles and dots will become events. Sensory actualities. Not real, yet indistinguishable from the real.'

Li Yuan stared at the open page and nodded, but it still didn't explain. Why this need for fictions? For taking away what was and filling it with something different? Wasn't life itself enough?

Ben was leaning close now, looking into his face, his eyes filled with an almost insane intensity, his voice a low whisper.

'It's like being a god. You can do whatever you want. Create whatever you want to create. Things that never happened. That never *could* happen.'

Li Yuan laughed uncomfortably. 'Something that never happened? But why should you want to do that? Isn't there enough diversity in the world as it is?'

Ben looked at him curiously, then looked away, as if disappointed. 'No. You miss my point.'

It was said quietly, almost as if it didn't matter. As if, in that brief instant between the look and the words, he had made his mind up about something.

'Then what *is* the point?' Li Yuan insisted, setting the book down on the padded innards of the casket.

Ben looked down, his hand reaching out to touch the apparatus. For the first time Li Yuan noticed that the hand was artificial. It seemed real, but the deeply etched ridge of skin gave it away. Once revealed, other signs added to the impression. There was an added subtlety of touch; a deftness of movement just beyond the human range.

'Your question is larger than you think, Li Yuan. It questions not merely what I do, but all art, all fiction, all dreams of other states. It asserts that "what is" is enough. My argument is that "what is" is insufficient. We need more than "what is". Much more.'

Li Yuan shrugged. 'Maybe. But this takes it too far, surely? It seems a kind of mockery. Life is good. Why seek this false perfection?'

'Do you really believe that, Li Yuan? Are you sure there's nothing my art could give you that life couldn't?'

Li Yuan turned away, as if stung. He was silent for some time, then he looked back, a grim expression of defiance changing his features. 'Only illusions. Nothing real.'

Ben shook his head. 'You're wrong. I could give you something so real, so solid and substantial that you could hold it in your arms – could taste it and smell it and never for a moment know that you were only dreaming.'

Li Yuan stared at him, aghast, then looked down. 'I don't believe you. It could never be that good.'

'Ah, but it will.'

Li Yuan lifted his head angrily. 'Can it give you back your father? Can it do that?'

The boy did not flinch. His eyes caught Li Yuan's and held them. 'Yes. Even that, if I wanted it.'

Li Yuan arrived at Tongjiang four hours later to find things in chaos, the audience hall packed with his Ministers and advisors. While the T'ang changed, Nan Ho went among the men, finding out what had been happening in their brief absence.

When Li Yuan returned to his study, Nan Ho was waiting for him, his face flushed, his whole manner extremely agitated.

'What is it, Nan Ho? What has got my Ministers in such a state?'

Nan Ho bowed low. 'It is not just your Ministers, *Chieh Hsia*. The whole of the Above is in uproar. They say that more than two hundred are ill already, and that more than a dozen have died.'

Li Yuan sat forward. 'What do you mean?'

Nan Ho looked up at him. 'There is an epidemic, *Chieh Hsia*, sweeping through the Minor Families. No one knows quite what it is...'

Li Yuan stood angrily and came round his desk. 'No one knows? Am I to believe this? Where are the Royal Surgeons? Have them come to me at once.'

Nan Ho lowered his head. 'They are outside, *Chieh Hsia*, but—'

'No buts, Master Nan. Get them in here now. If there is an epidemic we must act fast.'

Nan Ho brought them in, then stood back, letting his T'ang question the men directly.

The eight old men stood there, their ancient bodies bent forward awkwardly.

'Well?' he said, facing the most senior of them. 'What has been happening, Surgeon Yu? Why have you not been able to trace the source of this disease?'

'Chieh Hsia...' the old man began, his voice quavering. 'Forgive me, but the facts contradict themselves.'

'Nonsense!' Li Yuan barked, clearly angry. 'Do you know the cause of the disease or not?'

The old man shook his head, distressed. 'Forgive me, Chieh Hsia, but it is not possible. The Families are bred immune. For more than one hundred and fifty years...'

Li Yuan huffed impatiently. 'Impossible? Nothing is impossible! I've just come from Hal Shepherd's funeral. They killed him, remember? With a cancer. Something that, according to you, was quite impossible. So what have they come up with now?'

The old man glanced sideways at his colleagues, then spoke again. 'It seems, from our first tests, that what the victims are suffering from is what we term yang mei ping, "willow-plum sickness".'

Li Yuan laughed. 'A fancy name, Surgeon Yu, but what does it mean?'

Nan Ho answered for the old man. 'It is syphilis, Chieh Hsia. A sexually transmitted disease that affects the brain and drives its victims insane. This strain, apparently, is a particularly virulent and fast-working one. Besides sidestepping the natural immunity of its victims, it has a remarkably short incubation period. Many of its victims are dead within thirty hours of getting the dose.'

Surgeon Yu looked at Nan Ho gratefully, then nodded. 'That is so, Chieh Hsia. However, it seems that this particular strain affects only those of Han origin. As far as we can make out, no Hung Mao are affected.'

Li Yuan turned away, recognizing at once the implications of the thing. Willow-plum sickness... He had a vague recollection of reading about the disease. It was one of those many sicknesses the Hung Mao had brought with them when they had first opened China up, in the seventeenth and eighteenth centuries. But this was worse, far worse than anything those ancient sea traders had spread among the port women, because this time his kind had no natural immunity to it. None at all.

He turned back. 'Are you certain, Surgeon Yu?'

'As certain as we can be, Chieh Hsia.'

'Good. Then I want you to isolate each victim and question them as to who they have slept with in the past thirty days. Then I want all contacts traced and isolated. Understand?'

He looked past Yu at his Chancellor. 'Nan Ho... I want you to contact all the heads of the Minor Families and have them come here, at once. By my express order.'

Nan Ho bowed. '*Chieh Hsia*...'

And meanwhile he would call his fellow T'ang. For action must be taken. Immediate action, before the thing got out of hand.

Karr was buttoning his tunic when Chen came into the room, barely stopping to knock. He turned from the mirror, then stopped, seeing the look of delight on Chen's face.

'What is it?'

Chen handed Karr a file. 'It's our friend. There's no doubt about it. These are stills taken from a Security surveillance film thirty-two hours back at Nantes spaceport.'

Karr flipped the folder open and flicked through the stills a moment, then looked back at Chen, his face lit up. 'Then we've got him, neh?'

Chen's face fell. He shook his head.

'*What?*'

'I'm afraid not. It seems his man, Lehmann, picked him up and carried him out of there.'

'And no one intercepted him? Where were Security?'

'Waiting for orders.'

Karr made to speak, then understood. 'Gods... *Again?*'

Chen nodded.

'And the Security Captain. He committed suicide, neh?'

Chen sighed. 'That's right. It fits the pattern. I checked back in their surveillance records. The computer registers that a man matching DeVore's description passed through Nantes spaceport four times in the past month.'

'And there was no Security alert?'

'No. Nor would there have been. The machine was reprogrammed to ignore the instruction from Bremen. As he was wearing false retinas, the only way they could have got him was by direct facial recognition, and because they rely so heavily on computer-generated alerts, the chance of that was minimal.'

'So how did we get these?'

Chen laughed. 'It seems there was a fairly high-ranking Junior Minister on the same flight as DeVore. He complained about the incident direct to Bremen, and when they discovered they had no record of the event they instigated an immediate enquiry. This resulted.'

Karr sat down heavily, setting the file to one side, and began to pull on his boots. For a moment he was quiet, thoughtful, then he looked up again.

'Do we know where he'd been?'

'Boston. But who he saw there or what he was doing we don't yet know. Our friends in North American Security are looking into it right now.'

'And the assassins?' Karr asked, pulling on the other boot. 'Do we know who they were?'

Chen shrugged. 'The two Han look like Triad assassins, but the third... well, we have him on record as a probable *Ping Tiao* sympathizer.'

Karr looked up, raising his eyebrows. '*Ping Tiao*? But they don't exist any longer. At least, that's what our contacts down below tell us. Our friend Ebert is supposed to have wiped them out.'

Chen nodded. 'You don't think...?'

Karr laughed. 'Even Ebert wouldn't be stupid enough to try to work with the *Ping Tiao*. DeVore wouldn't let him.'

'So what do you think?'

Karr shook his head. 'We don't know enough, that's clear. Who, beside ourselves, would want DeVore dead?'

'Someone he's crossed?'

Karr laughed. 'Yes. But that could be anyone, neh? Anyone at all.'

Li Yuan looked out across the marbled expanse of the Hall of the Seven Ancestors and nodded to himself, satisfied. The space between the dragon pillars was packed. More than two thousand men – all the adult males of the Twenty-Nine – were gathered here this afternoon. All, that was, but those who had already succumbed to the sickness.

He sat there on the High Throne, dressed in the dragon robe of imperial yellow edged with blue. In one hand he held the Special Edict, in the other the bamboo cane with the silver cap that had been his brother's present to his father.

There was the faintest murmur from below, but when he stood the hall fell silent, followed a moment later by a loud rustling of expensive silks as, in a single movement, the great crowd knelt, touching their heads to the floor three times in the ritual *liu k'ou*. Li Yuan smiled bleakly, remembering another day, nine years ago, the day when his father had summoned the leaders of the Dispersionists before him, here in this very hall, and humbled them, making their leader, Lehmann, give up his friend, Wyatt. Much had changed since then, but once again the will of the T'ang had to be imposed. By agreement it was hoped, but by force if necessary.

Li Yuan came down, stopping three steps from the bottom, facing the five elderly men who stood at the front of the crowd. His Chancellor, Nan Ho, stood to the right, the list scrolled tightly in one hand. Behind him, just beyond the nearest of the dragon pillars, a troop of élite guards waited, their shaven heads bowed low.

He looked past the five Family heads at the great press of men behind them. All had their heads lowered, their eyes averted, acknowledging his supremacy. Right now they were obedient, but would they remain so when they knew his purpose? Would they understand the need for this, or would they defy him? He shivered, then looked back at the five who stood closest.

He saw how the hands of nephews and cousins reached from behind Chun Wu-chi, supporting him, keeping him from falling; saw how frail his once-father-in-law, Yin Tsu, had become; how the first signs of senility had crept into the eighty-three-year-old face of Pei Ro-hen. Only An Sheng and Hsiang Shao-erh, both men in their fifties, seemed robust. Even so, the Minor Families had thrived – a dozen, fifteen sons not uncommon amongst them – while the Seven had diminished. Why was that? he wondered for the first time. Was it merely the pressures of rule, the depredations of war and politics, or was it symptomatic of some much deeper malaise?

There was silence in the hall, but behind it he could feel the invisible pressure of their expectations. Many of them had heard rumours of the sickness; even so, most were wondering why he had summoned them. Why, in this unprecedented manner, they were standing here in the Great Hall at Tongjiang, waiting for him to speak.

Well, now they would know. He would put paid to all speculation.

'*Ch'un tzu!*' he began, his voice resonant, powerful. 'I have summoned you here today because we face a crisis – perhaps the greatest crisis the Families have ever faced.'

Li Yuan looked across the sea of lowered heads, aware of the power he exercised over these men, but conscious also of what that power rested upon. They obeyed him because they had agreed among themselves to obey him. Take away that agreement – that mandate – and what followed?

He took a breath then continued.

'More than fifty of our number are dead. Another three hundred, I am told, are sick or close to death. And the cause of this mysterious illness? Something we thought we had rid ourselves of long ago – *yang mei ping*. Willow-plum sickness!'

There was an audible murmur of surprise and a number of heads moved agitatedly, but as yet no one dared meet his eyes. He moved on, keeping his voice calm, letting the authority of his position fill his words.

'In the past, I am told, the disease would have killed only after long months of suffering, leading to blindness and eventual madness, but this is a new, more virulent strain – one that our Families are no longer immune to. It is a brain-killer. It can strike down a healthy man – or woman – in less than thirty hours, though, as is the way of such diseases, not all succumb immediately to the virus but become carriers. That, in itself, is horrible enough, but this strain, it seems, is particularly vile, for it is racially specific. It affects only we Han.'

Shocked faces were looking up at him now, forgetting all propriety. Deliberately ignoring this lapse, Li Yuan pressed on, saying what must be said.

'Such are the facts. What we must now ask ourselves is what can we do to combat this disease? There is no cure neither is there time to find one. No cure, that is, but the most drastic of preventative measures.'

Hsiang Shao-erh was looking up at him, his eyes half-lidded, deeply suspicious. 'What do you mean, *Chieh Hsia*?'

Li Yuan met the older man's gaze firmly. 'I mean that we must test everyone in this hall. Wives and children too. And then we must find those outside the Families – man or woman – who have been in contact with anyone from the Families.'

'In contact, *Chieh Hsia*?'

The words were framed politely, but he noted Hsiang's hostility. Hsiang had already lost his eldest son to the virus and it was clear that he saw the drift of Li Yuan's speech.

He answered unflinchingly. 'In *sexual* contact. How else do you think the disease was spread?'

Again he felt the ripples of shock pass through the hall. Despite his reference to willow-plum sickness, many had simply not understood until that moment. A low buzz ran from one end of the hall to the other.

'But surely, *Chieh Hsia*—?'

Li Yuan cut Hsiang off sharply, his patience snapping. 'Silence! All of you, be silent now! I have not finished.'

The hall fell silent, heads were lowered again, but only a pace or so from him Hsiang glared back at him, bristling with anger. Li Yuan looked past him, addressing the great mass.

'We must test everyone. We must track down every last victim – especially the carriers – of this disease.'

'And then?' The voice was Hsiang Shao-erh's. Stubborn, defiant.

Li Yuan looked back at him. 'And then they must die.'

The hall erupted. Li Yuan looked out across the seething crowd, seeing the angry opposition, but also the strong agreement, his words had engendered. Arguments raged on every side. Just beneath him, Hsiang Shao-erh and An Sheng were protesting loudly, their arms gesticulating, their faces dark with anger, while Yin Tsu and Pei Ro-han attempted to remonstrate with them. For a while he let it go on, knowing that this violent flood of feelings must be allowed its channel, then he raised one hand, palm outward. Slowly the hall fell silent again.

He looked down at Hsiang Shao-erh. 'You wish to say something, cousin?'

Hsiang took a pace forward, placing one foot on the first step of the High Throne, seeming almost to threaten his T'ang. He spat the words out angrily.

'I protest, *Chieh Hsia*! You cannot do this! We are Family, not *hsiao jen*! Never in our history have we been subjected to such humiliation! To make us take this test of yours would be to undermine our word, our honour as *ch'un tzu*! Why, it is tantamount to saying that we are all fornicators and cheats on our wives!'

Li Yuan shook his head. 'And the deaths? The spread of the disease? Are these things mere ghosts and idle rumours?'

'There are a few, I admit. Young bucks... but even so...'

'A *few!*' Li Yuan spat the words back angrily, almost contemptuously, taking a step forward, almost pushing his face into Hsiang's, forcing him to take a step back. 'You are a fool, Hsiang, to think of face at such a time! Do you really believe I would do this if it were not necessary? Do you think I would risk damaging my relationship with you, my cousins, if there were not some far greater threat?'

Hsiang opened his mouth, then closed it again, taken aback by the unexpected violence of Li Yuan's counter-attack.

'This is a war,' Li Yuan said, looking past him again, addressing the massed sons and cousins. 'And upon its outcome depends how Chung Kuo will be in years to come. Whether there will be good, stable rule – the rule of Seven and Twenty-Nine – or chaos. To think that we can fight such a war without losses – without sacrifices – is both ridiculous and untenable.'

He looked back directly at Hsiang. 'Do not mistake me, Hsiang Shao-erh. Face, honour, a man's word, these are the very things that bind our society in times of peace, and I would defend them before any man, yet in times of war we must let go sometimes of our high ideals, if but briefly. We must bow, like the reeds before the wind, or go down, like a great tree in a storm.'

Hsiang lowered his eyes. '*Chieh Hsia*...'

'Good. Then you will sign the paper, Hsiang Shao-erh?'

Hsiang looked up again. 'The paper?'

Nan Ho brought the scroll across. Li Yuan turned, offering it to Hsiang. 'Here. I have prepared a document. I would not have it said that the compact between Seven and Twenty-Nine was broken. There must be agreement between us, even in this matter.'

Li Yuan stood there, holding the document out towards Hsiang Shao-erh. As his father had, so he now seemed the very embodiment of imperial power; unyielding, like the famous rock in the Yellow River which, for centuries, had withstood the greatest of floods.

Hsiang stared at the scroll, then looked up at his T'ang, his voice smaller suddenly, more querulous. 'And if any here refuse?'

Li Yuan did not hesitate. 'Then the compact is ended, the Great Wheel broken.'

Hsiang shuddered. For a moment longer he stood there, hesitant, staring at the document. Then, suddenly, he lowered his head. 'Very well, *Chieh Hsia*. I will sign.'

★

Afterwards, while the Families were queuing to be tested, Nan Ho went to Li Yuan in his study.

'Forgive me, *Chieh Hsia*,' he said, bowing low, 'but I did not understand. Why did Hsiang Shao-erh oppose you just now? I would have thought, with his eldest son dead, he would have been the first to sanction your actions – to prevent the deaths of more of his sons.'

Li Yuan sighed. 'So it would have been, I'm sure, Master Nan, but the *chao tai hui* where the sickness was originally spread was held on Hsiang's estate. Oh, he had nothing to do with the organization of the affair – that was all his son, K'ai Fan's doing – neither was Hsiang Shao-erh responsible for the sickness itself. However, he *feels* responsible. Many among the Twenty-Nine blame him, irrational as that is. As a consequence he has lost great face. That display today was an attempt to regain his face. Unfortunately, I could not allow it. Now, I am afraid, I have made an enemy.'

'Things can be smoothed over, surely, *Chieh Hsia*? A gift, perhaps...'

Li Yuan shook his head. 'I made him challenge me. And then I broke him before his equals. It had to be done, but there is no repairing it. No, so we must watch ourselves from that quarter from henceforth. Wang Sau-leyan is sure to hear of what happened here today. No doubt he will try to exploit the division between Hsiang and me.'

The Chancellor shook his head, then looked up again. 'Forgive me, *Chieh Hsia*, but do you not think death too extreme a penalty? After all, it was not their fault that they picked up this sickness. Have you not considered, perhaps, castrating those found with the virus? Those, that is, who would not die of it anyway.'

'No, Master Nan. Had they been servants we might well have done that, but these are Family. Such a humiliation would have been worse than death for them. Besides, what of the women they have infected? What are we to do with them? Sew them up?'

Nan Ho gave a brief, uncomfortable laugh, then bowed his head. 'I had not thought, *Chieh Hsia*.'

Li Yuan smiled sadly. 'Never mind. Go now, Master Nan. Go and supervise the screening. I will expect you three hours from now to give your report on the proceedings.'

'*Chieh Hsia...*'

Li Yuan sat back. There were other things to consider now; other sicknesses to rid the world of. The Young Sons, for instance, and the virus of the Aristotle File. He sighed and leaned forward again, punching in the code that would connect him with Tsu Ma in Astrakhan.

It was time to act. Time to draw in the nets and see what fish they had caught.

Wu Shih, T'ang of North America, raised his eyes from the small screen inset into his desk and looked across at the huge image of Li Yuan's face that filled the facing wall.

He gave a deep sigh, then placed his hands palm down on the desk, clearly disturbed by what he had just seen.

'Well, cousin. I must thank you. The tape is quite conclusive. Even so, I feel nothing but sadness that it has come to this. I had hoped that I could persuade them somehow from their folly, but it is much more than mere folly, isn't it? More than boredom or high spirits. This can lead to one thing only – rebellion and the overthrow of the Seven. I have to act. You understand that?'

Li Yuan nodded. 'Of course,' he said sympathetically. 'Which is why I have already spoken with Tsu Ma. He agrees. And the sooner the better. The Sons of Benjamin Franklin are not the only group. There are similar factions in the other Cities, linked to the Young Sons. If we are to act, it would be best if we acted in concert, neh? Tonight, if possible. At twelfth bell.'

'And the other T'ang?'

Li Yuan shook his head. 'There's no time for that. Besides, if Wang Sau-leyan were to learn, it's likely there would be no one there to arrest. He has a funny way with "secrets".'

Wu Shih looked down, considering, then nodded. 'All right. Twelfth bell. And you will act elsewhere? You and Tsu Ma?'

'At twelfth bell.' He made to cut the connection.

'Li Yuan! Wait! What of the boy? Do you think they will suspect his role in this?'

Li Yuan laughed. 'How could they? Even he doesn't know what he has been these past few days.'

Wu Shih gave a small laugh. 'Even so, should I take steps to get him out?'

Li Yuan shook his head. 'No. Any such move might alert them. Ensure only that your men do not harm him by mistake.'

Wu Shih lowered his head slightly, a mark of respect that he had often made to Yuan's father, Li Shai Tung, and an implicit acknowledgment of where the real leadership lay within the Seven.

Li Yuan smiled. 'Then goodnight, cousin. We shall speak in the morning. Once things are better known.'

The Lever Mansion was a huge, two-storey house with gables, standing in its own wooded grounds. Outside it was dark, the house lights reflected brightly in the dark waters of the nearby lake. In the centre of the mansion's bold façade was a pillared entrance, its wide, double doors open, light spilling out on to a gravel drive. Dark sedans, some antique, some reproduction, lined the entrance road, their runners dressed in a black-suited livery that matched the ancient crest on the sides of the sedans. All evening they had gone back and forth, ferrying guests between the house and the transit, almost a *li* away.

The illusion was almost perfect. The darkness hid the walls of the surrounding decks, while above, a thick, dark blue cloth masked the ice of the stack's uppermost floor, like a starless night sky.

Kim stood there between the trees, in darkness, looking back at the house. This was the third time he had come to Richmond, to the Lever Mansion, but it was the first time he had seen the house in darkness. Tonight they were throwing a ball. A party for the elite of their City – the *Supernal*, as they called themselves. It was the first time he had heard the term used and it amused him to think of himself, so *low* in birth, mixing in such *high* company. He was not drunk – he took care never to touch alcohol or drugs – but merely mixing in the atmosphere of the house was enough to create a mild euphoria. The air was chill, sharp. In the trees nearby the leaves rustled in a mild, artificial breeze. Kim smiled, enjoying the strangeness of it all, and reached out to touch the smooth bark of one of the pines.

'Kim?'

A tall, elegant young man in old-fashioned evening dress stood at the edge of the gravel, calling him. It was Michael Lever.

'I'm here,' he said, stepping out from the trees. 'I was just getting some air.'

Lever greeted him, more than a ch'i taller than him, straight-backed and blond, an *American* ...

'Come on through,' he said, smiling. 'Father was asking after you.'

Kim let himself be ushered inside once more, through reception room and ballroom and out into a smaller, quieter space beyond. Leather doors closed behind him. The room was dimly lit, pervaded by the tart smell of cigar smoke. Old Man Lever was sitting on the far side of the room, beside the only lamp, his friends gathered about him in high-backed leather chairs. Old men, like himself. By the window stood a group of younger men. Michael joined them, accepting a drink from one, then turned back, looking across at Kim.

Charles Lever lit up a new cigar, then beckoned Kim over. 'Here, Kim. Take a seat.' He indicated the empty chair beside him. 'There are some people here – friends of mine – I want you to meet.'

Old men. The thought flashed through Kim's mind. *Old men, afraid of dying.*

He sat in the huge, uncomfortable chair, ill at ease, nodding acknowledgment to each of the men in turn; noting each face and placing it. These were big men. Powerful men. Each of them Lever's equal. So what had Lever said? What had Lever promised he could do for them?

'We were talking,' Lever said, turning in his chair to look at Kim. 'Chewing things over among ourselves. And I was telling my friends here about your new company. About *Chih Chu.* Potentially a nice little outfit, but small, undercapitalized.'

Kim looked down, surprised that Lever knew already.

Lever cleared his throat, then nodded, as if satisfied by his own evaluation of things. 'And I was saying what a shame it was. Because I've seen your like before, Kim. A hot property with plenty of good, strong ideas and lots of get-up-and-go, but nothing to back it up. There's a pattern to it, too. I've seen how they've built things up – how they've grown really fast. Up to a certain point. And then...' He shook his head and looked down at the cigar smouldering between his fingers. 'Then they've tried to move up a league. Into manufacturing. Because it's a shame to let the big industrials take so large a share of the cut. Galling, even.'

The young men by the window were watching him intently, almost suspiciously. Kim could feel their eyes on him; could almost sense what they were thinking. What would this mean for them? For if their fathers lived for ever...

'I've seen them try to take that step,' Lever continued. 'And I've seen them flounder, unable to cope with the sheer size of the market. I've watched the big Companies move in, like those sharks we were talking of, and gobble up the pieces. Because that's what it's really all about, Kim. Not ideas. Not potential. Not get-up-and-go. But money. Money and power.'

He paused and sucked at his cigar. All about him the old men nodded, but their eyes never left Kim's face.

'So I was saying to my friends here, let's make things happen a little differently this time. Use some of *our* money, *our* power to help this young man. Because it's a shame to see potential go to waste. A damn shame, if you ask me.'

He leaned back, drawing on the cigar, then puffed out a narrow stream of smoke. Kim waited, silent, not knowing what to say. He wanted nothing from these men. Neither money, nor power. But that was not the point. It was what they wanted from him that mattered here.

'CosTech has offered for your contract. Right?'

Kim opened his mouth, then snapped it shut. Of course Lever would know. He had spies, hadn't he? They all had spies. It was how things worked at this level. You weren't in business unless you knew what the competition was up to.

'Yes. But I haven't decided yet,' he lied, wanting to hear what they were going to offer. 'I'm meeting them again in two weeks to talk terms.'

Lever smiled, but it was a smile tinged with sourness. 'Working for the competition, eh?' He laughed. 'Rather you than me, boy.'

There was laughter from the gathered circle. Only by the window was there silence.

'But why's this, Kim? Why would you want to waste a year of your life slaving for CosTech when you could be pushing *Chih Chu* on to bigger things?'

Make your offer, Kim thought. *Spell it out. What you want. What you're offering. Make a deal, old man. Or would that embarrass you, being so direct?*

'You know what they've offered?' he asked.

Lever nodded. 'It's peanuts. An insult to your talent. And it ties you. Limits what you could do.'

Ah, thought Kim, *that's more to the point.* Working for CosTech, he could not work for ImmVac. And they needed him. The old men needed him, because, after a certain age, it was not possible to stop the ageing process. Not as things stood. They had to catch it before the molecular signal that triggered it. Afterwards was no good. What ImmVac had developed was no good for any of these men. The complex system of cell replication began to break down, slowly at first, but exponentially, until the genetic damage was irreparable. And then senility.

And what good was money or power against senility and death?

'I'm a physicist,' he said, looking at the old man directly. 'What good am I to you? You want a biochemist. Someone working in the field of defective protein manufacture. In cell repair. Not an engineer.'

Lever shook his head. 'You're good. People say you're the best. And you're young. You could learn. Specialize in self-repair mechanisms.' He stared at Kim fiercely. The cigar in his hand had gone out. 'We'll pay what you ask. Provide whatever you need.'

Kim rubbed at his eyes. The cigar smoke had made them sore. He wanted to say no and have an end to it, but knew these were not men he could readily say no to.

'Two weeks, Shih Lever. Give me two weeks, then I'll let you know.'

Lever narrowed his eyes, suspicious of the young, childlike man. 'Two weeks?'

'Yes. After all, you're asking me to change the direction of my life. And that's something I have to think about. I've got to consider what it means. What I might lose and what gain. I can't see it right now. Which is why I need to think it through.'

But he had thought it through already and dismissed it. He knew what he wanted; had known from the first moment he had glimpsed the vision of the web. Death – what was death beside that vision?

Lever looked to the other men in the room, then nodded his agreement. 'All right, Shih Ward. Two weeks it is.'

It was late. The crowd in the ballroom had thinned out, but the dancing went on. On the balcony overlooking the hall, a ten-man orchestra played a slow waltz, their bows rising and falling in the fragmented light. Kim stood at the back of the hall, beside Michael Lever, watching the couples move about the floor, realizing that this too was an illusion; a dream of ageless-ness. As if time could be restored, its flow reversed.

'I love their dresses,' he said, looking up at the tall young man. 'They're like jellyfish.'

Lever roared, then turned to his friends and repeated Kim's comment. In a moment their laughter joined his own. Lever turned back to Kim, wiping his eyes with the back of his hand.

'That's rich, Kim. Marvellous! Like jellyfish!' And again he burst into laughter.

Kim looked at him, surprised. What had he said? It was true, wasn't it? The bobbing movements of their many-layered dresses were like those of jellyfish in the ocean, even down to the frilled edges.

'I was only saying...' he began, but he never finished the sentence. At that moment the main lights came up. The orchestra played on for a moment or two, then ended in sudden disarray. The dancers stopped circling and stood there, looking towards the doorway at the far end of the ballroom. Suddenly it felt much colder in the hall. There was the sound of shouting from outside.

'What in hell's name?' Lever said, starting to make his way towards the doors. Then he stopped abruptly. Soldiers had come out on to the balcony above the dance floor. More came into the ballroom through the doorway. Security troops in powder-blue fatigues, black-helmeted, their visors down.

Kim felt his mouth go dry. Something was wrong.

The soldiers formed a line along the edge of the balcony and along the lower walls, covering the dancers with their weapons. Only a few of their number went among the dancers, their visors up, looking from face to face. Up above, on the balcony, a lieutenant began to read out a warrant for the arrest of fifteen men.

In the ballroom there was disbelief and anger. One young man jostled a Security guard and was brought down by a sharp blow with a rifle butt. When the soldiers went from the hall they took more than a dozen young men, Lever and his friends amongst them.

Kim, watching, saw the anger in surrounding faces after the soldiers had gone. More anger than he'd ever seen. And different, very different from the anger of the Clay. This anger smouldered like red-hot ashes fanned by a breath. It was a deep-rooted, enduring anger.

Beside Kim a young man's face was distorted, black with rage. 'He'll pay! The bastard will pay for this!' Others gathered about him, shouting, their fists clenched, the dance forgotten.

Kim stood there a moment longer, then turned away, going quickly from the hall. Things had changed. Suddenly, dramatically, the rules had changed, and he was no longer safe here. He passed through, glancing from side to side, seeing only outrage on the faces of those he passed. Outside he walked past the waiting sedans and on, out across the darkness towards the transit.

In a sober moment they would remember. Old Man Lever would remember. And in his anger, who knew how he would act? It was a time for taking sides, and he was Li Yuan's man.

He saw soldiers up ahead, guarding the transit entrance, and began to run, knowing his safety lay with them. But nearer the barrier he turned and looked back at the house, remembering the dresses bobbing to the music, the swish of lace in the air. And a circle of old men, offering him the earth.

Chapter 69

IN THE OPEN

Tolonen stood there at Haavikko's bedside, looking down at him, a faint smile on his lips. It was only two days since his own operation and he was still feeling weak, but he had had to come.

A nurse brought him a chair and he sat, content to wait until the young man woke. His new arm ached at the shoulder, despite the drugs, but it was feeling better than it had.

Besides, he was alive. Thanks to Haavikko.

The nurse hovered but he waved her away, then settled to watch the sleeping man.

All his life he had been self-reliant. All his life he had fought his own fights, keeping himself one step ahead of his enemies. But now he was growing old. At last he had proof of it. His old eyes had missed the discrepancy of the colour codings on the soldiers' chests – his reactions had been just that fraction of a second too slow – and he had lost his arm as a result. Almost his life.

He smiled, studying the young man. Haavikko was cradled in bandages, special healants creating new skin growth on his badly burned shoulder and back.

Tolonen shook his head as if to clear it, feeling both sad and happy at once. He had been told what Haavikko had done for him, like a son for a father; risking himself when all bonds of duty or obligation had long ago been severed between them.

Yes, he had sorely misjudged the boy.

Haavikko stirred and opened his eyes. 'Marshal...' He made to sit up, then winced and eased back, closing his eyes again. The blast had removed most of the skin at the top of his back and taken off his ear.

'Lie still, boy. Please. You need your rest.'

Haavikko opened his eyes again and looked up at the Marshal. 'Your arm...' he said, clearly pained by the sight.

Tolonen laughed gruffly. 'You like it? It hurts a bit just now, but that doesn't matter. I'm alive, that's the thing.' He sat back, his right hand reaching up to scratch at the stubble on his left cheek; an awkward, embarrassed gesture, indicative of just how hard the old man found it to deal with this. The warmth he felt towards the other man – that depth of reawakened feeling – brought him close to tears. He looked away a moment, controlling himself, then finished what he had meant to say. 'Thanks to you, Axel. Thanks to you.'

Axel smiled. His hands lay above the sheets. Long, fine hands, undamaged in the incident. Tolonen took one and squeezed it.

'I misjudged you, boy. I...'

Haavikko shook his head, a slight grimace of pain crossing his face. 'It doesn't matter. Really, sir. I...' He turned his head slightly, looking across the room to where his clothes hung on a peg. 'But there's something you must know. Something important.'

Tolonen smiled. 'Rest, my boy. There's plenty of time for other things...'

'No.' Haavikko swallowed drily. 'Over there, in my tunic, there's a package. I was bringing it to you when it happened. I'd pieced it all together.'

Tolonen shook his head, puzzled. 'Pieced what together?'

Haavikko looked up, pleading with his eyes. 'Just look. Please, sir. You don't have to read it all right now. Later, perhaps, when you feel up to it. But promise me you'll read it. Please, Marshal.'

Tolonen let go of Haavikko's hand, then got up heavily and went across. Just as Haavikko had said, there was a small package in the inner pocket of the tunic. He tugged at it until it came free, then went back, taking his seat again.

He held the package out, a query in his eyes. 'So what is this?'

Haavikko swallowed again and Tolonen, taking the hint, set the package down and picked up the glass by the bedside, giving Haavikko a few sips.

'Well?'

'Long ago you asked me to do something for you – to make a list of people who might have been involved in the assassination of Minister Lwo Kang. Do you remember?'

Tolonen laughed. 'Gods! That must have been eleven years ago. And you did that?'

Haavikko made the smallest movement of his head. 'That's how it began. But I extended it. I kept a record of anything I felt wasn't right – anything that didn't quite make sense to me. Then, recently, I teamed up with Kao Chen and your man Karr.'

'Good men,' Tolonen said, nodding his approval.

'Yes.' Haavikko smiled then grew serious again. 'Anyway, what you have there is the result of our investigations. My original list, my notes and a few other things. Computer files. Hologram images.'

Tolonen lifted the package and turned it in his hand, then set it down on his knee and reached out to take Haavikko's hand again. 'And you want me to look at it?'

'Yes...'

Tolonen considered a moment. He had promised Jelka he would dine with her later on, but maybe he would cancel that. He could always say he was tired. Jelka would understand. He smiled broadly at Haavikko. 'Of course. It's the very least I could do.'

Haavikko looked back at him, his eyes moist. 'Thank you,' he said, his voice almost a whisper. 'Thank you, sir.'

Tolonen sat there, clasping the young man's hand. The ache in his left shoulder was much stronger now. It was probably time for his medication, but he felt loath to leave the young man.

'I must go now,' he said softly. 'But I promise you I'll look at your files. Later. When it's quiet.'

Haavikko smiled, his eyes closed. Slowly his mouth relaxed. In a moment he was asleep.

Tolonen placed the young man's hand gently back on the sheets then got stiffly to his feet. Twice lucky, he thought, remembering the attack at Nanking spaceport. He made his way across, then turned, looking back, noticing for the first time just how pale Haavikko was. He stood there a moment longer, absently scratching at the dressing at his shoulder, then desisted, annoyed with himself.

He looked down at the silver arm and sighed, remembering how Jelka had fussed when she'd first seen it. But there was steel in her too. She had borne up bravely. So too this young man. Oh, he would make things up. He was determined on it. Would find a way of making things right again.

Tolonen yawned, then, smiling sadly to himself, turned away, leaving the young officer to sleep.

Tsu Ma lifted the dish and brushed his thumb across its silken, contoured surface. It was a perfect piece: black lacquer carved with two waterfowl against a background of lotus. Fourteenth century, from the last years of the Yuan dynasty. He smiled to himself, then turned to face Li Yuan.

'Two years they would labour to make one of these. Two years of a master craftsman's life. And at the end, this. This small fragment of dark perfection.'

Li Yuan looked across at him, turning from the view of the bay and the sugarloaf mountain beyond. He had not been listening, but he saw the lacquered dish in Tsu Ma's hands and nodded. 'That piece is beautiful. Hou Ti had many fine things.'

Tsu Ma held his eyes a moment. 'These days some think of them as primitive, ignorant men. Barbarians. But look at this. Is this barbarian?' He shook his head slowly, his eyes returning to the dish. 'As if the mere passage of years could make our species more sophisticated.'

Li Yuan laughed and came closer. 'Your point, Tsu Ma?'

Behind them, at the far side of the long room, the rest of the Seven were gathered, talking among themselves.

Tsu Ma set the dish down, letting his fingers rest in its shallow bowl, then looked up at Li Yuan again. 'Just that there are those here who think the future better than the past simply because it is the future. Who believe that change is good simply because it is change. They have no time for comparisons. Or for the kind of values expressed in the simplicity of this dish. No time for craft, control or discipline.' He lowered his voice a fraction. 'And I find that disturbing, Li Yuan. Dangerous, even.'

Li Yuan studied him a moment, then gave the barest nod of agreement. They had covered much ground that morning, but nothing yet of true significance. On the matters of the stewardships and the new immortality drugs he had bowed like the reed before the wind, not pushing his own viewpoint, merely ensuring that these matters were not finalized. Let them play their games of evading death, he thought; death would find them anyway, wherever they hid. As for the other, there was time enough to force his view on that.

'How deep is this feeling?'

Tsu Ma considered a moment, then leaned towards Li Yuan. 'Deep, cousin. Deep enough to trouble me.' He looked past the younger man, out beyond the window glass, seeing how the space between the bowl of hills was plugged with the white of the City's walls. 'They would do away with certain restraints.' He stretched his long neck, lifting his chin, then looked directly at Li Yuan. 'You'll see. This afternoon...'

The early afternoon sunlight fell across Li Yuan's arm and shoulder. 'It is the illness of our time. Change and the desire for change. But I had not thought...' Yuan smiled and broke off, seeing Chi Hsing, the T'ang of the Australias, approach.

The two men nodded, acknowledging the newcomer.

'Are you not eating, cousins?' Chi Hsing smiled and turned, summoning the waiters, then turned back. 'Before we resume, there is a matter I must raise with you. A change has been proposed to the scheduled itinerary.'

'A change?' Li Yuan said, raising his eyebrows slightly, but heavily emphasizing the word. Beside him Tsu Ma kept his amusement to himself, staring back mask-like at his fellow T'ang.

Chi Hsing was known for neither his intelligence nor his subtlety. In that regard he was much more his mother's child than his father's. He was a father now himself, of course. Two young sons, the eldest barely two, had blessed his first marriage, changing him considerably. He was less rash now than he'd been, and though he had secretly applauded Li Yuan's purge of the Ping Tiao, he also had misgivings about such actions. He feared for his sons, remembering what had happened in the War with the Dispersionists. Vengeance was fine, but now he wished only for peace.

Peace. So that he might see his sons grow to be men. Strong, fine men, as his father had been.

'Wang Sau-leyan has made a request,' he began, his eyes searching both their faces. 'And there are others here who wish to speak on the matter.' His eyes grew still, focused on Li Yuan.

'Go on, cousin.'

Chi Hsing bowed his head slightly. 'He wishes to discuss the arrests. The action you took in league with Wu Shih against the young sons.'

It was clear, by the way Chi Hsing stood there, that he expected Li Yuan to refuse. Indeed, it was within Li Yuan's rights to refuse Wang's request, as his father had done once before. But Li Yuan only smiled politely.

'I have no objection to that. Do you, Tsu Ma?'

'Not I.'

Li Yuan reached out and touched Chi Hsing's shoulder. 'It is best, after all, if these things are aired between us. In the open.'

Chi Hsing nodded, still hesitant, as if he expected Li Yuan to change his mind at any moment. Then, realizing he had achieved his end, he smiled.

'Good. That's very good, Li Yuan. As you say, it is best. In the open.' He nodded again, this time decisively, then turned and went across to where Wang Sau-leyan and their host, Hou Tung-po, T'ang of South America, were standing. Wang listened a moment, then looked across at Li Yuan, bowing his head slightly.

'In the open,' said Tsu Ma beneath his breath. 'You're like your father, Yuan. Devious.'

Li Yuan turned, surprised, then laughed, seeing the humour beneath the surface of Tsu Ma's words. 'Words are words, Tsu Ma. We must bend and shape them to our needs.'

Tsu Ma nodded, pleased with that. 'So it is in these troubled times, cousin. But history shall judge us by our actions.'

Wang Sau-leyan was leaning forward in his seat, his hands folded in his lap, his big, moon face looking from one to another as he spoke. He seemed calm, relaxed, his voice soft and deep, persuasive in its tones. Thus far he had said little that had not been said before, but now he turned the conversation.

'In this room, as in the rooms of the Twenty-Nine and the mansions of the Supernal, there are those who are questioning recent events. Some with anger, some with sadness and misgivings. Others fearfully, remembering things not long past. But every last one of them is concerned, wondering where it will stop. For myself, I believe it has already gone too far.'

Wu Shih made to interrupt, but Wang raised his hand. 'You will have your say, Wu Shih, and I shall listen. But first hear me out. This must be said, before it is too late for words.'

Tsu Ma reached into the pocket of his jacket and took out a slender silver case. 'Then talk, cousin. Let us hear what you have to say.'

There was an unconcealed hostility in the words that surprised Li Yuan. He watched Tsu Ma take a cheroot from the case then close it and slip it back into his pocket.

'Thank you, cousin,' said Wang, watching the older man light the cheroot and draw the first breath from it. He smiled tightly, then let his face fall blank again. 'As I said, there is anger and sadness and a great deal of fear. Unhealthy symptoms. Signs of a deep and bitter hostility towards us.'

Wu Shih grunted indignantly, but kept his silence. His cheeks burned red and his eyes bored into the side of Wang's softly rounded face.

'We have sown a harvest of discontent,' Wang went on. 'And I say we, because this affects us all. And yet I hesitate to use that plural, because it suggests consensus on our part. Suggests a commonly agreed-upon set of actions, discussed and debated here, in Council, as has always been our way.' He paused and looked about him, shaking his head. 'Instead I wake to find the world a different place from when I slept. And myself every bit as surprised as those who came begging audience, saying, "Why is my son arrested?"'

In the chair beside him, Hou Tung-po nodded his head vigorously. 'So it was for me. I was not notified, Li Yuan. Not consulted before you and Wu Shih acted. A poor choice was left to me, to seem a scoundrel or look a fool. Relations are bad between us and the Above. As bad as at any time during the last ten years. We must act to defuse this situation before it gets out of hand. We must make some gesture to placate the Above.'

There was a moment's silence, then Li Yuan spoke, his anger at Wang Sau-leyan's criticism barely contained.

'When a man saves his brother's life, does he say first, "Excuse me, brother, I would save your life, is that all right with you?" No, he acts, pushing his brother aside, out of the way of the falling rock. He *acts*! I make no apologies for my actions. Or for the lack of consultation. Surprise was a necessity. I could not risk informing *anyone*.'

He stood, going to the centre of their informal circle, looking down at Wang Sau-leyan.

'Perhaps you relish death, cousin Wang. For myself I would grow old in peace, no dagger to my throat.'

Wang laughed; a short, bitter laugh. 'Oh, yes, Li Yuan, you act like one destined to live long. For while your enemies multiply, your friends diminish.'

Li Yuan smiled back at him tightly. 'So it is in this world. But it is better to trust one's friends and know one's enemies. To act than to prevaricate.'

Wang Sau-leyan glared back at Li Yuan, infuriated by his words, all pretence of calm gone from him. 'Ai ya! – but must we all suffer for your rashness, cousin? Must we reap what you sow? You sound like your dead brother – hot-headed!'

For a moment there was a tense silence, then Li Yuan gave a soft laugh. 'Hot-headed, you say?' He shook his head. 'Not so, cousin. Not so. You ask for something to placate the Above, like a woman begging for her son's life. Has it come to that? Are we so weak we must beg for our existence? Are we not to crush what seeks to destroy us? It seems you have changed your tune, Wang Sau-leyan, for once you sought to lecture us...'

Wang was shaking his head. 'Young men, Li Yuan, that's all they are. Young men. Misguided, over-enthusiastic, that's all.' Wang looked beyond Li Yuan, a faint smile resting on his lips. 'It would defuse things if we let them go, and in time this thing would certainly blow over.'

'Blow over?' Li Yuan shook his head in disbelief. 'What must they do before you see it, cousin? Must they hold the gun to your head? This is no act of high spirits. This is revolution. Open rebellion. Don't you understand? It begins with ideas and it ends with bloodshed.' He paused, then took a step closer, pointing down at Wang. 'They would kill you, Wang Sau-leyan, T'ang of Africa, and set themselves up in your place. Just as they killed your eldest brothers. Or do you forget?'

Li Yuan stood there, breathing deeply, staring down at Wang Sau-leyan, forcing him to meet his eyes.

'Well? Do you still want appeasement?'

Wang nodded.

'And who else?' He looked at Hou Tung-po, then across to Chi Hsing. Both nodded, though neither met his eyes.

'And you, Wei Feng? What do you counsel?' He turned, facing the aged T'ang of East Asia. 'You, surely, know the depths of this problem.'

'You speak as if I had the casting vote, Li Yuan.'

'You have.' It was Tsu Ma who answered for Li Yuan. Beside him Wu Shih looked across, bowing his head in assent.

Wei Feng sighed and looked down. 'You know what I feel,' he began, his low, toneless voice picking out each word slowly, meticulously. 'You know my dislikes, my prejudices.' He looked up at Li Yuan. 'You must know, then, that what you did pleased me greatly.' He smiled sourly. 'However, that is not what is at issue here. What's at issue is our manner of conducting ourselves, Li Yuan. Not the action itself – with which I basically agree and on which I would support you at any other time – but the *way* in which you acted. As Wang Sau-leyan says, you acted without consulting us.'

He paused, considering, then spoke again. 'We are Seven, Li Yuan. Not One, but Seven. In that lies our strength. For seven generations now, our strength and the reason for peace in the world. For the strength of our society. Break that cohesion and you break it all.'

'You defer, then, Wei Feng?'

Wei Feng nodded. 'I say free the young men. Then do as Wang says. Make the best of a bad lot and seek conciliation.'

For a moment longer Li Yuan stood there, then he shrugged. 'So be it,' he said, looking across at Wang. 'I will hand my prisoners over to you, cousin, to do with as you will.'

He looked away, leaving it there, but in his head the words resounded. *Not One, but Seven. In that lies our strength.* He had never questioned it before, but now, standing there amidst his peers, he asked himself if it was really so.

He glanced at Wu Shih, seeing how the T'ang of North America was looking down, his anger unexpressed, and had his answer. The days of unanimity were gone, and what had made the Seven such a force had gone with them. What Wei Feng had said, that had been true once, back in his father's time, but now?

Seven... the word was hollow now, the Great Wheel broken. It had died with his father. Four against three – that was the new reality. He looked across at Wang Sau-leyan, seeing the gleam of triumph in his eyes, and knew. It was finished. Here, today, it had ended. And now they must find another path, another way of governing themselves. That was the truth. But the truth could not be spoken. Not yet, anyway, and certainly not here, in Council.

He smiled, suddenly relaxing, as if a great weight had been taken from his shoulders and turned his head, meeting Tsu Ma's eyes; seeing the light of understanding there.

'Shall we move on?' he said, looking about the circle of his fellow T'ang. 'Time presses and there's much to do.'

Yes, he thought; *but none of it matters now. From now on this is merely play, a mask to hide our real intentions. For all the real decisions will henceforth be made in secret.*

Out in the open. He laughed, recognizing finally the full irony of what he had said earlier, then turned, looking at Tsu Ma, and smiled, seeing his smile returned strongly. Yes. So it would be from now on. *In the open...*

It had been summer in Rio. In Tongjiang it was winter.

Li Yuan stood on the terrace, looking out over the frozen lake. He wore furs and gloves and thick leather boots, but his head was bare, snowflakes settling in his fine, dark hair. Below him the slope was deep in snow while on the far shore the trees of the orchard formed stark, tangled shapes against the white.

He looked up past the gentle slopes towards the distant mountains. Vast, sharp-edged escarpments of rock speared the colourless sky. He shivered then turned away, finding the bleakness of the view too close to his present mood.

He looked across at the palace, the stables beyond. His men were waiting on the veranda, talking amongst themselves beneath the great, shuttered windows. They did not like it here, he knew. This openness appalled them. They felt exposed, naked to all the primal things the City shut out behind its walls, but for him only this was real. The rest was but a game.

He had expected to find her here, or at least the memory of her, but there was nothing. Only the place itself remained, robbed of its scents, its vivid greenness, all human presence gone. As if all that had happened here had never been.

He shivered and looked down at his feet. A leaf clung to the ankle of his right boot. He removed his glove and stooped to pluck the wet and blackened leaf, then straightened up, feeling the icy cold against his flesh, the wetness in his palm. What did it all mean? He brushed the leaf away and pulled his glove back on, turning to walk back to the palace and the waiting transit.

Nothing, he decided. *It meant nothing.*

He flew south-west, over unbroken whiteness. Not snow this time but the endless City, three thousand li without a break, until they reached Kuang Chou, ancient Canton, at the mouth of the Pei River. Then, for a while, there was the blue of the South China Sea, before Hong Kong and, to its south-east, the island of T'ai Yueh Shan, where Yin Tsu had his estate.

He had put this off too long. But now it was time to see the child. To bestow his gift upon his past-wife's son.

Coded signals passed between the ship and the estate's defence system, then they came down, Yin Tsu greeting him in the hangar. He was kneeling, his forehead pressed to the cold metal of the grid as Li Yuan stepped down.

Li Yuan had changed on the flight down, shedding his furs and gloves and heavy boots in favour of thin satins of a fiery orange and slippers of the finest kid. Approaching the old man, he stopped, lifting his foot.

Yin Tsu took the offered foot with care and kissed it once, then once more, before releasing it.

'Yin Tsu, once-father, please.' He reached down and took the old man's hand, helping him up. Only then did Yin Tsu look at him.

'I am honoured by your visit, *Chieh Hsia.* What may I do for you?'

'Fei Yen... Is she still here with you?'

The old man nodded, his thin lips forming the faintest of smiles. 'Yes, *Chieh Hsia.* She is here. And the child.'

'Good. Good.' He hesitated a moment, feeling awkward, then spoke again. 'I'd like to see her. And... the child too. If she would see me.'

'Please. Come through.' Yin Tsu led the way, half turned towards Li Yuan in courtesy as he walked, bowed low, his hands held out but pressed together in an attitude of the deepest respect.

While he waited for her, he thought of what he would say. He had not seen her since the day he had insisted on the tests. Had she forgiven him for that?

He gritted his teeth, thinking on it, then turned to find her standing there. She was wearing a pale lemon-coloured dress, her dark hair hanging loose about her shoulders. The child was not with her.

'I...' he began, but the sight of her struck him dumb. She seemed more beautiful than ever, her face stronger, her breasts much fuller than he remembered them. As he had turned to face her she had bowed and now rested on one knee, her head lowered, awaiting his command.

'Fei Yen,' he said, but the words came out so softly that she did not hear them. He went across and touched her gently on the crown of her head, wanting to kiss her there, his cheek muscle twitching with the tension he felt this close to her. He stepped back, straightening up. 'Get up, Fei Yen. Please...'

She got up slowly, her dark eyes filled with awe of him. She had seen how powerful he was; how his servants laid their necks down for him to tread upon. Had seen and was afraid. This was not the boy she had known. No, he was no longer a child but a man: the cub a lion now, dressed in flame.

'You look well,' he said, aware of the inadequacy of the words.

'I wondered when you'd come. I knew you would.'

He nodded, surprised by how subdued she sounded. So different from before. 'And the child?'

'He's fine.' She looked away, biting her lip. 'He's sleeping now. Do you want to see him?' She glanced at him, aware of his hesitation. 'You don't have to. I know how you feel about all this.'

Do you? he thought; but he kept silent and simply nodded.

'Han,' she said. 'I called him Han. As you wished.'

She was watching him, trying to see what he made of it. His cheek muscle twitched once more and then lay still, his face a mask.

'Come,' she said after a moment, then led him through, down a high-ceilinged corridor to the nursery.

A girl sat beside the cot, her hands in her lap. At the entrance of her mistress she got up and bowed. Then she saw Li Yuan and abased herself, as Yin Tsu had done. Fei Yen dismissed her hurriedly, then turned to face Li Yuan again.

'Don't wake him, Yuan. He needs his sleep.'

He nodded and went close.

The child lay on its side, one hand up to its mouth, the other resting lightly against the bars at the side of the cot. A fine, dark down of hair covered its scalp, while about its neck lay a monitoring strip, the milky white band pulsing quickly, in time with the baby's heartbeat.

'But he's so... so *tiny!*' Li Yuan laughed, surprised. The baby's hands, his tiny, perfectly formed feet were like fine sculpture. Like miniatures in tarnished ivory.

'He's not six weeks yet,' she said, as if that explained the beauty of the child. Li Yuan wanted to reach out and hold one of those tiny hands, to feel its fingers stretch and close about his thumb.

He turned, looking at her, and suddenly all of the old bitterness and love were there, impurely mixed in what he was feeling. He hated her for this. Hated her for making him feel so much. Frustration made him grit his teeth and push past her, the feeling overwhelming him, making him want to cry out for the pain he felt.

As at first, he realized. It had always hurt him to be with her. She took too much. Left him so little of himself. And that was wrong. He could not be a T'ang and feel like this. No, it was better to feel nothing than to feel so much. He stood with his back to her, breathing deeply, trying to calm himself, to still the turmoil in his gut and put it all back behind the ice.

Where it belonged. Where it had to belong.

She was silent, waiting for him. When he turned back all trace of feeling had gone from his face. He looked across at the cot and the sleeping child, then back at her, his voice quiet, controlled.

'I want to give you something. For you and the child. It will be his when he comes of age, but until that time it is yours to administer.'

She lowered her head obediently.

'I want him to have the palace at Hei Shui.'

She looked up, wide-eyed with surprise. 'Li Yuan...' But he had raised his hand to silence her.

'The documents are drawn up. I want no arguments, Fei Yen. It's little enough compared to what he might have had.'

She turned her head away, unable to disguise the moment's bitterness, then nodded her acquiescence.

'Good.' He turned, looking at the cot once more. 'There will be an allowance, too. For both of you. You will not want for anything, Fei Yen. Neither you nor he.'

'My father...' she began, pride creeping back into her voice, but she cut it off, holding her tongue. She knew he need do nothing. The terms of the divorce were clear enough. Hers was the shame. In her actions lay the blame for how things were.

'Let it be so, then,' he said finally. 'Your father shall have the documents. And Han...' He said the name; said it and breathed deeply afterwards, a muscle jumping in his cheek. 'Han shall have Hei Shui.'

Tolonen looked up, his long face ashen, his grey eyes filled with a deep hurt. For a time he stared sightlessly at the wall, then, slowly, shook his head.

'I can't believe it,' he said quietly, pushing the file away from him. 'I just can't believe it. Hans...' His mouth creased into a grimace of pain. 'What will I say...? What will his father say?' Then he thought of Jelka and the betrothal and groaned. 'Gods, what a mess. What a stinking, horrible mess.'

The file on Hans Ebert was a slender dossier, not enough to convict a man in law, but enough to prove its case by any other measure. To an advocate it would have been merely a mass of circumstantial evidence, but that evidence pointed in one direction only.

Tolonen sighed, then rubbed at his eyes. Hans had been clever. Too clever, in fact, for the sum total of his cleverness was a sense of absence: of shadow where there should have been substance. Discrepancies in GenSyn funds. Payments to fellow officers. Unexplained absences in Ebert's service record – missing hours and days that, in three cases, linked up with dates given them by DeVore's man, Reid. Misplaced files on five of the eighteen younger sons arrested on Li Yuan's instructions only a day or so ago, all of which had, at some point, passed through Ebert's hands. Then there was the statement given by the girl in the Ebert household, Golden Heart, and, finally, the holograms.

The holograms seemed, on the surface of it, to be the most conclusive evidence, though in law, he knew, they held no real significance. It had been successfully claimed long ago that photographic and holographic evidence was unreliable, since GenSyn could make a perfect duplicate of anyone. This and the whole question of image-verification had relegated such 'information' to a secondary status in law.

But this was not something that would ever see a courtroom. Wider issues were at stake here. And older codes of conduct.

In one of the holograms Hans could be seen standing on the veranda of a skiing lodge, looking down at a figure on the snow below him. That

figure was DeVore. They were grainy shots, taken from a narrow triangu-
lation – perhaps as little as twenty degrees – and consequently the far side
of the three-dimensional image blurred into perfect whiteness, but that
incompleteness itself suggested that it was genuine, taken with two hand-
helds from a distance, who knew for what purpose – maybe blackmail. The
holograms had been found in storage in DeVore's stronghold, almost as
though they had been left to be found. In itself this might have led Security
to discount them as a subtle attempt to undermine Ebert's position, but
added to the other matters they were significant.

No, there was no *real* proof, but the circumstantial evidence was con-
siderable. Ebert had been working with the rebels; providing them with
funds; meeting with them; passing on information, and covering their
tracks where necessary.

Tolonen closed the file, then sat back, his hands trembling. He had
always trusted Ebert. When he had asked Haavikko to investigate he had
been thinking of three other officers. For him the question of Hans Ebert's
loyalty had never arisen. Not until this evening.

He shook his head. There were tears in his eyes now; tears running down
his furrowed cheeks. He gritted his teeth, tightening the muscles in his face,
but still the tears came. There was only one thing to do. He would have to go
and see Klaus. After all, this was Family. A matter of honour.

He let out a shuddering sigh, then shook his head, remembering. Jelka...
He had promised Jelka that he would dine with her at home tonight. He
glanced at the timer on the wall, then pulled himself up out of the chair,
throwing the file down on the bed. He was late already, but she would
understand. He would call Helga and explain. And maybe send Jelka a note
by messenger.

He shivered, feeling old beyond his years. He had been so wrong.
So very wrong. And not just once but twice now. First with DeVore and
then...

'Ach...' he muttered, then turned, angry with himself for his weakness,
pressing the button to summon his aide. He would bathe and dress and go
to see his old friend. For a father should know his son. Whatever kind of
creature he was.

★

It was just after three when Jelka woke. The apartment was in darkness, silent. For a while she lay there, trying to settle back into sleep, then abandoned the idea.

She slipped on a robe and went through to her father's room, forgetting for a moment. His bed was empty, the room tidy. Of course... She moved on, pausing outside her aunt and uncle's room, hearing their soft snoring from within. In the kitchen she found a handwritten note resting against the coffee machine. The sheet was folded in half, her name written on the front in her father's neat, upright hand. She sat at the table and read it through then smiled, thinking of him. She always felt such fear for him when he was out on business. More so since the latest attempt on his life.

She looked about her at the dark forms of the kitchen, feeling suddenly tense, restless. That sense of restlessness seemed almost her natural state these days. That and an underlying desire to break things. But she told no one of these feelings. She knew they had to do with Hans and the forthcoming marriage, but there was little she could do to salve them.

One thing she *could* do, however, was exercise. The gym was locked, but, unknown to her father, she had memorized the combination. She punched it in then went through, into darkness, the doors closing behind her automatically.

They had strengthened the walls since the attack on her and put in a special locking system, but otherwise the gym was much as it had been before the attack. She went across to the panel on the wall and switched on three of the spotlights over the wallbars, then shrugged off her robe and began to exercise, knowing that no one could hear her once the doors were closed.

There was a wall-length mirror at the far end of the gym. As she went through her routine, she caught glimpses of her naked figure as it moved between the three separate beams of light, her limbs flashing like spears of ice, her body twisting and turning intricately. And as she danced so she felt the tension drain from her, deriving a definite pleasure from her body's precise and disciplined movements. Faster she went and faster, like a dervish, crying out in delight as her feet pounded the floor, flicking her over in a somersault, then into a tight, high leap.

Afterwards she stood there, breathing deeply, trying not to laugh. *If he could only see me now...* She shook her head, then drew her hair back from her face.

She had begun a second routine when something caught her eye. She slowed, then stopped, facing the door, her whole body tensed.

The panel above the door was pulsing steadily. A feverish, silent pulse that meant one thing only. There were intruders in the apartment.

Lehmann read the note quickly, then crumpled it in his hand and threw it aside. Tolonen led a charmed life. Three times they had tried for him now and three times they had failed. Tonight, for instance, Ebert had assured him that he would be home, but for some reason he had not come. Lehmann cursed softly, then turned, going through to where they held the two captives.

They lay on the bed, face down, their plumply naked bodies bound at hand and foot. Beside them the two Han waited.

'Anything?' he asked, seeing the huge welts on the prisoners' backs, the burns on their arms where they had been tortured.

'Nothing,' one of the Han answered him. 'Nothing at all.'

Lehmann stood there a moment, wondering if he should try something more persuasive, then shrugged and gave the order, turning away, letting them get on with it.

Outside, in the corridor, he paused and looked about him, sniffing the air. Something nagged at him. They had searched the apartment thoroughly and there was no sign of the girl, so maybe she *had* gone. But then why the note?

He turned and looked down the corridor at the door to the gym. *In there?* he wondered. It was unlikely, but then so too was the possibility that the girl had gone. Her bed had been slept in, even if the covers were cold.

He stood at the control panel, studying it. It was a new doorlock, specially strengthened. Without the code there was no way of opening it. He was about to turn away when he realized that he didn't have to get inside to find out if she was there. There was a security viewscreen. Which meant that there were cameras inside.

It took only a moment to work out how to operate the screen, then he was staring into darkness, the cameras looking for forms amongst the shadows. He scanned the whole room once, then went back carefully, double-checking. Nothing. There was no one in the room.

He switched off the screen, satisfied now that she had gone. It was a shame. She would have made the perfect hostage. But as it was, the death of Tolonen's brother and sister-in-law would hurt the old man badly.

He went back through to where his men were waiting. They had finished now and were ready to go. He looked down at the corpses dispassionately, feeling nothing for them. Directly or indirectly they served a system that was rotten. This, then, was their fate. What they deserved. He leaned forward and spat in the face of the dead man, then looked up, meeting the eyes of the Han.

'All right. We've finished here. Let's go.'

They nodded, then filed out past him, their weapons sheathed, their eyes averted. Lehmann stood, looking about him, then drew his knife and followed them, out into the corridor.

Jelka waited in the darkness, fearing the worst, her cheeks wet, her stomach tight with anxiety. This was the nightmare come again. And this time it was much worse than before, for this time she could do nothing. Nothing but crouch there by the locked door, waiting.

In the past hour she learned how dreadful a thing inaction was – far worse than the terror of hiding. When she had been balanced on the perch above the camera it had been somehow easier – much easier – than the awful limbo of not-knowing that came afterwards. Then she could think to herself, In a few moments this will be over, the cameras will stop moving and I can drop to the floor again. But the waiting was different. Horribly different. The very quality of time changed subtly, becoming the implement by which she tortured herself, filling the darkness with her vile imaginings.

In the end her patience broke and she went out, afraid that they would still be there, waiting silently for her, but unable to stay in the gym a moment longer.

Outside it was dark, silent. A strange smell hung in the air. She went slowly down the corridor, feeling her way, crouching warily, prepared to strike out with hand or foot, but there was nothing. Only her fear.

At the first door she stopped, sniffing the air. The smell was stronger here, more sickly than in the corridor. She gritted her teeth and went inside, placing her feet carefully, staring into the darkness, trying to make out forms.

There were vague shapes on the floor close to her. She leaned towards them, then jerked her head back, giving a small cry, unable to stop herself. Even in the darkness she could tell. Could see the wire looped tightly about their throats.

She backed away, horrified, gasping for breath, her whole body shaking violently, uncontrollably. They were dead...

She turned and made to run, but her legs betrayed her. She stumbled and her outstretched hands met not the hard smoothness of the floor but the awful, yielding softness of dead flesh. She shrieked and scrambled up, then fell again, her horror mounting as she found herself tangled amongst the bodies that littered the floor.

She closed her eyes and reached out, taking the wall as her guide, small sounds of brute disgust forming at the back of her throat as she forced herself to tread over them.

She went out into the dimly lit corridor. The outside barrier was un-manned, the lift empty. She stood there a moment, beside the open doors, then went inside and pressed to go down. It was the same at the bottom of the deck. There were no guards anywhere, as if the whole contingent had been withdrawn. She went through into the control centre for the deck and sat at the console, trying to work out how to operate the board. Her first few attempts brought no response, then the screen lit up and a soft MekVoc asked for her Security code.

She stammered the number her father had made her memorize, then repeated it at the machine's request. At once a face filled the central screen.

'Nu *shi* Tolonen,' the duty officer said, recognizing her at once. 'What is it? You look—'

'Listen!' she said, interrupting him. 'There are no guards. The apartment has been attacked. They've...' She bit it off, unable to say, yet it seemed he understood.

'Stay where you are. I'll inform the General at once. We'll get a special unit over to you within the next ten minutes.' He was leaning out of screen as he spoke, tapping a scramble code into the machine next to him. Then he turned back, facing Jelka again. 'All right. They're on their way. The General will contact you directly. Stay by the board.' He paused and drew a breath. 'How long ago did this happen?'

'About an hour.' She shuddered, trying not to think of what she had left back up the levels. 'I think they've gone now. But there are...' She swallowed drily, then continued, steeling herself to say it. 'There are bodies. My aunt and uncle. Some others. I don't know who.' She took a shuddering breath, so close to tears again that she found it difficult to control herself.

'Listen to me, Jelka. Do exactly what I say. There should be a medical cupboard in the rest room next to you. You'll find some tranquillizers there. Take two. Only two. Then come back to the board and stay there. All right?'

She nodded and went off to do as she was told, but then she stopped and turned, looking back at the screen. Why was there no one here? Where *was* the guard unit? The pattern was all too familiar. Like the attack on the Wiring Project that time.

It hit her suddenly. This wasn't like the other attack on her. This had been set up. From inside. Someone had given the order for the unit to pull out. Someone at the top.

Which meant that she had to get out. Right away. Before they came for her.

Even as she turned and looked, the picture on the screen changed. Hans Ebert's face appeared, red-eyed, his cheeks unshaven. He had been summoned from his bed. 'Jelka? Is that you? Come closer. Come over to the board.'

In a trance she went across and stood there, staring down at the screen.

'Stay where you are. And don't worry. I'll be with you just as soon as I can.'

She stood there, a cold certainty transfixing her. Then, as his face vanished from the screen, she reached across and cut the connection. She laughed: a cold bitter laughter, then, not looking back, made her way across to the transit and went inside, pressing the down button.

It was ten minutes after four when Tolonen got to the Ebert Mansion. One of the goat-creatures greeted him and ushered him through to the study. It bowed low, then, in a deep, burred voice excused itself while it went to fetch its master. A moment later another of the creatures entered the room; taller, gaunter than the first, its dress immaculate. It came across to where the Marshal stood and asked him what he would have to drink.

'Nothing, thank you,' he answered, not looking at the beast.

'Would you like something to eat, Marshal?'

It stood close to him, almost at his elbow. He could hear its breathing, smell its heavy musk beneath the artifice of its cologne.

'No. Now leave me,' he said, waving it away.

'Is there anything I can do for you, Excellency?' it persisted, seeming not to have heard what he had said, or seen his gesture of dismissal.

Tolonen turned and shook his head, meeting the creature's pink eyes. He had not noticed before how repulsive the creatures were; how vile their combination of sophistication and brutality. 'I'm sorry,' he said tightly, controlling the irritation he was feeling, 'but please leave me alone. I want nothing, I assure you.'

He watched it go, then shuddered, wondering if this would be the last time he would come here; whether by this he ended it all between himself and his oldest friend. He looked around, trying to distract himself, aware that the moment was drawing close, but it was no good: the words he had come to say ran on inside his head, like an awful, unrelenting litany.

He hadn't long to wait. Klaus Ebert had doused his face, put on a robe and come down. He pushed the far doors open and strode into the room, smiling, his arms out to welcome his friend.

'You're damned early, Knut, but you're as welcome as ever.'

Ebert clasped Tolonen to him, then released him, standing back.

'What brings you here at this hour, Knut? All's well with you and yours, I hope?'

Tolonen smiled wanly, touched more than ever by the warmth and openness of the greeting, but the smile was fragile. Underlying it was a bitterness that he found hard to contain. He nodded, then found his voice. 'They were well when I left them, Klaus.'

He drew a breath, then shook his head once, violently, his face muscles tightening into a grimace. 'I rehearsed the words, but I can't...' He straightened his back, controlling his emotions. Then, with his right hand, he took the file from beneath his artificial arm and handed it across.

Ebert frowned. 'What's this, Knut?' He searched his friend's face for explanations, troubled now, but could find nothing there. His broad lips formed a kind of shrug, then he turned and went to his desk, pulling open the top drawer and taking out a small case. He sat, setting the file down on the broad desktop, then opened the case and drew out a pair of old-fashioned spectacles, settling them on the bridge of his nose.

He opened the file and began to read.

Tolonen went across and stood there on the far side of the desk, watching Ebert's face as he read. He had written out a copy of the file in his own hand, taking direct responsibility for the matter.

After a moment Ebert looked up at him, his eyes half-lidded. 'I don't understand this, Knut. It says...' He laughed briefly, awkwardly, then shook his head, watching Tolonen carefully all the while. 'You wouldn't...'

He looked down, then immediately looked up again, his mouth making the first motion of speech but saying nothing. There was a strange movement in his face as he struggled towards realization; a tightening of his lips, a brief flash of pain in his eyes.

Tolonen stood there silently, his right fist clenched tight, the nails digging into the soft palm, his own face taut with pain, waiting.

Ebert looked down again, but now there was a visible tremor in his hand as it traced the words, and after a moment a tear gathered then fell from his nose on to the sheet below. He turned the page and read on, the trembling spreading to his upper arms and shoulders. When he had finished he closed the folder slowly and took off his glasses before looking up at Tolonen. His eyes were red now, tear-rimmed, and his face had changed.

'Who else knows of this, Knut?'

Ebert's voice was soft. His eyes held no hatred of his old friend, no blame, only a deep, unfathomable hurt.

Tolonen swallowed. 'Three of us now.'

'And Li Yuan? Does he know yet?'

Tolonen shook his head. 'This is Family, Klaus. Your son.'

The man behind the desk considered that, then nodded slowly, a small sad smile forming on his lips. 'I thank you, Knut. I...' The trembling in his hands and arms returned. Then something broke in the old man and his face crumpled, his mouth opening in a silent howl of pain, the lower jaw drawn back. He pressed his palms into the desk's surface, trying to still the shaking, to control the pain that threatened to tear him apart. 'Why?' he said at last, looking up at the Marshal, his eyes beseeching him. 'What could he possibly have wanted that he didn't have?'

Tolonen shrugged. He had no answer to that. No understanding of it.

At that moment the door at the far end of the study opened. One of the goat-creatures stood there, a tray of drinks in one hand. For a second or two Klaus Ebert did nothing, then he turned in his seat and yelled at the beast.

'Get out, you bloody thing! *Get out!*'

It blanched, then turned and left hurriedly. There was the sound of breaking glass in the hallway outside.

Ebert turned back to face the Marshal, breathing deeply, his face a deep red. 'How long have I, Knut? How long before Li Yuan has to know?'

Tolonen shivered. They both knew what had to be done. 'Two days,' he said quietly. 'I can give you two days.'

Ebert nodded, then sat back in his chair, clasping his hands together tightly. 'Two days,' he repeated, as if to himself, and looked up at Tolonen again. 'I'm sorry, Knut. Sorry for Jelka's sake.'

'And I.'

Tolonen watched him a moment longer, then turned and left, knowing that there was nothing more to be said. His part in this was ended, his duty discharged, but for once he felt anything but satisfaction.

There were fires on the hillside. Bodies lay unmoving on the snow. In the skies above the mountains the dark, knife-like shapes of Security battleships moved slowly eastward, searching out any trace of warmth in the icy wasteland.

In the control room of the flagship sat Hans Ebert, Li Yuan's General. He was unshaven and his eyes were red-rimmed from lack of sleep. His uniform was undone at the collar and he had his feet up on the console in front of him. Above him a bank of nine screens showed the landscape down below. Over the image on the central screen ran bright red lines of data. From time to time a map would flash up, showing the current extent of the sweep.

Hans watched the screens vacantly, tired to the core. There were drugs he might have taken to ameliorate his condition, but he had chosen to ignore them, feeding his bitter disappointment.

There were five others in the low-ceilinged room with him, but all were silent, wary of their commander's dark mood. They went about their tasks deftly, quietly, careful not to draw his attention.

Eight strongholds had been taken. Another five had been found abandoned. DeVore's network was in tatters, more than three thousand of his men dead. What Karr had begun, he, in the space of six short hours, had finished. Moreover, Jelka was gone, probably dead, and all his dreams with her. His dreams of being king. King of the world.

'The lodge is up ahead, sir!'

He looked up sharply, then took his feet down from the desk. 'Good!' He bit the word out savagely, then relented. He turned, looking at the young officer who had reported it to him. 'Thanks...'

The officer saluted and turned smartly away. Ebert sat there a moment longer then hauled himself up on to his feet and went down the narrow corridor and out into the cockpit. Staring out through the broad, thickly slatted screen, he could see the mountain up ahead, the lodge high up on its western slopes.

It was a mere twelve months since he had met DeVore here, and now he was forced to return, the architect of his own undoing, following his T'ang's explicit orders. Silently he cursed Li Yuan. Cursed the whole damn business, his irritation and frustration rising to fever pitch as he stood there, watching the lodge draw closer.

They touched down less than half a li away, the twin turrets of the battle-ship pointed towards the lodge. Hans suited up then went down, on to the snow. He crossed the space slowly, a lonely figure in black, holding the bulky gun with both hands, the stock tucked into his shoulder. Fifty paces from the veranda he stopped, balancing the gun's barrel across his left forearm and flicking off the safety. Then, without a word, he emptied the cartridge into the side of the lodge.

The explosions were deafening. In seconds the lodge was a burning ruin, debris falling everywhere, sizzling in the snow as it fell, the concussions echoing back and forth between the mountains, starting small slides. He waited a moment longer, the weapon lowered, watching the flames, then turned and walked back, the heavy gun resting loosely on his shoulder.

CHUNG KUO

Chapter 70

THE SHATTERED LAND

Klaus Ebert waited in his study for his son. He had dismissed his servants and was alone in the huge, dimly lit room, his face expressionless. The file lay on the desk behind him, the only object on the big leather-topped desk. It had been fifteen hours since Tolonen's visit and he had done much in that time; but they had been long, dreadful hours, filled with foul anticipation.

Hans had been summoned twice. The first time he had sent word that he was on the T'ang's business and could not come, the second that he would be there within the hour. Between the two had been the old man's curtly worded message: '*Come now, or be nothing to me.*'

A bell rang in the corridor outside, the signal that his son had arrived. Ebert waited, his feet apart, his hands clasped behind his back. He was the picture of strength, of authority, his short grey hair combed back severely from his high forehead, but his grey-green eyes were lifeless.

There were footsteps on the tiled floor outside then a knock on the great oak door. Hans entered, followed by two young lieutenants. He crossed the room and stood there, only an arm's length from his father. The two officers stood by the door, at ease.

'Well, Father?' There was a trace of impatience, almost of insolence in the young man's tone.

Klaus Ebert narrowed his eyes and looked past his son at the two lieutenants. 'This is Family business,' he said to them. 'Please leave us.'

There was a moment's uncertainty in their faces. They looked at each other but made no move to go. Ebert stared at them a moment then looked at his son for explanation.

'They're under my direct orders, Father. They're not to leave me. Not for a moment.' His voice was condescending now, as if he were explaining something to an inferior.

Ebert looked at his son, seeing things he had never noticed before: the arrogance of his bearing; the slight surliness in the shapes his mouth formed; the lack of real depth in his clear blue eyes. It was as if he looked *at* you, but not into you. He saw only surfaces: only himself, reflected in others.

He felt something harden at the core of him. This was his son. This... *creature.* He hissed out a long breath, his chest feeling tight, then started forward, shouting at the two officers. 'Get *out,* damn you! Now! Before I throw you out!'

There was no hesitation this time. They jerked as if struck then turned, hurrying from the room. Klaus stared at the closed door a moment before turning to look at his son.

'There was no need for that...'

'There was *every* need!' he barked, and saw his son flinch slightly. 'I summon you and you excuse yourself. And then you have the nerve to bring your popinjay friends—'

'They're officers...' Hans began, interrupting, but the old man cut him off with a sharp gesture of his hand.

'Your... *friends.*' He turned to face his son, no longer concealing his anger. He bit the words out. 'To bring them *here,* Hans.' He pointed at the floor. 'Here, where only we come.' He took a breath, calming himself, then moved away, back to the desk. From there he turned and looked back at his son.

Hans was looking away from him, his irritation barely masked. 'Well? What *is* it, Father?'

The words were sharp, abrasive. Hans glanced at his father then resumed his rigid stance, his whole manner sullen, insolent, as if answering to a superior officer he detested.

So it has come to this? Ebert thought, growing still, studying his son. He looked down at the file and gritted his teeth. But he didn't need the

Marshal's carefully documented evidence. All that he needed was there, before him, for his own eyes to read.

'Well?' the young man insisted. 'You've summoned me from my duties, threatened to withhold from me what is mine by right and insulted my officers. I want to know why, Father. What have I done to warrant this treatment?'

Ebert laughed bitterly. 'My *son*,' he said, weighting the second word with all the irony he could muster, but what he felt was hurt – a deep, almost overwhelming feeling of hurt – and a sense of disillusionment that threatened to unhinge his mind. He stood up, then moved away from the desk, circling his son until he stood there with his back to the door.

'What have you done, Hans? What have you done?'

The young man turned, facing his father, his fists clenched at his sides. He seemed barely in control of himself. 'Yes, what *have* I done?'

Ebert pointed across at the desk. 'See that file?'

'So?' Hans made no move to look. 'You could have sent it to me. I would have read it.'

Ebert shook his head. 'No, Hans. I want you to read it now.'

There was a small movement in the young man's face, a moment's doubt, and then it cleared. He nodded and turned, taking his father's seat.

Ebert went across and locked the door, slipping the key into his pocket.

Hans was reading the first page, all colour drained from his face.

Why? the old man asked himself for the thousandth time that day. But in reality he knew. Selfishness. Greed. A cold self-interest. These things were deeply rooted in his son. He looked at him, his vision doubled, seeing both his son and the stranger who sat there wearing the T'ang's uniform. And, bitterly, he recognized the source.

Berta, he thought. *You're Berta's child.*

Hans closed the file. For a moment he was silent, staring down at the unmarked cover of the folder, then he looked up, meeting his father's eyes. 'So...' he said. There was sober calculation in his eyes: no guilt or regret, only simple cunning. 'What now, Father?'

Ebert kept the disgust he felt from his voice. 'You make no denial?'

'Would you believe me if I did?' Hans sat back, at ease now.

The old man shook his head.

Hans glanced at the file then looked back at his father. 'Who else knows, besides Tolonen?'

'His one-time lieutenant, Haavikko.' Ebert moved slowly, crossing the room in a half-circle that would bring him behind his son.

'Then Li Yuan has yet to be told?'

He nodded.

Hans seemed reassured. 'That's good. Then I could leave here this evening.' He turned in his seat, watching his father's slow progress across the room towards him. 'I could take a ship and hide out amongst the Colony planets.'

Ebert stopped. He was only paces from his son. 'That's what you want, is it? Exile? A safe passage?'

Hans laughed. 'What else? I can't argue with this.' He brushed the file with the fingertips of his left hand. 'Li Yuan would have me killed if I stayed.'

Ebert took another step. He was almost on top of his son now. 'And what if I said that that wasn't good enough? What if I said no? What would you do?'

The young man laughed uncomfortably. 'Why should you?' He leaned back, staring up at his father, puzzled now.

Ebert reached out, placing his hand gently on his son's shoulder.

'As a child I cradled you in my arms, saw you learn to walk and utter your first, stumbling words. As a boy you were more to me than all of this. You were my joy. My delight. As a man I was proud of you. You seemed the thing I'd always dreamed of.'

Hans licked at his top lip, then looked down. But there was no apology. 'Shall I go?'

The old man ignored the words. The pressure of his hand increased. His fingers gripped and held. Reaching out, he placed his other hand against Hans's neck, his thumb beneath the chin. Savagely, he pushed Hans's head up, forcing him to look into his face. When he spoke the words were sour, jagged-edged. 'But now all that means nothing.' He shook his head, his face brutal, pitiless. '*Nothing! Do you hear me, Hans?*'

Hans reached up to free himself from his father's grip, but the old man was unrelenting. His left hand slipped from the shoulder to join the other about his son's neck. At the same time he leaned forward, bearing down on the younger man, his big hands tightening their grip, his shoulder muscles straining.

Too late, the young man realized what was happening. He made a small, choked sound in his throat and began to struggle in the chair, his legs kicking out wildly, his hands beating then tearing at his father's arms and hands, trying to break the vice-like grip. Suddenly the chair went backwards. For a moment Hans was free, sprawled on the floor beneath his father's body, but then the old man had him again, his hands about his throat, his full weight pressing down on him, pushing the air from the young man's lungs.

For one frozen moment the old man's face filled the younger man's vision, the mouth gasping as it strained, spittle flecking the lips. The eyes were wide with horror, the cheeks suffused with blood. Sweat beaded the brow. Then, like a vast, dark wave, the pain became immense. His lungs burned in his chest and his eyes seemed about to burst.

And then release. Blackness...

He gasped air into his raw throat, coughing and wheezing, the pain in his neck so fierce that it made him groan aloud; a hoarse, animal sound.

After a moment he opened his eyes again and pulled himself up on to one elbow. His father lay beside him, dead, blood gouting from the hole in the back of his head.

He looked about, expecting to see his lieutenants, but they were not in the room. The door to his father's private suite was open, however, and there was movement inside. He called out – or tried to – then struggled up into a sitting position, feeling giddy, nauseous.

At the far end of the room a figure stepped into the doorway: tall as a man, but not a man. Its white silk jacket was spattered with blood, as were its trousers. It looked at the sitting man with half-lidded eyes, eyes that were as red as the blood on its clothes. Over one arm was a suit of Hans's father's clothes.

'Here, put these on,' said the goat-creature in its soft, animal voice. It crossed the room and stood there over him, offering the clothes.

He took them, staring at the beast, not understanding yet, letting it help him up and across the study to his father's room. There, in the doorway, he turned and looked back.

His father lay face down beside the fallen chair, the wound at the back of his head still wet and glistening in the half-light.

'We must go now,' said the beast, handing him a key, its breath like old malt.

He turned and met its eyes. It was smiling at him, showing its fine, straight teeth. He could sense the satisfaction it was feeling. Years of resentment had culminated in this act. He shuddered and closed his eyes, feeling faint.

'We have an hour, two at most,' it said, its three-toed hand moving to the side of Ebert's neck, tracing but not touching the welt-like bruise there. For a moment its eyes seemed almost tender.

He nodded and let it take him through. There was nothing for him here now. Nothing at all.

Karr looked up over his glass and met the young officer's eyes. 'What is it, Captain?'

'Forgive me, sir. I wouldn't normally come to you on a matter of this kind, but I think this will interest you.'

He held out a slender dossier. Karr stared at it a moment, then took it from him. Setting down his glass, he opened it. A moment later, he started forward, suddenly alert.

'When did this come in?'

'Twenty minutes back. Someone said you were down here in the Mess, sir, so I thought...'

Karr grinned at him fiercely. 'You did well, Captain. But what put you on to this?'

'The name sir. Mikhail Boden. It was one of the names we had as a suspect for the murder of a *Fu jen* Maitland six years ago. It seems she was Under-Secretary Lehmann's wife at one time. She was burned to death in her rooms. An incendiary device. Boden was there shortly before she died. His retinal print was in the door camera, which survived the blaze. When it appeared again, I thought I'd have a look at the visual image and see if it was the same man. As you can see, it wasn't.'

'No...' Karr got to his feet. The camera stills were of two quite different men, yet the retinal print was the same.

'How come the computer allowed the match?'

'It seems that the only detail it has to have a one hundred per cent mapping on is the retinal pattern. That's unchanging. The rest – facial hair, proportion of muscle and fat in the face – changes over the years. The computer is programmed to ignore those variations. As long as the underlying bone structure is roughly the same the computer will recognize it as being the same face.'

Karr laughed. 'And you know who this is?'

The young officer smiled back at Karr. 'I read my files, sir. It's DeVore, isn't it?'

'Yes. And he entered Salzburg *hsien* twenty, twenty-five minutes back, right?'

'Yes, sir.'

'Good. And you're tracking him?'

'Yes, sir. I've put two of my best men on to the job.'

'Excellent.'

Karr looked down at the dossier again. The gods knew why DeVore had made such an elementary mistake, but he had, so praise them for it. Taking the handset from his pocket, he tapped in Chen's combination, then, as Chen came on line, gave a small laugh. 'It's DeVore, Chen. I think we've got him. This time I really think we've got him!'

Tolonen was crouched in the middle of the room. The corpses were gone now, his men finished here, but still the room seemed filled with death. He looked up at the young officer, his face pulled tight with grief, his eyes staring out at nothing. 'I should have killed him... while I had the chance.' He shuddered and looked down at his big, square hands. 'If only I had known what mischief he was up to.'

'We'll track him, sir. Bring him back,' the officer assured him, watching his Marshal, deep concern in his clear grey eyes.

The old man shook his head then looked down again. Something had broken in him in the last few hours. His shoulders sagged, his hands – real and artificial – rested limply on his knees. All of the anger, all of the old blind rage that had fired him as a man had gone. There was no avenging this, whatever he said. The young officer had seen how the old man had looked, such tenderness and agony in his face as he had bent and gently touched the wire about his brother's neck. It was awful to see such things. More than could be borne.

The young man swallowed, his voice a sympathetic whisper. 'Can I get you anything, sir?'

Tolonen looked up at him again, seeming to see him for the first time.

There was a faint smile on his lips, but it was only the smallest flicker of warmth in the wasteland of his features.

'Is there any news?'

The young man shook his head. There was no trace of Jelka. It was as if she had vanished. Perhaps she was dead, or maybe Ebert had her after all. He hoped not. But she was nowhere in the City. An eighteen-hour Security trawl had found no trace of her.

He went through to the living-room, returning a moment later with two brandies. 'Here,' he said, handing one to the Marshal. 'This will help.'

Tolonen took the glass and stared at it a while, then drained it at a gulp. He looked up at the young officer, his face expressionless.

'Telling Li Yuan was hard.' His wide brow furrowed momentarily. 'I felt I had failed him. Betrayed him. It was bad. Worse than Han Ch'in's death. Much worse.'

'It wasn't your fault...'

Tolonen met his eyes a moment, before looking away and shaking his head. 'If not mine, then whose? I knew and didn't act. And this...' His mouth puckered momentarily and his fists clenched. He took a deep breath, then looked up again. 'This is the result.'

He was about to answer the Marshal, to say something to alleviate the old man's pain, when a three-tone signal sounded in his head. There was news. He narrowed his eyes, listening, then smiled; a huge grin of a smile.

'What is it?' Tolonen asked, getting to his feet.

'It's Viljanen, from Jakobstad. He says to tell you that Jelka is there. And safe.'

Jelka stood at the end of the old stone jetty, waiting for him. Waves crashed against the rocks across the bay. Above her the slate-grey sky was filled with huge thunderheads of cloud, black and menacing.

The island was in winter's grip. Snow covered everything. She stood there, above the deep green swell of the sea, wrapped in furs against the cold, only her face exposed to the bitter air. The boat was small and distant, rising and falling as she watched, labouring against the elements. Beyond it, its scale diminished by the distance, lay the cliff-like whiteness of the City, its topmost levels shrouded by low cloud.

Only as the boat came nearer could she hear the noise of its engine, a thin thread of regularity amidst the swirling chaos of wind and wave. Entering the bay, the engine noise changed, dropping an octave as the boat slowed, turning in towards the jetty. She saw him on the deck, looking across at her, and lifted her arm to wave.

They embraced on the path above the water, the old man hugging her to him fiercely, as if he would never again let her go. He pushed back her hood and kissed her on the crown, the brow, the lips, his hot tears coursing down her frozen face, cooling in her lashes and on her cheeks.

'Jelka... Jelka... I was so worried.'

She closed her eyes and held on to him. Snow had begun to fall, but he was warm and close and comforting. The familiar smell of him eased her tortured mind. She let him turn her and lead her back to the house.

He built a fire in the old grate then lit it, tending it until it was well ablaze. She sat, watching him in the half-light from the window, her hand clasping the pendant at her neck, the tiny *kuei* dragon seeming to burn against her palm.

Still kneeling, he half turned towards her, his face a mobile mask of black and orange, his grey hair glistening in the flickering light.

'How did you get here?' he asked gently. 'My men were looking for you everywhere.'

She smiled but did not answer him. Desperation created its own resources, and she had been desperate to get here. Besides, she wasn't sure. It was as if she had dreamed her journey here. She had known. Known that while the storm might rage on every side, here was safety, here the eye. And she had run for the eye. Here, where it was warm and safe.

He watched her a moment longer, his moist eyes filled with the fire's wavering light, then stood. He was old. Old, and weary to the bone. She went across and held him, laying her cheek against his neck, her arm about his waist. For a moment he rested against her, thoughtless, unmoving, then he shifted slightly, looking down into her face.

'But why here? Why did you come here?'

In her head there had been the memory of brine and leather and engine oils, the strong scent of pine; the memory of a circle of burned and blackened trees in the woods; of an ancient stone tower overlooking a boiling sea. These things, like ghosts, had summoned her.

She smiled. 'There was nowhere else.'

He nodded, then sighed deeply. 'Well... It's over now.'

'Over?'

His hand went to her face, holding her where the jawbone came down beneath the ear, his thumb stroking the soft flesh of her cheek. His own face was stiff, his chin raised awkwardly.

'I was wrong, Jelka. Wrong about many things, but most of all wrong to try to force you into something you didn't want.'

She knew at once what he meant. Hans. She felt herself go cold, thinking of him.

'I was blind. Stupid.' He shook his head slowly. His face muscles clenched and unclenched, then formed a grimace. This pained him. As much as the deaths.

She opened her lips to speak, but her mouth was dry. She nodded. She had tried to tell him.

'He's gone,' he said, after a moment. 'Hans has gone.'

For a moment she said nothing. Her face was blank, her eyes puzzled. 'Gone?'

Her father nodded. 'So it's over. Finished with.'

For a moment longer she held herself there, tensed against the news, afraid to believe him. Then, suddenly, she laughed, relief flooding her. She shivered, looking away from her father. *Gone. Hans was gone.* Again she laughed, but then the laughter died. She looked up suddenly, remembering.

'He told me to stay there. He was coming for me.'

She shivered again, more violently this time, her arm tightening about her father's waist, her hands gripping him hard. She looked up fiercely into his face.

'He would have killed me.'

'I know,' he said, pulling her face down against his neck, his arms wrapped tightly about her. His voice was anxious now, filled with sorrow and regret. 'I was wrong, my love. So very wrong. Gods forgive me, Jelka, I didn't know. I just didn't know...'

That night Jelka dreamed. The sky pressed down upon her head, solid and impenetrable. Voices clawed at her with hands of ragged metal, screeching their elemental anger. It was dark; a darkness laced with purple. She was alone on the tilted, broken land, the storm raging at every corner of the earth.

Each time the lightning struck she felt a tremor pass through her from head to toe, as sharp as splintered ice. And when the thunder growled it sounded in her bones, exploding with a suddenness that made her shudder.

Through the dark, its progress marked in searing flashes of sudden light, came the tower, its eyes like shattered panes of glass, its wooden spider limbs folding and stretching inexorably, bringing it closer.

She stood there, unable to move, watching it come. It seemed malefic, evil, its dark mouth crammed with splintered bone. She could hear it grunt and wheeze as it dragged its weight across the jagged, uneven ground. Closer it came, climbing the hill on which she stood, picking its way through the darkness.

In the sudden light she saw it, close now and laughing horribly, its crooked mouth smiling greedily at her. Its breath was foul, rolling up the hill to where she stood. The scent of rottenness itself.

As the darkness enfolded her again she cried out, knowing she was lost. Her cry rang out, louder than the storm, and for a moment afterwards there was silence. Light leaked slowly into that silence, as if her cry had cracked the darkness open at its seams.

Things took a shadowy form. The tower had stopped. It stood there, not far below her. She could hear its wheezing, scraping voice as it whispered to itself. Her sudden cry had startled it. Then, as she stared into the half-dark, the earth between her and the tower cracked and split. For a moment the land was still and silent and then something small and dark crawled from the dark mouth of the earth. A stooped little creature with eyes that burned like coals. Its wet, dark skin shone with an inner light and its limbs were short but strong, as though it had dug its way to the surface. As she watched, it climbed up on to its legs and stood there, facing the tower. In one hand it held a circle of glass backed with silver. Holding it up before it, it advanced.

Light flashed from the circle and where it touched the tower small leaves of bright red flame blossomed. The tower shrieked and stumbled backwards, but the small, dark creature kept advancing, light flashing from the circle in its hand, the tiny fires spreading, taking hold.

Screeching, the tower turned and began to run, its thin legs pumping awkwardly. Thick black smoke billowed up into the air above it, gathering in a dense layer beneath the solid sky. The noise of the tower burning, splitting, was fierce. Great cracks and pops filled the bright-lit silence.

The creature turned, looking at her, the glass lowered now. Its fiery eyes seemed both kind and sad. They seemed to see right through her, to the bone and the darkness beneath the bone.

She stared back at it as the darkness slowly returned, filling the space between the sky and the cracked and shattered land, until all she could see was the fallen tower, blazing in the distance, and, so close she could feel their warmth, two jewels of fire set into the soft and lambent flesh of the creature.

As she watched, it smiled and bowed its head to her. Then, its movements quick and fluid, it returned to the open crack and slipped down into the darkness of the earth.

For eighteen hours DeVore hadn't settled, but had moved on constantly, as if he knew that his only salvation lay in flight. His disguises had been tenuous at best and he had cashed in old friendships at a frightening rate, but all the while Karr had kept close on his tail. Then, suddenly, Karr had lost him. That had been in Danzig. It might have ended there, but DeVore got careless. For the second time that day he doubled up on an identity.

As a back-up, Karr had programmed the Security pass computer to 'tag' all past known aliases of DeVore – eight in all – with special priority 'screamers'. If DeVore used any of them, alarm bells would ring. It was the slimmest of chances and no one expected it to work, but for once it did. A day after Karr had lost the trail, DeVore gave himself away. A screamer sounded on one Joseph Ganz, who had moved up-level in one of the Amsterdam stacks. A random Security patrol had checked on his ID and passed him through, unaware of the 'tag'.

Karr was there in less than an hour. Chen was waiting for him, with a full Security battalion. He had sealed off all the surrounding stacks and put Security guards at every entrance to the transit lifts. The fast-track bolts were shut down and they were ready to go in.

There was no possibility that DeVore had gone far. All the local Security posts had been alerted at once. If DeVore was coming out, it would be by force this time, not guile. He had worn his last disguise.

Karr smiled fiercely and rubbed his big hands together. 'I have you now, old ghost. You won't slip away this time.'

There were five decks to check out. Chen planned to move through them carefully, one at a time, from the bottom up – fifty levels in all – but Karr knew already where he would find DeVore. At the very top of the City. He left Chen in charge of the sweep and went on up, alone, taking the transit to the uppermost deck.

He was an impressive sight, coming out of the transit: a seven *ch'i* giant, in full combat dress and carrying a fearsome array of weaponry. He walked slowly, searching faces, but knowing that he wouldn't find DeVore there, in the corridors. His quarry would be higher, holed up somewhere in one of the penthouse apartments. With an old friend, perhaps.

Karr lowered his visor and pressed out a code into his wrist comset. On to the transparent visor came a read-out. He thumbed it through as he walked, until he came upon a name he knew. *Stefan Cherkassky*. An old associate of DeVore's and a retired Security officer. Karr checked habitation details, moving towards the inter-level lifts. Cherkassky's apartment was on the far side of the deck and at the highest level. Just as he'd thought.

DeVore would be there.

Karr took a deep breath, considering. It would not be easy. DeVore was one of the best. He had been an excellent Security Major. In time he would have been General. But he'd had more ambitious plans than that. Karr had studied his file carefully and viewed training films of him in action. Karr respected few men, but DeVore demanded respect. Speed, size and age were on Karr's side, but DeVore was cunning. And strong too. A fox with the strength of a tiger.

People moved hurriedly out of Karr's way as he strode along. The lift emptied at his bark of command and he went up. He thumbed for a map, then thumbed again for Cherkassky's service record. The man may have retired, but he could still be dangerous. It did not pay to make assumptions.

Cherkassky, Stefan. The file extract appeared after a two-second delay. He took in the details at a glance, then cleared his visor and stopped.

He hadn't realized... This gave things a new complexion. The old man had been specially trained. Like Karr, he was an assassin.

Karr checked his guns, all the while staring down the wide, deserted corridor. He was less than a hundred *ch'i* from Cherkassky's apartment now. If they were being careful – and there was no reason to expect otherwise – they would know he was coming. There would have been an 'eye' close by the transit; someone to report back at once.

Which meant they would be waiting for him.

He switched to special lenses. At once his vision changed. Using lenses, he could pick out the shape of a tiny insect at five hundred *ch'i*. Squeezing the corners of his eyes, he adjusted them to medium range and checked all the surfaces ahead for signs of anti-personnel devices. It seemed clear, but for once he decided not to trust the visual scan. He set one of his hand lasers to low charge and raked it along the walls and floors, then along the ceiling. Nothing. Yet he still felt ill at ease. Some instinct held him back. He waited, breathing shallowly, counting to twenty in his head, then heard a sound behind him – so faint that it would have been easy to miss it. The faintest clicking, like a claw gently tapping the side of a porcelain bowl.

He tensed, listening, making sure, then turned fast and rolled to one side, just as the machine loosed off a burst of rapid fire. The wall exploded beside him as the heavy shells hit home. He cursed and fired back, the first few rounds wild, the next deadly accurate. The machine sputtered, then blew apart, hot fragments flying everywhere. A piece embedded itself in his side, another cracked the front of his visor.

There was no time to lose now. The machine was like the one they had used to attack Tolonen, but more deadly. A remote. Which meant they had seen him. Seen how good he was. He was using up his advantage.

He considered the situation as he ran. They knew he was coming. Knew what he was like, how fast, how agile he was. There was one of him and two of them. Older, yes, but more experienced than him. A Security Major and a special services assassin, now sixty-eight, but still fit and active, he was certain. On those facts alone it might seem he had little chance of succeeding. But there was one final factor: something they didn't know – that DeVore couldn't know, because it had never got on to Karr's service record. In his teens – before he had become a blood – he had been an athlete, perhaps the finest athlete the Net had ever produced. And he was better now. At twenty-nine he was fitter and faster than he'd ever been.

Karr slowed as he neared the end of the corridor. There was no tape to break this time but even so, his time was close to nine seconds. They wouldn't think...

He fired ahead of him, letting momentum take him through the door, rolling and springing up, turning in the next movement to find Cherkassky on the ceiling above the door, held there in an assassin's cradle. He was turning with his feet, but it wasn't fast enough. Karr shot away the strands, making Cherkassky tumble to the floor, all the while his eyes darting here and there, looking for DeVore. He skipped over the rubble and crouched above the winded assassin.

'Where is he? Tell me where he is.'

The old man laughed, then coughed blood. Karr shot him through the neck. DeVore had gone. Had traded on his final friendship. But he could not have gone far. Cherkassky hadn't been operating the machine. So...

Quickly, carefully, he checked the rest of the apartment. There was no sign of the controls here, so DeVore had them elsewhere. Somewhere close by. But where?

He pushed his helmet out into the corridor then, a moment later, popped his head round the corner to look. Nothing. There was a high-pitched screaming from a nearby apartment but he ignored it, stepping out into the corridor again. There was no way out overhead. The roof was sealed here. He had checked on that earlier. No. The only way out was down.

He glanced at his timer. It was only three minutes and forty-eight seconds since he had stood at the far end of the corridor. Was that time enough for DeVore to get to the lift? Possibly. But Karr had a hunch that he hadn't done that. DeVore would want to make sure he was safe, and that meant getting back at his pursuer.

He walked slowly down the corridor, keeping to the wall, the largest of his guns, an antique Westinghouse-Howitzer, pressed tight against his chest. He would take no chances with this bastard.

He was about to go on when he paused, noticing the silence. The screaming had stopped, suddenly, almost abruptly, in mid-scream. It had taken him a second or two to notice it, but then it hit him. He turned, lowering himself on to his haunches, as if about to spring. Two doors down the corridor, it had been. He went back slowly, his finger trembling against the hair-line trigger, making a small circle of the door until he stood on its far side, his back to Cherkassky's apartment.

He had two options now: to wait or to go in. Which would DeVore expect him to do? Was he waiting for Karr to come in, or was he about to come out? For a moment Karr stood there, tensed, considering, then he smiled. There was a third option: burn away the wall and see what lay behind it. He liked that. It meant he didn't have to go through a door.

He lay down, setting the big gun up in front of him, ejecting the standard explosive shells and slipping a cartridge of ice-penetrating charges into the loader. Then he squeezed the trigger, tracing a line of shells first up the wall, then along the top of it. The partition shuddered, like something alive, and began to peel away from where the charges had punctured holes in it. There was no sound from the other side of the wall; only silence and the roiling smoke.

He waited, easing his finger back and forth above the hair-trigger as the ice curled back, revealing the shattered room. Karr's eyes took in each and every detail, noting and discarding them. A young woman lay dead on the lounger, her pale limbs limp, her head at an odd angle, garrotted by the look of it. There was no sign of DeVore, but he had been there. The woman had been alive only a minute before.

Karr crawled into the room. A siren had begun to sound in the corridor. It would bring Chen and help. But Karr wanted to finish this now. DeVore was his. He had pursued him for so long now. And, orders or no, he would make sure of things this time.

He stopped, calling out.

'Surrender yourself, DeVore. Put your hands up and come out. You'll get a fair trial.'

It was a charade. Part of the game they had to play. But DeVore would pay no heed. They both knew now that this could only end in death. But it had to be said. Like the last words of a ritual.

His answer came a moment later. The door to the right hissed open a fraction and a grenade was lobbed into the room. Karr saw it curl in the air and recognized what it was. Dropping his gun, he placed his hands tight over his ears and pushed his face down into the floor. It was a concussion grenade. The shock of it ripped a hole in the floor and seemed to lift everything in the room into the air.

In a closed room it would have been devastating, but much of the force of it had gone out into the corridor. Karr got up, stunned but unhurt, his ears ringing. And then the door began to iris open.

Reactions took over. Karr buckled at the knees and rolled forward, picking up his gun on the way. DeVore was halfway out of the door, the gun at his hip already firing, when the butt of Karr's gun connected with his head. It was an ill-aimed blow that glanced off the side of his jaw, just below the ear, but the force of it was enough to send DeVore sprawling, the gun flying from his hands. Karr went across, his gun raised to aim another blow, but it was already too late. DeVore was dead, his jaw shattered, fragments of it pushed up into his brain.

Karr stood there a moment, looking down at his old enemy, all of the fierce indignation and anger he felt welling up in him again. He shuddered, then, anger getting the better of him, brought the gun down, once, twice, a third time, smashing the skull apart, spilling DeVore's brains across the floor.

'You bastard... You stinking, fucking bastard!'

Then, taking the small cloth bag from his top pocket, he undid the string and spilled the stones over the dead man. Three hundred and sixty-one black stones.

For Haavikko's sister, Vesa, and Chen's friend, Pavel; for Kao Jyan and Han Ch'in, Lwo Kang and Edmund Wyatt, and all the many others whose deaths were down to him.

Karr shuddered, then threw the cloth bag down. It was done. He could go home now and sleep.

Li Yuan stood in the deep shadow by the carp pool, darkness wrapped about him like a cloak. It had been a long and tiring day, but his mind was sharp and clear. He stared down through layers of darkness, following the languid movements of the carp. In their slow, deliberate motions it seemed he might read the deepest workings of his thoughts.

Much had happened. Out there, in the chill brightness of his study, all had seemed chaos. DeVore was dead and his warren of mountain fortresses destroyed. But Klaus Ebert was also dead and his son, the General, had fled. That had come as a shock to him, undermining his newfound certainty.

Here, in the darkness, however, he could see things in a better light. He had survived the worst his enemies could do. Fei Yen and young Han were safe. Soon he would have a General he could trust. These things comforted him. In the light of them, even Wang Sau-leyan's concessions to the Young Patriots seemed a minor thing.

For a while he let these things drift from him; let himself sink into the depths of memory, his mood dark and sorrowful, his heart weighed down by the necessities of his life. He had companionship in Tsu Ma and three wives to satisfy his carnal needs. Soon he would have a child – an heir, perhaps. But none of this was enough. So much was missing from his life. Fei Yen and Han Ch'in, so deeply missed that sometimes he would wake from sleep, his pillow wet with tears. Worst were the nightmares: images of his father's corpse, exposed, defenceless in its nakedness, painfully emaciated, the skin stretched pale across the frame of bone.

The fate of kings.

He turned and looked across at the single lamp beside the door. Its light was filtered through the green of fern and palm, the smoky darkness of the panels, as if through depths of water. He stared at it, reminded of something else – of the light on a windswept hillside in the Domain as a small group gathered about the unmarked grave. Sunlight on grass and the shadows in the depths of the earth. He had been so certain that day: certain that he didn't want to stop the flow of time and have the past returned to him, fresh, new again. But had Ben been right? Wasn't that the one thing men wanted most?

Some days he ached to bring it back. To have it whole and perfect. To sink back through the years and have it all again. The best of it. Before the cancer ate at it. Before the worm lay in the bone.

He bowed his head, smiling sadly at the thought. To succumb to that desire was worse than the desire itself. It was a weakness not to be tolerated. One had to go on, not back.

The quality of the light changed. His new Master of the Inner Chambers, Chan Teng, stood beside the doorway, silent, waiting to be noticed.

'What is it, Master Chan?'

'Your guest is here, *Chieh Hsia*.'

'Good.' He lifted a hand to dismiss the man, then changed his mind. 'Chan, tell me this. If you could recapture any moment from your past – if you could have it whole, perfect in every detail – would you want that?'

The middle-aged man was silent a while, then answered.

'There are, indeed, times when I wish for something past, *Chieh Hsia*.

Like all men. But it would be hard. Hard living in the "now" if "what was" were still to hand. The imperfection of a man's memories is a blessing.'

It was a good answer. A satisfactory answer. 'Thank you, Chan. There is wisdom in your words.'

Chan Teng bowed and turned to go, but at the door he turned back and looked across at his master.

'One last thing, *Chieh Hsia*. Such a gift might well prove useful. Might prove, for us, a blessing.'

Li Yuan came out into the light. 'How so?'

Chan lowered his eyes. 'Might its very perfection not prove a cage, a prison to the mind? Might we not snare our enemies in its sticky web?'

Li Yuan narrowed his eyes. He thought he could see what Chan Teng was saying, but he wanted to be sure. 'Go on, Chan. What are you suggesting?'

'Only this. That desire is a chain. If such a thing exists it might be used, not as a blessing but a curse. A poisoned gift. It would be the ultimate addiction. Few men would be safe from its attractions. Fewer still would recognize it for what it was. A drug. A way of escaping from what is here and now and real.'

Li Yuan took a deep breath, then nodded. 'We shall speak more on this, Chan. Meanwhile, ask my guest to come through. I shall see him here, beside the pool.'

Chan Teng bowed low, and turned away. Li Yuan stared down at the naked glow of the lamp, and moved his hand close, feeling its radiant warmth, tracing its rounded shape. How would it feel to live a memory? Like this? As real as this? He sighed. Perhaps, as Chan said, there was a use for Shepherd's art: a way of making his illusions serve the real. He drew his hand away, seeing how shadows formed between the fingers, how the glistening lines of the palm turned dull and lifeless.

To have Han and Fei again. To see his father smiling.

He shook his head, suddenly bitter. Best nothing. Better death than such sweet torment.

There was movement in the corridor outside. A figure appeared in the doorway. Li Yuan looked up, meeting Shepherd's eyes.

'Ben...'

Ben Shepherd looked about him at the room, then looked back at the young T'ang, a faint smile on his lips. 'How are you, Li Yuan? With all that's happened, I wasn't sure you'd remember our meeting.'

Li Yuan smiled and moved forward, greeting him. 'No. I'm glad you came. Indeed, our meeting is fortuitous, for there's something I want to ask you. Something only you can help me with.'

Ben raised an eyebrow. 'As mirror?'

Li Yuan nodded, struck once again by how quick, how penetrating Ben Shepherd was. He, if anyone, could make things clear to him.

Ben went to the edge of the pool. For a moment he stared down into the darkness of the water, following the slow movements of the fish, then he looked back at Li Yuan.

'Is it about Fei Yen and the child?'

Li Yuan shivered. 'Why should you think that?'

Ben smiled. 'Because, as I see it, there's nothing else that only I could help you with. If it were a matter of politics, there are a dozen able men to whom you might talk. Whereas the matter of your ex-wife and the child. Well... who could you talk to of that within your court? Who could you trust not to use what was said to gain some small advantage?'

Li Yuan bowed his head. It was true. He had not thought of it in quite such a calculated manner, but it was so.

'Well?' he said, meeting Ben's eyes.

Ben moved past him, crouching down to study the great tortoise shell with its ancient markings.

'There's an advantage to being outside things,' Ben said, his eyes searching the surface of the shell, tracing the fine patterning of cracks beneath the transparent glaze. 'You see events more clearly than those taking part in them. What's more, you learn to ask the right questions.' He turned his head, looking up at Li Yuan. 'For instance. Why, if Li Yuan knows who the father of his child is, has he not acted on that knowledge? Why has he not sought vengeance on the man? Of course, the assumption has always been that the child is not Li Yuan's. But why should that necessarily be the case? It was assumed by almost everyone that Li Yuan divorced Fei Yen to ensure the child of another man would have no legitimate claim upon the dragon throne, but why should that be so? What if that were merely a pretext? After all, it is not an easy thing to obtain a divorce when one is a T'ang. Infidelity, whilst a serious enough matter in itself, would be an insufficient reason. But to protect the line of inheritance...'

Li Yuan had been watching Ben, mesmerized, unable to look away. Now Ben released him.

'You always saw things clearly, didn't you?'

'To the bone.'

'And was I right?'

'To divorce Fei Yen? Yes. But the child... Well, I'll be frank and say that that puzzles me somewhat. I've thought about it often lately. He's *your* son, isn't he, Li Yuan?'

Li Yuan nodded.

'Then why disinherit him?'

Li Yuan looked down, thinking back to the evening when he had made that awful decision, recollecting the turmoil of his feelings. He had expected the worst – had steeled himself to face the awful fact of her betrayal – but then, when he had found it was his child, unquestionably *his*, he had been surprised to find himself not relieved but appalled, for in his mind he had already parted from her. Had cast her from him, like a broken bowl. For a long time he had sat there in an agony of indecision, unable to see things clearly. But then the memory of Han Ch'in had come to him; of his dead brother, there beside him in the orchard, a sprig of white blossom in his jet-black hair – and he had known, with a fierce certainty, what he must do.

He looked back at Ben, tears in his eyes. 'I wanted to protect him. Do you understand that, Ben? To keep him from harm. He was Han, you see. Han Ch'in reborn.' He shook his head. 'I know that doesn't make sense, but it's how I felt. How I still feel, every time I think about the child.'

He turned away, trying for a moment to control – to wall in – the immensity of his suffering. Then turned back, his face open, exposed to the other man, all of his grief and hope and suffering there on the surface for Ben's eyes to read.

'I couldn't save Han Ch'in. I was too young, too powerless. But my son...' He swallowed, then looked aside. 'If one good thing can come from my relationship with Fei Yen, let it be this: that my son can grow up safe from harm.'

Ben looked down, then, patting the shell familiarly, he stood. 'I see.' He walked back to the edge of the pool, then turned, facing Li Yuan again. 'Even so, you must have sons, Li Yuan. You have taken wives for that very purpose. Can you save them all? Can you keep them all from harm?'

Li Yuan was staring back at him. 'They will be sons...'

'And Fei's son, Han? Is he *so* different?'

Li Yuan looked aside, a slight bitterness in his face. 'Don't tease me, Ben. I thought you of all people would understand.'

Ben nodded. 'Oh, I do. But I wanted to make sure that you did. That you weren't trying to fool yourself over your real motives. You say the boy reminds you of Han. That may be so, and I understand your reasons for wanting to keep him out of harm's way. But it's more than that, isn't it? You still love Fei Yen. And the child... the child is the one real thing that came of your love.'

Li Yuan looked back at him gratefully.

Ben sighed. 'Oh, I understand clearly enough, Li Yuan. You wanted to *be* her, didn't you? To *become* her. And the child... that's the closest you'll ever come to it.'

Li Yuan shivered, acknowledging the truth. 'Then I was right to act as I did?'

Ben turned, looking down, watching the dark shapes of the carp move slowly in the depths. 'You remember the picture I drew for you, the day of your betrothal ceremony?'

Li Yuan swallowed. 'I do. The picture of Lord Yi and the ten suns – the ten dark birds in the *fu sang* tree.'

'Yes. I saw it then. Saw clearly what would come of it.'

'To the bone.'

Ben looked back at the young T'ang, seeing he understood. 'Yes. You remember. The mistake was made back there. You should never have married her. You should have left her as your dream, your ideal.' He shrugged. 'The rest, I'm afraid, was inevitable. And unfortunate, for some mistakes can never be rectified.'

Li Yuan moved closer, his hand resting loosely on Ben's arm, his eyes boring into Ben's, pleading for something that Ben could not give him.

'But what else *could* I have done?'

'Nothing,' Ben said. 'There was nothing else you could have done. But still it isn't right. You tried to shoot the moon, Li Yuan, like the great Lord Yi of legend. And what but sorrow could come of that?'

★

It was dawn in the Otzalen Alps and a cold wind blew down the valley from the north. Stefan Lehmann stood there on the open mountainside, his furs gathered tight about him, the hood pulled up over his head. He squinted into the shadows down below, trying to make out details, but it was hard to distinguish anything, so much had changed.

Where there had been snow-covered slopes and thick pine forest was now only barren rock – rock charred and fused to a glossy hardness in places. Down there where the entrance had been was now a crater almost a li across and half a li deep.

He went down, numbed by what he saw. Where the land folded and rose slightly he stopped, resting against a crag. All about him were the stumps of trees, charred and splintered by the explosions that had rent the mountain. He shuddered and found he could scarcely catch his breath.

All gone...

A thin veil of snow began to fall, flecks on the darkness below where he stood. He made himself go on, clambering down the treacherous slope until he stood there at the crater's edge, looking down into the great circle of its ashen bowl.

Shadow filled the crater like a liquid. Snowflakes drifted into that darkness and seemed to blink out of existence, their glistening brightness extinguished. He watched them fall, strangely touched by their beauty. For a time his mind refused to acknowledge what had been done. It was easier to stand there, emptied of all thought, all enterprise, and let the cold and delicate beauty of the day seep into the bones, like ice into the rock. But he knew that the beauty of it was a mask, austere and terrible. Inhumanly so. For, even as he watched, the whiteness spread, thickening, concealing the dark and glassy surface.

At his back the mountains thrust high into the thin, cold air. He looked up into the greyness of the sky, then turned, looking across at the nearest peaks. The early daylight threw them into sharp relief against the sky. Huge, jagged shapes they were, like the broken, time-bared jawbone of a giant. Beneath, the rest lay in shadow, in vast depths of blue shading into impenetrable darkness. Cloud drifted in between, casting whole slopes of white into sudden shade, obscuring the crisp, paleocrystic forms. He watched, conscious of the utter silence of that desolate place, his warm breath pluming in the frigid air. Then, abruptly, he turned away, beginning to climb the slope.

The rawness of the place appalled some part of him that wanted warmth and safety, yet the greater part of him – that part he termed his 'true self' – recognized itself in all of this. It was not a place for living, yet living things survived here, honed to the simplest of responses by the savagery of the climate; made lithe and fierce and cunning by necessity. So he, then. Rather this than the deadness of the City – that sterile womb from which nothing new came forth.

He reached the crest and paused, looking back. The past with all its complex schemes was gone. It lay behind him now. From here on he would do it his way; would become a kind of ghost, a messenger from the outside, flitting between the levels, singular and deadly.

A bleak smile came to his albinic eyes, touched the corners of his thin-lipped mouth. He felt no grief for what had happened, only new determination. This had not changed things so much as clarified them. He knew now what to do; how to harness all the hatred that he felt for them. Hatred enough to fill the whole of Chung Kuo with death.

The cloud moved slowly south. Suddenly he was in sunlight again. He turned to his right, looking up towards the summit. There, at the top of the world, an eagle circled the naked point of rock, its great wings extended fully. The sight was unexpected yet significant; another sign for him to read. He watched it for some time then moved on, descending into the valley, heading north again towards his scantily provisioned cave. It would be hard, but in the spring he would emerge again, leaner and hungrier than before but also purer, cleaner. Like a new-forged sword, cast in the fire and tempered in the ice.

He laughed – a cold, humourless sound – then gritted his teeth and began to make his way down, watching his footing, careful not to fall.

INTERLUDE   **DRAGON'S TEETH**

WINTER 2207

Without preparedness superiority is not real
superiority and there can be no initiative either.
Having grasped this point, a force which is
inferior but prepared can often defeat a superior
enemy by surprise attack.

—Mao Tse-tung, *On Protracted War*, May 1938

CHUNG KUO

t was dusk on Mars. On the Plain of Elysium it was minus seventy-six degrees and falling. Great swathes of shadow lay to the north, beneath the slopes of Chaos, stretching slowly, inexorably towards the great dome of Kang Kua City. Earth lay on the horizon, a circle of pure whiteness, back-lit by the sun. The evening star, they called it here. Chung Kuo. The place from which they had come, centuries before.

DeVore stood at the window of the tower, looking out across the great dome of Kang Kua towards the northern desert and the setting sun. The messenger had come an hour back, bringing news from Earth. He smiled. And so it had ended, his group surrounded, his pieces taken from the board. Even so, he was pleased with the way his play had gone. It was not often that one gained so much for so small a sacrifice.

He turned, looking back into the room. The morph sat at the table, its tautly muscled skin glistening in the dull red light. It was hunched forward, its hands placed either side of the board, as if considering its next play. So patient it was; filled with an inhuman watchfulness, with an inexhaustible capacity for waiting.

He went across and sat, facing the faceless creature. This was the latest of his creations; the closest yet to the human. Closest and yet furthest, for few could match it intellectually or physically.

He took a white stone from the bowl and leaned forward, placing it in *shang*, the south, cutting the line of black stones that extended from the corner.

'Your move,' he said, sitting back.

Each stone he placed activated a circuit beneath the board, registering in the creature's mind. Even so, the illusion that the morph had actually seen him place the stone was strong. Its shoulders tensed as it leaned closer, seeming to study the board, then it nodded and looked up, as if meeting his eyes.

Again it was only the copy – the counterfeit – of a gesture, for the smooth curve of its head was unmarked; like unmoulded clay, or a shell waiting to be formed.

So too its personality.

He looked away, a faint smile on his lips. Even in those few moments it had grown much darker. The lights of the great dome, barely evident before, now glowed warmly, filling the cold and barren darkness.

'Did you toast my death, Li Yuan?' he asked the darkness softly. 'Did you think it finally done between us?'

But it wasn't done. It was far from being done.

He thought back, remembering the day when he had sent the 'copy' out, two weeks after the assassination squad. It had never known; never for a moment considered itself anything but real. DeVore, it had called itself, fancying that that was what it had always been. And so, in a sense, it had. Was it not his genetic material, after all, that had gone into the being's making? Were they not his thoughts, his attitudes that had gone to shape its mind? Well, then, perhaps, in a very real sense, it *was* himself. An imperfect copy, perhaps, but good enough to fool all those it had had to face; even, when it turned to face the mirror, itself.

He watched the morph lay its stone, shadowing his own one line out while at the same time protecting the connection between its groups. He smiled, pleased. It was the move he himself would have made.

Shadowing... it was an important part of the game. As important, perhaps, as any of the final skirmishes. One had to sketch out one's territory well in advance, while at the same time plotting to break up one's opponent's future schemes: the one need balanced finely against the other.

DeVore leaned across and took a stone from the bowl, holding it a moment between his fingers, finding its cool, polished weight strangely satisfying, then set it down in *p'ing*, the east, beginning a new play.

He stood and went to the window again, looking out across the lambent hemisphere of the dome to the darkness beyond.

He had never returned from Mars. What had landed at Nanking ten years ago had been a copy – a thing so real that to call it artificial questioned definition – while he had remained here, perfecting his plays, watching, from this cold and distant world, how the thing he had made fared in his place.

It had been impressive. Indeed, it had exceeded all expectations. Whatever doubts he had harboured about its ability had quickly vanished. By all reports it had inherited his cunning along with many other of his traits. But in the end its resources had proved insufficient. It had been but a single man, fragile in all the ways a single man is fragile. Karr's rifle butt had split its skull and ended all its schemes. And so it was if one *were* single. But to amend the forgotten poet Whitman's words, he would contain multitudes: would be like the dragon's teeth that, when planted from the dragon's severed head, would sprout, producing a harvest of dragons, each fiercer, finer than its progenitor.

He breathed deeply then turned, looking at the morph again. Soon it would be time. They would take this unformed creature and mould it, mind and body, creating a being superior to those it would face back on Chung Kuo. A quicker, more cunning beast, unfettered by pity or love or obligation. A new model, better than the last.

But this time it would have another's face.

He went across, placing his hand on the creature's shoulder. Its flesh was warm, but the warmth was of the kind that communicated itself to the senses only after a moment or two: at first it had seemed cold, dead almost. Well, so it was, and yet, when they had finished with it, it would think itself alive; would defy God himself had He said, 'I *made* you.'

But whose face would he put to this one? Whose personality would furnish the empty chambers of its mind? He leaned across the creature to play another stone, furthering his line in *p'ing*, extending out towards *tsu*, the north. A T'ang? A general? Or something subtler – something much more unexpected?

DeVore smiled and straightened up, squeezing the creature's arm familiarly before he moved away. It would be interesting to see what they made of this one, for it was different in kind from the last. Was what his own imperfect copy had dreamed of. An *inheritor*. The first of a new species. A cleaner, purer being.

A dragon's tooth. A seed of destruction, floated across the vacuum of space. The first stone in a new, more terrifying game. He laughed, sensing the creature move behind him in the semi-dark, responding to the noise. Yes, the first... but not the last.

PART 17   **THE WHITE MOUNTAIN**

SUMMER 2208

Chi K'ang Tzu asked Confucius about government, saying, 'What would you think if, in order to move closer to those who possess the Way, I were to kill those who do not follow the Way?'
Confucius answered, 'In administering your government, what need is there for you to kill? Just desire the good in yourself and the common people will be good. The virtue of the gentleman is like wind; the virtue of the small man is like grass. Let the wind blow over the grass and it is sure to bend.'
—Confucius, *The Analects*, Book XII

'All warfare is based on deception.'
—Sun Tzu, *The Art of War*, Book I, Estimates

CHUNG KUO

Chapter 71

BETWEEN LIGHT AND SHADOW

Chen knelt patiently before the mirror as Wang Ti stood over him, brushing out his hair and separating it into bunches. He watched her fasten three of them at the scalp, her fingers tying the tiny knots with practised deftness. Then, with a glancing smile at his reflection, she began to braid the fourth into a tight, neat queue. As ever, he was surprised by the strength of her hands, their cleverness, and smiled to himself. A good woman, she was. The best a man could have.

'What are you thinking?' she asked, her fingers moving on to the second of the bunches, her eyes meeting his in the mirror.

'Just that a man needs a wife, Wang Ti. And that if all men had wives as good as mine this world would be a better place.'

She laughed; her soft, rough-edged peasant's laugh, which, like so many things she did, made him feel warm deep down inside. He lowered his eyes momentarily, thinking back. He had been dead before he had met her. Or as good as. Down there, below the Net, he had merely existed, eking out a living day by day, like a hungry ghost, tied to nothing, its belly filled with bile.

And now?

He smiled, noting the exaggerated curve of her belly in the mirror. In a month – six weeks at most – their fourth child would be born. A girl, the doctors said. A second girl. He shivered and turned his head slightly, trying to look across at the present he had bought her only the day before, but she pulled his head back firmly.

'Keep still. A minute and I'll be done.'

He smiled and held still, letting her finish.

'There,' she said, stepping back from him, satisfied. 'Now put on your tunic. It's on the bed, freshly pressed. I'll come and help you with your leggings in a while.'

Chen turned, about to object, but she had already gone to see to the children. He could hear them in the living-room, their voices competing with the trivee, his second son, the six-year-old Wu, arguing with the 'baby' of the family, Ch'iang Hsin, teasing her, as he so often did.

Chen laughed. Things were good. No, he thought; things had never been better. It was as if the gods had blessed him. First Wang Ti. Then the children. And now all this. He looked about him at the new apartment. Eight rooms they had. Eight rooms! And only four stacks out from Bremen Central! He laughed, surprised by it all, as if at any moment he might wake and find himself back there, beneath the Net, that all-pervading stench filling his nostrils, some pale, blind-eyed bug crawling across his body while he had slept. Back then, simply to be out of that hell had been the total of his ambitions. While this – this apartment that he rented in the upper third, in Level 224 – had seemed as far beyond his reach as the stars in the midnight sky.

He caught his breath, remembering, then shook his head. That moment on the roof of the solarium – how long ago had that been now? Ten years? No, twelve. And yet he remembered it as if it were yesterday. That glimpse of the stars, of the snow-capped mountains in the moonlight. And afterwards, the nightmare of the days that had followed. Yet here he was, not dead like his companion, Kao Jyan, but alive: the T'ang's man, rewarded for his loyalty.

He pulled on his tunic, then looked at himself in the mirror. It was the first time he had worn the azurite-blue ceremonial tunic and he felt awkward in it.

'Where's that rascal, Kao Chen?' he asked his image, noting how strange his hair looked now that it was braided, how odd his blunt, nondescript face seemed set against such elegant clothes.

'You look nice,' Wang Ti said from the doorway. 'You should wear your dress uniform more often, Chen. It suits you.'

He fingered the chest patch uncomfortably, tracing the shape of the young tiger there – the symbol of his rank as Captain in the T'ang's Security forces – then shook his head. 'It doesn't feel right, Wang Ti. I feel over-dressed. Even my hair.'

He sniffed-in deeply, then shook his head again. He should not have let Wang Ti talk him into having the implants. For all his adult life he had been happy shaving his scalp, wearing its bareness like a badge, but for once he had indulged her, knowing how little she asked of him. It was four months now since the operation had given him a full head of long, glistening black hair. Wang Ti had liked it from the first, of course, and for a while that had been enough for him, but now his discontent was surfacing again.

'Wang Ti...?' he began, then fell silent.

She came across, touching his arm, her smile of pride for once making him feel uncomfortable. 'What is it, husband?'

'Nothing...' he answered. 'It's nothing...'

'Then hold still. I'll do your leggings for you.'

The woman was leaning over the open conduit, reaching in with the fine-wire to adjust the tuning, when Leyden, the elder of the two Security men, came up with a bulb of *ch'a* for her. She set the wire down, looking across at him as she peeled off her elbow-length gloves.

'Thanks,' she said softly, and sipped at the steaming lip of the bulb.

'How much longer, Chi Li?'

Ywe Hao looked up, responding to the false name on her ID badge, then smiled. It was a beautiful smile; a warm, open smile that transformed her plain, rather narrow face. The old guard, seeing it, found himself smiling in return, then turned away, flustered. She laughed, knowing what he was thinking, but there was nothing mocking in her laughter, and when he turned back, a trace of red lingering in the paleness of his neck, he too was laughing.

'If you were my daughter...' he began.

'Go on. What would you do?' The smile remained, but fainter, a look of unfeigned curiosity in the young woman's eyes. Still watching him, she tilted her head back and ran one hand through her short dark hair. 'Tell me, Wolfgang Leyden. If I were your daughter...' And again there was laughter – as if she hadn't said this a dozen times before.

'Why... I'd lock you up, my girl. That's what I'd do!'

'You'd have to catch me first!'

He looked at her, the web of wrinkles about his eyes momentarily stark in the brightness of the overhead light, then he nodded, growing quieter. 'So I would... So I would ...'

Their nightly ritual over, they grew silent. She drained the bulb, then pulled on her gloves and got back to work, crouching there over the conduit while he knelt nearby, watching her clever hands search the tight cluster of filaments with the fine-wire, looking for weak signals.

There was a kind of natural fellowship between them. From the first – almost three weeks ago now – he had sensed something different in her; in the way she looked at him, perhaps. Or maybe simply because she, twenty years his junior, *had* looked at him; had noticed him and smiled her beautiful smile, making him feel both young and old, happy and sad. From that first day had come their game – the meaningless banter that, for him at least, was too fraught with meaning to be safe.

'There!' she said, looking up. 'One more of the fiddly little buggers done!'

Leyden nodded, but he was still remembering how her top teeth pulled down the pale flesh of her lower lip when she concentrated; how her eyes filled with a strange, almost passionate intensity. As if she saw things differently. Saw more finely, clearly than he.

'How many more?'

She sat back on her heels and drew in a deep breath. 'Eighty-seven junctions, one hundred and sixteen conduits, eleven switches and four main panels.' She smiled. 'Three weeks' work at the outside.'

She was part of a team of three sent in to give the deck its biannual service. The others were hard at work elsewhere – checking the transportation grid for faults; repairing the basic plumbing and service systems; cleaning out the massive vents that threaded these upper decks like giant cat's cradles. Their jobs were important, but hers was the vital one. She was the communications expert. In her hands rested the complex network of computer links that gave the deck its life. There were back-ups, of course, and it was hard to cause real damage, but it was still a delicate job – more like surgery than engineering.

'It's like a huge head,' she had told him. 'Full of fine nerves that carry messages. And it has to be treated like a living mind. Gently, carefully. It can be hurt, you know.' And he recalled how she had looked at him, real tenderness and concern in her face, as if the thing really were alive.

But now, looking at her, he thought, *Three weeks. Is that all? And what then? What will I do when you're gone?* Seeing him watching her, she leaned across and touched his arm gently.

'Thanks for the *ch'a*, but shouldn't you be checking on things?'

He laughed. 'As if anything ever happens.' But he sensed that he had outstayed his welcome and turned to go, stopping only at the far end of the long, dark shaft to look back at her.

She had moved on, further in towards the hub. Above her the overhead lamp, secure on its track and attached to her waist by a slender, web-like thread, threw a bright, golden light over her dark, neat head as she bent down, working on the next conduit in the line. For a moment longer he watched her, her head bobbing like a swimmer's between light and shadow, then turned, sighing, to descend the rungs.

Chen sat there, watching the screen in the corner while Wang Ti dressed the children. The set was tuned to the local MidText channel and showed a group of a dozen or so dignitaries on a raised platform, a great mass of people gathered in the Main in front of them. It was a live broadcast, from Hannover, two hundred *li* to the south-east.

At the front of the group on-screen was the T'ang's Chancellor, Nan Ho, there on his master's behalf to open the first of the new Jade Phoenix Health Centres. Behind him stood the *Hsien L'ing*, the Chief Magistrate of Hannover *Hsien*, Shou Chen-hai, a tall man with a patrician air and a high-domed head that shone damply in the overhead lights. The Chancellor was speaking, a great scroll held out before him, outlining Li Yuan's 'new deal' for the Lowers, dwelling in particular upon the T'ang's plan to build one hundred and fifty of the new Health Centres throughout the lower third.

'About time,' said Wang Ti, not looking up from where she sat, lacing up her young daughter's dress. 'They've neglected things far too long. You remember the problems we had when Jyan was born. Why, I almost gave birth to him in the reception hall. And that was back then. Things have got a lot worse in the years since.'

Chen grunted, remembering; yet he felt uneasy at the implied criticism of his T'ang. 'Li Yuan means only well,' he said. 'There are those who would not do one tenth as much.'

Wang Ti looked across at him, a measured look in her eyes, then looked away. 'I'm sure that's so, but there are rumours...'

Chen turned his head abruptly, the stiff collar of his jacket chafing his neck. '*Rumours?* About the T'ang?'

Wang Ti laughed, pushing Ch'iang Hsin away from her. 'No. Of course not. And yet his hands...'

Chen frowned. 'His hands?'

Wang Ti got up slowly, putting a hand to her lower back. 'They say that some grow fat on the T'ang's generosity, while others get but the crumbs from his table.'

'I don't follow you, Wang Ti.'

She indicated the figures on the screen. 'Our friend, the *Hsien L'ing*. It is said he has bought himself many things these past six months. Bronzes and statues and silks for his concubines. And more besides...'

Chen's face had hardened. 'You *know* this, Wang Ti? For a certainty?'

'No. But the rumours...'

Chen stood, angered. 'Rumours! Kuan Yin preserve us! Would you risk all this over some piece of ill-founded tittle-tattle?'

The three children were staring up at him, astonished. As for Wang Ti, she lowered her head, her whole manner suddenly submissive.

'Forgive me, husband, I...'

The sharp movement of his hand silenced her. He turned, agitated, and went to the set, jabbing a finger angrily at the power button. At once the room was silent. He turned back, facing her, his face suffused with anger.

'I am surprised at you, Wang Ti. To slander a good man like Shou Chen-hai. Do you know for a fact what the *Hsien L'ing* has or hasn't bought? Have you been inside his mansion? Besides, he is a rich man. Why should he not have such things? Why are you so quick to believe he has used the T'ang's money and not his own? What evidence have you?'

He huffed impatiently. 'Can't you see how foolish this is? How danger-ous? Gods, if you were to repeat to the wrong ear what you've just said to me, we would all be in trouble! Do you want that? Do you want us to lose all we've worked so long and hard to build? Because it's still a crime to damage a man's reputation with false allegations. Demotion, that's what I'm talking about, Wang Ti. Demotion. Back below the Net.'

Wang Ti gave a tiny shudder, then nodded. 'Forgive me, Kao Chen. I was wrong to say what I did. I will say no more about the *Hsien L'ing*.'

Chen stared at her a moment longer, letting his anger drain from him, then nodded, satisfied. 'Good. Then we'll say no more. Now hurry or we'll be late. I promised Karr we'd be there by second bell.'

Shou Chen-hai looked about him nervously, then, satisfied that everything was prepared, forced himself to relax.

The T'ang's Chancellor had departed an hour past, but though Nan Ho was high, high enough to have the ear of a T'ang, Shou's next guest – a man never seen on the media – was in many ways more important.

For Shou it had begun a year back, when he had been appointed to the Chair of the Finance Committee for the new Health Centre. He had seen then where it might lead... if he was clever enough, audacious enough. He had heard of the merchant some time before and, his mind made up, had gone out of his way to win his friendship. But it was only when *Shih* Novacek had finally called on him, impressed more by his persistence than his gifts or offers of help, that he had had a chance to win him to his scheme. And now, this afternoon, that friendship would bear its first fruit.

Novacek had briefed him fully on how to behave. Even so, Shou's hands trembled with a mixture of fear and excitement at the thought of entertaining a Red Pole, a real-life 426, like on the trivee serials. He called the Chief Steward over and wiped his hands on the towel the man held out for him, dabbing his forehead nervously. When he had first considered all this he had imagined a meeting with the Big Boss, the 489 himself, but Novacek had quickly disillusioned him. The Triad bosses rarely met the people they dealt with. They were careful to use intermediaries. Men like Novacek, or like their Red Poles, the 'Executioners' of the Triads; cultured, discreet men with the manners of Mandarins and the instincts of sharks.

The curtains at the far end of the long room swished back and four young, muscular-looking Han entered, Novacek just behind. They wore yellow headbands with a wheel – the symbol of the Big Circle Triad – embroidered in blue silk above the forehead. Novacek looked across and smiled reassuringly. Again, Shou had been prepared for this – even so, the thought of being 'checked out' by the Red Pole was faintly disturbing.

They worked with an impressive thoroughness, as if it were much more than simple precaution. But then, if what *Shih* Novacek said was true, theirs was a cut-throat world down there, and those who succeeded were not merely the strongest but the most careful.

Novacek came across, bowing to Shou Chen-hai. 'You have done well, *Hsien L'ing* Shou,' he said, indicating the spread Shou had prepared.

Shou returned Novacek's bow, immensely gratified by the merchant's praise. 'It is but the humblest fare, I am afraid.'

Novacek came closer, lowering his voice. 'Remember what I said. Do not smile at our friend when he comes. Nor should you show any sign of familiarity. Yao Tzu, like most Red Poles, is a proud man – he has great face – but understandably so. One does not become a Red Pole through family influence or by sitting exams. The *Hung Mun*, the Secret Societies, are a different kind of school – the very toughest of schools, you might say, and our friend, the Red Pole, is its finest graduate. If any other man were qualified for the job, *he* would be Red Pole and our friend Yao Tzu would be dead. You understand?'

Shou Chen-hai bowed his head, swallowing nervously, made aware once again of the risks he was taking even in meeting this man. His eyes went to the *Hung Mao*'s face. 'You will sit beside me, *Shih* Novacek?'

Novacek smiled reassuringly. 'Do not worry, *Hsien L'ing* Shou. Just do as I've said and all will be well.'

Shou Chen-hai gave a tiny shudder, then bowed again, grateful that the merchant had agreed to this favour. It would cost him, he knew, but if his scheme succeeded it would be a small price to pay.

At the entrance to the kitchen one of the runners appeared again, giving a brief hand-signal to one of his compatriots. At once the young man turned and disappeared through the curtain.

'All's well, it seems,' Novacek said, turning back. 'Come, let's go across. Our friend the Red Pole will be here any moment now.'

Little was said during the meal. Yao Tzu sat, expressionless, facing Shou Chen-hai across the main table, one of his henchmen seated either side of him. If what Novacek said was true, the Red Pole himself would be unarmed, but that didn't mean that he was unprepared for trouble.

The henchmen were big, vicious-looking brutes who sat there, eating nothing. They merely stared at Shou; stared and stared until his initial discomfort became something else – a cold, debilitating dread that seeped into his bones. It was something Novacek had not prepared him for and he wondered why. But he let nothing show. His fear and discomfort, his uncertainty and self-doubt were kept hidden behind the thickness of his face.

He watched the Red Pole wipe at his lips delicately with the cloth, then look across at him. Yao Tzu had tiny, almost childlike features; his nose and ears and mouth dainty, like those of a young woman, his eyes like two painted marbles in a pock-marked face that was almost *Hung Mao* in its paleness. He stared at Shou Chen-hai with an impersonal hostility that seemed of a piece with the rest of him. Meeting that gaze, Shou realized that there was nothing this man would not do. Nothing that could ever make him lose a moment's sleep at night. It was this that made him so good at what he did – that made him a 426, an Executioner.

He almost smiled, but stopped himself, waiting, as he'd been told, for Yao Tzu to speak first. But instead of speaking, the Red Pole half-turned in his seat and clicked his fingers. At once one of his men came across and placed a slender case on the table by Yao Tzu's left hand.

Yao Tzu looked up, then pushed the case towards him.

Shou glanced at Novacek, then drew the case closer, looking to the Red Pole for permission to open it. At the man's brief nod, he undid the catches and lifted the lid. Inside, embedded in bright red padded silk, were three rows of tiny black-wrapped packages, Han pictograms embossed on the wrappings in red and blue and yellow – a row of each colour. He stared at them a moment, then looked up, meeting the Red Pole's eyes. Again he had to fight down the impulse to smile – to try to make some kind of personal contact with the man facing him – but he felt exultant. If these were what he thought they were... He glanced at Novacek for confirmation, then looked back at the Red Pole, bowing his head.

For the first time in over an hour, Yao Tzu spoke.

'You understand, then, Shou Chen-hai? You have there the complete range of our latest drugs, designed to suit every need, manufactured to the very highest quality in our laboratories. At present there is nothing like them in the whole of Chung Kuo. We will supply you with whatever you require for the first two months, free of charge, and you in turn will provide the capsules without payment to your contacts in the Above. After that time, however, we begin to charge for whatever we supply. Not much, of course – nothing like what you will be charging your friends, neh? – but enough to keep us both happy.'

Shou Chen-hai gave the smallest nod, his throat dry, his hands trembling where they rested either side of the case. 'And my idea?'

Yao Tzu looked down. 'Your scheme has our approval, *Hsien L'ing* Shou. Indeed, we had been looking for some while to move in this direction. It is fortunate for us both that our interests coincide so closely, neh?'

'And the other bosses... they'll not contest you?'

It was his deepest worry – the one thing that had kept him sleepless night after night – and now he had blurted it out. For a moment he thought he had said the wrong thing, but beside him Novacek was silent, and there was no sign in the Red Pole's face that he had been offended; even so, Shou sensed a new tension about the table.

'It will be dealt with,' Yao Tzu answered stiffly, meeting his eyes. 'When the well is deep, many can draw from it, neh? Besides, it is better to make money than fight a war. I am certain the other bosses will feel the same.'

Shou let the tension drain from him. Then it was agreed. Again he felt a wave of pure elation wash through him.

Yao Tzu was watching him coldly. 'You, of course, will be responsible for your end of things. You will take care of recruitment and marketing. You will also provide all tea money.'

Shou bowed his head, concealing his disappointment. He had hoped they would help him out in respect of 'tea money' – bribes; had assumed that they would pay well to buy his contacts, but it was clear they saw things differently. His funds were large, admittedly, since he had tapped into the Health Project finances, but they were far from infinite and he had had extensive experience already of dealing with officials. They were like whores, only whores were cheap.

He looked up, meeting the Red Pole's stare with sudden confidence, knowing he had not been wrong all those months back. He, Shou Chen-hai, was destined for great things. And his sons would be great men, too. Maybe even Ministers.

When they had gone he sat there, studying the contents of the case.

If what he had heard was true, this lot alone was worth half a million. He touched his tongue to his teeth thoughtfully, then lifted one of the tiny packages from its bed.

It was identical in size to all the others, its waxy, midnight-black wrapper heat-sealed on the reverse with the blue wheel logo of the Big Circle. The only difference was the marking on the front. In this instance the pictograms were in red. *Pan shuai ch'i*, it read – 'half-life'. The others had similarly strange names. He set it in its place and sat back, staring thoughtfully into the distance. He was still sitting there when Novacek came back.

'What are these?'

Novacek hesitated, then laughed. 'You know what they are.'

'I know they're drugs, but why are they so different? He said there was nothing like them in Chung Kuo. Why? I need to know if I'm going to sell them.'

Novacek studied him a moment, then nodded. 'Okay, Shou Chen-hai. Let me tell you what's happening... what's *really* happening here.'

'It's all pipes now,' said Vasska, his voice coming from the darkness close by. 'The shit goes down and the water comes up. Water and shit. Growth and decay. Old processes, but mechanized now. Forced into narrow pipes.'

A warm, throaty laughter greeted Vasska's comment. 'Don't we just know it,' said Erika, her knees rubbing against Ywe Hao's in the cramped space.

'They fool themselves,' Vasska continued, warming to his theme. 'But it isn't a real living space, it's a bloody machine. Switch it off and they'd die, they're so cut off from things.'

'And we're so different?'

Ywe Hao's comment was sharp, her irritation with Vasska mixed up with a fear that they might be overheard. They were high up here, at the very top of the stack, under the roof itself, but who knew what tricks acoustics played in the ventilation system? She glanced at the faintly glowing figure at her wrist and gritted her teeth.

'Yes, we're different,' said Vasska, leaning closer, so that she could feel his breath on her cheek. 'We're different because we want to tear it down. To level it all and get back to the earth.'

It was close to an insult. As if she had forgotten – she, who had been in the movement a good five years longer than this... this *boy*! Neither was it what she had really meant. They too were cut off. They too had lived their lives inside the machine. So what if they only *thought* they were different?

She was about to respond, but Erika leaned forward, touching her arm. 'How much longer, Chi Li? I'm stifling.'

It was true. The small space at the hub hadn't been designed for three.

'Another five at least,' she said, covering Erika's hand with her own. She liked the woman, for all her faults, whereas Vasska... Vasska was a pain. She had met his sort before. Zealots. Bigots. They used the *Yu* ideology as a substitute for thinking. The rest was common talk. Shit and water. Narrow pipes. These were the catch-phrases of the old *Ping Tiao* intelligentsia. As if *she* needed such reminders.

She closed her eyes a moment, thinking. The three of them had been together as a team for only six weeks now – the first three of those in training and in what they termed 'assimilation'. Vasska, Erika – those weren't their real names, any more than her own was Chi Li, the name on her ID badge. Those were the names of dead men and women in the Maintenance Service; men and women whose identities the *Yu* had stolen for their use. Neither would she ever learn their real names. They were strangers, brought in from other *Yu* cells for this mission. Once they were finished here she would never see them again.

It was a necessary system, and it worked, but it had its drawbacks. From the start Vasska had challenged her. He had never said as much, but it was clear that he resented her leadership. Even though there was supposed equality between men and women in the movement, the men still expected to be the leaders – the doers and the thinkers, the formulators of policy and the agents of what had been decided. Vasska was one such. He stopped short of open dissent, but not far. He was surly, sullen, argumentative. Time and again she had been forced to give him explicit orders. And he, in return, had questioned her loyalty to the cause and to the underlying dogma of the *Yu* ideology; questioned it until she, in her quiet moments, had begun to ask herself, *Do* I believe in what I'm doing? Do I believe in Mach's vision of the new order that is to come once the City has been levelled? And though she did, it had grown harder than ever to say as much – as though such lip-service might make her like Vasska.

For a while there was only the sound of their breathing and the faint, ever-present hum of the life systems. Then, prefacing his remark with an unpleasantly insinuating laugh, Vasska spoke again. 'So how's your boy-friend, Chi Li? How's... *Wolf*-gang?' And he made the older man's name sound petty and ridiculous.

'Shut up, Vasska,' said Erika, defusing the sudden tension. Then, leaning closer to Ywe Hao, she whispered, 'Open the vent. Let's look. It's almost time.'

In the dark Ywe Hao smiled, grateful for Erika's intervention, then turned and slipped the catch. Light spilled into the cramped, dark space, revealing the huddle of their limbs.

'What can you see?'

For a moment it was too bright. Then, when her eyes had focused, she found she was looking down into Main from a place some fifty or sixty ch'i overhead. It was late and the day's crowds had gone from Main, leaving only a handful of revellers and one or two workers, making their way to their night-shift occupations. Ywe Hao looked beyond these to a small doorway to her left at the far end of Main. It was barely visible from where she was, yet even as her eyes went to it, a figure stepped out, raising a hand in parting.

'That's him!' she said in an urgent whisper. 'Vasska, get going. I want that lift secured.' Dismissing him, she turned, looking into the strong, feminine face close to her own. 'Well? What do you think?'

Erika considered, then nodded, a tight, tense smile lighting her features. 'If it's like last time we've thirty minutes, forty at the outside. Time enough to secure the place and get things ready.'

'Good. Then let's get moving. There won't be another opportunity as good as this.'

Ywe Hao looked about her, then nodded, satisfied. The rooms looked normal, no sign of the earlier struggle visible. Four of the servants were locked away in the pantry, bound hand and foot and sedated. In another room she had placed the women and children of the household, taking care to administer the exact dosage to the boys. Now she turned, facing the fifth member of the household staff, the Chief Steward, the number *yi* – one

– emblazoned in red on the green chest patch he wore on his pure white *pau*. He stared back at her, his eyes wide with fear, his head slightly lowered, wondering what she would do next. Earlier she had taped a sticky-bomb to the back of his neck, promising him that at the slightest sign or word of warning, she would set it off.

'Remember,' she said reassuringly, 'it's not you we want, Steward Wong. Do as I say and you'll live. But Shou Chen-hai must suspect nothing. He'll be back from seeing the girl soon, so run his bath and tend to him as normal. But remember, we shall be watching your every movement.'

The Steward bowed his head.

'Good.' She turned, double-checking the room, then patted the pocket of her tunic. The papers were inside – the pamphlet explaining their reasons for the execution and the official death warrant, signed by all five members of the High Council of the *Yu*. These would be left on Shou's body for Security to find. Meanwhile, friends sympathetic to the cause would be distributing copies of the pamphlet throughout the Lowers. More than fifty million in all, paid for from the coffers of the long-defunct *Ping Tiao*. Money that Mach had sifted away after Helmstadt and before the débâcle at Bremen that had brought about the *Ping Tiao*'s demise.

'Okay. You know what to say? Good. Then get to work. I want things prepared for when he returns.'

She joined Erika at the desk in the tiny surveillance room. At once she picked up the figure of the Chief Steward as he made his way down the corridor to the main bathroom. Keeping an eye on what he did, she glanced at the other screens, once more appalled by the luxury, by the sheer waste of what she saw. Shou Chen-hai's family was no bigger than many in the Mids and Lowers, and yet he had all this: twenty-four rooms, including no less than two kitchens and three private bathrooms. It was disgraceful. An insult to those he was meant to serve. But that was not why she was here, for there were many who lived as Shou Chen-hai lived, unaware of the suffering their greed relied upon. No, there were specific reasons for singling out Shou Chen-hai.

She shuddered, indignation fuelling her anger. Shou Chen-hai was a cheat. And not just any cheat. His cheating was on a grand scale and would result in untold suffering: in children not receiving treatment for debilitating diseases; in good men bleeding to death in overcrowded Accident

Clinics; in mothers dying in childbirth because the facilities promised by the T'ang had not been built. She laughed coldly. That ceremony earlier had been a sham. The T'ang's Chancellor had been shown around the new wards and operating theatres as if they were typical of what existed in the rest of the facility. But she had seen with her own eyes the empty wards, the unbuilt theatres, the empty spaces where real and solid things ought to have been. Only a fifth of the promised facility had been built. The rest did not exist – would *never* exist – because Shou Chen-hai and his friends had taken the allocated funds and spent them on their own personal schemes. She shook her head slowly, still astonished by the scale of the deception. It was not unheard of for officials to take ten, even fifteen per cent of any project. It was even, in this crazy world of theirs, *expected*. But eighty per cent! Four *billion* yuan! Ywe Hao gritted her teeth. It could not be tolerated. Shou Chen-hai had to be made an example of, else countless more would suffer while such as Shou grew bloated on their suffering.

She turned, looking at Erika. 'Who is Shou seeing?'

Erika smiled, her eyes never leaving the screen. 'One of his underling's daughters. A young thing of thirteen. The mother knows but condones it. And who can blame her?'

'No...' Yet Ywe Hao felt sick at the thought. It was another instance of Shou's rottenness; of his corrupt use of the power given him. Power... that was what was at fault here. Power, given over into the hands of petty, unscrupulous men. Men who were not fit to run a brothel, let alone a *Hsien*.

She drew her knife and stared at it, wondering what it would feel like to thrust it into Shou Chen-hai, and whether that would be enough to assuage the anger she felt. No. She could kill a million Shous and it would not be enough. Yet it was a start. A sign, to be read by High and Low alike.

She turned the knife in her hand, tested the sharpness of the edge, then sheathed it again. 'Are you ready?'

Erika laughed. 'Don't worry about me. Just worry whether Vasska's done his job and covered the lifts.'

'Yes...' she said, then tensed, seeing the unmistakable figure of Shou Chen-hai at the far end of the approach corridor. 'But first our man...'

★

The ceremony was far advanced. In the small and crowded room there was an expectant silence as the New Confucian official turned back, facing the couple.

Karr was dressed in his ceremonial uniform, the close-fitting azurite-blue tunic emphasizing his massive frame. His close-cropped head was bare, but about his neck hung the huge golden dragon pendant of the *chia ch'eng*. It had been awarded to him by the T'ang himself at a private ceremony only two months earlier and Karr wore it now with pride, knowing it was the highest honour a commoner could attain outside government, making him Honorary Assistant to the Royal Household.

Beside Karr, soon to be his wife, stood the woman he had met at the Dragon Cloud teahouse six months before, Marie Enge. In contrast to Karr she wore bright scarlet silks, a simple one-piece, tied at the waist. The effect, though simple, was stunning. She looked the perfect mate for the big man.

Karr turned, meeting her eyes briefly, smiling, then turned back to face the official, listening attentively as the wizen-faced old man spelt out the marriage duties.

'I must remind you that in public it is neither seemly nor appropriate to show your love. Your remarks must be restrained and considerate to the feelings of those about you. Love must be kept in bounds. It must not be allowed to interfere with the husband's work or with his duties to the family. As for you, Marie Enge, you must perform your household duties as a good wife, without reproach or complaint. In social gatherings you should not sit with your husband but should remain aloof. As a wife, all ties of blood are broken. You will become part of your husband's household.'

The old man paused, becoming, for a moment, less formal.

'I am told that among the young it has become unfashionable to view things in this light, but there is much to be said for our traditions. They bring stability and peace, and peace breeds contentment and happiness. In your particular cases, Gregor Karr and Marie Enge, I realize that there are no families to consider. For you the great chain of family was broken, from no fault of your own. And yet these traditions are still relevant, for in time you will have children. You will be family. And so the chain will be re-forged, the ties re-made. By this ceremony you re-enter the great tidal flow of life in Chung Kuo. By taking part in these most ancient of rituals, you reaffirm their strength and purpose.'

Chen, looking on from Karr's left, felt a tiny shiver ripple down his spine at the words. So it had been for him when he had married Wang Ti. It had been like being re-born. No longer simply Chen, but *Kao* Chen, Head of the Kao family, linked to the future by the sons he would have. Sons who would sweep his grave and enact the rituals. In marrying he had become an ancestor. He smiled, feeling deeply for Karr at that moment, enjoying the way the big man looked at his bride, knowing that this was a marriage made in heaven.

Afterwards he went across, holding Karr to him fiercely. 'I am so pleased for you, Gregor. I always hoped...' He stopped, choked by the sudden upsurge of feeling.

Karr laughed, then pushed him back to arm's length. 'What's this, my friend? Tears? No... this is a time for joy, for today my heart is fuller than it has ever been.'

He turned, raising a hand. At the signal the doors behind him were thrown open, revealing a long, high-ceilinged room, all crystal and lace, the tables set for two hundred guests.

'Well, dear friends, let us go through. There is food and drink, and later there will be dancing.' He looked across at his bride, smiling broadly, holding out his hand until she joined him. 'So... welcome, everyone. Tonight we celebrate!'

The golden eye of the security camera swivelled in its dragon-mouth socket, following Shou Chen-hai as he approached. Moments later the door hissed back. Beyond it, in the tiled entrance hall, the Chief Steward was waiting, head bowed, a silken indoor robe over one arm.

Shou Chen-hai let Wong Pao-yi remove his outside garments and help him on with the lightweight *pau*. He breathed deeply, enjoying the cool silence of the anteroom, then turned, looking at his servant. 'Where is everyone?'

Wong Pao-yi lowered his head. 'Your first wife, Shou Wen-lo, is visiting her mother, Excellency. She will be back in the morning. Your second wife, Shou He, has taken the boys to buy new robes. She called not long ago to say she would be another hour.'

Shou nodded, satisfied. 'And Yue Mi?'

The old servant hesitated. 'She is asleep, Excellency. Would you have me wake her and send her to your room?'

Shou laughed. 'No, Steward Wong. Later, perhaps. Just now I'd like a bath.'

Wong Pao-yi bowed his head again. 'It is already poured, Excellency. If you will come through, I will see to your needs personally.'

'There's no need. Just bring me a drink.'

Alone in the bathroom, he kicked off his thin briefs, then set the wine cup down and peeled the *pau* over his head. Naked, he stretched, feeling good, then lifted his wine cup, toasting himself. The girl had been good. Much less tense than before. Much more willing to please him. Doubtless that was her mother's doing. Well, perhaps he would reward the mother. Send her some small gift to encourage her. Or maybe he would have them both next time, mother and daughter, in the same bed.

The thought made him laugh, but as he turned he slowed, sensing another presence in the corridor outside.

'Wong Pao-yi? Is that you?'

He took a step forward, then stopped, the heavy porcelain wine cup falling from his hand, clattering against the side of the bath.

'What the fuck...?'

It was a man, dressed in the orange and yellow work fatigues of Maintenance, standing there, a handgun raised and pointed at him.

'Wong Pao-yi!' Shou called, staring back at the man, conscious of his nakedness, his vulnerability. 'Wong Pao-yi, where are you?'

The man laughed softly and shook his head. 'Been having fun, Shou Chen-hai? Been fucking little girls, have we?'

Anger made Shou take two more steps before he remembered the gun. He stopped, frowning, seeing the odd look of enjoyment on the man's face.

'What do you want?' he asked. 'All I have is in the safe in the study. Cards, cash, a few other bits and pieces...'

'I'm no thief, Shou Chen-hai. If I were, I'd have taken you earlier, in the corridors.'

Shou nodded, forcing himself to stay calm. If this were one of the rival Triad bosses trying to muscle in on the deal he had made with the Big Circle, then it would not do to show any fear in front of one of their messenger boys. He puffed out his chest, wearing his nakedness like a badge of courage.

'Who sent you? Fat Wong? Li the Lidless? Or was it Whiskers Lu?'

The man waved the gun impatiently and thrust a piece of paper at him. Shou Chen-hai turned his head slightly, not understanding, but at second prompting took the paper. Looking down at it, his stomach turned over.

It was a terrorist pamphlet. Itemizing his crimes. Saying why they had had to kill him.

'Look, I...' Shou began. But there was no arguing with this. No way of dealing with these bastards. His only chance was to jump the man. But as if he knew this, the man took a step backwards, pulling back the safety. He was watching Shou intently, his eyes gloating now.

'Been having *fun*?' the man insisted, jerking the gun forward, making Shou jump and give a tiny whimper of fright. 'Been fucking little girls?'

Was that it? Was it someone hired by his underling, Fang Shuo? And was all this business with the pamphlets merely a cover? He put out one hand, as if to fend off the man.

'I'll pay you. Pay you lots. Much more than Fang Shuo paid you. Look, I'll take you to the safe now. I'll...'

'Shut up!'

The man's mouth was formed into a snarl, but his eyes were cold and pitiless and Shou Chen-hai knew at once he had been mistaken. He was a terrorist. There was no mistaking that mad gleam, that uncompromising fanaticism.

'Your kind revolt me,' he said, raising the gun and pointing it at Shou's forehead. 'You think you can buy anything. You think...' He stopped and turned abruptly, following Shou's eyes.

A second figure had come into the corridor. She too wore the orange and yellow of Maintenance. Taking one look at how things were, she raised her gun and came forward.

'What the fuck do you think you're doing?'

The man gave a visible shudder of anger then turned back, facing Shou Chen-hai. Even so, his face had changed; had lost its look of hideous amusement. Shou could see immediately how things stood between the two – could sense the acid resentment in the man – and at once began working on a way to use it. But it was too late.

Ywe Hao pointed her gun and fired, twice, then, a moment later, a third time, standing over the slumped, lifeless body to make sure it was dead. There was blood on the ceramic tiles. Blood in the glass-like water of the bath. She turned and looked at Vasska, her anger making her voice shrill.

'You fucking idiot! I've had to send Erika to do what you should have done. Now go! Go and link up with her. Now!'

The man huffed out his resentment, but lowered his gun and began to turn away. He was two steps across the room when he stopped and turned back.

'Someone's coming! I can hear footsteps!'

She looked up at him, shaking her head. He was such a fool. Such a bloody amateur. Why did she have to get him on her team? Quickly she placed the papers on the corpse. Then, straightening up, she went out past Vasska and into the corridor. At the far end a man had come into view – barefoot, it seemed, and in his indoor clothes. As he came closer, she recognized who it was. It was the Security guard, Leyden.

'No...' she said softly. 'Please, no...' But he kept coming. A few paces from her, he stopped.

'Chi Li... What's going on? I thought I heard shots. I...'

His voice tapered off. He was frowning and looking at the gun in her hand, part of him understanding, another part refusing to understand.

She shook her head. There wasn't time to tie him up. No time even to argue with him. Training and instinct told her to shoot him and get out, but something held her back. Vasska, coming alongside her, looked at the man and raised his gun.

'No...' she said, reaching out to restrain his hand. 'Let him go. He's not armed.'

Vasska laughed. 'You're a fool. Soft, too,' he sneered, forgetting what she had done in the other room. 'Let's kill him and get out.'

Leyden was looking frightened now. He glanced from one to the other and began to back away. Vasska stepped forward, throwing off Ywe Hao's arm, and aimed his gun. But he didn't have a chance to fire it. Two more shots rang out and he fell forward, dead.

Leyden looked at Ywe Hao, his eyes wide, his mouth open.

'Go!' she said, her eyes pleading with him. 'Go, before I have to kill you, too!' And she raised her gun at him – the gun that had killed Shou Chen-hai and Vasska. He hesitated only a moment, then turned and ran, back up the corridor. She watched him go – heard his footsteps sound long after he was out of sight – then, stepping over Vasska's corpse, walked slowly down the corridor, the gun held out in front of her.

The lights had been dimmed in the reception room, a space cleared for dancing. A small troupe of Han musicians had set up their instruments in one corner and were playing a sprightly tune, their faces beaming as they watched the dancers whirl about the floor.

Chen stood to one side, watching as Karr led his new wife through the dance. He had never seen the big man so happy; never seen that broad mouth smile so much, those blue eyes sparkle so vividly. Marie, facing him, seemed almost breathless with happiness. She gasped and laughed and threw her head back, screeching with delight. And all about them the crowd pressed close, sharing their happiness. Chen grinned and turned his head, looking across at his own family. Jyan and young Wu were sitting at a nearby table, sipping their drinks through straws, their eyes taking in everything. Beside them sat Wang Ti, her heavily swollen belly forcing her to sit straight-backed, her legs apart. Even so, she seemed not to notice her discomfort as she held Ch'iang Hsin's hands, twirling her baby daughter this way and that to the rhythms of the music.

Chen smiled, then took a deep swig of his beer. It felt good to be able to let go. To relax and not have to worry about what the morning would bring. The last six months had been murderously busy, getting the new squad ready for active service, but after tonight both Karr and he were on a week's furlough. Chen yawned, then put his hand up to smooth his head, surprised, for the briefest moment, that his fingers met not flesh but a soft covering of hair. He lowered his hand, frowning. A lifetime's habits were hard to shift. He was always forgetting...

He made his way back, catching Karr's eye as he circled the dance floor, lifting his glass in salute.

'Are you all right?' he asked Wang Ti, crouching at her side. 'If you're feeling tired...?'

She smiled. 'No, I'm fine. Just keep an eye on the boys. Make sure they don't drink anything they shouldn't. Especially Wu. He's a mischievous little soul.'

Chen grinned. 'Okay. But if you want anything, just let me know, eh? And if you get tired...'

'Don't nag me, husband. Who's carrying this thing – you or me? I'll tell you straight enough when I want to go. All right?'

Chen nodded, satisfied, then straightened up. As he did, the door at the far end swung open and a uniformed guard came into the room. Chen narrowed his eyes, noting at once that the man was a special services courier. In one hand he held a Security folder. As he came into the room he looked about him, then swept off his cap, recognizing Karr.

Chen went across, intercepting him. 'I am Captain Kao,' he said, standing between Karr and the man. 'What is your business here?'

The courier bowed. 'Forgive me, Captain, but I have sealed orders for Major Karr. From Marshal Tolonen. I was told to give them directly into the Major's hands.'

Chen shook his head. 'But this is his wedding night. Surely...?' Then he caught up with what the man had said. *From Tolonen...*

'What has been happening?'

The courier shrugged. 'Forgive me, Captain, but I am unaware of the contents, only that it is a matter of the utmost urgency.'

Chen stood back, letting the man pass, watching as he made his way through the dancers to stand before Karr.

Karr frowned, then, with a shrug, tore open the wallet and pulled out the printed documents. For a moment he was still, reading; then, grim-faced, he came across.

'What is it?' Chen asked, disturbed by the sudden change in Karr's mood.

Karr sighed, then handed Chen the photostat of the terrorist pamphlet. 'I'm sorry, Chen, but we've work to do. It looks like the *Ping Tiao* are active again. They've assassinated a senior official. A man named Shou Chen-hai.'

'Shou Chen-hai...' Chen looked up from the pamphlet, his mouth fallen open. 'The *Hsien L'ing* from Hannover?'

Karr's eyes widened. 'That's right. You knew him?'

But Chen had turned and was looking at Wang Ti, remembering what she had said only that morning – the argument they had had over the rumours of the man's corruption. And now the man was dead; murdered by assassins. He turned back. 'But your wedding night...?'

Karr smiled. 'Marie will understand. Besides, it will be sweeter for the waiting, neh?' And, turning away, the big man went across.

The first corpse lay where it had fallen, on its back on the bathroom floor. The face was unmarked, the eyes closed, as if sleeping, but the chest was a mess. The first two high-velocity shells had torn the ribcage apart and spattered the heart and most of the left lung over the far wall, but whoever had killed him had wanted to make absolutely sure. A third shot had been fired into the man's gut after he had fallen, haemorrhaging the stomach and large intestine and destroying the left kidney.

Chen had already seen the computer simulation produced by the medical examiner on the scene, but he had wanted to see the damage for himself; to try to picture what had happened. He knelt there a moment longer, studying the dead man, fingering the fine silk of his bathrobe, then looked across at the fallen wine cup, the faintly pink water of the low-edged marble bath. The medical report showed that Shou Chen-hai had recently had sex. As for the wine, he had barely sipped at the cup before he had dropped it, presumably in surprise, for it lay some way from the body, the thick stoneware chipped.

He stood and took a step back, taking in the whole of the scene, then turned, looking out into the hallway where the second corpse lay, face down, the back of the orange and yellow Maintenance worksuit stained red in a figure-of-eight where the wounds had overlapped. Chen shook his head, trying to piece it together, but as yet it made no sense. The second corpse was supposedly a terrorist. His ID was faked and, as expected, they had found a fish pendant about his neck, a copy of the pamphlet in his pocket. But was that what they had been meant to find? Was this, in fact, a Triad killing and the rest of it a front, meant to send them off on the wrong track? It would certainly make sense of the explicit mention in the pamphlet of Shou's dealings with the Big Circle. If a rival Triad boss wanted to discredit Iron Mu or, more likely, to frighten off those who might think of dealing with him, what better way than to resurrect old fears of fanatical terrorists who struck like ghosts between the levels?

Because the *Ping Tiao* were ghosts. They had been destroyed – their cells smashed, their leaders killed – less than six months ago. It was not possible that they could have rebuilt themselves in so short a time.

Chen took the copy of the pamphlet from his tunic pocket and unfolded it. There was no mention of the *Ping Tiao* anywhere on the pamphlet, but the Han pictogram for the word 'fish' – *Yu* – the symbol of the old *Ping Tiao* was prominent in several places, and the printing and style of the pamphlet were familiar. Even if the *Ping Tiao* itself had not survived, part of it – one man, perhaps, the brain and eye behind the original organization – had come through. Unless this was an intricate fake: a mask, designed to confuse them and throw them off the scent. But why do that?

He walked through, skirting the corpse. First Level was meant to be immune from attack – a haven from such violence. But that myth had just been blown. Whoever it was, *Ko Ming* or Triad, had just sent a ripple of fear throughout the whole of City Europe.

Karr was coming out of a room to his right. Seeing Chen, he beckoned him inside.

They had set up an Operations Room here by the main entrance. The room had been a store-cupboard, but they had cleared it and moved in their own equipment. Karr's desk was at one end of the tiny room, piled high with tapes and papers. In a chair in front of it sat a middle-aged man wearing the uniform of Deck Security.

'This is Wolfgang Leyden,' Karr said, taking his seat on the far side of the desk. 'It seems he knew the team who were responsible for this. More than that, he was witness to one of the killings.'

Chen stared at the man in disbelief. 'I don't understand.'

Karr looked to the man. 'Leyden, tell Captain Kao what you just told me.'

Slowly, and with a faint tremor in his voice, Leyden repeated his story.

'Well?' said Karr. 'Have you ever heard the like?'

Chen shook his head. 'No. But it makes sense. I had begun to think this was some kind of Triad operation. One of the big bosses cutting-in on another's deals, but now...' Now he understood. The *Ping Tiao* really were back. Or something like them. 'What else have we got?'

Karr looked up. 'Surprisingly little. The woman did a thorough job on the deck communications system. For the three weeks they were here there's no visual record of them.'

Chen laughed. 'That isn't possible.'

'That's what I thought. You've got Security guards checking the screens all the time. They'd notice if anything were being blanked out, neh? But that's not what she did. The cameras were working, but nothing was being stored by the deck computer. The term for it is a "white-out". It would only get noticed if someone wanted to refer back to something on the tapes, and with so little happening at this level, it's rare that Security have to make checks. I looked at their log. It was almost nine weeks since they last called anything from memory. You see, there's no crime this high up. At least, nothing that would show as being crime.'

Chen frowned. 'You said "she" just then when you were talking about the tampering with the computer system. How do we know that?'

Leyden spoke up. 'She was good. I've seen them before, many times, but none of them were as good as her. I sat and watched her while she was at work. It was like she was part of the system.' He paused, looking away, a sudden wistfulness in his face. 'She was such a nice girl. I... I don't understand.'

Chen leaned towards him. 'You're certain it happened as you said? The other... Vasska, you say his name was... he had already drawn his gun when she shot him?'

Leyden nodded. 'He was going to kill me, but she wouldn't let him. His gun was pointed at me. At my head.' He looked up, his eyes searching Chen's face. 'You'll kill her, won't you? You'll track her down and kill her.'

Chen looked down, disturbed by the accusation in Leyden's voice.

'I've read their pamphlet,' Leyden went on, 'and it's true. I've seen them come here for meetings. Businessmen. And others. Others who had no legitimate business to be here. And I've seen the things he's bought these past eight months. Things beyond his means. So maybe they were right...'

Karr raised a hand. 'Take care what you say, friend. Captain Kao here and I... we understand how you feel. The girl saved your life and you're grateful to her. But there are others who will be less understanding. They will take your gratitude for sympathy with the girl's ideals. I would advise you to keep your opinion of the *Hsien L'ing* to yourself, *Shih* Leyden. As for your account...'

Karr hesitated, noting the guard who had appeared at the door. 'Yes?'

The guard snapped to attention, bowing his head. 'Forgive me, Major, but an official from the *T'ing Wei* has arrived.'

'Shit,' Karr said under his breath. 'So soon?'

The *T'ing Wei* was the Superintendent of Trials, and his department was responsible for keeping the wheels of justice turning in City Europe, yet it was in the department's other role – as the official mouthpiece of the State – that it was most active.

Karr turned to Leyden. 'Forgive me, but I must attend to this. However, as I was about to say, your account will be entered in the official record and, if the matter comes to trial, will be offered in mitigation of the woman's crime. That said, I'm afraid I can't vouch that she'll ever come to trial. State policy towards terrorism is, and must be, of the severest kind. To have exposed Shou Chen-hai would have been one thing, to murder him another.'

Leyden shuddered, then stood, bowing his head first to Karr and then to Chen. As he left, Chen looked across at Karr.

'The T'ing Wei were bloody quick getting here. What do you think they want?'

Karr snorted in disgust. 'To meddle in things, as ever. To bugger things up and muddy the clearest of streams. What else are they good for?'

Chen laughed. 'Then we'll be giving them our full cooperation?'

Karr nodded. 'And dropping our pants for good measure, neh?'

The two men roared with laughter. They were still laughing when the official from the T'ing Wei entered, trailing four youthful, effeminate-looking assistants. All five were Han, and all had that unmistakable air of self-contained arrogance that was the hallmark of the T'ing Wei – a kind of brutal elegance that was reflected in their clothes and manners.

The official looked about him distastefully, then began to speak, not deigning to look at Karr.

'I understand that a pamphlet has been circulated linking the Hsien L'ing with certain nefarious organizations.'

Karr picked up a copy of the pamphlet and made to offer it, but the official ignored him.

'Our task here is to make sure that the truth is known. That this scurrilous tissue of lies is revealed for what it is and the reputation of the late Shou Chen-hai returned to its former glorious condition.'

Karr stared at the official a moment, then laughed. 'Then I'm afraid you have your work cut out, Shih... ?'

'My name is Yen T'ung,' the official answered coldly, turning to take a folder from one of his assistants, 'and I am Third Secretary to the Minister, Peng Lu-Hsing.'

'Well, Third Secretary Yen, I have to inform you that it seems the accusations are true. Our friend the *Hsien L'ing* has been having meetings with people with whom a man of his... reputation... ought not to have associated. As for the funds relating to the Phoenix Health Centre...'

Yen T'ung stepped forward, placing the folder carefully, almost delicately, on the edge of Karr's desk.

'Forgive me, Major Karr, but inside you will find the official report on the murder of Shou Chen-hai. It answers all of the points raised as well as several others. Moreover, it paints a full and healthy picture of the dead man.' Yen T'ung stepped back, brushing his left hand against his silks, as if to cleanse it. 'Copies of the report will be distributed to the media at twelfth bell tomorrow. Shortly afterwards I shall be making a statement regarding the capture of those responsible for this heinous crime.'

'A statement?' For once Karr looked nonplussed. 'Are you saying that we have until twelfth bell tomorrow to find the culprits?'

Yen T'ung snapped his fingers. At once another of his assistants opened the case he was carrying and handed him a scroll. With a flourish, Yen T'ung unfurled it and read.

'"We have been informed by our Security sources that the four man Triad assassination squad responsible for the murder of the *Hsien L'ing* of Hannover, Shou Chen-hai, were, in the early hours of this morning, surrounded by forces loyal to the T'ang and, after a brief struggle, subdued and captured."'

'I see,' Karr said, after a moment. 'Then we're to let things drop?'

'Not at all, Major Karr. Your investigations will continue as before, but from henceforth any discoveries made will be screened by my office. I have the authority to that effect right here.' He took a document from another of his assistants and handed it across.

Karr studied the authority a moment, then looked up again. 'Then we're to paint black white, is that it?'

Yen T'ung was silent, a fixed smile on his lips.

'And the guard Leyden's account?'

Yen T'ung raised an eyebrow in query.

'We have a witness who saw exactly what happened. His account—'

'Will be screened by this office. Now, if you will excuse me, Major Karr, there is much to be done.'

Karr watched the Third Secretary and his retinue depart, then sat back heavily, looking up at Chen.

'Can you believe that? The arrogance of the little shit. And they've got it all worked out beforehand. Every last little detail.'

Chen shook his head. 'It won't work. Not this time.'

'Why not? The T'ing Wei are pretty good at their job, and even if you and I don't like what they do or the way they go about it, it is necessary. Terrorist propaganda has to be countered. It softens public opinion and that makes our job easier.'

'Maybe, but this time I've a feeling that they're up against people who are better at this than them.'

'What do you mean?'

Chen hesitated, then said what had been on his mind all along. 'Wang Ti. She knew about Shou Chen-hai. When we were getting ready this morning, she commented on him – on his corruption. It was most unlike her. Usually she has nothing to do with such tittle-tattle, but it seems that the rumours were unusually strong. I suspect someone seeded them long before the assassination. And then there are the pamphlets.'

Karr nodded. Yes, it would be hard to counter the effect of the pamphlets. In the past they had been circulated on a small scale, but reports were coming in that millions of the things had been distributed throughout the Lowers. All of which spoke of a much larger scale of activity than before. And the assassination itself was far more subtle, far better planned than previous Ping Tiao attacks. Far more audacious. Whoever was behind this had learned a great deal from past mistakes.

Chen had gone to the door. He pulled it shut then turned, looking back at Karr. 'So what now? Where do we begin?'

Karr lifted the pamphlet. 'We begin with this. I want to know how much of it is true and I want to know how our friends the terrorists got hold of the information.'

'And the two women?'

Karr smiled. 'We've good descriptions on both of them from several sources – Leyden, the wives and servants, the three guards who tried to intercept them at the lift. We'll get one of our experts to run a face match and see what comes out of the files. Then we'll dig a little deeper. See what turns up.'

'And then?'

It seemed an innocuous question, but Karr knew what Chen meant. If they got to the girl, what would they do? Would they kill her? Would they hand her over, to be tortured and disposed of at the whim of the T'ing Wei official, Yen T'ung? Or was there something else they might do? Something that was not strictly by the book?

Karr sat back, sighing heavily. 'I don't know, Chen. Let's find her first, neh? Then we'll decide.'

It was a dark and empty place, echoing silent, its ceiling lost in the blackness overhead. They were gathered at one end, a single lamp placed at the centre of the circle of chairs. There were nine of them, including Ywe Hao, and they spoke softly, leaning towards the lamp, their faces moving from darkness into light, features forming from the anonymity of shadow. Just now the one called Edel was speaking.

'Is there any doubt?' he said, looking across at Ywe Hao as he spoke. 'There are many who have heard the guard's story. How she killed my brother – shot him in the back – and spared the guard.'

'So you say,' said Mach, his long, thin face stretching towards the light. 'But have you witnesses to bring forward? Written statements?'

Edel laughed scathingly, moving back into shadow. 'As if they'd come here! As if they'd risk their names on paper to satisfy a Yu court!'

'No Yu, even? Or is it only your say-so? Chi Li denies your charge. Without proof it is her word against yours.'

'Send someone. Get proof.'

A woman leaned forward, one of the Council of Five. Her face, etched in the light like a woodcut, showed strong, determined features. Her voice, when she spoke, was hard, uncompromising. 'You know we cannot do that. You know also that you broke our strictest orders by going yourself.'

'He was my brother!'

'We are all brothers.'

'Not all, it seems. Some are murderers.'

There was a moment's silence, then Mach leaned forward. 'You asked for this hearing, Edel. As was your right. But you have made accusations without supporting evidence. You have brought the reputation of a good and proven comrade into question. She has answered your charges fully and still you persist. Such, one might argue, is your duty as a brother. But do not add insolence to the list of things against you.'

Edel stood. His voice boomed, echoing in the dark and empty space. 'So it's *wrong* to want justice, is it? Wrong to want to unmask this murdering bitch?'

His finger pointed unerringly across the circle at Ywe Hao, who kept her head lowered, the lamplight shining in the crown of her dark, neat hair. This tableau held for a moment, then, without another word, Edel sat back again, putting his trembling hands on his knees. From the fierce look of hatred in his eyes there was no doubting he believed what he said.

'Chi Li?' asked the woman, looking at her. 'You stand by your account?'

Ywe Hao looked up, the lamp's light catching in her dark, liquid eyes. 'Vasska was a fool. Erika and I barely got out alive. There was a patrol at the lift he should have secured. We had to shoot our way out. Erika was badly wounded. These are facts. If I could, I would have killed him for that. For risking others' lives. But I didn't. Shou Chen-hai killed him. Killed him before I could get to him.'

So ran the official Security report, given to the media. Edel had done nothing, provided nothing, to seriously counter this. His evidence was rumour, hearsay, the kind of romantic legend that often attached itself to this kind of event. The Five made their decision and gave it.

'I find no case proven,' said Mach, standing. 'You must apologize, Edel, or leave the *Yu*. That is our law.'

Edel also stood, but there was no apology. Instead he leaned forward and spat across the lamp at Ywe Hao. It fell short, but at once Veda, the female Council member, stepped forward and pushed Edel back. She spoke quickly, harshly.

'That's it. You have proved there's no place for you here. Go! And say nothing, do nothing to harm the *Yu*. The merest word and we shall hear of it. And then...' She raised one finger to her throat and drew it across.

Sullenly, glaring back at Ywe Hao, Edel left the circle and walked slowly across the factory floor, stopping only in the brightness of the doorway at the far end to look back, as if to say it wasn't over yet.

When he'd gone, Mach signalled to one of the men at his side to follow Edel. 'Best do it now, Klaus. Veda's warning will have no effect on him. He is past reasoning.'

The man nodded, then ran across the dark floor, following Edel, his knife already drawn. Mach turned, facing Ywe Hao.

'I'm sorry, Chi Li. This has been a sad day for us all.'

But Ywe Hao was watching the man disappear in pursuit of Edel and asking herself if her lie had been worth the life of another man; if this barter, his life for hers, could in any way be justified. And as if in answer, she saw Leyden again, standing there, terrified, facing Edel's brother, the man she had only known as Vasska, and knew she had been right to spare the guard and kill her comrade. As right as she had been in killing Shou Chen-hai.

Veda came and stood by her, taking her hand, her words soft, comforting. 'It's all right, Chi Li. It wasn't your fault.'

But the thing was, she had enjoyed killing Vasska. Had wanted to kill him. And how could she live with that?

'Listen,' said Mach, coming close, turning her to face him. 'I have another task for you. There's a place the younger sons use. A place called the Dragonfly Club...'

CHUNG KUO

Chapter 72

DRAGONFLIES

The Pavilion of Elegant Sound rested on a great spur of pale rock, the delicately carved tips of its six sweeping gables spread out like the arms of white-robed giants raised in supplication to Heaven. To either side twin bridges spanned the ravine, the ancient wood of the handrails worn smooth like polished jade by a million pilgrims' hands.

A dark, lush greenery clothed the flank of Mount Emei about the ancient building, filtering the early morning sunlight, while below, long, twisted limbs of rock reached down to a shadowed gorge, their dark, eroded forms slick with the spray of the two tiny falls that met in a frenzy of mist and whiteness at their foot. Farther out, a great heart-shaped rock, as black as night itself, sat peacefully amidst the chill, crystal-clear flow.

Standing at the low, wooden balustrade, Li Yuan looked down into the waters. For more than a thousand years travellers had stopped here on their long journey up the sacred mountain, to rest and contemplate the perfection of this place. Here two rivers met, the black dragon merging with the white, forming a swirl of dark and light – a perfect, natural *tai ch'i*.

He turned, looking across. Tsu Ma stood by the table on the far side of the Pavilion, pouring wine. They were alone, the nearest servants five hundred *ch'i* distant, guarding the approaches. From the gorge below came the melodious sounds of the falls, from the trees surrounding them the sweet, fluting calls of wild birds. Li Yuan breathed in deeply, inhaling the heady scent of pine and cypress that filled the air. It was beautiful: a place of perfect harmony and repose. He smiled. It was like Tsu Ma to choose such a place for their meeting.

Tsu Ma came across, handing Li Yuan one of the cups. For a moment he stood there, looking out past Li Yuan at the beauty of the gorge, then turned to face him, placing a hand lightly on his shoulder. 'Life is good, neh, Yuan?'

Li Yuan's smile broadened. 'Here one might dream of an older, simpler age.'

Tsu Ma grunted. 'Things have never been simple for those who have to rule. Some problems are eternal. It is said that even the great Hung Wu, founder of the Ming dynasty, slept poorly at night. Population pressures, famines, civil unrest, the corruption of Ministers, court intrigues, the ambitions of rivals – these were as much his problems as they are ours. Neither was he much more successful at solving them.'

Li Yuan frowned. 'Then you think we should do nothing?'

'On the contrary. As T'ang, it is our purpose in this life to attempt the impossible – to try to impose some kind of order on the chaos of this world. There would be no justification for our existence were it not so. And where would we be then?'

Li Yuan laughed, then took a sip of wine, growing serious again. 'And in Council tomorrow? How are we to play that?'

Tsu Ma smiled. Tomorrow's was an important meeting; perhaps the most important since Li Shai Tung's death nine months earlier.

'With regard to GenSyn, I think you are right, Yuan. Wang Sau-leyan's proposal must be opposed. His idea of a governing committee of seven – one member appointed by each T'ang – whilst fair in principle would prove unworkable in practice. Wang's appointment would be but a front for his own guiding hand. He would seize upon the slightest excuse – the most petty of internal divisions on policy – to use his veto. It would have the effect of closing GenSyn down, and as few of GenSyn's facilities are based in City Africa, our cousin would escape relatively unscathed, while you would be harmed greatly. Which is why I shall support your counter-proposal of a single independent stewardship.'

'And my candidate?'

Tsu Ma smiled. 'I can see no reason why Wang should object to Wei Feng's man, Sheng, taking charge. No. It's the perfect choice. Wang would not dare suggest that Minister Sheng is unsuited for the post. It would be tantamount to a slur on Sheng's master, the T'ang of East Asia! And even our moon-faced cousin would not dare risk that.'

Li Yuan joined in with Tsu Ma's laughter, but deep down he was not so sure. Wang Sau-leyan made much of his power to offend. His sense of *hsiao* – of filial submission – was weak. If the man *had* dared to have his father killed, his brother driven to suicide, what else might he not do? And yet the question of GenSyn was the least of the items that was to be discussed. As Tsu Ma knew, Li Yuan was prepared to concede ground in this instance if Wang would give way on more important matters.

'Do you think the balance of Council will be against us on the other measures?'

Tsu Ma stared into his cup, then shrugged. 'It is hard to say. I have tried to sound Wu Shih and Wei Feng on the question of the changes, but they have been strangely reticent. On any other matter we might guarantee their support, but on this I am afraid they see things differently.'

Li Yuan huffed, exasperated. Without those concessions provided by the changes to the Edict and the reopening of the House, there was no chance of striking a deal with the Above over population controls. The three items worked as a package or not at all. The Edict changes were the sweetener, creating new prosperity for the merchant classes, whereas the reopening of the House would not only satisfy the growing call for proper representation of the Above in government but would provide the vehicle for the passage of new laws. Laws controlling the number of children a man might have. Laws that the Seven might find it difficult to implement without Above support.

Tsu Ma looked at Yuan ruefully. 'And the perversity of it is that Wang Sau-leyan will oppose us not because he disagrees – after all, he has made it quite clear that he would like to see changes to the Edict, the House reopened – but because it is his will to oppose us.'

Li Yuan nodded. 'Maybe so. But there is something else, cousin Ma. Something I have not mentioned before now.'

Tsu Ma smiled, intrigued. 'Which is?'

Li Yuan laughed quietly, but his expression was sombre, almost regretful. 'First fill my cup, then I will tell you a tale about a nobleman and a T'ang and a scheme they have hatched to make all plans of mine mere idle talk.'

★

It was all much dirtier than she remembered it. Dirtier and more crowded. Ywe Hao stood there, her back to the barrier, and breathed out slowly. Two boys, no taller than her knee, stood beside her, looking up at her. Their faces were black with dirt, their heads covered in sores and stubble. Their small hands were held up to her, palms open, begging. They said nothing, but their eyes were eloquent. Even so, she shooed them from her, knowing that to feed two would bring a hundred more.

Main had become a kind of encampment. The shops she remembered from her childhood had been turned into sleeping quarters, their empty fronts covered with sheets. There was rubbish everywhere, and the plain, clean walls she had glimpsed in memory were covered with graffiti and posters for a hundred different political groupings.

There was no sign anywhere of Security, but men wearing armbands stood at the intersections and about Main itself, wielding ugly-looking clubs. Against the walls families huddled or lay, mother and father on the outside, children between. These last were mainly Han. They called them 'little t'ang' down here, the irony savage, for these t'ang had nothing – only the handouts from Above. And an unfair share of that.

It had been only eight years since she had come from here. How could it have changed so much in that brief time?

Ywe Hao pushed across Main, jostled by surly, ill-featured men who looked at her with undisguised calculation. One of them came across and grabbed her arm. She shook herself free and reached out with a quicksilver movement that surprised him. 'Don't...' she warned, pushing him away. He backed off, understanding what she was. Others saw it too and a whisper went out, but she was gone by then, down a side corridor that, unlike the rest, seemed little changed. At the far end was her mother's place.

The room was squalid. Three families were huddled into it. She knew none of them. Angry, worried, she came out into the corridor and stood there, her heart pounding. *She hadn't thought...*

From across the corridor an old man called to her. 'Is that you, Ywe Hao? Is that really you?'

She laughed and went across. To either side people were watching her, standing in doorways, or out in the corridor itself. There was no privacy anywhere down here.

It was her Uncle Chang. Her mother's brother. She went to him and held him tightly to her, so glad to see him that for the moment she forgot they had parted badly.

'Come in, girl! Come in out of the way!' He looked past her almost haughtily at the watching faces, sniffing loudly before ushering her inside and sliding back the panel.

It was quieter inside. While her uncle crouched at the k'ang, preparing ch'a, she looked about her. Most of the floor was taken up by three bedrolls, made neatly, tidily. To her left, beside the door panel, was a small table containing holos and 2-Ds of the family. In a saucer in front of them was the stub of a burnt candle. The room smelled of cheap incense.

'Where's mother?'

Her uncle looked round at her and smiled. 'At market. With Su Chen.'

'Su Chen?'

He looked away, embarrassed. 'My wife,' he said. 'Didn't you hear?'

She almost laughed. Hear? How would she hear? For years she hadn't known a thing. Had lived in fear of anyone finding out anything about them. But she had never stopped thinking of them. Wondering how they were.

'And how is she?'

'Older,' he answered distractedly, then grunted his satisfaction at getting the k'ang to work. Ywe Hao could see he did little here. There was a vid unit in the corner, but it was dead. She looked at it, then back at him, wondering how he filled his days.

She had been right to get out. It was like death here. Like slow suffocation. The thought brought back the memory of the last time she had been here. The argument. She turned her face away, gritting her teeth.

The tiny silver fish hung on a chain about her neck, resting between her breasts, its metal cool against her flesh. It was like a talisman against this place; the promise of something better.

Her uncle finished pottering about and sat back on the edge of the nearest bedroll. 'So how are you?' His eyes looked her up and down. Weak, watery eyes, watching her from an old man's face. He had been younger, stronger, when she'd last seen him, but the expression in the eyes was no different. They wanted things.

He was a weak man, and his weakness made him spiteful. She had lived out her childhood avoiding his spitefulness; avoiding the wanting in his eyes. From his pettiness she had forged her inner strength.

'I'm fine,' she said. And what else? That she was an expert killer now? One of the most wanted people in the City?

'No man? No children, then?'

Again she wanted to laugh at him. He had never understood.

'No. No man. No children,' she said, after a moment. 'Only myself.'

She crouched beside the table, studying the small collection of portraits. There was one of her, much younger, there beside her dead brother.

'I thought mother didn't need this.'

'She gets comfort from it. You'd not deny her that?'

There was a holo of her father; one she had never seen before. No doubt her mother had bought the image from the public records. There was a file date at the foot of it that told her that the holo had been made almost eight years before she had been born. He would have been – what? – twenty. She shivered and straightened up, then turned, looking down at her uncle. 'Do you need money?'

She saw at once that she had been too direct. He avoided her eyes, but there was a curious tenseness in him that told her he had been thinking of little else. But to admit it... that was something different. He was still her uncle. In his head she was still a little girl, dependent on him. He shrugged, not meeting her eyes. 'Maybe... It would be nice to get a few things.'

She was about to say something more when the panel behind her slid back and her mother stepped into the room. 'Chang, I...'

The old woman paused, then turned to face Ywe Hao, confused. At first it didn't register, then her face lit up. She dropped the package she was carrying and opened her arms wide. 'Hao! My little Hao!'

Ywe Hao laughed and hugged her mother tightly, stooping to do so. She had forgotten how small her mother was. 'Mama...' she said, looking into her eyes and laughing again. 'How have you been?'

'How have I been?' The old lady shook her head. Her eyes were brimming with tears and she was trembling with emotion. 'Oh, dear gods, Hao, it's so good to see you. All these years...' There was a little sob, then, with another laugh and a sniff, she pointed to the beds. 'Sit down. I'll cook you something. You must be hungry.'

Ywe Hao laughed, but did as she was told, squatting beside her uncle on the bedroll. From the doorway Su Chen, unintroduced, looked on bewildered. But no one thought to explain things to her. After a while she pulled the door closed and sat on the far side of her husband. Meanwhile, the old lady pottered at the *k'ang*, turning every now and then to glance at her daughter, wiping her eyes before turning back, laughing softly to herself.

Later, after eating, they sat and talked, and for a time, it seemed almost as though the long years of parting had not happened; that this day and the last were stitched together like points on a folded cloth. But when, finally, she left them, she knew at last that there was no returning. She had gone beyond this, to a place where even a mother's love could not keep her.

Looking back at Main, she saw the changes everywhere. Time had injured this place, and there seemed no way to heal it. Best then to tear it down. Level by level. Maybe then they would have a chance. Once they had rid themselves of Cities.

Shivering, more alone now than she had been for many years, she turned from it and stepped into the transit, going up, away from her past.

The dark, heart-shaped rock was embedded deep into the earth beneath the pool, like the last tooth in an ancient's jaw. Its surface was scored and pitted, darker in places than in others, its long flank, where it faced the Pavilion, smoother than those that faced away; like a dark, polished glass, misted by the spray from the tiny falls. At its foot the cold, clear waters of the pool swirled lazily over an uneven surface of rock, converting the white-water turbulence of the two rivers' convergence into a single, placid flow.

From the rock one could see the two figures in the Pavilion; might note their gestures and hear the murmur of their words beneath the hiss and rush of the falling water. Tsu Ma was talking now, his hand moving to his mouth every so often, a thin thread of dark smoke rising in the air. He seemed intensely agitated, angered even, and his voice rose momentarily, carrying over the sound of the falls.

'It is all very well *knowing*, Yuan, but how will you get proof? If this is true, it is most serious. Wang Sau-leyan must be called to account for this. His conduct is outrageous!'

Li Yuan turned to face his fellow T'ang. 'No, Cousin Ma. Think what damage it would do to confront Wang openly. At best he might be forced to abdicate, and that would leave us with the problem of a successor – a problem that would make the GenSyn inheritance question a mere trifle, and the gods know that is proving hard enough! At worst he might defy us. If he did, and Hou Tung-po and Chi Hsing backed him, we could find ourselves at war among ourselves.'

'That cannot be.'

'No. But for once the threat to expose Wang might prove more potent than the actuality. If so, we might still use this to our benefit.'

'You mean, as a bargaining counter?'

Li Yuan laughed; a hard, clear laughter. 'Nothing so subtle. I mean we blackmail the bastard. Force him to give us what we want.'

'And if he won't?'

'He will. Like us all, he enjoys being a T'ang. Besides, he knows he is too weak, his friends in Council unprepared for such a war. Oh, he will fight if we push him to it, but only if he must. Meanwhile he plays his games and bides his time, hoping to profit from our failures. But this once he has over-stretched himself. This once we have him.'

'Good. But how do you plan to use this knowledge?'

Li Yuan looked outward. 'First we must let things take their course. Hsiang Shao-erh meets with our cousin Wang on his estate in Tao Yuan an hour from now. My friend in Wang's household will be there at that meeting. By tonight I will know what transpired. And tomorrow, after Council, we can confront Wang with what we know. That is, if we need to. If we haven't already achieved what we want by other, more direct means.'

'And your... *friend*? Will he be safe? Don't you think Wang might suspect there is a spy in his household?'

Li Yuan laughed. 'That is the clever part. I have arranged to have Hsiang Shao-erh arrested on his return home. It will seem as if he had... *volunteered* the information. As, indeed, he will.'

Tsu Ma nodded thoughtfully. 'Good. Then let us get back. All this talking has given me an appetite.'

Li Yuan smiled, then looked about him, conscious once more of the beauty of the shadowed gorge, the harmony of tree and rock and water. And yet that beauty was somehow insufficient.

He grasped the smooth wood of the rail, looking out at the great, heart-shaped rock that rested, so solid and substantial, at the centre of the flow, and felt a tiny tremor pass through him. This place, the morning light, gave him a sense of great peace, of oneness with things, and yet, at the same time, he was filled with a seething mass of fears and expectations and hopes. And these, coursing like twin streams in his blood, made him feel odd, distanced from himself. To be so at rest and yet to feel such impatience, was that not strange? And yet, was that not the condition of all things? Was that not what the great Tao taught? Maybe, but it was rare to feel it so intensely in the blood.

Like a dragonfly hovering above the surface of a stream.

Tsu Ma was watching him from the bridge. 'Yuan? Are you coming?'

Li Yuan turned, momentarily abstracted from the scene, then, with the vaguest nod, he moved from the rail, following his friend.

And maybe peace never came. Maybe, like life, it was all illusion, as the ancient Buddhists claimed. Or maybe it was himself. Maybe it was his own life that was out of balance. On the bridge he turned, looking back, seeing how the great swirl of white drifted out into the black, how its violent energy was stilled and channelled by the rock.

Then he turned back, walking on through the shadow of the trees, the dark image of the rock embedded at the centre of his thoughts.

It was midday and the sky over Northern Hunan was the cloudless blue of early spring. In the garden of the palace at Tao Yuan, Wang Sau-leyan sat on a tall throne, indolently picking from the bowls of delicacies on the table at his side while he listened to the man who stood, head bowed, before him.

The throne was mounted on an ancient sedan, the long arms carved like rearing dragons, the thick base shaped like a map of the ancient Middle Kingdom, back before the world had changed. Wang had had them set him down at the very heart of the garden, the elegant whiteness of the three-tiered Pagoda of Profound Significance to his right, the stream, with its eight gently arching bridges, partly concealed beyond a stand of ancient junipers to his left.

To one side Sun Li Hua, newly promoted to Master of the Royal Household, stood in the shadow of the junipers, his arms folded into his powder-blue sleeves, his head lowered, waiting to do his master's bidding.

The man who stood before Wang was a tall, elegant-looking Han in his mid-fifties. His name was Hsiang Shao-erh and he was Head of the Hsiang family of City Europe, Li Yuan's bondsman – his blood vassal. But today he was here, speaking to his master's enemy. Offering him friendship. And more...

For an hour Hsiang had prevaricated; had talked of many things, but never of the one thing he had come to raise. Now, tiring of his polite evasions, Wang Sau-leyan looked up, wiping his fingers on a square of bright red silk as he spoke.

'Yes, cousin, but why are you here? What do you want from me?'

For the second time that day Hsiang was taken aback. Earlier, when Wang had invited him outdoors to talk, his mouth had flapped uselessly, trying to find the words that would not offend the T'ang; that might make clear this was a matter best discussed behind closed doors or not at all. But Wang had insisted and Hsiang had had to bow his head and follow, concealing his discomfort.

Now, however, Hsiang was feeling much more than simple discomfort. He glanced up, then looked away, troubled by Wang Sau-leyan's directness. For him this was a major step. Once taken, it could not be reversed. Even to be here today was a kind of betrayal. But this next...

With a tiny shudder, Hsiang came to the point.

'Forgive me, *Chieh Hsia*, but I am here because I can do you a great service.' He lifted his head slightly, meeting Wang's eyes tentatively. 'There is one we both... dislike immensely. One who has offended us gravely. He...'

Wang raised an eyebrow. 'Go on, Hsiang Shao-erh...'

Hsiang looked down. 'You know what happened, *Chieh Hsia*?'

Wang nodded, a faint smile on his lips. He did indeed. And, strangely enough, it was one of the few things he actually admired Li Yuan for. Faced with similar circumstances – with an outbreak of a deadly strain of syphilis – he would have acted exactly as Li Yuan had done, even to the point of offending his own Family Heads. But that was not the issue. Hsiang Shao-erh was here because – quite rightly – he assumed Wang hated Li Yuan as much as he did. But though Hsiang's loss of face before his peers had been a great thing, it was as nothing beside this act of betrayal.

Hsiang looked up, steeling himself, his voice hardening as he recalled his humiliation; his anger momentarily overcoming the fear he felt. 'Then you understand why I am here, *Chieh Hsia*.'

Wang shook his head. 'You will have to be less opaque, cousin. You talk of one who has offended us both. Can you be more specific?'

Hsiang was staring at him now. But Wang merely turned aside, picking a lychee from one of the bowls and chewing leisurely at the soft, moist fruit before looking back at Hsiang.

'Well?'

Hsiang shook his head slightly, as if waking, then stammered his answer. 'Li Yuan. I mean Li Yuan.'

'Ah...' Wang nodded. 'But I still don't follow you, cousin. You said there was some great service you could do me.'

Hsiang's head fell. He had clearly not expected it to be so hard. For a time he seemed to struggle against some inner demon, then he straightened, pushing out his chest exaggeratedly, his eyes meeting Wang's.

'We are tied, you and I. Tied by our hatred of this man. There must be some way of using that hatred, surely?'

Wang's eyes narrowed slightly. 'It is true. I dislike my cousin. Hatred may be too strong a word, but...' He leaned forward, spitting out the seeds. 'Well, let me put it bluntly, Hsiang Shao-erh. Li Yuan is a T'ang. My equal and your master. So what are you suggesting?'

It could not have been put more explicitly, and Wang could see how Hsiang's eyes widened fearfully before he looked down again. Wang reached out and took another fruit, waiting, enjoying the moment. Would Hsiang dare take the next step, or would he draw back?

'I...' Hsiang shuddered. His hands pulled at the silk over his thighs. Then, after another titanic inner struggle, he looked up again. 'There is a substance I have heard of. An illegal substance that was developed, I am told, in the laboratories of SimFic.'

'A substance?'

Hsiang moved his head uncomfortably. 'Yes, *Chieh Hsia*. Something that destroys the female's ability to produce eggs.'

'A ...' Wang sat back, staring up into the blueness. 'And this substance? You have it, I take it?'

Hsiang shook his head. 'No, *Chieh Hsia*. It was taken in a raid on one of *Shih* Berdichev's establishments. Your late father's Security forces undertook that raid, I believe, yet the substance...'

'Was destroyed, I should think,' Wang said brusquely. 'But tell me, cousin. Had it existed – had there been some of this substance remaining, held, perhaps, illegally, in defiance of the Edict – what would you have done with it?'

Again it was too direct. Again Hsiang shied back like a frightened horse. Yet the desire for revenge – that burning need in him to reverse the humiliation he had suffered at Li Yuan's hands – drove him on. He spoke quickly, nervously, forcing the words out before his courage failed.

'I plan to hold a party, *Chieh Hsia*. In celebration of Li Yuan's official birthday. He will accept, naturally, and his wives will accompany him. It is there that I will administer this substance to them.'

Wang Sau-leyan had been sitting forward, listening attentively. Now he sat back, laughing. 'You mean, they will sit there calmly while you spoon it down their throats?'

Hsiang shook his head irritably. 'No, *Chieh Hsia*. I... The substance will be in their drinks.'

'Oh, of course!' Wang let out another burst of laughter. 'And the *She tou*, the official taster – what will he have been doing all this while?'

Hsiang looked down, biting back his obvious anger at Wang Sau-leyan's mockery. 'I am told this substance is tasteless, *Chieh Hsia*. That even a *She tou* would be unable to detect any trace of its presence.'

Wang sat forward, suddenly more conciliatory. He looked across at Sun Li Hua, then back at Hsiang Shao-erh, smiling.

'Let me make this absolutely clear, Hsiang Shao-erh. What you are suggesting is that I provide you with a special substance – an illegal substance – that you will then administer secretly to Li Yuan's three wives. A substance that will prevent them from ovulating.'

Hsiang swallowed deeply, then nodded. 'That is it, *Chieh Hsia*.'

'And if our young friend marries again?'

Hsiang laughed uneasily. '*Chieh Hsia*?'

'If Li Yuan casts off these three and marries again?'

Hsiang's mouth worked uselessly.

Wang shook his head. 'No matter. In the short term your scheme will deny Li Yuan sons. Will kill them even before they are born, neh?'

Hsiang shuddered. 'As he killed mine, *Chieh Hsia*.'

It was not strictly true. Hsiang's sons had killed themselves. Or, at least, had fallen ill from the *yang mei ping* – the willow-plum sickness – that had spread among the Minor Families after the entertainment at Hsiang's estate.

If Li Yuan had helped Hsiang's sons end their worthless lives a few days earlier than otherwise, that was more to his credit than to theirs. They had been fated anyway. But Wang was unconcerned with such sophistry. All that concerned him was how he might use this. Hsiang's sense of humiliation made him useful, almost the perfect means of getting back at Li Yuan. *Almost.*

Wang Sau-leyan leaned forward, thrusting out his right hand, the matt black surface of the *Ywe Lung*, the ring of power, resting like a saddle on the index finger.

Hsiang stared at it a moment, not understanding, then, meeting Wang's eyes, he quickly knelt, drawing the ring to his lips and kissing it once, twice, a third time before he released it, his head remaining bowed before the T'ang of Africa.

Karr had washed and put on a fresh uniform ready for the meeting. He turned from the sink and looked across. Marie was in the other room, standing before the full-length mirror. In the lamp's light her skin was a pale ivory, the long line of her backbone prominent as she leaned forward.

For a moment he was perfectly still, watching her, a thrill of delight rippling through him. She was so strong, so perfectly formed. He felt his flesh stir and gave a soft laugh, going across.

He closed his eyes, embracing her from behind, the warm softness of her skin, that sense of silk over steel, intoxicating. She turned, folding into his arms, her face coming up to meet his in a kiss.

'You must go,' she said, smiling.

'Must I?'

'Yes, you must. Besides, haven't you had enough?'

He shook his head, his smile broadening. 'No. But you're right. I must go. There's much to be done.'

Her smile changed to a look of concern. 'You should have slept...'

He laughed. 'And you'd have let me?'

She shook her head.

'No. And neither could I with you beside me.'

'The time will come...'

He laughed. 'I can't imagine it, but...

She lifted her hand. 'Here.'

He took the two pills from her and swallowed them down. They would keep him awake, alert, for another twelve to fifteen hours – long enough to get things done. Then he could sleep. If she'd let him.

'Is it important?' Marie asked, a note of curiosity creeping into her voice.

'It is the T'ang's business,' he answered cryptically, stone-faced, then laughed. 'You must learn patience, my love. There are things I have to do... well, they're not always pleasant...'

She put a finger to his lips. 'I understand. Now go. I'll be here, waiting, when you get back.'

He stood back from her, at arm's length, his hands kneading her shoulders gently, then bent forward, kissing her breasts. 'Until then...'

She shivered, then came close again, going up on tiptoe to kiss the bridge of his nose. 'Take care, my love, whatever it is.'

'Okay, Major Karr. You can take off the blindfold.'

Karr looked about him, genuinely surprised. 'Where are we? First Level?'

The servant lowered his head respectfully, but there was a smile on his face. He was too wary, too experienced in his master's service, to be caught by such a blatant attempt to elicit information, but he was also aware that, blindfolded as he was, Karr knew he had been taken down the levels, not up.

'If you would follow me...'

Karr smiled and followed, taken aback by the elegance of the rooms through which they passed. He had not thought such luxury existed here just above the Net, but it was not really that surprising. He had read the report on the United Bamboo; had seen the financial estimates for the last five years. With an annual turnover of one hundred and fifteen billion *yuan*, Fat Wong, the big boss of United Bamboo, could afford luxuries like these. Even so, it was unexpected to find them in such a setting. Like finding an oasis on Mars.

Karr looked down, noting that the floor mosaic mirrored that of the ceiling overhead. Nine long, thick canes of bamboo were gripped by a single, giant hand, the ivory yellow of the canes and the hand contrasted against the brilliant emerald green of a paddy field. Karr smiled, thinking of how often he had seen that symbol, on the headbands of dead runners trapped in Security ambushes, or on the packaging of illicitly smuggled goods that had made their way up from the Net. And now he was to meet the head behind that grasping hand – the 489 himself.

The servant had stopped. Now he turned, facing Karr again, and bowed deeply. 'Forgive me, Major Karr, but I must leave you here. If you would go through, my master will be with you in a while.'

Karr went through, past a comfortably furnished anteroom and out into a long, spacious gallery with a moon door at each end. Here, on the facing walls, were displayed the banners of the thirty or more minor Triads that the United Bamboo had conquered or assimilated over the centuries. Karr made his way down the row, stopping at the last of the banners.

He reached up, touching the ancient silk gently, delicately, conscious that it was much older than the others that hung there. The peacock blue of the banner had faded, but the golden triangle at its centre still held something of its former glory. In the blue beside each face of the triangle was embroidered a Han word, the original red of the pictograms transformed by time into a dull mauvish-brown, like ancient bloodstains. He gave a little shudder, then offered the words softly to the air.

'Tian. Nan Jen. Tu.'

Heaven. Man. Earth. He turned, then stopped, noticing the figure that stood inside the moon door at the far end of the gallery.

'You walk quietly, Wong Yi-sun. Like a bird.'

Fat Wong smiled, then came forward, his cloth-clad feet making no sound on the tiles.

'I am delighted to meet you, Major Karr. Your reputation precedes you.'

Contrary to public expectations, Fat Wong was not fat at all. Quite the contrary – he was a compact, wiry-looking man who, in his peach silks and bound white feet, looked more like a successful First Level businessman than the reputedly savage leader of one of the seven biggest Triads in City Europe. Karr had read the file and seen holos of Wong; even so, he found himself unprepared for the softspokenness of the man, for the air of sophistication that seemed to emanate from him.

'I am honoured that you would see me, Wong Yi-sun. A thousand blessings upon your sons.'

'And yours, Major. I understand you are recently married. A fine, strong woman, I am told.' Wong's smile broadened. 'I am happy for you. Give her my best regards. A man needs a strong wife in these unhappy times, neh?'

Karr bowed his head. 'Thank you, Wong Yi-sun. I will pass on your kind words.'

Fat Wong smiled and let his eyes move from Karr's figure for the first time since he had entered the room. Released from his gaze, Karr had a better opportunity of studying the man. Seen side on, one began to notice those qualities that had made Wong Yi-sun a 489. There was a certain sharpness to his features, a restrained tautness, that equated with reports on him. When he was younger, it was said, he had gone into a rival's bedroom and cut off the man's head with a hatchet, even as he was making love to his wife, then had taken the woman for his own. Later, he had taken the name Fat Wong, because, he claimed, the world was a place where worm ate worm, and only the biggest, fattest worm came out on top. From then on he had worked day and night to be that worm – to be the fattest of them all. And now he was. Or almost.

'I noticed you were admiring the ancient silk, Major. Do you know the history of the banner?'

Karr smiled. 'I have heard something of your history, Wong Yi-sun, but of that banner I am quite ignorant. It looks very old.'

Wong moved past Karr, standing beneath the banner, then turned, smiling up at the big man.

'It is indeed. More than four hundred years old, in fact. You say you know our history, Major Karr, but did you realize just how old we are? Before the City was, we were. When the City no longer is, we shall remain.'

Wong Yi-sun moved down the row of banners, then turned, facing Karr again.

'People call us criminals. They say we seek to destroy the social fabric of Chung Kuo, but they lie. Our roots are deep. We were founded in the late seventeenth century by the five monks of the Fu Chou monastery – honourable, loyal men, whose only desire was to overthrow the Ch'ing, the Manchu – and replace them with the rightful rulers of Chung Kuo, the Ming. Such was our purpose for a hundred years. Before the Manchu drove us underground, persecuting our members and cutting off our resources. After that we were left with no choice. We had to improvise.'

Karr smiled inwardly. *Improvise*. It was a wonderfully subtle euphemism for the crudest of businesses: the business of murder and prostitution, gambling, drugs and protection.

'So you see, Major Karr, we have always been loyal to the traditions of Chung Kuo. Which is why we are always pleased to do business with the Seven. We are not their enemies. All we wish is to maintain order in those lawless regions that have escaped the long grasp of the T'ang.'

'And the banner?'

Fat Wong smiled. 'The banner comes from Fu Chou monastery. It is the great ancestor of all such banners. And whoever leads the Great Council holds the banner.'

Wong turned slightly, his stance suggesting that Karr should join him. Karr hesitated, then went across, his mind racing. Fat Wong *wanted* something. Something big. But to ask for help directly was impossible for Wong: for to admit to any weakness – to admit that there was something, *anything* beyond his grasp – would involve him in an enormous loss of face. And face was everything down here. As Above.

Karr shivered, filled with a sudden certainty. Yes. Something was happening down here. In that veiled allusion to the Triad Council and the banner, Fat Wong had revealed more than he'd intended. Karr looked at him in profile and knew he was right. Fat Wong was under pressure. But from whom? From inside his own Triad, or from without – from another of the 489s?

He followed Wong through, up a broad flight of steps and out into a huge, subtly lit room.

Steps led down into a sunken garden, at the centre of which was a tiny, circular pool. Within the pool seven golden fish seemed to float, as if suspended in glass. But the garden and the pool were not the most striking things about the room, for the eye was drawn beyond them to where one whole wall – a wall fifty *ch'i* in length, ten in height – seemed to look out on to the West Lake at Hang Chou, providing a panoramic view of its pale, lace-like bridges and pagodas, its willow-strewn islands and ancient temples. Here it was perpetually spring, the scent of jasmine and apple blossom heavy in the cool, moist air.

From somewhere distant, music sounded, carried on the breeze that blew gently through the room. For a moment the illusion was so perfect that Karr held himself still, enthralled by it. Then, realizing Wong was watching him, he went down the steps and stood at the edge of the pool.

'You know why I have come here, Wong Yi-sun?'

'I understand you want some information. About the *Ko Ming* who assassinated the *Hsien L'ing*.'

'We thought you might know something about this group – for instance, whether or not they were related to the *Ping Tiao*.'

'Because they share the same symbol?' Wong sniffed, his face suddenly ugly. 'I don't know what your investigations have thrown up, Major Karr, but let me tell you this, the *Hsien L'ing* was meddling in things he ought never to have been involved in.'

Karr kept his face a mask, but behind it he felt an intense curiosity. What had Shou Chen-hai been involved in that could possibly anger Fat Wong? For there was no doubting that Wong Yi-sun was furious.

'And the *Ko Ming*?'

Fat Wong gulped savagely at his drink then took a deep breath, calming himself. 'Your assassins are called the *Yu*. Beyond that I cannot say. Only that their name echoes throughout the Lowers.'

Karr nodded thoughtfully. 'That is unusual, neh?'

Wong met Karr's eyes steadily. 'You are right, Major Karr. They are something different. We have not seen their like for many years. I...'

Wong paused, looking beyond Karr, towards the arched doorway. 'Come,' he said brusquely, one hand waving the servant on.

The servant handed Wong something, then leaned close, whispering.

For a moment Wong stared at the three tiny packages, his hand trembling with anger, then he thrust his hand out, offering them to Karr.

'These are yours, I understand.'

Karr nodded. 'We found them in the *Hsien L'ing*'s apartment. I thought they might interest you.'

Wong narrowed his eyes. 'You know what was in them?'

Again Karr nodded. They had had them analysed and knew they were something special. But what did Fat Wong know about them? Karr watched the movement in his face and began to understand. Wong hadn't been sure. He had only suspected until he had seen the packages. But now he knew.

Wong turned away and stood there, as if staring out across the lake. A wisp of his jet-black hair moved gently in the breeze. 'They have over-stretched themselves this time. They have sought to destroy the balance...'

Then, as if he realized he had said too much, he turned back, giving a tiny shrug. But, though Fat Wong smiled, his eyes gave him away. This was what had been worrying him. This was the big something he could not deal with on his own. He had been the biggest, fattest worm until now. The keeper of the ancient banner. But now the Big Circle were making their bid to oust him; a bid financed by the revenue from new drugs, new markets.

But what did Fat Wong want? Did he want help to crush the Big Circle? Or did he want something else – some other arrangement that would keep the Big Circle in their place while keeping him supreme? And, beyond that, what would his own master, Li Yuan, want from such a deal? That was, if he wanted anything but to keep the Triads in their place.

Fat Wong closed his hand over the three tiny packets then threw them down, into the water. Reaching inside his silks, he withdrew a slender envelope.

'Give this to your T'ang,' he said, handing it across.

'And what am I to say?'

'That I am his friend. His very good friend.'

On the table by the bed was a holo plinth. Mach knelt, then placed his hand on the pad. Nothing. He turned slightly, looking up at Ywe Hao, curious. She leaned across him, holding her fingertips against the pad. At once two tiny figures formed in the air above the plinth.

'My brother,' she explained. 'He died in an industrial accident. At least, that's what the official inquiry concluded. But that's not the story his friends told at the time. He was a union organizer. Eighteen he was. Four years older than me. My big brother. They say the *pan chang* threw him from a balcony. Eight levels he fell, into machinery. There wasn't much left of him when they pulled him out. Just bits.'

Mach took a breath, then nodded. For a moment longer Ywe Hao stared at the two tiny images, then drew her hand back, the pain in her eyes sharp, undiminished by the years.

'I wanted to see,' he said, looking about him again. 'I wanted to be sure.'

'Sure?'

'About you.'

'Ah...'

He smiled. 'Besides which, I've got to brief you.'

She frowned, then stood, moving back slightly. 'About what?'

'The attack on the Dragonfly Club. We're bringing it forward.' He went over to his pack and took out a hefty-looking folder, handing it to her.

She looked down at the folder, then back at Mach. 'What's this?'

'It's a full dossier. It's not pleasant reading, I'm afraid, but, then, it's not meant to be. But you have to understand why we need to do this.'

'And the raid? When do we go in?'

'Tonight.'

'*Tonight*? But I thought you said it would take at least a week to set this up.'

'That's what I thought. But our man is on duty tonight.'

She frowned. 'But we've not had time to rehearse things. We'd be going in blind.'

Mach shook his head. 'Let me explain. When I gave you this assignment I had already allocated a team leader. But after what happened I wanted to give you a chance. An opportunity to prove yourself.'

She made to speak, but he silenced her.

'Hear me out. I know what happened the other day. I know you killed Vasska. But it doesn't matter. You were right. The other matter... his brother... that's unfortunate, but we'll deal with it. What was important was that you did the right thing. If you'd let him kill the guard... well, it would have done us great harm, neh?'

She hesitated, then nodded, but he could see she was unhappy with his over-simplification of events. Which was good. It showed that she hadn't acted callously. He took the folder from her lap and opened it up, turning one of the still photographs towards her.

'This is why we're going in tonight. To put an end to this kind of thing. But it has to be done carefully. That's why I've drafted you in to lead the team. Not to organize the raid – your team know exactly what they have to do. No, your role is to keep it all damped down. To make sure the right people are punished. I don't want anyone getting over-excited. We have to get this right. If we get it wrong, we're fucked, understand me?'

She nodded, but her eyes stayed on the photo of the mutilated child. After a moment she looked up at him, the disgust in her eyes touched with profound sadness. 'What makes them do this, Jan? How in the gods' names could anyone do this to a little boy?'

He shook his head. 'I don't know. It's how they are.' He put his hand gently to her cheek. 'All I know is that all that anger you feel, all that disgust and indignation... well, it's a healthy thing. I want to harness that. To give it every opportunity to express itself.'

He let his hand fall away. 'You know, you remind me of an old friend. She was like you. Strong. Certain about what she did.'

Ywe Hao shivered, then looked down again. 'What about my cover?'

Mach smiled, impressed by her professionalism, then turned, pointing across at the pack beside the door. 'It's all in there. All you need to do is read the file. Someone will come for you at eleven. You go in at second bell.'

He sat back. 'There's a lot there, but read it all. Especially the statements by the parents. As I said, you need to know why you're there. It'll make it easier to do what you have to do.'

She nodded.

'Good. Now I must go. My shift begins in an hour and I've got to get back and change. Good luck, Ywe Hao. May Kuan Yin smile on you tonight.'

In the torchlit silence of the Hall of Eternal Peace and Tranquillity, Li Yuan knelt on the cold stone tiles, facing the hologram of his father. Thin threads of smoke from the offering sticks drifted slowly upwards, their rosewood scent merging with the chill dampness of the ancient room. Beyond the ghostly radiant figure of the dead T'ang, the red lacquer of the carved screen seemed to shimmer, as if it shared something of the old man's insubstantiality, the *Ywe Lung* at its centre flickering, as if, at any moment, it might vanish, leaving a smoking circle of nothingness.

Li Shai Tung stood there as in life, the frailty of his latter days shrugged off, the certainty he had once professed shaping each ghostly gesture as he spoke.

'Your dreams have meaning, Yuan. They are like the most loyal of ministers. They tell us not what we would have them say, but that which is true. We can deny them, can banish them to the furthest reaches of our selves, but we cannot kill them, not without killing ourselves.'

Li Yuan looked up, meeting his dead father's eyes. 'And is that what we have done? Is that why things are so wrong?'

Li Shai Tung sniffed loudly, then leaned heavily on his cane, as if considering his son's words, but tonight Yuan was more than ever conscious of what lay behind the illusion. In the slender case beneath the image, logic circuits had instantly located and selected from a score of possible responses, pre-programmed guidelines determining their choice. It seemed spontaneous, yet the words were given – were as predetermined as the fall of a rock or the decay of atoms. And the delay? That too was deliberate; was a machine-created mimicry of something that had once been real.

Even so, the sense of his father was strong. And though the eyes were blank, unseeing – were not eyes at all, but mere smoke and light – they seemed to see right through him; through to the tiny core of unrest that had robbed him of sleep and brought him here at this unearthly hour.

'Father?'

The old man lifted his head slightly, as if, momentarily, he had been lost in his thoughts. Then, unexpectedly, he gave a soft laugh.

'Dreams. Maybe that's all we have, Yuan. Dreams. The City itself, was that not a dream? The dream of our ancestors made tangible. And our long-held belief in peace, in order and stability, was that not also a dream? Was any of it ever real?'

Li Yuan frowned, disturbed by his father's words. For a moment his mind went back to the evening of his father's death, recalling how sickly thin his body had been, how weak and vulnerable death had found him.

'But what does it mean, Father? How am I to read my dream?'

The dead T'ang stared at his son, then gave a tiny shudder. 'You say you dreamt of dragonflies?'

Li Yuan nodded. 'Of great, emerald-green dragonflies, swarming on the river bank. Thousand upon thousand of them. Beautiful creatures, their wings like glass, their bodies like burnished jade. The sun shone down on them and yet the wind blew cold. And as I watched, they began to fall, first one, and then another, until the river was choked with their struggling forms. And even as I watched they stiffened and the brilliant greenness was leached from their bodies, until they were a hideous grey, their flesh flaking from them like ash. And still the wind blew, carrying the ash away, covering the fields, clogging every pool and stream, until all was grey and ashen.'

'And then?'

'And then I woke, afraid, my heart pounding.'

'Ah...' The T'ang put one hand to his beard, his long fingers pulling distractedly at the tightly braided strands, then shook his head. 'That is a strange and powerful dream, *erh tzu*. You ask me what it means, yet I fear you know already.' He looked up, meeting his son's eyes. 'Old glassy, he is the very symbol of summer, neh? And the colour green symbolizes spring. Furthermore, it is said that when the colour green figures in a dream, the dream will end happily. Yet in your dream the green turns to ash. Summer dies. The cold wind blows. How are you to read this but as an ill omen?'

Li Yuan looked down sharply, a cold fear washing through him. He had hoped against hope that there was some other way to read his dream, but his father's words merely confirmed his own worst fears. The drag-onfly, though the emblem of summer, was also a symbol of weakness and instability, of all the worst excesses of a soft and easy life. Moreover, it was said that they swarmed in vast numbers just before the storm.

Yet was the dream anything more than a reflection of his innermost fears? He thought of his father's words – of dreams as loyal ministers, utter-ing truths that could not otherwise be faced. Was that the case here? Had this dream been sent to make him face the truth?

'Then what am I to do?'

The dead T'ang looked at him and laughed. 'Do, Yuan? Why, you must wear stout clothes and learn to whistle in the wind. You must look to your wives and children. And then...'

'And then, Father?'

The old man looked away, as if he'd done. 'Spring will come, *erh tzu*. Even in your darkest hour, remember that. Spring always comes.'

Li Yuan hesitated, waiting for something more, but his father's eyes were closed now, his mouth silent. Yuan leaned forward and took the burning spills from the porcelain jar. At once the image shrank, taking its place beside the other tiny, glowing images of his ancestors.

He stood, looking about him at the torch-lit stillness of the hall – at the grey stone of the huge, funerary couch to his right, at the carved pillars and tablets and lacquered screens – then turned away, angry with himself. There was so much to be done – the note from Minister Heng, the packet from Fat Wong, the last few preparations for Council – yet here he was, moping like a child before his dead father's image. And to what end?

He clenched his fist, then slowly let it open. No. His anger could not be sustained. Neither would the dream be denied that easily. If he closed his eyes he could see them – a thousand bright, flickering shapes in the morning sunlight, their wings like curtains of the finest lace. Layer upon layer of flickering, sunlit lace...

'Chieh Hsia...'

Li Yuan turned, almost staggering, then collected himself, facing his Chancellor.

'Yes, Chancellor Nan. What is it?'

Nan Ho bowed low. 'News has come, Chieh Hsia. The news you were waiting for.'

He was suddenly alert. 'From Tao Yuan? We have word?'

'More than that, Chieh Hsia. A tape has come. A tape of the meeting between Wang and Hsiang.'

'A tape...' Li Yuan laughed, filled with a sudden elation that was every bit as powerful as his previous mood of despair. 'Then we have him, neh? We have him where we want him.'

The doorman had done his job. The outer door slid back at her touch. Inside it was pitch black, the security cameras dead. Ywe Hao turned, then nodded, letting the rest of the team move past her silently.

The doorman was in the cubicle to the left, face down on the floor, his hands on his head. One of the team was crouched there already, binding him at hand and foot.

She went quickly to the end of the hallway, conscious of the others forming up to either side of the door. She waited until the last of them joined her, then stepped forward, knocking loudly on the inner door.

There was a small eye-hatch near the top of the reinforced door. She faced it, clicking on the helmet lamp and holding up her ID. The call had gone out half an hour ago, when the outer power had 'failed', so they were expecting her.

The hatch cover slid back, part of a face staring out from the square of brightness within.

'Move the card closer.'

She did as she was told.

'Shit...' The face moved away; spoke to someone inside. 'It's a fuckin' woman.'

'Is there a problem?'

The face turned back to her. 'This is a men's club. Women aren't sup-posed to come in.'

She took a breath, then nodded. 'I understand. But look. I've only got to cut the power from the box inside. I can do the repairs out here in the hallway.'

The guard turned, consulting someone inside, then turned back. 'Okay, but be quick, neh? And keep your eyes to yourself or there'll be a report going in to your superior.'

Slowly the door slid back, spilling light into the hallway. The guard moved back, letting Ywe Hao pass, his hand coming up, meaning to point across at the box, but he never completed the gesture. Her punch felled him like a sack.

She turned, looking about her, getting her bearings. It was a big, hex-agonal room, corridors going off on every side. In its centre was a circular sunken pool of bright red tile, five steps leading down into its depths.

The young men in the pool seemed unaware of her entrance. There were eight of them, naked as newborns. One of them was straddling another over the edge of the pool, his buttocks moving urgently, but no one seemed to care. Behind him the others played and laughed with an abandon that was clearly drug-induced.

She took it all in at a glance, but what she was really looking for was the second guard – the one her fallen friend had been speaking to. She felt the hairs on her neck rise as she was unable to locate him, then she saw move-ment, a brief flash of green between the hinges of the screen to her right.

She fired twice through the screen, the noise muted by the thick carpet-ing underfoot, the heavy tapestries that adorned the walls, but it was loud enough to wake the young men from their reverie.

The others stood behind her now, masked figures clothed from head to toe in black. At her signal they fanned out, making for the branching corridors.

She crossed the room slowly, the gun held loosely in her hand, until she stood on the tiled lip of the pool. They had backed away from her, the drug-elation dying in their eyes as they began to realize what was happen-ing. The copulating couple had drawn apart and were staring wide-eyed at her, signs of their recent passion still evident. Others had raised their hands in the universal gesture of surrender.

'Out!' she barked, lifting the gun sharply.

They jerked at the sound of her voice, then began to scramble back, abashed now at their nakedness, fear beginning to penetrate the drug-haze of their eyes.

She knew them all. Faces and names and histories. She looked from face to face, forcing them to meet her gaze. They were so young. Barely out of childhood, it seemed. Even so, she felt no sympathy for them, only disgust.

There were noises from the rest of the club now; thumps and angry shouts and a brief snatch of shrieking that broke off abruptly. A moment later one of the team reappeared at the entrance to one of the corridors.

'Chi Li! Come quickly...'

'What is it?' she said as calmly as she could, tilting her head slightly, indicating her prisoners.

He looked beyond her, understanding, then came across, lowering his voice. 'It's Hsao Yen. He's gone crazy. You'd better stop him.' He drew the gun from his belt. 'Go on. I'll guard these.'

She could hear Hsao Yen long before she saw him, standing over the young man in the doorway, a stream of obscenities falling from his lips as he leaned forward, striking the prisoner's head and shoulders time and again with his rifle butt.

'Hsao Yen!' she yelled. '*Ai ya!* What are you doing?'

He turned, confronting her, his face livid with anger, then jerked his arm out, pointing beyond the fallen man.

She moved past him, looking into the room, then drew back, shuddering, meeting Hsao Yen's eyes almost fearfully. 'He did that?'

Hsao Yen nodded. 'Yes...'

He made to strike the fallen man again, but Ywe Hao stopped his hand, speaking to him gently. 'I understand. But let's do this properly, neh? After all, that's what we came here for. To put an end to this.'

Hsao Yen looked down at the bloodied figure beneath him and shivered. 'All right. As you say.'

She nodded, then looked past him, torn by what she saw. 'And the boy? He's dead, I take it.'

Hsao Yen shuddered, his anger transformed suddenly to pain. 'How could he do that, Chi Li? How could he do that to a child?'

She shook her head, unable to understand. 'I don't know, Hsao Yen. I simply don't know.'

They were lined up beside the pool when she returned, three dozen of them, servants included. The masked figures of the Yu stood off to one side, their automatic pistols raised. She had two of their number hold up their beaten fellow, then went down the line, separating out the servants.

'Tu Li-shan, Rooke… take them through to the kitchens. I want them gagged and bound. But don't harm them. Understand?'

Ywe Hao turned back, facing the remaining men. There were twenty-three of them. Fewer than she had hoped to find here. Looking down the line, she noted the absence of several of the faces from the files. A shame, she thought, looking at them coldly. She would have liked to have caught them all; every last one of the nasty little bastards. But this would do.

'Strip off!' she barked angrily, conscious that more than half of them were naked already, then turned away, taking the thickly wadded envelope from within her tunic. These were the warrants. She unfolded them and flicked through them, taking out those that weren't needed and slipping them back into the envelope, then turned back, facing them again.

They were watching her, fearful now, several of them crying openly, their limbs trembling badly. She went slowly down the line, handing each of them a single sheet of paper; watching as they looked down, then looked back up at her again, mouths open, a new kind of fear in their eyes.

They were death warrants, individually drafted, a photograph of the condemned attached to each sheet. She handed out the last, then stood back, waiting, wondering if any of them would have the balls at the last to say something, to try to argue their way out of this, perhaps even to fight. But one glance down the line told her enough.

For a moment she tried to turn things round: to see it from their viewpoint; maybe even to elicit some small trace of sympathy from deep within herself. But there was nothing. She had seen too much; read too much: her anger had hardened to something dark, impenetrable. They were evil, gutless little shits. And what they had done here – the suffering they had caused – was too vast, too hideous, to forgive.

Ywe Hao pulled the mask aside, letting them view her face for the first time, letting them see the disgust she felt, then walked back to the end of the line and stood facing the first of them. Taking the paper from his shaking hands, she began, looking directly into his face, not even glancing at the paper, reciting from memory the sentence of the Yu inner council, before placing the gun against his temple and pulling the trigger.

Fifth bell was sounding as Wang Sau-leyan stood at the head of the steps, looking down into the dimly lit cellar. It was a huge, dark space, poorly ventilated and foul-smelling. From its depths came a steady groaning, a distinctly human sound, half-articulate with pained confession. The semblance of words drifted up to him, mixing with the foul taste in his mouth, making him shudder with distaste and spread his fan before his face.

Seeing him there, Hung Mien-lo tore himself away from the bench and hurried across.

'Chieh Hsia,' he said, bowing low. 'We are honoured by your presence.'

The T'ang descended the uneven steps slowly, with an almost finicky care. At the bottom he glared at his Chancellor, as if words could not express the vulgarity of this.

It was old-fashioned and barbaric, yet in that lay its effectiveness. Torture was torture. Sophistication had nothing to do with it. Terror was of the essence. And this place, with its dank, foul-smelling miasma, was perfect for the purposes of torture. It stank of hopelessness.

The bench was an ordinary workman's bench from an earlier age. Its hard wooden frame was scrubbed clean and four dark iron spikes – each as long as a man's arm – jutted from the yellow wood, one at each corner, the polished metal thick at the base, tapering to a needle-sharp point. The prisoner's hands and feet were secured against these spikes with coils of fine, strong chain that bit into the flesh and made it bleed. Across his naked chest a series of heated wires had been bound, pulling tight and searing the flesh even as they cooled, making the prisoner gasp and struggle for each breath; each painful movement chafing the cutting wires against the blood-raw flesh.

One eye had been put out. Burned in its blackened socket. The shaven head was criss-crossed with razor-fine scars. Both ears had been severed. All four limbs were badly scarred and bruised, broken bone pushing through the skin in several places. There were no nails on hands or feet and the tendons of each finger had been cut neatly, individually, with a surgeon's skill.

Lastly, the man's genitals had been removed and the amputation sealed with a wad of hot tar.

Wang Sau-leyan looked, then turned away, moving his fan rapidly before his face, but Hung Mien-lo had seen, mixed in with the horror, the revulsion, a look of genuine satisfaction.

The prisoner looked up, his one good eye moving between the two men. Its movements seemed automatic, intent only on knowing where the pain would come from next. All recognition was gone from it. It saw only blood and heat and broken bone. Wang Sau-leyan, looking down at it, knew it from childhood. It was the eye of his father's Master of the Royal Household, Sun Li Hua.

'You have his confession?'

'Yes, *Chieh Hsia*,' Hung answered, one hand resting lightly on the bench. 'He babbled like a frightened child when I first brought him down. He couldn't take much pain. Just the thought of it and the words spilled from him like a songbird.'

And yet he's still alive, Wang thought. *How can he still be alive when all this has been done to him?* Even so, he deserved no pity. Sun Li Hua had sold him to another. To Li Yuan, his enemy.

Just as he sold my father to me.

Wang leaned over and spat on the scarred and wounded body. And the eye, following the movement, was passive, indifferent to the gesture, as though to say, *Is that all? Is there to be no pain this time?*

They moved on, looking at the other benches. Some were less damaged than Sun Li Hua, others were barely alive – hacked apart piece by piece, like hunks of animal product on a butcher's table. They were all old and trusted servants; all long-serving and 'loyal' men of his father's household. And Li Yuan had bought them all. No wonder the bastard had been able to anticipate him in Council these last few times.

Wang turned, facing his Chancellor.

'Well, *Chieh Hsia*?' Hung Mien-lo asked. 'Are you pleased?'

There was an unpleasant smile on the Chancellor's features, as if to say there was nothing he liked better than inflicting pain on others. And Wang Sau-leyan, seeing it, nodded and turned quickly away, mounting the steps in twos, hurriedly, lest his face betray his true feelings.

It was a side of Hung Mien-lo he would never have suspected. Or was there another reason? It was said that Hung and Sun had never got on. So maybe it was that. Whatever, there would come a time of reckoning. And then Hung Mien-lo would really learn to smile. As a corpse smiled.

Li Yuan stood at the window, letting himself be dressed. Outside the garden lay half in shadow, half in light, the dew-misted top leaves of the nearby rhododendron bushes glittering in the dawn's first light. He held himself still as the maid drew the sashes tight about his waist, then turned, facing his Master of the Inner Chambers.

'And have you no idea what they want, Master Chan?'

Chan Teng bowed low. 'None at all, *Chieh Hsia*. Only that the Marshal said it was of the utmost urgency. That I was to wake you if you were not awake already.'

Li Yuan turned away, hiding the smile that came to his lips at the thought of Tolonen's bluntness. Even so, he felt a ripple of trepidation run down his spine.

They were waiting in his study. Impatient to hear what had happened, he crossed the room quickly and stood before them.

'Well, Knut? What is it?'

Tolonen held out a file. Li Yuan took it and flicked it open. After a moment he looked up, giving a small, strange laugh. 'How odd. Only last night, I dreamed of dragonflies. And now this...' He studied Tolonen a moment, his eyes narrowed. 'But why show me this? It's nasty, certainly, but it is hardly the kind of thing to wake a T'ang about, surely?'

Tolonen bowed his head, acceding the point. 'In ordinary circumstances that would be so, *Chieh Hsia*. But this is a matter of the utmost importance. The beginning of something we would do well to take very seriously indeed.'

'So what makes this different?'

Nan Ho lowered his head again. 'This, *Chieh Hsia*.'

Li Yuan set the file down on a nearby chair, then took the pamphlet from his Chancellor. It was a single large sheet that had been folded into four, the ice-paper no more than a few mols thick, the print poor, uneven. He realized at once that it had been hand set; that whoever had produced this had wanted to avoid even the slightest chance of being traced through the computer network.

He shrugged. 'It's interesting, but I still don't understand.'

Nan Ho smiled tautly. 'Forgive me, *Chieh Hsia*, but it is not so much the pamphlet as the numbers in which it has been distributed. It's hard to estimate exactly how many copies went out, but latest Security estimates place it at between a quarter of a billion and a billion.'

Li Yuan laughed. 'Impossible! How would they print that number? How distribute them? Come to that, how on earth would they finance it?'

And yet he saw how grave the old man looked.

'This is something new, *Chieh Hsia*. Something dangerous. Which is why we must deal with it at once. That is why I came. To seek your permission to make the elimination of this new group our number one priority.'

Li Yuan stared at his Marshal a moment, then turned away. A billion pamphlets. If that were true it was certainly something to be concerned about. But was Tolonen right to be so worried, or was he overreacting? He went to his desk and sat, considering things.

'What is Major Karr doing right now?'

Tolonen smiled. 'Karr is on their trail already, *Chieh Hsia*. I put him in charge of investigating the murder of the *Hsien L'ing*, Shou Chen-hai.'

'And?'

Tolonen shook his head. 'And nothing, I'm afraid. Our investigations have so far drawn a blank.'

'All right. But I want Karr in charge, Knut, and I want a daily report on my desk concerning any and every development. You will make sure he gets whatever resources he needs.'

'Of course, *Chieh Hsia*.'

He watched Tolonen go, then turned his attention to his Chancellor.

'Was there something else?'

The Chancellor hesitated, as if weighing something up, then came forward, taking a small package from within his robes and offering it to his T'ang, his head lowered, his eyes averted. 'I was not certain whether to give this to you, *Chieh Hsia*.'

Li Yuan took the package, smiling, then felt his breath catch in his throat. There was the faintest scent from the silk. The scent of *mei hua*. Of plum blossom.

'Thank you, Nan Ho. I...'

But the Chancellor had already gone. Even as Li Yuan looked up, the door was closing on the far side of the room.

He sat back, staring at the tiny package on his desk. It was from her. From Fei Yen. Though there were no markings on the wrapping, he knew no other would have used that scent. No one else would have used his Chancellor as a messenger.

He shuddered, surprised by the intensity of what he felt. Then, leaning forward, his hand trembling, he began to unfasten the wrappings, curious and yet afraid of what was inside.

There was a note, and beneath the note a tiny tape. He unfolded it and read the brief message, then lifted the tape gingerly, his eyes drawn to the gold-leaf pictograms embossed into the black of the casing. *Han Ch'in*, they read. His son.

He swallowed, then closed his eyes. What did she want? Why was she doing this to him? For a moment he closed his hand tightly on the tiny cassette, as if to break it, then loosened his grip. No. He would have to see it. Suddenly he realized just how much he had wanted to go to the estate at Hei Shui and simply stand there, unobserved, watching his child at play.

Even so, the question still remained. What did she want? He went to the long window. Already the sun was higher, the shadows on the eastern lawn much shorter. He breathed deeply, watching the sunlight flicker on the surface of the pond, then shook his head. Maybe she didn't know. Maybe she didn't understand what power she had over him, even now. Maybe it *was* a simple act of kindness...

He laughed quietly. No. Whatever it was, it wasn't that. Or not simply that. He turned, looking across at the tape, the note, then turned back again, staring outward. Whatever, it would have to wait. Right now he must prepare himself, clearing his mind of everything but the struggle ahead. Tonight, after Council, he could relax; might let himself succumb to his weakness. But not before. Not until he had dealt with Wang Sau-leyan.

He sighed and turned from the window, making his way back to his rooms and the waiting maids.

Out on the pond, in the early morning light, a dragonfly hovered over the water, its wings flickering like molten sunlight, its body a bright irides-cent green.

CHUNG KUO

Chapter 73

IN A DARKENED EYE

It was just after seven in the morning, but in the Black Heart business was brisk. At the huge centre table a crowd of men pressed close, taking bets on the two tiny contestants crouched in the tight beam of the spotlight.

They were mantises, brought up from the Clay, their long, translucent bodies raised threateningly, switchblade forelegs extended before their tiny, vicious-looking heads as they circled slowly. To Chen, watching from the edge of the crowd, it was an ugly, chilling sight. He had seen men – Triad gangsters – behave in this manner, their every movement suggestive of a deadly stillness. Men whose eyes were dead, who cared only for the perfection of the kill. Here, in these cold, unsympathetic creatures, was their model; the paradigm of their behaviour. He shuddered. To model oneself on such a thing – what made a man reduce himself so much?

As he watched, the larger of the creatures struck out, its forelegs moving in a blur as it tried to catch and pin its opponent. There was a roar of excitement from the watching men, but the attack faltered, the smaller mantis struggling free. It scuttled back, twitching, making small, answering feints with its forelegs.

Chen looked about him, sickened by the glow of excitement in every face, then came away, returning to the table in the corner.

'So what's happened?'

Karr looked up from the map, smiling wearily. 'It's gone cold. And this time even our Triad friends can't help us.'

Chen leaned across, putting his finger down where the map was marked with a red line – a line that ended abruptly at the entrance to the stack in which the Black Heart was located. 'We've tracked them this far, right? And then there's nothing. It's a white-out, right?'

Karr nodded. 'The cameras were working, but the storage system had been tampered with. There was nothing on record but white light.'

'Right. And there's no trace of either of them coming out of this stack, correct? The records have been checked for facial recognition?'

Again Karr nodded.

'Then what else remains? No one broke the seals and went down to the Net, and no one got out by flyer. Which means they *must* be here.'

Karr laughed. 'But they're not. We've searched the place from top to bottom and found nothing. We've taken the place apart.'

Chen smiled enigmatically. 'Which leaves what?'

Karr shrugged. 'Maybe they were ghosts.'

Chen nodded. 'Or maybe the images on the tape were. What if someone tampered with the computer storage system down the line?' He traced the red line back with his finger, stopping at the point where it took a sixty-degree turn. 'What if our friends turned off earlier? Or went straight on? Have we checked the records from the surrounding stacks?'

'I've done it. And there's nothing. They just disappeared.'

At the gaming table things had changed dramatically. Beneath the spot-light's glare the smaller mantis seemed to be winning. It had pinned the larger creature's forelegs to the ground, trapping it, but it could not take advantage of its position without releasing its opponent. For a long time it was still, then, with a suddenness that surprised the hushed watchers, it moved back, meaning to strike at once and cripple its enemy. But the larger beast had waited for that moment. The instant it felt the relentless pressure of the other's forelegs lapse, it snapped back, springing up from the floor, its back legs powering it into the smaller insect. The snap of its forelegs was followed instantly by the crunch of its opponent's brittle flesh. It was over. The smaller mantis was dead.

For a moment they looked across, distracted by the uproar, then Karr turned back, his blue eyes filled with doubt. 'Come... there's nothing here.'

They were getting up as a messenger came across; one of the Triad men they had met earlier. Bowing, he handed Karr a sheet of computer printout – a copy of a Security report timed at 4.24 a.m.

Karr studied it a moment, then laughed. 'Just when I thought it had died on us. Look, Chen! Look what the gods have sent us!'

Chen took the printout. It was a report on a new terrorist attack. On a place called the Dragonfly Club. The details were sketchy, but one fact stood out – a computer face-recognition match. Chen stared at Karr. 'It's the woman! Chi Li, or whatever her name is!'

'Yes,' Karr laughed, his gloom dispelled for the first time in two days. 'So let's get there, neh? Before the trail goes cold.'

Ywe Hao woke, her heart pounding, and threw back the sheet. Disoriented, she sat up, staring about her. What in the gods' names...?

Then she saw it – the winking red light of the warning circuit. Its high-pitched alarm must have woken her. She spun about, looking to see what time it was: 7.13. She had been asleep less than an hour.

Dressing took fifteen seconds, locating and checking her gun another ten. Then she was at the door, breathing deeply, preparing herself, as the door slid slowly back.

The corridor was empty. She walked quickly, her gun held out before her, knowing they would have to use this corridor.

At the intersection she slowed, hearing footsteps, but they were from the left. The warning had come from her friends – the two boys at the lift – which meant her assailants would be coming from that direction; from the corridor directly ahead. She put the gun away and let the old man pass, then went to the right, breaking into a run, heading for the inter-level steps.

There was urgent whispering in the corridor behind her at the intersection. She flattened herself against the wall, holding her breath. Then the voices were gone, heading towards her apartment.

Vasska's brother, Edel. She was certain of it.

She was eight, nine steps up the flight when she remembered the case. She stopped, annoyed with herself. But there hadn't been time. If she'd stopped to dig it out from the back of the cupboard she would have lost valuable seconds. Would have run into them in the corridor. Even so, she couldn't leave it there. The dossier on the raid was in it.

A group of Han students passed her on the steps, heading for their morning classes, their sing-song chatter filling the stairwell briefly. Then she was alone again. For a moment longer she hesitated, then she went up, heading for the maintenance room at the top of the deck.

Karr looked about him at the ruins. It was the same pattern as before – broken security cameras, deserted guard-posts, secured lifts, the terrorists' trail cleverly covered by white-outs. All spoke of a highly-organized operation, planned well in advance and carried out with a professionalism that even the T'ang's own élite would have found hard to match.

Not only that, but the Yu chose their targets well. Even here, amidst this chaos, they had taken care to identify their victims. Twenty-four men had died here, all but one of them – a guard – regular members of the Club, each of them 'tagged' by the Yu, brief histories of their worthless lives tied about their necks. The second guard had simply been beaten and tied up, while the servants had again been left unharmed. Such discrimination was impressive and the rumour of it – passed from mouth to ear, in defiance of the explicit warnings of the T'ing Wei – had thus far served to discredit every effort of that Ministry to portray the terrorists as uncaring, sadistic killers, their victims as undeserving innocents.

He shook his head, then went across. 'Anything new?' he asked, looking past Chen at the last of the corpses.

'Nothing,' Chen answered, his weary smile a reminder that they had been on duty more than thirty hours. 'The only remarkable thing is the similarity of the wounds. My guess is that there was some kind of ritual involved.'

Karr grimaced. 'Yes. These men weren't just killed, they were executed. And, if our Ko Ming friends are right, for good reason.'

Chen looked away, a shudder of disgust passing through him. He too had seen the holos the assassins had left – studies of their victims with young boys taken from the Lowers. Scenes of degradation and torture. Scenes that the T'ing Wei were certain to keep from popular consumption.

Which was to say nothing of the mutilated corpse of the child they had found in the room at the far end of the club.

Karr leaned across, touching Chen's arm. 'We're waiting on lab reports, word from our Triad contacts. There's little we can do just now, so why don't you go home? Spend some time with that wife of yours, or take young Jyan to the Palace of Dreams. They tell me there's a new historical.'

Chen laughed. 'And Marie? I thought this was supposed to be your honeymoon?'

Karr grinned. 'Marie understands. It's why she married me.'

Chen shook his head. 'And I thought I was mad.' He laughed. 'Okay. But let me know as soon as something happens.'

Karr nodded. 'All right. Now go.'

He watched Chen leave, then stood, feeling the emotional weight of what had happened here bearing down on him. It was rare that he was affected by such scenes, rarer still that he felt any sympathy for the perpetrators, but for once he was. The *Yu* had done society a great service here tonight. Had rid Chung Kuo of the kind of scum he had met so often below the Net.

He breathed out heavily, recalling Chen's disgust, knowing, at the very core of him, that this was what all healthy, decent men *ought* to feel. And yet the T'ing Wei would try to twist it, until these good-for-nothing perverts, this shit masquerading as men, were portrayed as shining examples of good citizenship.

Yes, he had seen the holos. Had felt his guts wrenched by the distress in the young boys' eyes, by that helpless, unanswered plea. He shuddered. The oven man had them now. And no evidence remained but for that small, pathetic corpse and these mementoes – these perverse records of a foul desire.

And was he to watch it being whitewashed? Made pure and sparkling by a parcel of lies? He spat, angered by the injustice of it. Was this why he had become Tolonen's man? For this?

Everywhere he looked he found the signature of decadence; of sons given everything by their fathers – everything but time and attention. No wonder they turned out as they did, lacking any sense of value. No wonder they pissed their time away, drinking and gambling and whoring – for inside them there was nothing. Nothing *real*, anyway. Some of them were even clever enough to realize as much, yet all their efforts to fill that nothingness were pointless. The nothingness was vast, unbounded. To fill it was like trying to carry water in a sieve.

Karr sighed, angered by the sheer waste of it all. He had seen enough to know that it was not even their fault; they had had no choice but to be as they were – spoilt and corrupt, vacuous and sardonic. They had been given no other model to emulate, and now it was too late.

He found the sheer sumptuousness of the room abhorrent. His own taste was for the simple, the austere. Here, confronted by its opposite, he found himself baring his teeth, as if at an enemy. Then, realizing what he was doing, he laughed uncomfortably and turned, forcing himself to be still.

It would be no easy task tracking down the *Yu*, for they were unlike any of the other *Ko Ming* groups currently operating in City Europe. They were fuelled not by simple hatred – by that obsessive urge to destroy that had fired the *Ping Tiao* and their like – but by a powerful indignation and a strong sense of injustice. The first *Ko Ming* emperor, Mao Tse-tung, had once said something about true revolutionaries being the fish that swam in the great sea of the people. Well, these *Yu* – these 'fish' – were certainly that. They had learned from past excesses. Learned that the people cared who died and who was spared. Discrimination – *moral* discrimination – was their most potent tool, and they took great pains to be in the right. At least, from where he stood, it looked like that, and the failure of the *T'ing Wei* to mould public opinion seemed to confirm his gut instinct.

And now this. Karr looked about him. Last night's raid – this devastatingly direct strike against the corrupt heart of the Above – would do much to bolster the good opinion of the masses. Yes, he could imagine the face of the *T'ing Wei*'s Third Secretary, Yen T'ung, when he learned of this. Karr laughed, then fell silent, for his laughter, like the tenor of his thoughts, was indicative of a deep inner division.

His duty was clear. As Tolonen's man he owed unswerving loyalty. If the Marshal asked him to track down the *Yu*, he would track them down. But for the first time ever he found himself torn, for his instinct was for the *Yu*, not against them. If one of those boys had been *his* son...

But he was Tolonen's man; bound by the strongest of oaths. Sworn to defend the Seven against *Ko Ming* activity, of whatever kind.

He spoke softly to the empty room. 'Which is why I must find you, Chi Li, even if, secretly, I admire what you have done here. For I am the T'ang's man, and you are the T'ang's enemy. A *Ko Ming*.'

And when he found her? Karr looked down, troubled. When he found her he would kill her. Swiftly, mercifully, and with honour.

*

The first of them was facing Ywe Hao as she came through the door. He fell back, clutching his ruined stomach, the sound of the gun's detonation echoing in the corridor outside. The second came out of the kitchen. She shot him twice in the chest, even as he fumbled for his weapon. Edel was behind him. He came at her with a small butcher's knife, his face twisted with hatred. She blew his hand off, then shot him through the temple. He fell at her feet, his legs kicking impotently.

She looked about her. There had been five of them, according to her lookouts. So where were the others?

There was shouting outside. Any time now Security would investigate. She went through to the kitchen, then came back, spotting the case on the bed. Good. They'd taken nothing. It was only when she lifted it that she realized she was wrong. They *had* taken something. The case was empty.

'Shit...'

She looked about her, trying to work out what to do. Where would they have taken the dossiers? What would they have wanted them for?

There were footsteps, coming down the corridor.

She threw the case down and crossed the room, standing beside the open door, clicking the spent clip from the handle of her gun. Outside the footsteps stopped.

'Edel? Is that you?'

She nodded to herself, then slipped a new clip into the handle. The longer she waited, the more jittery they'd get. At the same time, they might just be waiting for her to put her head round the door.

She smiled. It was the kind of dilemma she understood.

She counted. At eight she turned and went low, the gun kicking noisily in her hand as she moved out into the corridor.

*

Overhead, tiny armies, tens of thousands strong, fought against a hazed background of mountains, the roar of battle faint against the hubbub of noise in the crowded Main. The giant hologram was suspended in the air above the entrance to the Golden Emperor's Palace of Eternal Dreams.

Crowds were pushing out from the Holo-Palace while others queued to get in, their necks – young and old alike – craned back to watch the battle overhead. As Kao Chen pushed through, ushering his son before him, he smiled, seeing how his head strained up and back, trying to glimpse the air-show.

'Well, Jyan? What did you think?'

The ten-year-old looked up at his father and beamed a smile. 'It was wonderful! That moment when Liu Pang raised his banner and the whole army roared his name. That was great!'

Chen laughed. 'Yes, wasn't it? And to think he was but Ch'en She, a poor man, before he became Son of Heaven! Liu Pang, founder of the great Han dynasty!'

Jyan nodded eagerly. 'They should teach it like that at school. It's far more interesting than all that poetry.'

Chen smiled, easing his way through the crowds. 'Maybe, but not all poetry is bad. You'll understand that when you're older.'

Jyan made a face, making Chen laugh. He too had always preferred history to poetry but, then, he'd never had Jyan's chances, Jyan's education. No, things would be different for Jyan. Very different.

He slowed, then leaned close again. 'Do you want to eat out, Jyan, or shall we get back?'

Jyan hesitated, then smiled. 'Let's get back, neh? Mother will be waiting, and I want to tell her all about it. That battle between Liu Pang and the Hegemon King was brilliant. It was like it was really real. All those horsemen and everything!'

Chen nodded. 'Yes... it was, wasn't it? I wonder how they did that?'

'Oh, it's easy,' Jyan said, pulling him on by the hand. 'We learned all about it in school ages ago. It's all done with computer images and simulated movement.'

'Simulated movement, eh?' Chen laughed, letting himself be pulled through the crowds and into one of the quieter corridors. 'Still, it seemed real enough. I was wincing myself once or twice during some of those close-up fight scenes.'

Jyan laughed, then fell silent, slowing to a halt.

'What is it?' Chen said, looking up ahead.

'Those two...' Jyan whispered. 'Come. Let's go back. We'll take the south corridor and cut through.'

Chen glanced at Jyan, then looked back down the corridor. The two young men – Han, in their mid teens – were leaning against the wall, pretending to be talking.

Chen bent down, lowering his voice. 'Who are they?'

Jyan met his eyes. 'They're senior boys at my school – part of a *tong*, a gang. They call themselves the Green Banner Guardians.'

'So what do they want?'

'I don't know. All I know is that they're trouble.'

'You've not done anything, then, Jyan? Nothing I should know of?'

Jyan looked back at him clear-eyed. 'Nothing, Father. I swear to you.'

'Good. Then we've nothing to fear, have we?' He straightened up. 'Do you want me to hold your hand?'

Jyan shook his head.

Chen smiled, understanding. 'Okay. Then let's go.'

They were almost level with the two when they turned and stepped out, blocking their way. 'Where do you think you're going, shit-brains?' the taller of them said, smirking at Jyan.

'What do you want?' Chen asked, keeping the anger from his voice.

'Shut your mouth, *lao jen*,' said the second of them, moving closer. 'We've business with the boy. He owes us money.'

Chen made himself relax. So that was it. They were out of funds and thought they could shake down one of the junior boys. He smiled and touched the tiny eye on his tunic's lapel, activating it. 'I don't think my son has any business with you, friend. So be on your way.'

The first youth laughed; a false, high laugh that was clearly a signal. At the sound of it, four more youths stepped out from doorways behind him.

'As I said, the boy owes us money. Twenty *yuan*.'

Chen put his left arm out, moving Jyan back, behind him. 'You have proof of this?'

'Not on me,' the first youth said, his face ugly now, his body movements suddenly more menacing. 'But he does. And I want it. So unless you want to call me a liar...'

Chen smiled, moving his body slightly, so that the camera would capture all their faces. 'Oh, I'm sure there's no need for that, friend. But I'm afraid my son doesn't have a single *fen* on him, let alone twenty *yuan*.'

The youth's eyes flickered to the side, then looked back at Chen, a smile coming to his lips. 'Well, what about you, *lao jen*? They say a father is responsible for his son's debts. I reckon you're good for twenty *yuan*.'

Chen smiled and shook his head, taking a step back. 'I've spent my money, friend. Now let us pass. Our home is up ahead.'

There was a peel of mocking laughter from behind the two youths. The taller of them stepped forward, resting his hand lightly on Chen's shoulder.

'I'm sorry... *friend*... but I don't believe you. I saw the note you paid with at the picture house. You can't have spent it all, can you?'

Chen looked at the hand on his shoulder. It was a thin, ugly hand. It would be easy – and immensely satisfying – to take it from his shoulder and crush it. But he could not do that. He was an officer of the T'ang. And besides, Jyan had to learn the right way of doing things.

Chen took a breath, then bowed his head, taking the slender, crumpled note from his pocket and handing it to the youth.

'Good...' The youth squeezed Chen's shoulder reassuringly, then turned, holding the note up triumphantly for his friends to see. They whooped and jeered, making hand gestures at Chen. Then, with a final, mocking bow, the youth turned and strolled arrogantly away, his friends parting before him, one of them turning to send a final gesture of contempt.

Chen watched them go, then turned, looking down at his son. Jyan was standing there sullenly, his head turned away, held stiffly.

'I had to...' Chen began, but Jyan shook his head violently.

'You let them piss on us!'

Chen felt himself go still. He had never heard Jyan swear in front of him before. Neither had he heard that tone of anger – of hurt and fierce disapproval.

'There were six of them. Someone would have got hurt.'

Jyan looked up, glaring at him. '*You*, you mean!'

It wasn't what he'd meant, but he didn't argue. He took a breath, spelling it out clearly, trying to make his son understand. 'I am an officer of the T'ang's Security forces, Jyan, and I am off duty. I am not empowered to brawl in the corridors.'

'They pissed on us,' Jyan said again, glaring at his father, close to tears now. 'And you let them get away with it. You just handed the money over to them, like some low-level oaf!'

Chen lifted his hand abruptly, then let it fall. 'You don't understand, Jyan. I've got it all on camera. I...'

Jyan gave a huff of derision and turned, beginning to walk away.

'Jyan! Listen to me!'

The boy shook his head, not looking back. 'You let them piss on us!'

Chen stood there a moment longer, watching him, shaking his head, then began to follow.

Back at the apartment, he went through to the end bedroom. Wang Ti was seated on the bed, packing his kit.

'Where is he?' he said quietly.

She looked up at him, then pointed to the closed door of Jyan's room. 'There,' she mouthed. 'But leave him be.'

He looked at her, then looked down, sighing heavily. Seeing that, she stopped and came across, holding him to her. 'What is it?' she asked quietly.

He closed the door behind him, then told her what had happened, explaining what he planned to do. If he acted now, they could trace the note to the youths. That and the evidence of the camera eye would be enough to have the boys demoted to a lower deck. It was the proper way of doing things. The effective way, for it rid the level of that kind of scum. But for once he felt a strong sense of dissatisfaction.

'You were right, Chen,' she said softly. 'And what you did was right. There must be laws. We cannot live as they did in the old days. It would be like the Net up here if it were otherwise.'

'I know,' he said, 'but I let him down. I could see it in his face. He thinks I am a coward.'

Wang Ti shook her head, pained. 'And you, Chen? Do you consider yourself a coward? No. You are *kwai*, husband. Whatever clothes you wear, you will always be *kwai*. But sometimes it is right to avoid trouble. You have said so yourself. Sometimes one must bend like a reed.'

'Ai ya...' He turned his head aside, but she drew it gently back.

'Let him be, Chen. He'll come round. Just now his head is filled with heroics. That film you took him to see. His imagination was racing with it. But life is not like that. Sometimes one must concede to get one's way.'

He stared back at her, knowing she was right, but some part of him couldn't help thinking that he should have acted. Should have crushed the boy's hand and broken a few of their hot heads. To teach them a lesson.

And impress his son...

He looked down. 'It hurts, Wang Ti. To have him look at me like that. To have him say those things...'

She touched his cheek tenderly, her caress, like her voice, a balm. 'I know, my love. But that too is a kind of bravery, no? To face that hurt and conquer it. For the good. Knowing you did right.' She smiled. 'He'll come round, Chen. I know he will. He's a good boy and he loves you. So just leave him be a while, neh?'

He nodded. 'Well... I'd best get Deck Security on to it. I've got to report back in a few hours, so there's not much time.'

She smiled and turned away, returning to her packing. 'And, Chen?'

'Yes?' he said, turning at the door, looking back at her.

'Don't do anything silly. Remember what I said. You know what you are. Let that be enough.'

He hesitated, then nodded. But even as he turned away he knew it wasn't. *Damn them!* he thought, wondering what it was that twisted men's souls so much that they could not exist without tormenting others.

In the long, broad hallway that led to the Hall of the Serene Ultimate it was cool and silent and dimly lit. From the dark, animal mouths of cressets set high in the blood-red walls, naked, oil-fed flames gave off a thin, watery glow that flickered on the tiled mosaic of the floor and gave a dozen wavering shadows to the slender pillars that lined each side. The long shapes of dragons coiled upwards about these pillars in alternating reds and greens, stretching towards the heavens of the ceiling where, in the flicker of dark and light, a battle between gods and demons raged in bas relief.

Between the pillars stood the guards, unmoving, at attention. Light glimmered dimly on their burnished armour, revealing the living moistness of their eyes. They faced the outer doors prepared, their lives a wall, defending their lords and masters.

At their backs was a second double door, locked now. Beyond it, the Seven sat in conference. There it was warmer, brighter. Each T'ang sat easy in a padded chair, relaxed, their ceremonial silks the only outward sign of ritual. Wang Sau-leyan, host of this Council, was talking, discussing the package of proposals Li Yuan had set before them.

Li Yuan sat facing Wang, a hard knot of tension in his chest. Earlier, he had been taken aback by the unexpected warmth of the young T'ang of Africa's greeting. He had come expecting coldness, even overt hostility, but Wang's embrace, his easy laughter had thrown him. And so now. For while his words seemed fair – seemed to endorse, even to embrace Li Yuan's scheme for the days ahead – Li Yuan could not shed the habit of suspicion. Wang Sau-leyan was such a consummate actor – such a *natural* politician – that to take anything he did or said at face value was to leave oneself open, unguarded, vulnerable to the next twist or turn of his mood.

Li Yuan eased back into the cushions, forcing himself to relax, trying to see through the veil of Wang's words. Beside him, he could sense Tsu Ma shift in his chair.

'And so...' Wang said, looking across at Li Yuan again, his smile clear, untroubled, 'my feeling is that we must support Li Yuan's ideas. To do otherwise would be unwise, maybe even disastrous.' He looked about him, raising his plump hands in a gesture of acceptance. 'I realize that I have argued otherwise in the past, but in the last six months I have come to see that we must face these problems *now*, before it is too late. That we must deal with them resolutely, with the will to overcome all difficulties.'

Li Yuan was aware of how closely Wang's words echoed his father's. But was that deliberate on Wang's part or mere unconscious echo?

He looked up, noting how Wang was watching him, and nodded.

'Good,' Wang said, turning to face Wu Shih and Wei Feng, understanding that only those two alone remained to be convinced. 'In that case, I propose that we draft a much fuller document to be agreed and ratified by us at the next meeting of this Council.'

Li Yuan looked to Tsu Ma, surprised. Was that it? Was there to be no sting in the tail?

Tsu Ma leaned forward, a soft laugh forming a prologue to his words. 'I am glad that we see eye to eye on this matter, cousin, but let me make this clear. Are you proposing that we adopt Li Yuan's package of measures, or are you suggesting some... *alteration* of their substance?'

Wang Sau-leyan's smile was disarming. 'In essence I see nothing wrong with Li Yuan's proposals, yet in matters of this kind we must make sure that the fine detail – the drafting of the laws themselves – are to our satisfaction, neh? To allow too little would be as bad as to allow too much. The changes to the Edict must be regulated finely, as must the laws on population growth. The *balance* must be right, would you not agree, Wei Feng?'

Wei Feng, addressed unexpectedly, considered the matter a moment. He was looking old these days, markedly tired, and for the last meeting he had let his eldest son, Wei Chan Yin, sit in for him. But this time, in view of the importance of the meeting, he had decided to attend in person. He sat forward slightly, clearly in pain, and nodded.

'That is so, Wang Sau-leyan. And I am gratified to hear you talk of balance. I have heard many things today that I thought not to hear in my lifetime, yet I cannot say you are wrong. Things have changed these last ten years. And if it takes this package of measures to set things right, we must pursue this course, as my cousin Wang says, resolutely and with the will to overcome all difficulties. Yet we would do well to take our own counsel on the extent and nature of these changes before we make them. We must understand the likely outcome of our actions.'

Wang bowed his head respectfully. 'I agree, honoured cousin. There is great wisdom in your words. And that is why I propose that a joint committee be set up to investigate the likely consequences of such measures. Moreover, might I suggest that my cousin, Wei Feng's man, Minister Sheng, be appointed Head of that committee, reporting back directly to this Council with his findings.'

Li Yuan stared at Tsu Ma, astonished. Minister Sheng! It was Sheng whom he and Tsu Ma had planned to propose as the new Steward for GenSyn – Sheng who was the linchpin of their scheme to keep the company from financial ruin – but somehow Wang Sau-leyan had found out, and now he had pre-empted them, robbing them of their candidate, knowing they had prepared no other. Wei Feng was nodding, immensely pleased by the suggestion. A moment later a vote had carried the decision unanimously, bringing them on to the next piece of business, the question of GenSyn and how it was to be administered.

'But first let us eat,' Wang said, lifting his bulky figure from the chair. 'I don't know about you, cousins, but I could eat an ox, raw if necessary.'

There was laughter, but it was not shared by Li Yuan or Tsu Ma – they were still reeling from the shock of Wang's final twist. Li Yuan looked across, meeting Wang's eyes. Before they had been clear, but now there was a hardness, a small gleam of satisfaction in them.

Li Yuan bit back his anger, then leaned forward and picked up the silk-bound folder, gripping it tightly as he made his way across and out on to the balcony. Only minutes ago he had decided not to use what he knew, but now he was determined.

No. He was not finished yet. Let Wang Sau-leyan savour his tiny victory, for this day would see him humbled, his power in Council broken for all time.

And nothing – *nothing* – would stop him now.

At that moment, twenty thousand *li* away, at Nanking spaceport, a tall Han, wearing the outworld fashions of the Mars Colony, was stepping down from the interplanetary craft *Wuhan*. He had been through one exhaustive security check on board the ship, but another lay ahead. Ever since the attempt on Marshal Tolonen's life, security had been tight at Nanking.

He joined the queue, staring out across the massive landing pit dispassionately. The tests inside the ship had interested him. They were looking for abnormalities; for differences in the rib structure and the upper chest; signs of unusual brain scan patterns. He had had to produce a sample of his urine and his faecal matter. Likewise he had had to spit into a small ceramic dish. And afterwards the guard had looked up at him and smiled. 'It's all right,' he'd said, laughing, as if he'd cracked the joke a thousand times, 'you're human.'

As if that meant anything.

'Tuan Wen-ch'ang...'

He stepped forward, presenting his papers. The guard ignored them, taking his hand and placing it on to a lit-up pad on the desk in front of him. After a moment the guard released his hand, then brought round a swivel arm. Tuan put his eye to the cup at the end, holding it there a moment longer than was necessary for the machine to take a retinal scan.

'Okay,' the guard said, then leaned across, taking Tuan's papers. Holding them under the high-density light, he looked for signs of tampering or falsification. Satisfied, he slipped the pass into the slim black box at his side. A moment later it popped out again. At Security Central in Bremen the computer had entered Tuan Wen-ch'ang's personal details into the mainframe.

'All right. You're authorized for unobstructed passage in the four Cities in which you have business, full access granted between Level 150 and First Level.'

Tuan gave the slightest bow then walked on, pocketing his papers.

Deep inside he felt mild amusement. It had been much easier than he had expected. But he understood why. This whole society had been conditioned not to anticipate; to think of how things were and had always been, not of their potential. Their security procedures, for instance. They were testing for something that was already redundant; that was as outmoded as the tests they used to find it. On Mars things were different. There the pace was faster. Things had moved on.

He climbed aboard the courtesy train and sat there, waiting, his patience inexhaustible, his path through the great labyrinth of the City mapped out clearly in his head, as if already travelled. It was four hours by bolt to Luo Yang, then another hour and a half north to Yang Ch'ian on the edge of the City, only a hundred li from Wang Sau-leyan's palace at Tao Yuan. But the central computer records would show something else; would show him travelling south down the coast to catch the inter-continental shuttle from Fuchow to Darwin. And if the central computer said it was so, who would argue with it? Who would bother to check whether it reflected anything real – anything happening in the solid, physical world?

Outwardly Tuan Wen-ch'ang's face remained placid, almost inscrutable in its mask-like quality, yet deep down he was smiling. Yes, they had had all kinds of things bred out of them down here. Things that the species needed if it were to evolve beyond its present state. And that was why he was here. To remind them of what could be done. To shake them up a little.

And to push things one stage further.

Beyond the one-way glass the two youths sat, their backs to the wall, their hands bound. The preliminary interrogation was over. Now it was time to take things further.

Chen followed the sergeant through, watching how the two boys glanced at him, seeing the uniform, then looked again, their eyes widening as they recognized who he was.

'Ai ya...' the younger of them murmured beneath his breath, but the tall, thin youth – the ringleader – was silent.

'Well, my friends,' the sergeant said, a warm, ironic tone to his voice, 'you've met your accuser before, but I don't think you knew his name. So let me present Captain Kao of the T'ang's special élite force.'

The thin youth's eyes came up, meeting Chen's briefly.

Good, thought Chen. *So now you understand.*

'All right,' he said brusquely. 'You have had your chance to confess. Now you will be taken before a specially convened panel of judges who will decide the matter.' He paused. 'Your families will be present.'

He saw the sudden bitterness in the thin youth's face. 'You bastard,' the boy said quietly. 'You fucking bastard.'

Again, he let it pass. He was the T'ang's man, after all.

They took them down, under armed escort, to the meeting hall at the far end of the deck. There, in closed session, the three judges were waiting, seated behind their high lecterns. To one side of the hall, on chairs set apart from the rest, sat the four accomplices. Behind them were the families – men, women and children – numbering several hundred in all.

All this, Chen thought, looking about him, surprised by the size of the gathering. *All this because I willed it. Because I wanted things to be done properly.*

And yet it didn't feel right. He should have broken the little bastard's hand. Should have given him a simple lesson in power. Whereas this...

It began. Chen sat there, to the side, while the judges went through the evidence, questioning the boys and noting down their replies. It was a cold, almost clinical process. Yet when Chen stood to give his statement, he could feel the silent pressure of all those eyes, accusing him, angry at him for disturbing the balance of their lives. He felt his face grow numb, his heart begin to hammer, but he saw it through. He was *kwai*, after all. Besides, it was not he who had threatened another; who had extorted money and then lied about it.

He stared at the two youths, the desire to lash out – to smash their ugly little faces – almost too much for him. The darkness afterwards came as a relief. He sat there, barely conscious of the film being shown on the screen behind the judges – the film he had taken only hours before – yet when the lights came up again, it was hard to turn and confront that wall of hostile faces.

He listened carefully as the senior judge summed up the case, then, steeling himself, stood for the verdict. There was a moment's silence, then an angry murmur of disapproval as the two ringleaders were sent down, demoted fifty levels, their families fined heavily, their accomplices fined and ordered to do one hundred days' community service.

Chen looked across, conscious of the pointing fingers, the accusing eyes, and even when the senior judge admonished the families, increasing the fines and calling upon the Heads to bring their clans to order, he felt no better. Maybe they were right. Maybe it was too harsh. But that wasn't really the point. It was the kind of punishment, not the degree, that felt wrong.

As the families left, Chen stood there by the door, letting them jostle him as they filed past, staring back at his accusers, defying them to understand.

You saw what your sons did. You have seen what they've become. Why blame me for your children's failings?

And yet they did.

Ts'ui Wei, father of the ringleader, came across, leaning menacingly over Chen. 'Well, Captain Kao, are you *satisfied* with what you have done here today?'

Chen stared back at him silently.

Ts'ui Wei's lips curled slightly, the expression the mirror image of his son's disdainful sneer. 'I am sure you feel proud of yourself, Captain. You have upheld the law. But you have to live here, neh? You have children, *neh*?'

Chen felt himself go cold with anger. 'Are you threatening me, *Shih* Ts'ui?'

Ts'ui Wei leaned back, smiling; a hideously cynical smile. 'You misunderstand me, Captain. I am a law-abiding man. But one must live, neh?'

Chen turned away, biting back his anger, leaving before he did something he would regret. As Wang Ti said, he should be content to have done his part and helped cleanse his level. Yet as he made his way back it was anger, not satisfaction that he felt. That and a profound sense of wrongness. And as he walked, his hand went to his queue, feeling the thick braid of hair then tugging at it, as if to pull it from his head.

It was after three when they called Karr from his bed. There had been a shootout at one of the stacks east-south-east of Augsburg *Hsien*. Five men were dead, all visitors to the stack. That alone would not have been significant enough to wake him, but, some hours later a sack had been found near one of the inter-deck lifts. A sack containing a full *Yu* dossier on the Dragonfly Club. Now, less than thirty minutes later, Karr stood in the bedroom of the two-roomed apartment, trying to work out what had happened.

As he stood there the deck's duty officer knocked and entered. He bowed and handed Karr two printouts.

'Ywe Hao...' Karr mouthed softly, studying the flat, black and white image of the apartment's occupant; noting at once how like the artist's impression of the Yu terrorist, Chi Li, she was. This was her. There was no doubting it. But who were the others?

The security scans on the five victims had revealed little. They were from various parts of the City – though mostly from the north-central hsien. All were engineers or technicians in the maintenance industries: occupations that allowed them free access at this level. Apart from that their past conduct had been exemplary. According to the record, they were fine, upstanding citizens, but the record was clearly wrong.

So what was this? A rival faction, muscling in on the action? Or had there been a split in the ranks of the Yu – some internal struggle for power, culminating in this? After all he'd seen of such Ko Ming groups it would not have surprised him, but for once the explanation didn't seem to fit.

'What do the cameras show?'

'They're being processed and collated, sir. We should have them in the next ten to fifteen minutes.'

'And the woman – this Ywe Hao – she's on them, neh?'

'I sent a squad up to where she was last seen by the cameras, but there was no sign of her, sir. She vanished.'

'Vanished?' Karr shook his head. 'How do you mean?'

The man glanced away uneasily. 'Our cameras saw her enter the maintenance room at the top of the deck. After that there's no sign of her. Neither of the cameras on the main conduit picked her up.'

'So she must be there, neh?'

'No, sir. I had my men check that straight away. The room's empty and there's no sign of her in the conduit itself.'

Karr sighed. It was clear he would have to look for himself. 'You said earlier that she may have been warned – that there was a lookout of some kind...'

'Two young boys, sir.'

'I see. And you've traced them, neh?'

'They're in custody, sir. Would you like to see them?'

Karr looked about him at the mess. 'Your men have finished here, I take it?'

The Captain nodded.

'Good. Then clear this up first. Remove the corpses and put some cloths down. I don't want our young friends upset, understand me?'

'Sir!'

'Oh, and, Captain... have one of your men run a file on the movements of our friend Ywe Hao over the last three months. With particular attention to those occasions when she doesn't show up on camera.'

The Captain frowned but nodded. 'As you wish, Major.'

'Good. And bring me some *ch'a*. A large *chung* if you have one. We may be here some while.'

Chen stood there in the doorway, looking about him at the carnage. 'Kuan Yin! What happened here?'

Karr smiled tiredly. 'It looks like some kind of inter-factional rivalry. As to whether it's two separate groups or a struggle within the Yu, maybe that's something we'll discover, if and when we find the woman. As for the woman herself, I'm certain she was involved in both the Hannover assassination and the attack on the Dragonfly Club. I've asked for files on her movements over the last three months. If I'm right about her, then there ought to be blanks on the tape corresponding with the white-outs surrounding the terrorist incidents. We've no next-of-kin details, which is unusual, but you can do a little digging on that, neh? Oh, yes, and the Duty Captain is going to bring two young boys here. They were the woman's lookouts. I want you to question them and find out what they know about her. But be easy on them. I don't think they understood for a moment what they were in on.'

'And you, Gregor? What will you be doing?'

Karr straightened up, then laughed. 'First I'm going to finish this excellent *ch'a*, then I'm going to find out how a full-grown woman can disappear into thin air.'

★

'And so, cousins, we come to the question of the GenSyn inheritance.' Wang looked about him, his eyes resting briefly on Li Yuan and Tsu Ma before they settled on the ageing T'ang of East Asia, Wei Feng. 'As I see it, this matter has been allowed to drag on far too long. As a result the company has been harmed, its share price reduced dramatically on the Index. Our immediate concern, therefore, must be to provide GenSyn with a stable administrative framework, thus removing the uncertainties that are presently plaguing the company. After that...'

Li Yuan cleared his throat. 'Forgive me for interrupting, cousin, but, before we debate this matter at any length, I would like to call for a further postponement.'

Wang laughed, a small sound of disbelief. 'Forgive me, cousin, but did I hear you correctly? A *further* postponement?'

'If it would please my cousins. It is clear that we need more time to find a satisfactory solution. Another month or two.'

Wang sat forward, his face suddenly hard. 'Forgive me, cousin, but I do not understand. Since Klaus Ebert's death, this matter has been brought before this Council twice. On both occasions there was a unanimous agreement to postpone. For good reason, for no solution was forthcoming. But now we have the answer. Hou Tung-po's proposal is the solution we were looking for.'

Tsu Ma's laugh was heavily sardonic. 'You call that a solution, cousin? It sounds to me like a bureaucratic nightmare – a recipe not for stability but for certain financial disaster.'

Hou Tung-po sat forward, his face red with anger, but Wang's raised hand silenced him.

'Had this matter not been raised before, Tsu Ma, and were there not already a satisfactory solution before us – one you will have a full opportunity to debate – I would understand your desire to look for other answers, but the time for prevarication is past. As I was saying, we must act now or see the company damaged, perhaps irreparably.'

Wang paused, looking to Wei Feng, appealing to the old man directly. As things stood, Hou Tung-po and Chi Ling would support Wang, while Tsu Ma and Wu Shih would line up behind Li Yuan. If it came to a fight, Wei Feng held the casting vote.

Wang smiled, softening his stance.

'Besides, what objections could my cousins possibly have to the idea of a ruling committee? Would that not give us each a fair say in the running of the company? Would that not demonstrate – more clearly than anything – that the Seven have full confidence in the continuing prosperity of GenSyn?'

Li Yuan looked away. Whilst in terms of holdings it was second behind the giant MedFac company on the Hang Seng Index, GenSyn was, without doubt, the single most important commercial concern on Chung Kuo, and, as Tsu Ma had rightly said, any weakening of the company would affect him far more than it did Wang Sau-leyan.

But that could not be said. Not openly. For to say as much would give Wang the chance to get back at Li Yuan for his family's special relationship with GenSyn – a relationship which, though it had existed for a century or more, was, in truth, against the spirit of the Seven.

Li Yuan sat back, meeting Tsu Ma's eyes. They would have to give way. Minister Sheng had been their winning card, and Wang had already taken him from their hand.

'Cousin Wang,' he said coldly. 'I concede. Let us adopt cousin Hou's proposal. As you say, what possible objection could we have to such a scheme?'

He drew a breath, finding comfort in the presence of the silk-bound folder in his lap – in the thought of the humiliation he would shortly inflict on Wang. Then – from nowhere, it seemed – a new thought came to him. He leaned forward again, the sheer outrageousness of the idea making him want to laugh aloud.

'Indeed,' he said softly, 'let me make my own proposal. If the Council permits, I would like to suggest that Marshal Tolonen be replaced in his high post and appointed as Head of the ruling committee of GenSyn.' He looked at Wang directly. 'As my cousin argued so eloquently, we need to boost the market's confidence, and what clearer sign could we give than to make a man of such experience and integrity the head of our committee?'

He saw the movement in Wang's face and knew he had him. Wang could object, of course, but on what grounds? On the unsuitability of the candidate? No. For to argue that would be to argue that their original ratification of Tolonen as Marshal had been wrong, and that he could not – *would not* – do.

Li Yuan looked about him, seeing the nods of agreement from all sides – even from Wang's own allies – and knew he had succeeded in limiting the damage. With Tolonen in charge there was a much greater chance of things getting done. It would mean a loss of influence in the Council of Generals, but that was as nothing beside the potential loss of GenSyn's revenues.

He met Wang's eyes, triumphant, but Wang had not finished.

'I am delighted that my cousin recognizes the urgency of this matter. However, I am concerned whether my cousin really means what he says. It would not, after all, be the first time that he has promised this Council something, only to go back on his word.'

Li Yuan started forward, outraged by Wang's words. All around him there was a buzz of astonishment and indignation. But it was Wei Feng who spoke first, his deeply lined face grown stern and rock-like as he sat stiffly upright in his chair. His gruff voice boomed, all sign of frailty gone from it.

'You had best explain yourself, Wang Sau-leyan, or withdraw your words. I have never heard the like!'

'No?' Wang stood in a flurry of silks, looking about him defiantly. 'Nor would you have, cousin, had there not been good reason. I am talking of Li Yuan's promise to this Council that he would release the young sons – a promise that my cousins, Wu Shih and Tsu Ma were also party to.' He shifted his bulk, looking about the circle of his fellow T'ang. 'It is six months since they gave that promise and what has happened? Are the sons back with their fathers? Is the matter resolved, the grievance of those high citizens settled? No. The fathers remain unappeased, rightfully angry that – after giving our word – their sons remain imprisoned.'

Li Yuan stood, facing Wang. 'There is good reason why the sons have not been released, and you know it.'

'Know it?' Wang laughed contemptuously. 'All I know is that you gave your word. Immediately, you said.'

'And so it would have been had the paperwork gone smoothly.'

'*Paperwork...* ?' Wang's mocking laughter goaded Wu Shih to rise and stand beside Li Yuan, his fists clenched, his face livid.

'You know as well as any of us why there have been delays, Wang Sau-leyan! Considering the gravity of the circumstances, the terms of release were laughable. All we asked of the fathers was that they should sign a bond of good behaviour. It was the very minimum we could have asked for, and yet they refused, quibbling over the wording of the papers.'

'With every right, if what I've heard is true...'

Wu Shih bristled. 'And what *have* you heard, *cousin?*'

Wang Sau-leyan half turned, then turned back, moving a step closer, his face thrust almost into Wu Shih's. 'That it has been your officials and not the fathers who have quibbled over the precise wording of these... *bonds*. That they have dragged their heels and delayed until even the best man's patience would be frayed. That they have found every excuse – however absurd – not to come to terms. In short, that they have been ordered to delay matters.'

'*Ordered?*' Wu Shih shuddered with rage, then lifted his hand, as if to strike Wang, but Li Yuan put out his arm, coming between them.

'Cousins...' he said urgently, 'let us remember where we are.' He turned his head, staring fiercely at Wang. 'We will achieve nothing by hurling insults at each other.'

'You gave your word,' Wang said, defiantly, meeting his eyes coldly. 'All three of you. Immediately, you said. Without conditions.' He took a breath, then turned away, taking his seat.

Wu Shih glared at Wang a moment longer then stepped back, his disgust at his cousin no longer concealed. Li Yuan stood there, feeling the tensions that flowed like electric currents in the air about him and knew – for the first time knew beyond all doubt – that this was a breach that could never be healed. He took his seat again, leaning down to lift the folder from where it had fallen.

'Wang Sau-leyan,' he began, looking across at his moon-faced cousin, calm now that he had taken the first step, 'there is a small matter I would like to raise before we continue. A matter of... etiquette.'

Wang Sau-leyan smiled. 'As you wish, cousin.'

Li Yuan opened the folder, looking down at the wafer-thin piece of black plastic. It was the template of a hologrammic image: the image of Wang Sau-leyan in the garden at Tao Yuan, meeting with Li Yuan's bondsman, Hsiang Shao-erh. There were other things in the folder – a taped copy of their conversation, and the testimony of Wang's Master of the Royal Household, Sun Li Hua, but it was the holo that was the most damning piece of evidence.

He made to offer it to Wang, but Wang shook his head. 'I know what it is, Li Yuan. You have no need to show me.'

Li Yuan gave a small laugh of astonishment. What was this? Was Wang admitting his treachery?

With what seemed like resignation, Wang pulled himself up out of the chair and went to the double doors, unlocking them and throwing them open. At his summons a servant approached, head bowed, bearing a large, white lacquered box. Wang took it and turned, facing his fellow T'ang.

'I wondered when you would come to this,' he said, approaching to within an arm's length of where Li Yuan was sitting. 'Here. I was saving this for you. As for the traitor, Sun, he has found peace. After telling me everything, of course.'

Li Yuan took the box, his heart pounding.

He opened it and stared, horrified. From within the bright red wrappings of the box Hsiang Shao-erh stared back at him, his eyes like pale grey, bloated moons in an unnaturally white face, the lids peeled back. And then, slowly, very slowly, as in a dream, the lips began to move.

'Forgive... me... *Chieh... Hsia...* I... confess... my... treachery... and... ask... you... not... to... punish... my... kin... for... my... abjec ... unworthiness...' There was a tiny shudder from the severed head, and then it went on, the flat, almost gravelly whisper like the voice of stone itself. 'Forgive... them... *Chieh... Hsia...* I... beg... you... Forgive... them...'

Li Yuan looked up, seeing his horror reflected in every face but one. Then, with a shudder of revulsion, he dropped the box, watching it fall, the frozen head roll unevenly across the thick pile of the carpet until it lay still, resting on its cheek beside Wang Sau-leyan's foot. Bending down, the T'ang of Africa lifted it and held it up, offering it to Li Yuan, the smile on his face like the rictus of a corpse.

'This is yours, I believe, cousin.' Then he began to laugh, his laughter rolling from him in great waves. 'Yours...'

'What's your name?'

'Kung Lao.'

'And yours?'

'Kung Yi-lung.'

'You're brothers, then?'

The nine-year-old, Yi-lung, shook his head. 'Cousins,' he said quietly, still not sure of this man who, despite his air of kindness, wore the T'ang's uniform.

Chen sat back slightly, smiling. 'Okay. You were friends of Ywe Hao's, weren't you? You helped her when those men came, didn't you?'

He saw how the younger of the two, Lao, looked at his cousin before he nodded.

'Good. You probably saved her life.'

He saw how they looked down at that; how, again, they glanced at each other, still not sure what this was all about.

'She must have been a very good friend for you to do that for her, Yi-lung. Why was that? How did you come to be friends?'

Yi-lung kept his head lowered. 'She was kind to us,' he mumbled, the words offered reluctantly.

'Kind?' Chen gave a soft laugh, recalling what Karr had said about the guard, Leyden, and how she had probably spared his life. 'Yes, I can imagine that. But how did you meet her?'

No answer. He tried another tack.

'That's a nice machine she's got. A MedRes Network-6. I'd like one like that, wouldn't you? A top-of-the-range machine. It was strange, though. She was using it to record news items.'

'That was our project,' the younger boy, Lao, said, without thinking, then fell quiet again.

'Your project? For school, you mean?'

Both boys nodded. Yi-lung spoke for them. 'She was helping us with it. She always did. She took the time. Not like the rest of them. Any time we had a problem we could go to her.'

Chen took a deep breath. 'And that's why you liked her?'

Both boys were looking at him now, a strange earnestness in their young faces.

'She was funny,' Lao said reflectively. 'It wasn't all work with her. She made it fun. Turned it all into a game. We learned a lot from her, but she wasn't like the teachers.'

'That's right,' Yi-lung offered, warming to things. 'They made every-thing seem dull and grey, but she brought it all alive for us. She made it all make sense.'

'Sense?' Chen felt a slight tightening in his stomach. 'How do you mean, Yi-lung? What kind of things did she say to you?'

Yi-lung looked down, as if he sensed there was some deeper purpose behind Chen's question. 'Nothing,' he said evasively.

'Nothing?' Chen laughed, letting go, knowing he would get nothing if he pushed. 'Look, I'm just interested, that's all. Ywe Hao's gone missing and we'd like to find her. To help her. If we can find out what kind of woman she was...'

'Are you tracking her down?'

Chen studied the two a moment, then leaned forward, deciding to take them into his confidence. 'Ywe Hao's in trouble. Those men who came tried to kill her, but she got away. So, yes, Kung Lao, we have to find her. Have to track her down, if that's how you want to put it. But the more we know – the more good things we know about her – the better it will be for her. That's why you have to tell me all you can about her. To help her.'

Lao looked at his cousin, then nodded. 'Okay. We'll tell you. But you must promise, Captain Kao. Promise that once you find her you'll help her all you can.'

He looked back at the two boys, momentarily seeing something of his own sons in them, then nodded. 'I promise. All right? Now tell me. When did you first meet Ywe Hao, and how did you come to be friends?'

The maintenance room was empty, the hatch on the back wall locked, the warning light beside it glowing red in the half-light. Karr crouched down, squeezing through the low doorway, then stood there, perfectly still, listening, sniffing the air. There was the faintest scent of sweat. And something else... something he didn't recognize. He went across, putting his ear against the hatch. Nothing. Or almost nothing. There was a faint hum – a low, pulsing vibration.

He paused a moment, studying the hatchway, realizing it would be a tight squeeze; that he would be vulnerable momentarily if she was waiting just the other side. But the odds were that she was far away by now.

He ducked into the opening backwards, head first, forcing his shoulders through the narrow space diagonally, then grabbed the safety bar overhead and heaved himself up, twisting sideways. He dropped and spun round quickly, his weapon out, but even as he turned, he had to check himself, staggering, realizing suddenly that the platform was only five *ch'i* in width and that beyond...

Beyond was a drop of half a li.

He drew back, breathing slowly. The conduit was fifty ch'i across, a great diamond-shaped space, one of the six great hollowed columns which stood at the corners of the stack, holding it all up. Pipes went up into the darkness overhead, massive pipes twenty, thirty times the girth of a man, each pipe like a great tree, thick branches stretching off on every side, criss-crossing the open space. Service lights speckled the walls of the great conduit above and below, but their effect was not so much to illuminate the scene as to emphasize its essential darkness.

It was a cold, sombre place, a place of shadows and silence. Or so it seemed in those first few moments. But then he heard it – the sound that underlay all others throughout the City – the sound of great engines, pushing the water up the levels from the great reservoirs below, and of others, filtering what came down. There was a palpable hum, a vibration in the air itself. And a trace of that same indefinable scent he had caught a hint of in the room earlier, but stronger here. Much stronger.

Poking his head out over the edge, he looked down, then moved back, craning his neck, trying to see up into the shadows.

Which way? Had she gone up or down?

He looked about him, locating the cameras, then frowned, puzzled. There was no way the cameras wouldn't have seen her come out of the room and on to the platform. No chance at all. Which meant that either she hadn't gone into the maintenance room in the first place or those cameras had been tampered with. And she *had* gone into the room.

For a moment Karr stared at the camera just across from him, then, struck by the absurdity of it, he laughed. It was all too bloody easy. Since the City had first been built Security had been dependent on their eyes – their security cameras – to be their watchdogs and do most of their surveillance work for them, not questioning for a moment how satisfactory such a system was, merely using it, as they'd been taught. But the *Yu* had recognized how vulnerable such a network was – how easily manipulated. They had seen just how easy it was to blind an eye or feed it false information. All they needed was access. And who had access? Technicians. Maintenance technicians. Like the five dead men. And the girl. And others. Hundreds of others. Every last one of them tampering with the network, creating gaps in the vision of the world.

False eyes they'd made. False eyes. Like in *wei chi*, where a group of stones was only safe if it had two eyes, and where the object was to blind an eye and take a group, or to lull one's opponent into a false sense of security, by letting them think they had an eye, whereas, in fact...

Pulling his visor down, he leaned out, searching the walls for heat traces.

Nothing. As he'd expected, the trail was cold. He raised the visor, sighing heavily. What he really needed was sleep. Twelve hours if possible, four if he was lucky. The drugs he was taking to keep awake had a limited effect. Thought processes deteriorated, reflexes slowed. If he didn't find her soon...

He leaned back, steadying himself with one hand, then stopped, looking down. His fingers were resting in something soft and sticky. He raised them to his mouth, tasting them. It was blood, recently congealed.

Hers? It had to be. No one else had come here in the last few hours. So maybe she'd been wounded in the fire-fight. He shook his head, puzzled. If that were so, why hadn't they found a trail of blood in the corridors outside?

Unless they hadn't looked.

He went to the edge of the platform, feeling underneath, his fingers searching until, at the top of the service ladder, three rungs down, they met a second patch of stickiness.

Down. She had gone down.

Karr smiled, then, drawing his gun, turned and clambered over the edge, swinging out, his booted feet reaching for the ladder.

Towards the bottom of the shaft it became more difficult. The smaller service pipes that branched from the huge arterials proliferated, making it necessary for Karr to clamber out, away from the wall, searching for a way down.

The trail of blood had ended higher up, on a platform thirty levels down from where he had first discovered it. He had spent twenty minutes searching for further traces, but there had been nothing. It was only when he had trusted to instinct and gone down that he had found something – the wrapping of a field dressing pad, wedged tightly into a niche in the conduit wall.

It was possible that she had gone out through one of the maintenance hatches and into the deck beyond. Possible but unlikely. Not with all the nearby stacks on special security alert. Neither would she have doubled back. She had lost a lot of blood. In her weakened state the climb would have been too much.

Besides which, his instinct told him where he would find her.

Karr moved on, working his way down, alert for the smallest movement, the least deviation in the slow, rhythmic pulse that filled the air. That sound seemed to grow in intensity as he went down, a deep vibration that was as much within his bones as in the air. He paused, looking up through the tangled mesh of pipework, imagining the great two-li-high conduit as a giant flute – a huge k'un-ti – reverberating on the very edge of audibility: producing one single, unending note in a song written for titans.

He went down, taking greater care now, conscious that the bottom of the shaft could not be far away. Even so, he was surprised when, easing his way between a nest of overlapping pipes, his feet met nothing. For a moment he held himself there, muscles straining, as his feet searched blindly for purchase, then drew himself up again.

He crouched, staring down through the tangle of pipework. Below him there was nothing. Nothing but darkness.

In all probability she was down there, in the darkness, waiting for him. But how far down? Twenty ch'i? Thirty? He pulled his visor down and switched to ultra-violet. At once his vision was filled with a strong red glow. Of course... he had felt it earlier – that warmth coming up from below. That was where the great pumps were – just beneath. Karr raised the visor and shook his head. It was no use. She could move about as much as she wanted against that bright backdrop of warmth, knowing that she could not be seen. Neither could he use a lamp. That would only give his own position away, long before he'd have the chance to find her.

What then? A flash bomb? A disabling gas?

The last made sense, but still he hesitated. Then, making up his mind, he turned, making his way across to the wall.

There would be a way down. A ladder. He would find it and descend, into the darkness.

He went down, tensed, listening for the slightest movement from below, his booted feet finding the rungs with a delicacy surprising in so big a man. His body was half-turned towards the central darkness, his weapon drawn, ready for use. Even so, it was a great risk he was taking and he knew it. She didn't have night-sight – he was fairly sure of that – but, if she *was* down there, there was the distinct possibility that she would see him first, if only as a shadow against the shadows.

He stopped, crouching on the ladder, one hand going down. His foot had met something. Something hard but yielding.

It was mesh. A strong security mesh, stretched across the shaft. He reached out, searching the surface. Yes, there – the raised edge of a gate, set into the mesh. He traced it round. There was a slight indentation on the edge farthest from the ladder, where a spanner-key fitted, but it was locked. Worse, it was bolted from beneath. If he was to go any further he would have to break it open.

He straightened up, gripping the rung tightly, preparing himself, then brought his foot down hard. With a sharp crack it gave, taking him with it, his hand torn from the rung, his body twisting about.

He fell. Instinctively, he curled into a ball, preparing for impact, but it came sooner than he'd expected, jarring him.

He rolled to one side, then sat up, sucking in a ragged breath, his left shoulder aching.

If she was there...

He closed his eyes, willing the pain to subside, then got up on to his knees. For the briefest moment he felt giddy, disoriented, then his head cleared. His gun... he had lost his gun.

In the silent darkness he waited, tensed, straining to hear the click of a safety or the rattle of a grenade, but there was nothing, only the deep, rhythmic pulse of the pumps, immediately beneath. And something else – something so faint he thought at first he was imagining it.

Karr got to his feet unsteadily, then, feeling his way blindly, he went towards the sound.

The wall was closer than he'd thought. For a moment his hands searched fruitlessly, then found what they'd been looking for. A passageway – a small, low-ceilinged tunnel barely broad enough for him to squeeze into. He stood there a moment, listening. Yes, it came from here. He could hear it clearly now.

Turning side on, he ducked inside, moving slowly down the cramped passageway, his head scraping the ceiling. Halfway down he stopped, listening again. The sound was closer now, its regular rhythm unmistakable. Reaching out, his fingers connected with a grill. He recognized it at once. It was a storage cupboard, inset into the wall, like those they had in the dormitories.

Slipping his fingers through the grill, he lifted it, easing it slowly back and up into the slot at the top. He paused, listening again, his hand resting against the bottom edge of the niche, then began to move his fingers inward, searching...

Almost at once they met something warm. He drew them back a fraction, conscious of the slight change in the pattern of the woman's breathing. He waited for it to regularize, then reached out again, exploring the shape. It was a hand, the fingers pointing to the left. He reached beyond it, searching, then smiled, his fingers closing about a harder, colder object. Her gun.

For a moment he rested, his eyes closed, listening to the simple rhythm of the woman's breathing, the deep reverberation of the pumps. In the darkness they seemed to form a kind of counterpoint and for a moment he felt himself at ease, the two sounds connecting somewhere deep within him, Yin and Yang, balancing each other.

The moment passed. Karr opened his eyes into the darkness and shivered. It was a shame. He would have liked it to have ended otherwise, but it was not to be. He checked the gun, then pulled his visor down, clicking on the lamp. At once the cramped niche filled with light and shadow.

Karr caught his breath, studying the woman. She lay on her side, her face towards the entrance, one hand folded across her breasts. In the pearled glow of the lamp she was quite beautiful, her asiatic features softened in sleep, her strength – the perfect bone structure of her face and shoulders – somehow emphasized. *Like Marie*, he thought, surprised by the notion. As he watched she stirred, moving her head slightly, her eyes flickering beneath the lids in dream.

Again he shivered, recalling what the guard, Leyden, had said about her, and what the two boys had told Chen. At the same time he could see the murdered youth at the Dragonfly Club and the soft, hideous excess of that place, and for a moment he was confused. Was she *really* his enemy? Was this strong, beautiful creature really so different from himself?

He looked away, reminding himself of the oath of loyalty he had made to his T'ang. Then, steeling himself, he raised the gun, placing it a mere finger's length from her sleeping face, clicking off the safety.

The sound woke her. She smiled and stretched, turning towards him.

For a moment her dark eyes stared out dreamily, then, with a blink of realization, she grew still.

He hesitated, wanting to explain, wanting, just this once, for her to understand. 'I—'

'Don't,' she said quietly. 'Please...'

The words did something to him. He drew the gun back, staring at her, then, changing its setting, he leaned forward again, placing it to her temple.

Afterwards he stood there, out in the darkness of the main shaft, the mesh overhead glittering in the upturned light from his visor, and tried to come to terms with what he'd done. He had been resolved to kill her; to end it cleanly, honourably. But, faced with her, hearing her voice, he had found himself unmanned – incapable of doing what he'd planned.

He turned, looking back at the shadowed entrance to the passageway. All this while he had been operating under a communications blackout, so in theory he might still kill her or let her go and no one would be the wiser. But he knew now that he would do what his duty required of him and deliver her, stunned, her wrists and ankles bound, into captivity.

Whether it felt right or not. Because that was his job – the thing Tolonen had chosen him to do all those years ago.

Karr sighed, then, raising his right hand, held down the two tiny blisters on the wrist, reactivating the inbuilt comset.

'Kao Chen,' he said softly, 'can you read me?'

There was a moment's silence, then the reply came, sounding directly in his head. 'Gregor... thank the gods. Where are you?'

He smiled, comforted by the sound of Chen's voice. 'Listen. I've got her. She's bound and unconscious, but I don't think I can get her out of here on my own. I'll need assistance.'

'Okay. I'll get on to that straight away. But where are you? There's been no trace of you for almost two hours. We were worried.'

Karr laughed quietly. 'Wait. There's a plaque here somewhere.' He lowered his visor, looking about, then went across. 'All right. You'll need two men and some lifting equipment – pulleys and the like.'

'Yes,' Chen said, growing impatient. 'I'll do all that. But tell me where you are. You must have some idea.'

'It's Level 31,' Karr said, turning back, playing the beam on to the surface of the plaque, making sure. 'Level 31, Dachau *Hsien*.'

Chapter 74

THE DEAD BROTHER

L i Yuan stood on the high terrace at Hei Shui, looking out across the lake. He had come unannounced. Behind him stood his eight retainers, their black silks merging with the shadows.

A light breeze feathered the surface of the lake, making the tall reeds at the shoreline sway, the cormorants bob gently on the water. The sky was a perfect blue, the distant mountains hard, clear shapes of black. Sunlight rested like a honeyed gauze over everything, glinting off the long sweep of steps, the white stone arches of the bridge. On the far bank, beyond the lush green of the water meadow, Fei Yen's maids moved among the trees of the orchard, preparing their mistress for the audience.

From where he stood he could see the child's cot – a large, sedan-like thing of pastel-coloured cushions and veils. Seeing it had made his heart beat faster, the darkness at the pit of his stomach harden like a stone.

He turned, impatient. 'Come,' he said brusquely, then turned back, skipping down the broad steps, his men following like shadows on the white stone.

They met on the narrow bridge, a body's length separating them. Fei Yen stood there, her head lowered. Behind her came her maids, the cot balanced between four of them.

As Li Yuan took a step closer, Fei Yen knelt, touching her head to the stone. Behind her, her maids did the same.

'*Chieh Hsia*...'

She was dressed in a simple *chi pao* of pale lemon, embroidered with butterflies. Her head was bare, her fine, dark hair secured in a tightly braided bun at the crown. As she looked up again, he noticed a faint colour at her neck.

'Your gift...' he began, then stopped, hearing a sound from within the cot.

She turned her head, following his gaze, then looked back at him. 'He's waking.'

He looked at her without recognition, then looked back at the cot. Stepping past, he moved between the kneeling maids and, crouching, drew back the veil at the side of the cot. Inside, amidst a downy nest of cushions, young Han was waking. He lay on his side, one tiny, delicate hand reaching out to grip the edge of the cot. His eyes – two tiny, rounded centres of perfect, liquid blackness – were open, staring up at him.

Li Yuan caught his breath, astonished by the likeness. 'Han Ch'in...' he said softly.

Fei Yen came and knelt beside him, smiling down at the child, evoking a happy gurgle of recognition. 'Do you wish to hold him, *Chieh Hsia*?'

He hesitated, staring down at the child, engulfed by a pain of longing so strong it threatened to unhinge him, then nodded, unable to form the words.

She leaned past, brushing against him, the faint waft of her perfume, the warmth of the momentary contact bringing him back to himself, making him realize that it was her there beside him. He shivered, appalled by the strength of what he was feeling, knowing suddenly that it had been wrong for him to come. A weakness. But now he had no choice. As she lifted the child and turned towards him, he felt the pain return, sharper than before.

'Your son,' she said, so faintly that only he caught the words.

The child nestled in his arms contentedly, so small and frail and vulnerable that his face creased with pain at the thought that anyone might harm him. Nine months old, he was – a mere thirty-nine weeks – yet already he was the image of Yuan's brother, Han Ch'in, dead these last ten years.

Li Yuan stood, then turned, cradling the child, cooing softly to him as he moved between the kneeling maids. Reaching the balustrade, he stood there, looking down at the bank, his eyes half-lidded, trying to see. But there was nothing. No younger self stood there, his heart in his throat, watching as a youthful Han Ch'in strode purposefully through the short grass, like a proud young animal, making towards the bridge and his betrothed.

Li Yuan frowned then turned, staring across the water meadow, but again there was nothing. No tent, no tethered horse or archery target. It had gone, all of it, as if it had never been. And yet there was the child, so like his long-dead brother that it was as if he had not died but simply been away, on a long journey.

'Where have you been, Han Ch'in?' he asked softly, almost inaudibly, feeling the warm breeze on his cheek; watching it stir and lift the fine dark hair that covered the child's perfect, ivory brow. 'Where have you been all these years?'

Yet even as he uttered the words he knew he was deluding himself. This was not Tongjiang, and his brother Han Ch'in was dead. He had helped bury him. No, this was someone else. A stranger to the great world. A whole new cycle of creation. His son, fated to be a stranger.

He shivered again, pained by the necessity of what he must do, then turned, looking back at Fei Yen.

She was watching him, her hands at her neck, her eyes misted, moved by the sight of him holding the child, all calculation gone from her. That surprised him – that she was as unprepared for this as he. Whatever she had intended by her gift – whether to wound him or provoke a sense of guilt – she had never expected this.

Beyond her stood his men, like eight dark statues in the late morning sunlight, watching, waiting in silence for their lord.

He went back to her, handing her the child. 'He is a good child, neh?'

She met his eyes, suddenly curious, wondering what he had meant by coming, then lowered her head. 'Like his father,' she said quietly.

He looked away, conscious for the first time of her beauty. 'You will send me a tape each year, on the child's birthday. I wish...' He hesitated, his mouth suddenly dry. He looked back at her. 'If he is ill, I want to know.'

She gave a small bow. 'As you wish, Chieh Hsia.'

'And, Fei Yen...'

She looked up, her eyes momentarily unguarded. 'Chieh Hsia?'

He hesitated, studying her face, the depth of what he had once felt for her there again, just below the surface, then shook his head. 'Just that you must do nothing beyond that. What was between us is past. You must not try to rekindle it. Do you understand me clearly?'

For a moment she held his eyes, as if to deny him, then, with a familiar little motion of her head, she looked away, her voice harder than before.

'As you wish, *Chieh Hsia*.'

A screen had been set up between the pillars at the far end of the hall, like a great white banner gripped between the teeth of dragons. Wang Sau-leyan's Audience Chair had been set before it, some twenty *ch'i* back. He went to it and climbed up, taking his place, then looked across at his Chancellor. 'Well?'

Hung Mien-lo shuddered, then, turning towards the back of the hall, lifted a trembling hand.

At once the lights in the hall faded. A moment later the screen was lit with a pure white light. Only as the camera panned back slightly did Wang Sau-leyan realize that he was looking at something – at the pale stone face of something. Then, as the border of green and grey and blue came into stronger focus, he realized what it was. A tomb. The door to a tomb.

And not just any tomb. It was his family's tomb at Tao Yuan, in the walled garden behind the eastern palace. He shivered, one hand clutching at his stomach, a tense feeling of dread growing in him by the moment. 'What...?'

The query was uncompleted. Even as he watched, the faintest web of cracks formed on the pure white surface of the stone. For the briefest moment these darkened, broadening, tiny chips of whiteness falling away as the stone began to crumble. Then, with a suddenness that made him jerk back, the door split asunder, revealing the inner darkness.

He stared at the screen, horrified, his throat constricted, his heart hammering in his chest. For a moment there was nothing – nothing but the darkness – and then the darkness moved, a shadow forming on the ragged edge of stone. It was a hand.

Wang Sau-leyan was shaking now, his whole body trembling, but he could not look away. Slowly, as in his worst nightmare, the figure pulled itself up out of the darkness of the tomb, like a drowned man dragging himself up from the depths of the ocean bed. For a moment it stood there, faintly outlined by the morning sunlight, a simple shape of darkness against the utter blackness beyond, then it staggered forward, into the full brightness of the sun.

Wang groaned. '*Kuan Yin...*'

It was his brother, Wang Ta-hung. His brother, lain in a bed of stone these last twenty months. But he had grown in the tomb, becoming the man he had never been in life. The figure stretched in the sunlight, earth falling from its shrouds, then looked about it, blinking into the new day.

'It cannot be,' Wang Sau-leyan said softly, breathlessly. 'I had him killed, his copy destroyed.'

'And yet his vault was empty, *Chieh Hsia*.'

The corpse stood there, swaying slightly, its face up to the sun. Then, with what seemed like a drunken lurch, it started forward again, trailing earth.

'And the earth?'

'Is real earth, *Chieh Hsia*. I had it analysed.'

Wang stared at the screen, horrified, watching the slow, ungainly procession of his brother's corpse. There was no doubting it. It was his brother, but grown large and muscular, more like his elder brothers than the weakling he had been in life. As it staggered across the grass towards the locked gate and the watching camera, the sound of it – a hoarse, snuffling noise – grew louder step by step.

The gate fell away, the seasoned wood shattering as if rotten, torn brutally from its solid, iron hinges. Immediately the image shifted to another camera, watching the figure come on, up the broad pathway beside the eastern palace and then down the steps, into the central gardens.

'Did no one try to stop it?' Wang asked, his mouth dry.

Hung's voice was small. 'No one knew, *Chieh Hsia*. The first time an alarm sounded was when it broke through the main gate. The guards there were terrified. They ran from it. And who can blame them?'

For once Wang Sau-leyan did not argue. Watching the figure stumble on he felt the urge to hide – somewhere deep and dark and safe – or to run and keep running, even to the ends of the earth. The hair stood up on his neck, and his hands shook like those of an old man. He had never felt so afraid. Never, even as a child.

And yet it could not be his brother. Even as he feared it, a part of his mind rejected it.

He put his hands out, gripping the arms of the chair, willing himself to be calm, but it was hard. The image on the screen was powerful, more

powerful than his reasoning mind could bear. His brother was dead – he
had seen that with his eyes; touched the cold and lifeless flesh – and yet here
he was once more, reborn – a new man, his eyes agleam with life, his body
glowing with a strange, unearthly power.

He shuddered, then tore his eyes from the screen, looking down into the
pale, terrified face of his Chancellor.

'So where is it now, Hung? Where in the gods' names is it now?'

Hung Mien-lo looked up at him, wide-eyed, and gave the tiniest shrug.
'In the hills, *Chieh Hsia*. Somewhere in the hills.'

Ywe Hao was standing with her back to Karr, naked, her hands secured
behind her back, her ankles bound. To her right, against the bare wall, was
an empty examination couch. Beyond the woman, at the far end of the cell,
two medical staff were preparing their instruments at a long table.

Karr cleared his throat, embarrassed, even a touch angry, at the way they
were treating her. It had never worried him before – normally the creatures
he had to deal with deserved such treatment – but this time it was different.
He glanced at the woman uneasily, disturbed by her nakedness, and, as he
moved past her, met her eyes briefly, conscious once more of the strength
there, the defiance, even, perhaps, a slight air of moral superiority.

He stood by the table, looking at the instruments laid out on the white
cloth. 'What are these for, Surgeon Wu?'

He knew what they were for. He had seen them used a hundred, maybe
a thousand times. But that was not what he meant.

Wu looked up at him, surprised. 'Forgive me, Major...?'

Karr turned, facing him. 'Did anyone instruct you to bring these?'

The old man gave a short laugh. 'No, Major Karr. But it is standard practice at an interrogation. I assumed...'

'You will assume nothing,' Karr said, angry that his explicit instructions
had not been acted on. 'You'll pack them up and leave. But first you'll give
the prisoner a full medical examination.'

'It is most irregular, Major—' the old man began, affronted by the
request, but Karr barked at him angrily.

'This is *my* investigation, Surgeon Wu, and you'll do as I say! Now get to
it. I want a report ready for my signature in twenty minutes.'

Karr stood by the door, his back turned on the girl, while the old man and his assistant did their work. Only when they'd finished did he turn back.

The girl lay on the couch, naked, the very straightness of her posture, like the look in her eyes, a gesture of defiance. Karr stared at her a moment, then looked away, a feeling of unease eating at him. If the truth were told, he admired her. Admired the way she had lain there, suffering all the indignities they had put her through, and yet had retained her sense of self-pride. In that she reminded him of Marie.

He looked away, disturbed at where his thoughts had led him. Marie was no terrorist, after all. Yet the thought was valid. He had only to glance at the girl – at the way she held herself – and he could see the similarities. It was not a physical resemblance – though both were fine, strong women – but some inward quality that showed itself in every movement, every gesture.

He went across and opened one of the store cupboards on the far side of the room, then returned, laying the sheet over her, covering her nakedness. She stared up at him a moment, surprised, then looked away.

'You will be moved to another cell,' he said, looking about him at the appalling bareness of the room. 'Somewhere more comfortable than this.'

He looked back at her, seeing how her body was tensed beneath the sheet. She didn't trust him. But, then, why should she? He was her enemy. He may have shown her some small kindness now, but ultimately it was his role to destroy her, and she knew that.

Maybe this was just as cruel. Maybe he should just have let this butcher, Wu, get on with things. But some instinct in him cried out against that. She was not like the others he had had to act against – not like DeVore or Berdichev. There he had known exactly where he stood, but here...

He turned away, angry with himself. Angry that he found himself so much in sympathy with her; that she reminded him so much of his Marie. Was it merely that? That deep resemblance? If so, it was reason enough to ask to be taken off the case. But he wasn't sure it *was*. Rather, it was some likeness to himself; the same thing he had seen in Marie, perhaps – that had made him want her for his mate. Yet if that were so, what did it say about him? Had things changed so much – had *he* changed so much – that he could now see eye to eye with his master's enemies?

He looked back at her – at the clear, female shape of her beneath the sheet – and felt a slight tremor pass through him. Was he deluding himself – making it harder for himself – by seeing in her some reflection of his own deep-rooted unease? Was it that? For if it were...

'Major Karr?'

He turned. Surgeon Wu stood there, the medical report on the table beside him.

Karr picked it up, studying it carefully, then took the pen and signed, giving the under-copy to the surgeon.

'Okay. You can go now, Wu. I'll finish off here.'

Wu's lips and eyes formed a brief, knowing smile. 'As you wish, Major Karr.' Then, bowing his head, he departed, his assistant – silent, colourless, like a pale shadow of the old man – following two paces behind.

Karr turned back to the woman. 'Is there anything you need?'

She looked at him a moment. 'My freedom? A new identity, perhaps?' She fell silent, a look of sour resignation on her face. 'No, Major Karr. There's nothing I need.'

He hesitated, then nodded. 'We'll move you in the next hour or so. Then, later, I'll be back to question you. We know a great deal anyway, but it would be best for you...'

'*Best* for me?' She stared back at him, a look of disbelief in her eyes. 'Do what you must, Major Karr, but never tell me what's best for me. Because you just don't know. You haven't any idea.'

He felt a shiver pass through him. She was right. This much was fated. Was like a script from which they both must read. But best...? He turned away. This was their fate, but at least he could make it easy for her once they had done – make it painless and clean. That much he could do, little as it was.

In Tao Yuan, in the walled burial ground of the Wang clan, it was raining. Beneath a sky of dense grey-black cloud, Wang Sau-leyan stood before the open tomb, his cloak pulled tight about him, staring wide-eyed into the darkness below.

Hung Mien-lo, watching from nearby, felt the hairs rise on the back of his neck. So it was true. The tomb had been breached from within, the stone casket that had held Wang Ta-hung shattered like a plaster god. And the contents?

He shuddered. There were footprints in the earth, traces of fibre, but nothing conclusive. Nothing to link the missing corpse with the damage to the tomb. Unless one believed the film.

On the flight over from Alexandria they had talked it through, the T'ang's insistence bordering on madness. The dead did not rise, he argued, so it was something else. Someone had set this up, to frighten him and try to undermine him. But how? And who?

Li Yuan was the obvious candidate – he had most to gain from such a move – but equally he had had least opportunity. Hung's spies had kept a close watch on the young T'ang of Europe and no sign of anything relating to this matter had emerged – not even the smallest hint.

Tsu Ma, then? Again, he had motive enough, and it was true that Hung's spies in the Tsu household were less effective than in any other of the palaces, but somehow it seemed at odds with Tsu Ma's nature. With Tsu Ma even his deviousness had a quality of directness to it.

So who did that leave? Mach? The thought was preposterous. As for the other T'ang, they had no real motive – even Wu Shih. Sun Li Hua had had motive enough, but he was dead, his family slaughtered, to the third generation.

All of which made the reality of this – the shattered slabs, the empty casket – that much more disturbing. Besides which, the thing was out there somewhere, a strong, powerful creature, capable of splitting stone and lifting a slab four times the weight of a man.

Something inhuman.

He watched the T'ang go inside and turned away, looking about him at the layout of the rain-swept garden. Unless it was the real Wang Ta-hung, it would have had to get inside the tomb before it could break out so spectacularly, so how would it have done that?

Hung Mien-lo paced to and fro slowly, trying to work things out. It was possible that the being had been there a long time – placed there at the time of Wang Ta-hung's burial ceremony, or before. But that was unlikely. Unless it was a machine it would have had to eat, and he had yet to see a machine as lifelike as the one that had burst from the tomb.

So how? How would something have got into the tomb without them seeing it?

He called the head of the team across and questioned him. It seemed that the security cameras here worked on a simple principle. For most of the time the cameras were inactive, but at the least noise or sign of movement they would focus on the source of the disturbance, following it until it left their field of vision. In the dark it was programmed to respond to the heat traces of intruders.

The advantage of such a system was that it was easy to check each camera's output. There was no need to reel through hours of static film; one had only to look at what was there.

Hung could see how that made sense... normally. Yet what if, just this once, something cold and silent had crept in through the darkness?

He went across, looking down into the tomb. At the foot of the steps, in the candlelit interior, Wang was standing beside the broken casket, staring down into its emptiness. Sensing Hung there, above him, Wang Sau-leyan turned, looking up. 'He's dead. I felt him. He was cold.'

The T'ang's words sent a shiver down his spine. *Something cold...* He backed away, bowing low, as Wang came up the steps.

'You'll find out who did this, Master Hung. And you'll find that thing... whatever it is. But until you do, you can consider yourself demoted, without title. Understand me?'

Hung met the T'ang's eyes, then let his head drop, giving a silent nod of acquiescence.

'Good. Then set to it. This business makes my flesh creep.'

And mine, thought Hung Mien-lo, concealing the bitter anger he was feeling. *And mine.*

Since the fire that had destroyed it, Deck Fourteen of Central Bremen stack had been rebuilt, though not to the old pattern. Out of respect for those who had died here, it had been converted into a memorial park, landscaped to resemble the ancient water gardens – the Chuo Cheng Yuan – at Su Chou. Guards walked the narrow paths, accompanied by their wives and children, or alone, enjoying the peaceful harmony of the lake, the rocks, the delicate bridges and stilted pavilions. From time to time one or more would stop beside the great t'ing, named 'Beautiful Snow, Beautiful Clouds' after its original, and stare up at the great stone – the Stone of Enduring Sorrow – that had been placed there by the young T'ang only months before, reading the red-painted names cut into its broad, pale grey flank. The names of all eleven thousand and eighteen men, women and children who had been killed here by the *Ping Tiao*.

Further down, on the far side of the lotus lake, a stone boat jutted from the bank. This was the teahouse, Travelling by Sea. At one of the stone benches near the prow Karr sat, alone, a *chung* of the house's finest *ch'a* before him. Nearby two of his guards made sure he was not disturbed.

From where Karr sat, he could see the Stone, its shape partially obscured by the willows on the far bank, its top edge blunted like a filed tooth. He stared at it a while, trying to fit it into the context of recent events.

He sipped at his *ch'a*, his unease returning stronger than ever. However he tried to argue it, it didn't feel right. Ywe Hao would never have done this. Would never, for a moment, have countenanced killing so many innocent people. No. He had read what she had written about her brother and been touched by it. Had heard what the guard, Leyden, had said about her. Had watched the tape of Chen's interview with the two boys – her young lookouts – and seen the fierce love for her in their eyes. Finally he had seen with his own eyes what had happened at the Dragonfly Club, and in his heart of hearts he could find no wrong in what she had done.

She was a killer, yes, but, then, so was he, and who was to say what justified the act of killing, what made it right or wrong? He killed to order, she for conscience's sake, and who could say which of those was right, which wrong?

And now this – this latest twist. He looked down at the scroll on the table beside the *chung* and shook his head. He should have killed her while he'd still had the chance. No one would have known. No one but himself.

He set his bowl down angrily, splashing the *ch'a*. Where the hell was Chen? What in the gods' names was keeping him?

But when he turned, it was to find Chen there, moving past the guards to greet him.

'So what's been happening?'

'This...' Karr said, pushing the scroll across to him.

Chen unfurled it and began to read.

'They've taken it out of our hands,' Karr said, his voice low and angry. 'They've pushed us aside, and I want to know why.'

Chen looked up, puzzled by his friend's reaction. 'All it says here is that we are to hand her over to the T'ing Wei. That is strange, I agree, but not totally unheard of.'

Karr shook his head. 'No. Look further down. The second to last paragraph. Read it. See what it says.'

Chen looked back at the scroll, reading the relevant paragraph quickly, then looked up again, frowning. 'That can't be right, surely? SimFic? They are to hand her over to SimFic? What is Tolonen thinking of?'

'It's not the Marshal. Look. There at the bottom of the scroll. That's the Chancellor's seal. Which means Li Yuan must have authorized this.'

Chen sat back, astonished. 'But why? It makes no sense.'

Karr shook his head. 'No. It makes sense. It's just that we don't know how it fits together yet.'

'And you want to know?'

'Yes.'

'But isn't that outside our jurisdiction?'

Karr leaned towards him. 'I've done a bit of digging and it seems that the T'ing Wei are to hand her over to SimFic's African operation.'

Chen frowned. 'Africa?'

'Yes. But listen. It seems she's destined for a special unit in East Africa. A place named Kibwezi. The gods alone know what they do there or why they want her, but it's certainly important – important enough to warrant the T'ang's direct intervention. And that's why I called for you. I've another job for you – another task for our friend Tong Chou.'

Tong Chou was Chen's alias. The name he had used in the Plantations when he had gone in there after DeVore.

Chen took a long breath. Wang Ti was close to term: the child was due some time in the next few weeks and he had hoped to be there at the birth. But this was his duty. What he was paid to do. He met Karr's eyes, nodding. 'All right. When do I start?'

'Tomorrow. The documentation is being prepared. You're to be transferred to Kibwezi from the European arm of SimFic. All the relevant background information will be with you by tonight.'

'And the woman? Ywe Hao? Am I to accompany her?'

Karr shook his head. 'No. That would seem too circumstantial, neh? Besides which, the transfer won't be made for another few days yet. It'll give you time to find out what's going on over there.'

'And how will I report back?'

'You won't. Not until you have to come out.'

Chen considered. It sounded dangerous, but no more dangerous than before. He nodded. 'And when I have to come out – what do I do?'

'You'll send a message. A letter to Wang Ti. And then we'll come in and get you out.'

'I see...' Chen sat back, looking past the big man thoughtfully. 'And the woman, Ywe Hao... am I to intercede?'

Karr dropped his eyes. 'Not in any circumstances. You are to observe, nothing more. Our involvement must not be suspected. If the T'ang were to hear...'

'I understand.'

'Good. Then get on home, Kao Chen. You'll want to be with Wang Ti and the children, neh?' Karr smiled. 'And don't go worrying. Wang Ti will be fine. I'll keep an eye on her while you're gone.'

Chen stood, smiling. 'I am grateful. That will ease my mind greatly.'

'Good. Oh, and before you go... what did you find out down there? Who had Ywe Hao been meeting?'

Chen reached into his tunic pocket and took out the two framed pictures he had removed from the uncle's apartment: the portraits of Ywe Hao's mother with her husband, and that of Ywe Hao with her brother. He looked at them a moment, then handed them across.

Karr stared at the pictures, surprised. 'But they're dead. She told me they were dead.'

Chen sighed. 'The father's dead. The brother too. But the mother is alive, and an uncle. That's who she went to see. Her family.'

Karr stared at them a moment longer, then nodded. 'All right. Get going, then. I'll speak to you later.'

When Chen had gone, Karr got up and went to the prow of the stone boat, staring out across the water at the Stone. He could not save her. No. That had been taken out of his hands. But there was something he could do for her: one small but significant gesture, not to set things right, but to make things better – maybe to give her comfort at the last.

He looked down at the portraits one last time, then let them fall into the water, smiling, knowing what to do.

★

Li Yuan looked about him at the empty stalls, sniffing the warm darkness. On whim, he had summoned the Steward of the Eastern Palace and had him bring the keys, then had gone inside, alone, conscious that he had not been here since the day he had killed the horses.

Though the stalls had been cleaned and disinfected, the tiled floors cleared of straw, the scent of horses was strong; was in each brick and tile and wooden strut of the ancient building. And if he closed his eyes...

If he closed his eyes... He shivered and looked about him again, seeing how the moonlight silvered the huge square of the entrance; how it lay like a glistening layer of dew on the end posts of the stalls.

'I must have horses...' he said softly, speaking to himself. 'I must ride again and go hawking. I have kept too much to my office. I had forgotten...'

Forgotten what?

How to live, came the answer. *You sent her away, yet still she holds you back. You must break the chain, Li Yuan. You must learn to forget her. You have wives, Li Yuan – good wives. And soon you will have children.*

He nodded, then went across quickly, standing in the doorway, holding on to the great wooden upright, looking up at the moon.

The moon was high and almost full. As he watched, a ragged wisp of cloud drifted like a net across its surface. He laughed, surprised by the sudden joy he felt, and looked to the north-east, towards Wang Sau-leyan's palace at Tao Yuan, fifteen hundred li in the distance.

'Who hates you more than I, cousin Wang? Who hates you enough to send your brother's ghost to haunt you?'

And was it that which had brought this sudden feeling of well-being? No, for the mood seemed unconnected to event – was a sea change, like the sunlight on the waters after the violence of the storm.

He went out on to the gravelled parade ground and turned full circle, his arms out, his eyes closed, remembering. It had been the morning of his twelfth birthday and his father had summoned all the servants. If he closed his eyes he could see it; could see his father standing there, tall and imperious, the grooms lined up before the doors, the Chief Groom, Hung Feng-chan, steadying the horse and offering him the halter.

He stopped, getting back his breath. Had that happened? Had that been him that morning, refusing to mount the horse his father had given him, claiming his brother's horse instead? He nodded slowly. Yes, it had.

He walked on, stopping where the path fell away beneath the high wall of the East Gardens, looking out towards the hills and the ruined temple, remembering.

For so long now he had held it all back, afraid. But there was nothing to be afraid of. Only ghosts. And he could live with those.

A figure appeared on the balcony of the East Gardens, above him and to his left. He turned, looking up. It was his First Wife, Mien Shan. He went across and climbed the steps, meeting her at the top.

'Forgive me, my lord,' she began, bowing her head low, the picture of obedience. 'You were gone so long. I thought...'

He smiled and reached out, taking her hands. 'I had not forgotten, Mien Shan. It was just that it was such a perfect night I thought I would walk beneath the moon. Come, join me.'

For a time they walked in silence, following the fragrant pathways, holding hands beneath the moon. Then, suddenly, he turned, facing her, drawing her close. She was so small, so daintily made, the scent of her so sweet that it stirred his blood. He kissed her, crushing her body against his own, then lifted her, laughing at her tiny cry of surprise.

'Come, my wife,' he said, smiling down into her face, seeing how two tiny moons floated in the darkness of her eyes. 'I have been away from your bed too long. Tonight we will make up for that, neh? And tomorrow... Tomorrow we shall buy horses for the stables.'

The morph stood at the entrance to the cave, looking out across the moon-lit plain below. The flicker of torches, scattered here and there across the darkened fields, betrayed the positions of the search parties. All day it had watched them, as they had criss-crossed the great plain, scouring every last copse and stream on the estate. They would be tired now and hungry. If it amplified its hearing it could make out their voices, small and distant on the wind – the throaty encouragement of a sergeant or the muttered complaints of a guard.

It turned, focusing on the foothills just below where it stood. Down there among the rocks, less than a li away, a six-man party was searching the lower slopes, scanning the network of caves with heat-tracing devices. But they would find nothing. Nothing but the odd fox or rabbit, that was.

For the morph was cold, almost as cold as the rocks surrounding it, its body heat shielded beneath thick layers of insulating flesh.

In the centre of the plain, some thirty li distant, was the palace of Tao Yuan. Extending its vision, it looked, searching, sharpening its focus until it found what it was looking for – the figure of the Chancellor, there in the south garden, crouched over a map table in the flickering half-light of a brazier, surrounded by his men.

'Keep looking, Hung Mien-lo,' it said quietly, coldly amused by all this activity. 'For your master will not sleep until I'm found.'

No, and that would suit its purpose well. For it was not here to hurt Wang Sau-leyan but to engage his imagination, like a seed, planted in the soft earth of the young T'ang's mind. It nodded to himself, remembering DeVore's final words to it on Mars.

You are the first stone, Tuan Wen-ch'ang. The first in a whole new game. And whilst it may be months, years even, before I play again in that part of the board, you are nonetheless crucial to my scheme, for you are the stone within, placed deep inside my opponent's territory – a single white stone, embedded in the darkness of his skull, shining like a tiny moon.

It was true. He was a stone, a dragon's tooth, a seed. And in time the seed would germinate and grow, sprouting dark tendrils in the young T'ang's head. And then, when it was time...

The morph turned, its tautly muscled skin glistening in the silvered light, the smooth dome of its near-featureless head tilted back, its pale eyes searching for handholds, as it began to climb.

CHUNG KUO

Chapter 75

WHITE MOUNTAIN

The rocket came down at Nairobi, on a strip dominated by the surrounding mountains. It was late afternoon, but the air was dry and unbearably hot after the coolness of the ship. Chen stood there a moment, then made hurriedly for the shelter of the buildings a hundred ch'i off. He made it, gasping from the effort, his shirt soaked with sweat.

'Welcome to Africa!' one of the guards said, then laughed, taking Chen's ID.

They took a skimmer south-east, over the old, deserted town, heading for Kibwezi. Chen stared out through one of the skimmer's side windows. Below him was a rugged wilderness of green and brown, stretching to the horizon in every direction. Huge bodies of rock thrust up from the plain, their sides creased and ancient-looking, like the flanks of giant, slumbering beasts. He shivered and took a deep breath. It was all so raw. He had been expecting something like the Plantations. Something neat and ordered. He had not imagined it would be so primitive.

Kibwezi Station was a collection of low buildings surrounded by a high wire fence, guard towers standing like machine-sentinels at each corner. The skimmer came in low over the central complex and dropped on to a small, hexagonal landing pad. Beside the pad was an incongruous-looking building; a long, old-fashioned construction made of wood, with a high, steeply sloping roof. Two men stood on the verandah, watching the skimmer land. As it settled one of them came down the open, slatted steps and out on to the pad; a slightly built *Hung Mao* in his late twenties. As Chen stepped down, the man moved between the guards and took his pack, offering a hand.

'Welcome to Kibwezi, Tong Chou. I'm Michael Drake. I'll be showing you the ropes. But come inside. This damned heat...'

Chen nodded, looking around him at the low, featureless buildings. Then he saw it. 'Kuan Yin!' he said, moving out of the skimmer's shadow. 'What's that?'

Drake came and stood beside him. 'Kilimanjaro, they call it. The White Mountain.'

Chen stared out across the distance. Beyond the fence the land fell away. In the late afternoon it seemed filled with blue, like a sea. Thick mist obscured much of it, but from the mist rose up a giant shape of blue and white, flat-topped and massive. It rose up and up above that mist, higher than anything Chen had ever seen. Higher, it seemed, than the City itself. Chen wiped at his brow with the back of his hand and swore.

Drake smiled and touched his arm familiarly. 'Anyway, come. It's far too hot to be standing out here.'

Inside, Chen squinted into shadow, then made out the second man, seated behind a desk at the far end.

'Come in, Tong Chou. Your appointment came as something of a surprise – we're usually given much more notice – but you're welcome all the same. So... take a seat. What's your poison?'

'My... ?' Then he understood. 'Just a beer, if you have one. Thanks.' He crossed the room and sat in the chair nearest the desk, feeling suddenly disoriented, adrift from normality.

There was a window behind the desk, but like all the windows in the room it had a blind, and the blind was pulled down. The room was chill after the outside, the low hum of the air-conditioning the only background noise. The man leaned forward, motioning to Drake to bring the drink, then switched on the old-fashioned desk lamp.

'Let me introduce myself. My name is Laslo Debrenceni and I'm Acting Administrator of Kibwezi Station.'

The man half rose from his chair, extending his hand.

Debrenceni was a tall, broad-shouldered *Hung Mao* in his late forties, a few strands of thin blond hair combed ineffectually across his sun-bronzed pate.

He had a wide, pleasant mouth and soft green eyes above a straight nose.

Drake returned with the drinks, handing Chen a tall glass beaded with chill drops of water. Chen raised his glass in a toast, then took a long sip, feeling refreshed.

'Good,' said Debrenceni, as if he had said something. 'The first thing to do is get you acclimatized. You're used to the City. To corridors and levels and the regular patterning of each day. But here... well, things are different.' He smiled enigmatically. 'Very different.'

The White Mountain filled the sky. As the skimmer came closer it seemed to rise from the very bowels of the earth and tower over them. Chen pressed forward, staring up through the cockpit's glass, looking for the summit, but the rock went up and up, climbing out of sight.

'How big is it?' he asked, whispering, awed by the great mass of rock.

Drake looked up from the controls and laughed. 'About twelve li at the summit, but the plateau is less... no more than ten. There are actually two craters – Kebo and Mawensi. The whole thing is some five li across at the top, filled with glaciers and ice sheets.'

'Glaciers?' Chen had never heard the term before.

'A river of ice – real ice, I mean, not plastic. It rests on top like the icing on some monstrous cake.' He looked down at the controls again. 'You can see it from up to four hundred li away. If you'd known it was here you could have seen it from Nairobi.'

Chen looked out, watching the mountain grow. They were above its lower slopes now, the vast fists of rock below them like speckles on the flank of the sleeping mountain.

'How old is it?'

'Old,' said Drake, softer than before, as if the sheer scale of the mountain was affecting him too. 'It was formed long before Mankind came along. Our distant ancestors probably looked at it from the plains and wondered what it was.'

Chen narrowed his eyes.

'We'll need breathing apparatus when we're up there,' Drake continued. 'The air's thin and it's best to take no chances when you're used to air-conditioning and corridors.'

Again there was that faint but good-natured mockery in Drake's voice that seemed to say, You'll find out, boy, it's different out here.

Masked, Chen stood in the crater of Kebo, looking across the dark throat of the inner crater towards the crater wall and, beyond it, the high cliffs and terraces of the northern glacier. No, he thought, looking out at it, not a river but a city. A vast, tiered city of ice, gleaming in the midday sun.

He had seen wonders enough already: perfect, delicate flowers of ice in the deeply shadowed caves beneath the shattered rocks at the crater's rim, and the yellowed, steaming mouths of fumeroles, rank-smelling crystals of yellow sulphur clustered obscenely about each vent. In one place he had come upon fresh snow, formed by the action of wind and cold into strange fields of knee-high and razor-sharp fronds. *Neige penitant*, Drake had called it. *Snow in prayer.* He had stood on the inner crater's edge, staring down into its ashen mouth, four hundred *ch'i* deep, and tried to imagine the forces that had formed this vast, unnatural edifice. And failed. He had seen wonders, all right, but this, this over-towering wall of ice, impressed him most.

'Five more minutes and we'd best get back,' Drake said, coming over and standing next to him. 'There's more to show you, but it'll have to wait. There are some things back at Kibwezi you need to see first. This...' he raised an arm, indicating the vastness of the mountain '... is an exercise in perspective, if you like. It makes the rest easier. Much easier.'

Chen stared at him, not understanding. But there was a look in the other's masked face that suggested discomfort, maybe even pain.

'If you ever need to, come here. Sit a while and think. Then go back to things.' Drake turned, staring off into the hazed distance. 'It helps. I know. I've done it myself a few times now.'

Chen was silent a while, watching him. Then, as if he had suddenly tired of the place, he reached out and touched Drake's arm. 'Okay. Let's get back.'

The guards entered first. A moment later two servants entered the cell, carrying a tall-backed sedan chair and its occupant. Four others – young Han dressed in the blue of officialdom – followed, the strong, acridly sweet scent of their perfume filling the cell.

The sedan was set down on the far side of the room, a dozen paces from where Ywe Hao sat, her wrists and ankles bound.

She leaned forward slightly, tensed. From his dress – from the cut of his robes and the elaborate design on his chest patch – she could tell this was a high official. And from his manner – from the brutal elegance of his deportment – she could guess which Ministry he represented. The T'ing Wei, the Superintendency of Trials.

'I am Yen T'ung,' the official said, not looking at her, 'Third Secretary to the Minister, and I am here to give judgment on your case.'

She caught her breath, surprised by the suddenness of his announcement, then gave the smallest nod, her head suddenly clear of all illusions. They had decided her fate already, in her absence. That was what Mach had warned her to expect. It was just that that business with Karr – his kindness and the show of respect he had made to her – had muddied the clear waters of her understanding. But now she knew. It was War. Them and us. And no possibility of compromise. She had known that since her brother's death. Since that day at the hearing when the overseer had been cleared of all blame, after all that had been said.

She lifted her head, studying the official, noting how he held a silk before his nose, how his lips formed the faintest moue of distaste.

The Third Secretary snapped his fingers. At once one of the four young men produced a scroll. Yen T'ung took it and unfurled it with a flourish. Then, looking at her for the first time, he began to read.

'I, Ywe Hao, hereby confess that on the seventh day of June in the year two thousand two hundred and eight I did, with full knowledge of my actions, murder the honourable Shou Chen-hai, *Hsien L'ing* to his most high eminence, Li Yuan, Grand Counsellor and T'ang of City Europe. Further, I confess that on the ninth day of the same month I was responsible for the raid on the Dragonfly Club and the subsequent murder of the following innocent citizens...'

She closed her eyes, listening to the list of names, seeing their faces vividly once more, the fear or resignation in their eyes as they had stood before her, naked and trembling. And, for the first time since that evening, she felt the smallest twinge of pity for them – of sympathy for their suffering in those final moments.

The list finished, Yen T'ung paused. She looked up and found his eyes were on her; eyes that were cruel and strangely hard in that soft face.

'Furthermore,' he continued, speaking the words without looking at the scroll, 'I, Ywe Hao, daughter of Ywe Kai-chang and Ywe Sha...'

She felt her stomach fall away. Her parents... Kuan Yin! How had they found that out?

'... confess also to the charge of belonging to an illegal organization and to plotting the downfall of his most high eminence—'

She stood, shouting back at him. 'This is a lie! I have confessed nothing!'

The guards dragged her down on to the stool again. Across from her Yen T'ung stared at her as one might stare at an insect, with an expression of profound disgust.

'What you have to say has no significance here. You are here only to listen to your confession and to sign it when I have done.'

She laughed. 'You are a liar, Yen T'ung, in the pay of liars, and nothing in heaven or earth could induce me to sign your piece of paper.'

There was a flash of anger in his eyes. He raised a hand irritably. At the signal one of his young men crossed the room and slapped her across the face, once, then again; stinging blows that brought tears to her eyes. With a bow to his master, the man retreated behind the sedan.

Yen T'ung sat back slightly, taking a deep breath. 'Good. Now you will be quiet, woman. If you utter another word I will have you gagged.'

She glared back at him, forcing her anger to be pure, to be the perfect expression of her defiance. But he had yet to finish.

'Besides,' he said softly, 'there is no real need for you to sign.'

He turned the document, letting her see. There at the foot of it was her signature – or, at least, a perfect copy of it.

'So now you understand. You must confess and we must read your confession back to you, and then you must sign it. That is the law. And now all that is done, and you, Ywe Hao, no longer exist. Likewise your family. All data has been erased from the official record.'

She stared back at him, gripped by a sudden numbness. Her mother... they had killed her mother. She could see it in his face.

In a kind of daze she watched them lift the chair and carry the official from the room.

'You bastard!' she cried out, her voice filled with pain. 'She knew nothing!'

The door slammed.

Nothing...

'Come,' one of the guards said softly, almost gently. 'It's time.'

Outside was heat – fifty *ch'i* of heat. Through a gate in the wire fencing, a flight of a dozen shallow steps led down into the bunkers. There the icy coolness was a shock after the thirty-eight degrees outside. Stepping inside was like momentarily losing vision. Chen stopped there, just inside the doorway, his heart pounding from exertion, waiting for his vision to normalize, then moved on slowly, conscious of the echo of his footsteps on the hard concrete floor. He looked about him at the bareness of the walls, the plain unpainted metal doors, and frowned. Bracket lights on the long, low-ceilinged walls gleamed dimly, barely illuminating the intense shadow. His first impression was that the place was empty, but that, like the loss of vision, was only momentary. A floor below – through a dark, circular hole cut into the floor – were the cells. Down there were kept a thousand prisoners, fifty to a cell, each shackled to the floor at wrist and ankle, the shortness of the chains making them crouch on all fours like animals.

It was Chen's first time below. Drake stood beside him, silent, letting him judge things for himself. The cells were simple divisions of the open-plan floor – no walls, only lines of bars, each partitioned space reached by a door of bars set into the line. All was visible at a glance, all the misery and degradation of these thin and naked people. And that, perhaps, was the worst of it – the openness, the appalling openness. Two lines of cells, one to the left and one to the right. And between, not recognized until he came to them, were the hydrants. To hose down the cells and swill the excrement and blood, the piss and vomit, down the huge, grated drains that were central to the floor of each cell.

Chen looked on, mute, appalled, then turned to face Drake. But Drake had changed. Or, rather, Drake's face had changed; had grown harder, more brutish, as if in coming here he had cast off the social mask he wore above, to reveal his true face; an older, darker, more barbaric face.

Chen moved on, willing himself to walk, not to stop or turn back. He turned his head, looking from side to side as he walked down the line of cells, seeing how the prisoners backed away – as far as their chains allowed. Not knowing him, yet fearing him. Knowing him for a guard.

At the end he turned and went to the nearest cell, standing at the bars and staring into the gloom, grimacing with the pain and horror he was feeling. He had thought at first there were only men, but there were women too, their limbs painfully emaciated, their stomachs swollen, signs of torture and beatings marking every one of them. Most were shaven-headed. Some slouched or simply lay there, clearly hurt, but from none came even the slightest whimper of sound. It was as if the very power to complain, to cry out in anguish against what was being done to them, had been taken from them.

He had never seen... never imagined...

Shuddering, he turned away, but they were everywhere he looked, their pale, uncomplaining eyes watching him. His eyes looked for Drake and found him there, at the far end.

'Is...?' he began, then laughed strangely and grew quiet. But the question remained close to his tongue and he found he had to ask it, whether these thousand witnesses heard him or not. 'Is this what we do?'

Drake came closer. 'Yes,' he said softly. 'This is what we do. What we're contracted to do.'

Chen shivered violently, looking about him, freshly appalled by the passive suffering of the prisoners; by the incomprehensible acceptance in every wasted face. 'I don't understand,' he said, after a moment. 'What are we trying to do here?'

His voice betrayed the true depth of his bewilderment. He was suddenly a child again, innocent, stripped bare before the sheer horror of it.

'I'm sorry,' Drake said, coming closer. His face was less brutish now, almost compassionate; but his compassion did not extend beyond Chen. 'There's no other way. You have to come down here and see it for yourself. What you're feeling now... we've all felt that. Deep down we still do. But you have to have that first shock. It's... necessary.'

'Necessary?' Chen laughed, but the sound seemed inappropriate. It died in his throat. He felt sick, unclean.

'Yes. And afterwards... once it's sunk in... we can begin to explain it all. And then you'll see.'

But Chen didn't see. He looked at Drake afresh, as if he had never seen him before that moment, and began to edge round him, towards the steps and the clean, abrasive heat outside, and when Drake reached out to touch his arm, he backed away, as if the hand that reached for him were something alien and unclean.

'This is vile. It's...'

But there wasn't a word for it. He turned and ran, back up the steps and out – out through icy coolness to the blistering heat.

It was late night. A single lamp burned in the long, wood-walled room. Chen sat in a low chair across from Debrenceni, silent, listening, the drink in his hand untouched.

'They're dead. Officially, that is. In the records they've already been executed. But here we find a use for them. Test out a few theories.' He cleared his throat. 'We've been doing it for years, actually. At first it was all quite unofficial. Back in the days when Berdichev ran things there was a much greater need to be discreet about these things. But now...'

Debrenceni shrugged, then reached out to take the wine jug and refill his cup. There was a dreadful irony in his voice – a sense of profound mistrust in the words even as he offered them. He sipped at his cup then sat back again, his pale green eyes resting on Chen's face.

'We could say no, of course. Break contract and find ourselves dumped one morning in the Net, brain-wiped and helpless. That's one option. The moral option, you might call it. But it's not much of a choice. We do it because we must. Because our "side" demands that someone does it, and we've been given the short straw. Those we deal with here are murderers, of course – though I've found that that doesn't help when you're thinking about it. After all, what are we? I guess the point is that they started it. They *began* the killing. As for us, well, I guess we're merely finishing what they began.'

He sighed. 'Look, you'll find a dozen rationalizations while you're here. A hundred different ways of evading things and lying to yourself. But trust to your first instinct, your first response. Never – whatever you do – question that. Your first response was the right one. The natural one. It's what we've grown used to here that's unnatural. It may *seem* natural after a while, but it isn't. Remember that in the weeks to come.'

'I see.'

'Some forget,' Debrenceni said, leaning forward, his voice lowered. 'Some even *enjoy* it.'

Chen breathed in deeply. 'Like Drake, you mean?'

'No. There you're wrong. Michael feels it greatly, more than any of us, perhaps. I've often wondered how he's managed to stand it. The mountain helps, of course. It helps us all. Somewhere to go. Somewhere to sit and think things through, *above* the world and all its pettiness.'

Chen gave the barest nod. 'Who are they? The prisoners, I mean. Where do they come from?'

Debrenceni smiled. 'I thought you understood. They're terrorists. Hot-heads and troublemakers. This is where they send them now. All of the State's enemies.'

Kibwezi Station was larger than Chen had first imagined. It stretched back beneath the surface boundary of the perimeter fence and deep into the earth, layer beneath layer. Dark cells lay next to stark-lit, cluttered rooms, while bare, low-ceilinged spaces led through to crowded guard rooms, banked high with monitor screens and the red and green flicker of trace lights. All was linked somehow, interlaced by a labyrinth of narrow corridors and winding stairwells. At first it had seemed very different from the City, a place that made that greater world of levels seem spacious – open-ended – by comparison, and yet, in its condensation and contrasts, it was very much a distillation of the City. At the lowest level were the laboratories and operating theatres – the 'dark heart of things', as Drake called it, with that sharp, abrasive laugh that was already grating on Chen's nerves. The sound of a dark, uneasy humour.

It was Chen's first shift in the theatres. Gowned and masked, he stood beneath the glare of the operating lights and waited, not quite knowing what to expect, watching the tall figure of Debrenceni washing his hands at the sink. After a while two others came in and nodded to him, crossing the room to wash up before they began. Then, when all were masked and ready, Debrenceni turned and nodded to the ceiling camera. A moment later two of the guards wheeled in a trolley.

The prisoner was strapped tightly to the trolley, his body covered with a simple green cloth, only his shaved head showing. From where Chen stood he could see nothing of the man's features, only the transparency of the flesh, the tight knit of the skull's plates in the harsh overhead light. Then, with a small jerk of realization that transcended the horrifying unreality he had been experiencing since coming into the room, he saw that the man was still conscious. The head turned slightly, as if to try to see what was behind it. There was a momentary glint of brightness, of a moist, penetratingly blue eye, straining to see, then the neck muscles relaxed and the head lay still, kept in place by the bands that formed a kind of brace about it.

Chen watched as one of the others leaned across and tightened the bands, bringing one loose-hanging strap across the mouth and tying it, then fastening a second across the brow, so that the head was held rigid. Satisfied, the man worked his way round the body, tightening each of the bonds, making sure there would be no movement once things began.

Dry-mouthed, Chen looked at Debrenceni and saw that he too was busy, methodically laying out his scalpels on a white cloth. Finished, the Administrator looked up and, smiling with his eyes, indicated that he was ready.

For a moment the sheer unreality of what was happening threatened to overwhelm Chen. His whole body felt cold and his blood seemed to pulse strongly in his head and hands. Then, with a small, embarrassed laugh, he saw what he had not noticed before. It was not a man. The prisoner on the trolley was a woman.

Debrenceni worked swiftly, confidently, inserting the needle at four different points in the skull and pushing in a small amount of local anaesthetic. Then, with a deftness Chen had not imagined him capable of, Debrenceni began to cut into the skull, using a hot-wire drill to sink down through the bone. The pale, long hands moved delicately, almost tenderly over the woman's naked skull, seeking and finding the exact points where he would open the flesh and drill down towards the softer tissues beneath. Chen stood at the head of the trolley, watching everything, seeing how one of the assistants mopped and staunched the bleeding while the other passed the instruments. It was all so skilful and so gentle. And then it was done, the twelve slender filaments in place, ready for attachment.

Debrenceni studied the skull a moment, his fingers checking his own work. Then he nodded and, taking a spray from the cloth, coated the skull with a thin, almost plastic layer that glistened wetly under the harsh light. It had the sweet, unexpected scent of some exotic fruit.

Chen came round and looked into the woman's face. She had been quiet throughout and had made little movement, even when the tiny, hand-held drill let out its high, nerve-tormenting whine. He had expected screams, the outward signs of struggle, but there had been nothing; only her stillness, and that unnerving silence.

Her eyes were open. As he leant over her, her eyes met his and the pupils dilated, focusing on him. He jerked his head back, shocked after all to find her conscious and undrugged, and looked across at Debrenceni, not understanding.

They had drilled into her skull...

He watched, suddenly frightened. None of this added up. Her reactions were wrong. As they fitted the spiderish helmet, connecting its filaments to those now sprouting from the pale, scarred field of her skull, his mind feverishly sought its own connections. He glanced down at her hands and saw, for the first time, how they were twitching, as if in response to some internal stimulus. For a moment it seemed to mean something – to *suggest* something – then it slipped away, leaving only a sense of wrongness, of things not connecting properly.

When the helmet was in place, Debrenceni had them lower the height of the trolley and sit the woman up, adjusting the frame and cushions to accommodate her new position. In doing this the cover slipped down, exposing the paleness of her shoulders and arms, her small firm breasts, the smoothness of her stomach. She had a young body. Her face, in contrast, seemed old and abstract, the legs of the metal spider forming a cage about it.

Chen stared at her, as if seeing her anew. Before he had been viewing her only in the abstract. Now he saw how frail and vulnerable she was; how individual and particular her flesh. But there was something more – something that made him turn from the sight of her, embarrassed. He had been aroused. Just looking at her he had felt a strong, immediate response. He felt ashamed, but the fact was there and, turned from her, he faced it. Her helpless exposure had made him want her. Not casually or coldly, but with a sudden fierceness that had caught him off guard.

Beneath his pity for her was desire. Even now it made him want to turn and look at her – to feast his eyes on her helpless nakedness. He shuddered, loathing himself. It was hideous; more so for being so unexpected, so incontestable.

When he turned back his eyes avoided the woman. But Debrenceni had seen. He was watching Chen pensively, the mask pulled down from his face. His eyes met Chen's squarely, unflinchingly.

'They say a job like this dehumanizes the people who do it, Tong Chou. But you'll learn otherwise. I can see it in you now, as I've seen it in others who've come here. Piece by piece it comes back to us. What we *really* are. Not the ideal but the reality. The full, human reality of what we are. Animals that think.'

Chen looked away, hurt – inexplicably hurt. Not knowing why. As if even Debrenceni's understanding were suddenly too much to bear. And, for the second time since his arrival, he found himself stumbling out into the corridor, away from something that, even as he fled it, he knew he could not escape.

Up above, day had turned to night. It was warm and damp and a full moon bathed the open space between the complex and the huts with a rich, silvery light. In the distance the dark shadow of Kilimanjaro dominated the sky-line, an intense black against the velvet blue.

Debrenceni stood there, taking deep breaths of the warm, invigorating air. The moonlight seemed to shroud him in silver and for the briefest moment he seemed insubstantial, like a projection cast against a pure black backcloth. Chen made to put out his hand, then drew it back, feeling foolish.

Debrenceni's voice floated across to him. 'You should have stayed. You would have found it interesting. It's not an operation I've done that often and this one went very well. You see, I was wiring her.'

Chen frowned. Many of the senior officers in Security were wired – adapted for linking-up to a comset – or, like Tolonen, had special slots surgically implanted behind their ears so that tapes could be direct-inputted. But this had been different.

Debrenceni saw the doubt in Chen's face and laughed. 'Oh, it's nothing so crude as the usual stuff. No, this is the next evolutionary step. A pretty obvious one, but one that – for equally obvious reasons – we've not taken before now. This kind of wiring needs no input connections. It uses a pulsed signal. That means the connection can be made at a distance. All you need is the correct access code.'

'But that sounds...' Chen stopped. He had been about to say that it sounded an excellent idea, but some of its ramifications had struck him. The existence of a direct-input connection gave the subject a choice. They could plug in or not. Without that there was no choice. He – or she – became merely another machine, the control of which was effectively placed in the hands of someone else.

He shivered. So *that* was what they were doing here. That was why they were working on sentenced prisoners and not on volunteers. He looked back at Debrenceni, aghast.

'Good,' Debrenceni said, yet he seemed genuinely pained by Chen's realization.

Chen looked down, suddenly tired of the charade, wishing he could tell Debrenceni who he really was and why he was there; angry that he should be made a party to this vileness. For a moment his anger extended even to Karr for sending him in, knowing nothing; for making him have to feel his way out of this labyrinth of half-guessed truths. Then, with a tiny shudder, he shut it out.

Debrenceni turned, facing Chen fully. Moonlight silvered his skull, reduced his face to a mask of dark and light. 'An idea has two faces. One acceptable, the other not. Here we experiment not only on perfecting the wiring technique but on making the idea of it acceptable.'

'And once you've perfected things?' Chen asked, a tightness forming at the pit of his stomach.

Debrenceni stared back at him a moment, then turned away, his moonlit outline stark against the distant mountain's shape. But he was silent. And Chen, watching him, felt suddenly alone and fearful and very, very small.

Chen watched them being led in between the guards; three men and two women, loosely shackled to each other with lengths of fine chain, their clothes unwashed, their heads unshaven.

She was there, of course, hanging back between the first two males, her head turned from him, her eyes downcast.

Drake took the clipboard from the guard and flicked through the flimsy sheets, barely glancing at them. Then, with a satisfied nod, he came across, handing the board to Chen.

'The names are false. As for the rest, there's probably nothing we can use. Security still think it's possible to extract factual material from situations of duress, but we know better. Hurt a man and he'll confess to anything. But it doesn't really matter. We're not really interested in who they were or what they did. That's all in the past.'

Chen grunted, then looked up from the clipboard, seeing how the prisoners were watching him, as if, by handing him the board, Drake had established him as the man in charge. He handed the clipboard back and took a step closer to the prisoners. At once the guards moved forward, raising their guns, as if to intercede, but their presence did little to reassure him. It wasn't that he was afraid – he had been in far more dangerous situations, many a time – yet he had never had to face such violent hatred, such open hostility. He could feel it emanating from the five. Could see it burning in their eyes. And yet they had never met him before this moment.

'Which one first?' Drake asked, coming alongside.

Chen hesitated. 'The girl,' he said finally. 'The one who calls herself Chi Li.'

His voice was strong, resonant. The very sound of it gave him sudden confidence. He saw at once how his outward calm, the very tone of his voice, impressed them. There was fear and respect behind their hatred now. He turned away, as if he had done with them.

He heard the guards unshackle the girl and pull her away. There were murmurs of protest and the sounds of a brief struggle, but when Chen turned back she was standing away from the others, at the far end of the cell.

'Good,' he said. 'I'll see the others later.'

The others were led out, a single guard remaining inside the cell, his back to the door.

He studied the girl. Without her chains she seemed less defiant. More vulnerable. As if sensing his thoughts, she straightened up, facing him squarely.

'Try anything and I'll break both your legs,' he said, seeing how her eyes moved to assess how things stood. 'No one can help you now but yourself. Cooperate and things will be fine. Fight us and we'll destroy you.'

The words were glib – were the words Drake had taught him to say in this situation – but they sounded strangely sinister now that things were real. Rehearsing them, he had thought them stagey, melodramatic, like something out of an old Han opera, but now, alone with the prisoner, they had a potency that chilled him as he said them. He saw the effect they had on her. Saw the hesitation as she tensed and then relaxed. He wanted to smile, but didn't. Karr was right. She was an attractive woman, even with that damage to her face. Her very toughness had a beauty to it.

'What do you want to do?' Drake asked.

Chen took a step closer. 'We'll just talk for now.'

The girl was watching him uncertainly. She had been beaten badly. There were bruises on her arms and face, unhealed cuts on the left side of her neck. Chen felt a sudden anger. All this had been done since she'd been released to SimFic. Moreover, there was a tightness about her mouth that suggested she had been raped. He shivered, then spoke the words that had come into his head.

'Have they told you that you're dead?'

Behind him Drake drew in a breath. The line was impromptu. Was not scripted for this first interview.

The girl looked down, smiling, but when she looked up again Chen was still watching her, his face unchanged.

'Did you think this was just another Security cell?' he asked, harsher now, angry, his anger directed suddenly at her – at the childlike vulnerability beneath her outward strength; at the simple fact that she was there, forcing him to do this to her.

The girl shrugged, saying nothing, but Chen could see the sweat beading her brow. He took a step closer; close enough for her to hit out at him, if she dared.

'We do things here. Strange things. We take you apart and put you back together again. But different.'

She was staring at him now, curiosity getting the better of her. His voice was calm, matter-of-fact, as if what he was saying to her was quite ordinary, but the words were horrible in their implication and the very normality of his voice seemed cruel.

'Stop it,' she said softly. 'Just do what you're going to do.'

Her eyes pleaded with him, like the hurt eyes of a child; the same expression Ch'iang Hsin sometimes had when he teased her. That similarity – between this stranger and his youngest child – made him pull back; made him realize that his honesty was hurting her. Yet he was here to hurt. That was his job here. Whether he played the role or not, the hurt itself was real.

He turned from her.

Drake was watching him strangely, his eyes half-lidded. *What are you up to?* he seemed to be saying.

Chen met his eyes. 'She'll do.'

Drake frowned. 'But you've not seen the others…'

Chen smiled. '*She'll do.*' He was still smiling when she kicked him in the kidneys.

She was beaten and stripped and thrown into a cell. For five days she languished there, in total darkness. Morning and night a guard would come and check on her, passing her meal through the hatch and taking the old tray away. Otherwise she was left alone. There was no bed, no sink, no pot to crap into, only a metal grill set into one corner of the floor. She used it, reluctantly at first, then with growing indifference. What did it matter, after all? There were worse things in life than having to crap into a hole.

For the first few days she didn't mind. After a lifetime spent in close proximity to people it was something of a relief to be left alone, almost a luxury. But from the third day on it was hard.

On the sixth day they took her from the cell, out into a brightness that made her screw her eyes tight, tiny spears of pain lancing her head. Outside, they hosed her down and disinfected her, then threw her into another cell, shackling her to the floor at wrist and ankle.

She lay there for a time, letting her eyes grow accustomed to the light. After the foetid darkness of the tiny cell she had the sense of space about her, yet when finally she looked up, it was to find herself eye to eye with a naked man. He was crouched on all fours before her, his eyes lit with a feral glint, his penis jutting stiffly from between his legs. She drew back sharply, the sudden movement checked by her chains. And then she saw them.

She looked about her, appalled. There were forty, maybe fifty naked people in the cell with her, men and women both. All were shackled to the floor at wrist and ankle. Some met her eyes, but it was without curiosity, almost without recognition. Others simply lay there, listless. As she watched, one of them raised herself on her haunches and let loose a bright stream of urine, then lay still again, like an animal at rest.

She shuddered. So this was it. This was her fate, her final humiliation, to become like these poor souls. She turned back, looking at her neighbour. He was leaning towards her, grunting, his face brutal with need, straining against his chains, trying to get at her. One hand was clutched about his penis, jerking it back and forth urgently.

'Stop it,' she said softly. 'Please...' But it was as if he was beyond the reach of words. She watched him, horrified; watched his face grow pained, his movements growing more frantic, and then, with a great moan of pain, he came, his semen spurting across the space between them.

She dropped her eyes, her face burning, her heart pounding in her chest. For a moment – for the briefest moment – she had felt herself respond; had felt something in her begin to surface, as if to answer that fierce, animal need in his face.

She lay there, letting her pulse slow, her thoughts grow still, then lifted her head, almost afraid to look at him again. He lay quietly now, no more than two ch'i from her, his shoulders rising and falling gently with each breath. She watched him, feeling immense pity, wondering who he was and what crime he had been sent here for.

For a time he lay still, soft snores revealing he was sleeping, then, with a tiny whimper, he turned slightly, moving on to his side. As he did she saw the brand on his upper arm; saw it and caught her breath, her soul shrivelling up inside her.

It was a fish. A stylized fish.

Chen stood in the doorway to the Mess, looking into the deeply shadowed room. There was the low buzz of conversation, the smell of mild euphorics. Sitting at the bar, alone, a tall glass at his elbow, was Debrenceni. Seeing Chen, he lifted his hand and waved him across.

'How are the kidneys?'

Chen laughed. 'Sore, but no serious damage. She connected badly.'

'I know. I saw it.' Debrenceni was serious a moment longer, then he smiled. 'You did well, despite that. It looked as if you'd been doing the job for years.'

Chen dropped his head. He had been in the sick bay for the last six days, the first two in acute pain.

'What do you want to drink?'

Chen looked up. 'I'd best not.'

'No. Maybe not.' Debrenceni raised his glass, saluting Chen. 'You were right about the girl, though.'

'I know.' He hesitated, then, 'Have you wired her yet?'

'No. Not yet.' Debrenceni sat back a little on his stool, studying him. 'You know, you were lucky she didn't kill you. If the Security forces hadn't worked her over before we'd got her, she probably would have.'

Chen nodded, conscious of the irony. 'What happened to her?'

'Nothing. I thought we'd wait until you got back on duty.'

It was not what Chen had expected. 'You want me to carry on? Even after what happened?'

'No. *Because* of what happened.' Debrenceni laid his hand lightly on Chen's shoulder. 'We see things through here, Tong Chou. To the bitter, ineluctable end.'

'Ineluctable?'

'Ineluctable,' repeated Debrenceni solemnly. 'That from which one cannot escape by struggling.'

'Ah...' In his mind Chen could see the girl and picture the slow working out of her fate. *Ineluctable*. Like the gravity of a black hole or the long, slow process of entropy. Things his son, Jyan, had told him of. He gave a tiny, bitter laugh.

Debrenceni smiled tightly, removing his hand from Chen's shoulder. 'You understand, then?'

'Do I have a choice?'

'No one here has a choice.'

'Then I understand.'

'Good. Then we'll start in the morning. At six sharp. I want you to bring her from the cells. I'll be in the theatre. Understand?'

It was late when Chen returned to his room. He felt frayed and irritable. More than that, he felt ashamed and – for the first time since he'd come to Kibwezi – guilty of some awfulness that would outweigh a lifetime's atonement. He sat heavily on his bed and let his head fall into his hands. Today had been the day. Before now he had been able to distance himself from what had been happening. Even that last time, facing her in the cell, it had not really touched him. It had been something abstract; something happening to someone else – Tong Chou, perhaps – who inhabited his skin. But now he knew. It was himself. No one else had led her there and strapped her down, awaiting surgery. It was no stranger who had looked down at her while they had cut her open and put things in her head.

'That was *me*,' he said, shuddering. 'That was *me* in there.'

He sat up, drawing his feet under him, then shook his head in disbelief. And yet he had to believe. It had been too real – too *personal* – for disbelief.

He swallowed deeply. Drake had warned him. Drake had said it would be like this. One day fine, the next the whole world totally different; like some dark, evil trick played on your eyesight, making you see nothing but death. Well, Drake was right. Now he too could see it. Death. Everywhere death. And he a servant of it.

There was a knocking at the door.

'Go away!'

The knocking came again. Then a voice. 'Tong Chou? Are you all right?'

He turned and lay down, facing the wall. 'Go away...'

Ywe Hao had never run so far, or been so afraid. As she ran she seemed to balance two fears in the pit of her stomach: her fear of what lay behind outweighing her fear of the dark into which she ran. Instinct took her towards the City. Even in the dark she could see its massive shape against the skyline, blotting out the light-scattered velvet backdrop.

It was colder than she had ever thought it could be. And darker. As she ran she whimpered, not daring to look back. When the first light of morning coloured the sky at her back she found herself climbing a gradual slope. Her pace had slowed, but still she feared to stop and rest. At any moment they would discover her absence. Then they would be out, after her.

As the light intensified, she slowed, then stopped and turned, looking back. For a while she stood there, her mouth open. Then, as the coldness, the stark openness of the place struck her, she shuddered violently. It was so open. So appallingly open. Another kind of fear, far greater than anything she had known before, made her take a backward step.

The whole of the distant horizon was on fire. Even as she watched, the sun's edge pushed up into the sky, so vast, so threatening, it took her breath. She turned, away from it, horrified, then saw, in the first light, what lay ahead.

At first the ground rose slowly, scattered with rock. Then it seemed to climb more steeply until, with a suddenness that was every bit as frightening as anything she had so far seen, it ended in a thick, choking veil of whiteness. Her eyes went upward... No, not a veil, a wall. A solid wall of white that seemed soft, almost insubstantial. Again she shuddered, not understanding, a deep-rooted, primitive fear of such things making her crouch into herself. And still her eyes went up until, beyond the wall's upper lip, she saw the massive summit of the shape she had run towards throughout the night. The City...

Again she sensed a wrongness to what she saw. The shape of it seemed... Seemed what? Her arms were making strange little jerking movements and her legs felt weak. Gritting her teeth, she tried to get her mind to work, to triumph over the dark, mindless fear that was washing over her, wave after wave. For a moment she seemed to come to herself again.

What was wrong? What in the gods' names was it?

And then she understood. The shape of it was wrong. The rough, tapered, irregular look of it. Whereas... Again her mouth fell open. But if it wasn't the City... then what in hell's name was it?

For a moment longer she stood there, swaying slightly, caught between two impulses, then, hesitant, glancing back at the growing circle of fire, she began to run again. And as she ran – the dark image of the sun's half-circle stamped across her vision – the wall of mist came down to meet her.

It was just after dawn when the two cruisers lifted from the pad and banked away over the compound, heading north-west, towards the mountain. Chen was in the second craft, Drake at the controls beside him. On Chen's wrist, scarcely bigger than a standard Security field comset, was the tracer unit. He glanced at it, then stared steadily out through the windscreen, watching the grassy plain flicker by fifty ch'i below.

'We're going to kill her, aren't we?'

Drake glanced at him. 'She was dead before she came here. Remember that.'

Chen shook his head. 'That's just words. No, what I mean is that *we* are going to kill *her*. Us. Personally.'

'In a manner of speaking.'

'No. Not in a manner of speaking. This is real. We're going out to kill her. I've been trying not to think about it, but I can't help it. It seems...' He shook his head. 'It's just that some days I can't believe it's me, doing this. I'm a good man. At least, I thought I was.'

Drake was silent, hunched over the controls as if concentrating, but Chen could see he was thinking; chewing over what he'd said.

'So?' Chen prompted.

'So we set down, do our job, get back. That's it.'

Again Chen stared at Drake for a long time, not sure even what he was looking for. Whatever it was, it wasn't there. He looked down at the tiny screen. Below the central glass were two buttons. They looked innocuous enough, but he wasn't sure. Only Drake knew what they were for.

He looked away, holding his tongue. Maybe it was best to see it as Drake saw it. As just another job to be done. But his disquiet remained, and, as the mountain grew larger through the front screen, his sense of unreality grew with it.

It was all so impersonal. As if what they were tracking was a thing, another kind of machine – one that ran. But Chen had seen her close; had looked into her eyes and stared down into her face while Debrenceni had been operating. He had seen just how vulnerable she was.

How human...

He had put on the suit's heater and pulled the helmet visor down – even so, his feet felt like ice and his cheeks were frozen. A cold breeze blew across the mountain now, shredding the mist in places, but generally it was thick, like a flaw in seeing itself.

There was a faint buzz on his headset, then a voice came through. 'It's clearing up here. We can see right up the mountain now, to the summit.'

Chen stared up the slope, as if to penetrate the dense mist, then glanced back at Drake. 'What now?'

Drake nodded distractedly, then spoke into his lip-mike. 'Move to within a hundred *ch'i*. It looks like she's stopped. Gustaffson, you go to the north of where she is. Palmer, come round to the east. Tong Chou and I will take the other points. That way we've got a perfect grid.'

Drake turned, looking up the mountain. 'Okay. Let's give this thing a proper test.'

Chen spoke to Drake's back. 'The trace ought to be built into a visor display. This thing's vulnerable when you're climbing. Clumsy, too.'

'You're right,' Drake answered, beginning to climb. 'It's a bloody nuisance. It should be made part of the standard Security headgear, with direct computer input from a distance.'

'You mean wire the guards, too?'

Drake paused, mist wreathing his figure. 'Why not? That way you could have the coordinator at a distance, out of danger. It would make the team less vulnerable. The runner couldn't get at the head – the brains behind it.'

Halfway up, Drake turned, pointing across. 'Over there. Keep going until you're due south of her. Then wait. I'll tell you what to do.'

Chen went across, moving slowly over the difficult terrain, then stopped, his screen indicating that he was directly south of the trace, approximately a hundred ch'i down. He signalled back, then waited, listening as the others confirmed they were in place. The mist had cleared up where he was and he had eye contact with both Gustaffson and Palmer. There was no sign of the runner.

Drake's voice sounded in his headset. 'You should be clear any minute. We'll start when you are.'

Chen waited, while the mist slowly thinned out around him. Then, quite suddenly, he could see the mountain above him, the twin peaks of Kebo and Mawensi white against the vivid blue of the sky. He shivered, looking across, picking out the others against the slope.

'I see you,' Drake said, before he could say anything. 'Good. Now come up the slope a little way. We'll close to fifty now. Palmer, Gustaffson, you do the same.'

Chen walked forward slowly, conscious of the others as they closed on him. Above him was a steep shelf of bare earth. As he came closer he lost sight, first of Drake, then of the other two.

'I'll have to come up,' he said into his lip-mike. 'I can't see a thing from down here.'

He scrambled up and stood there, on the level ground above the shelf, where the thick grass began. He was only twenty *ch'i* from the trace signal now. The others stood back at fifty, watching him.

'Where is she?' he said, softer than before.

'Exactly where the trace shows she is,' said Drake into his head. 'In that depression just ahead of you.'

He had seen it already, but it looked too shallow to hide a woman.

'Palmer?' It was Drake again. Chen listened. 'I want you to test the left-hand signal on your handset. Turn it slowly to the left.'

Chen waited, watching the shallow pit in front of him. It seemed as if nothing had happened.

'Good,' said Drake. 'Now you, Gustaffson. I want you to press both your controls at the same time. Hold them down firmly for about twenty seconds. Okay?'

This time there was a noise from the depression. A low moaning that increased as the seconds passed. Then it cut off abruptly. Chen shuddered. 'What was that?'

'Just testing,' Drake answered. 'Each of our signals is two-way. They transmit, but they also have a second function. Palmer's cuts off all motor activity in the cortex. Gustaffson's works on what we call the pain gate, stimulating nerves at the stem of the brain.'

'And yours?' asked Chen. He could hear the breathing of the others on the line as they listened in.

'Mine's the subtlest. I can talk to our runner. Directly. Into her head.'

The line went silent. From the depression in front of Chen came a sudden whimper of pure fear. Then Drake was speaking again. 'Okay. You can move the signal back to its starting position. Our runner is ready to come out.'

There was a tense moment of waiting then from the front of the shallow pit a head bobbed up. Wearily, in obvious pain, the woman pulled herself up out of the deep hole at the front lip of the shallow depression. As her head came up and round she looked directly at Chen. For a moment she stood there, swaying, then she collapsed and sat back, pain and tiredness etched in her ravaged face. She looked ragged and exhausted. Her legs and arms were covered in contusions and weeping cuts.

Drake must have spoken to her again, for she jerked visibly and looked round, finding him. Then she looked about her, seeing the others. Her head dropped and for a moment she just sat there, breathing heavily, her arms loose at her sides.

'Okay,' Drake said. 'Let's wrap things up.'

Chen turned and looked across at Drake. In the now brilliant sunlight he seemed a cold and alien figure. His suit, like all of them, was non-reflective. Only the visor sparkled menacingly. Just now he was moving closer in. Twenty ch'i from the woman he stopped. Chen watched as Drake made Palmer test his signal again. As it switched off, the woman fell awkwardly to one side. Then, moments later, she pushed herself up again, looking round, wondering what had happened to her. Then it was Gustaffson's turn. He saw how the woman's face changed, her teeth clamped together, her whole body arching as she kicked out in dreadful pain.

When she sat up again, her face twitched visibly. Something had broken in her. Her eyes, when they looked at him now, seemed lost.

He looked across at Drake, appalled, but Drake was talking to her again. Chen could see his lips moving, then looked back and saw the woman try to cover her ears, a look of pure terror on her face.

Slowly, painfully, she got up and, looking straight at Chen, clambered over the lip and began to make her way towards him, almost hopping now, each touch of her damaged leg against the ground causing her face to buckle in pain. But still she came.

He made to step back, but Drake's voice was suddenly in his headset, on the discreet channel. 'Your turn,' it said. 'Just hold down the left-hand button and touch the right.'

She was less than two body-lengths away from him now, reaching out to him. He looked down at the tiny screen, then held and touched.

The air was filled with a soft, wet sound of exploding matter. As if someone had fired a gun off in the middle of a giant fruit. And there, where the signal had been, there was nothing.

He looked up. The body was already falling, the shoulders and upper chest ruined by the explosion that had taken off the head. He turned away, sickened, but the stench of burned flesh was in his nostrils and gobbets of her ruptured, bloodied flesh were spattered all over his suit and visor. He stumbled and almost went down the steep, bare bank, but stopped there on the edge, swaying, keeping his balance, telling himself quietly that he would not be sick, over and over again.

After a while he turned and, looking past the body, met Drake's eyes. 'You bastard... why did she come at me? What did you say to her?'

Drake pulled off his helmet and threw it down. 'I told her you'd help her,' he said, then laughed strangely. 'And you did. You bloody well did.'

Chapter 76

FLAMES IN A GLASS

'Wang Ti?'

Chen stood just inside the door, surprised to find the apartment in darkness. He put out his hand, searching the wall, then slowly brought up the lights. Things looked normal, everything in its place. He released a breath. For the briefest moment...

He went out into the kitchen and filled the kettle, then plugged it in. As he turned, reaching up to get the *ch'a* pot, he heard a noise. A cough.

He went out, into the brightness of the living room. 'Wang Ti?' he called softly, looking across at the darkened doorway of their bedroom. 'Is that you?'

The cough came again, a strong, racking cough that ended with a tiny moan.

He went across and looked into the room. It was Wang Ti beneath the covers, he could see that at once. But Wang Ti as he had never seen her before, her hair unkempt, her brow beaded with sweat. Wang Ti, who had never suffered a day's illness in her life.

'Wang Ti?'

She moaned, turning her head slightly on the pillow. 'Nmmm...'

He looked about him, conscious that something was missing, but not knowing what. 'Wang Ti?'

Her eyes opened slowly. Seeing him, she moaned and turned away, pulling the sheet up over her head.

'Wang Ti?' he said gently, moving closer. 'Where are the children?'

Her voice was small, muffled by the sheets. 'I sent them below. To Uncle Mai.'

'Ahh...' He crouched down. 'And you, my love?'

She hesitated, then answered in that same small, frightened voice. 'I am fine, husband.'

Something in the way she said it – in the way her determination to be a dutiful, uncomplaining wife faltered before the immensity of her suffering – made him go cold inside. Something had happened.

He pulled back the sheet, studying her face in the half-light. It was almost unrecognizable. Her mouth – a strong mouth, made for laughter – was twisted into a thin-lipped grimace of pain. Her eyes – normally so warm and reassuring – were screwed tightly shut as if to wall-in all the misery she felt, the lids heavy and discoloured. Pained by the sight, he put his fingers to her cheek, wanting to comfort her, then drew them back, surprised. She had been crying.

There was a moment's blankness, then he felt his stomach fall away. 'The child...'

Wang Ti nodded, then buried her face in the pillow, beginning to sob, her body convulsing under the sheets.

He sat on the bed beside her, holding her to him, trying to comfort her, but his mind was in shock. 'No...' he said, after a while. 'You have always been so strong. And the child was well. Surgeon Fan said so.'

She lay there quietly – so quiet that it frightened him. Then it was true. She had lost the child.

'When was this?'

'A week ago.'

'A week! Ai ya!' He sat back, staring sightlessly into the shadows, thinking of her anguish, her suffering, and him not there. 'But why wasn't I told? Why didn't Karr send word? I should have been here.'

She put out a hand, touching his chest. 'He wanted to. He begged me to, but I would not let him. Your job...'

He looked back at her. She was watching him now, her puffed and blood-red eyes filled with pity. The sight of her – of her concern *for him* – made his chest tighten with love. 'Oh, Wang Ti, my little pigeon... what in the gods' names happened?'

She shuddered and looked away again. 'No one came,' she said quietly. 'I waited, but no one came...'

He shook his head. 'But the Surgeon... We paid him specially to come.'

'There were complications,' she said, afraid to meet his eyes. 'I waited. Three hours I waited, but he never came. Jyan tried...'

'Never came?' Chen said, outraged. 'He was notified and never came?'

She gave a tight little nod. 'I got Jyan to run up to the Medical Centre, but no one was free.' She met his eyes briefly, then looked away again, forcing the words out in a tiny, frightened voice. 'Or so they said. But Jyan says that they were sitting there, in a room beyond the reception area, laughing – drinking ch'a and laughing – while my baby was dying.'

Chen felt himself go cold again; but this time it was the coldness of anger. Of intense, almost blinding anger. 'And no one came?'

She shook her head, her face cracking again. He held her tightly, letting her cry in his arms, his own face wet with tears. 'My poor love,' he said. 'My poor, poor love.' But deep inside his anger had hardened into something else – into a cold, clear rage. He could picture them, sitting there, laughing and drinking ch'a while his baby daughter was dying. Could see their well-fed, laughing faces and wanted to smash them, to feel their cheekbones shatter beneath his fist.

And young Jyan... How had it been for him, knowing that his mother was in trouble, his baby sister dying, and he impotent to act? How had that felt? Chen groaned. They had had such hopes. Such plans. How could it all have gone so wrong?

He looked about him at the familiar room, the thought of the dead child an agony, burning in his chest. 'No...' he said softly, shaking his head. 'Nooooo!'

He stood, his fists bunched at his sides. 'I will go and see Surgeon Fan.'

Wang Ti looked up, frightened. 'No, Chen. Please. You will solve nothing that way.'

He shook his head. 'The bastard should have come. It is only two decks down. Three hours... Where could he have been for three hours?'

'Chen ...' She put out a hand, trying to restrain him, but he moved back, away from her.

'No, Wang Ti. Not this time. This time I do it my way.'

'You don't understand...' she began. 'Karr knows everything. He has all the evidence. He was going to meet you...'

She fell silent, seeing that he was no longer listening. His face was set, like the face of a statue.

'He killed my daughter,' he said softly. 'He let her die. And you, Wang Ti... you might have died too.'

She trembled. It was true. She had almost died, forcing the baby from her – no, *would* have died, had Jyan not thought to contact Karr and bring the big man to her aid.

She let her head fall back. Maybe Chen was right. Maybe, this once, it was right to act – to hit back at those who had harmed them, and damn the consequences. Better that, perhaps, than let it fester deep inside. Better that than have him shamed a second time before his son.

She closed her eyes, pained by the memory of all that had happened. It had been awful here without him. Awful beyond belief.

She felt his breath on her cheek, his lips pressed gently to her brow, and shivered.

'I must go,' he said quietly, letting his hand rest softly on her flank. 'You understand?'

She nodded, holding back the tears, wanting to be brave for him this once. But it was hard, and when he was gone she broke down again, sobbing loudly, uncontrollably, the memory of his touch glowing warmly in the darkness.

The room was cold and brightly lit, white tiles on the walls and floor emphasizing the starkness of the place. In the centre of the room was a dissecting table. Beside the table stood the three surgeons who had carried out the post mortem, their heads bowed, waiting.

The corpse on the table was badly burned, the limbs disfigured, the head and upper torso crushed; even so, the body could still be identified as GenSyn. In three separate places the flesh had been peeled back to the bone, revealing the distinctive GenSyn marking – the bright red 'G' forming a not-quite-closed circle with a tiny blue 'S' within.

They had cornered it finally in the caves to the north of the estate. There, Hung Mien-lo and a small group of élite guards had fought it for an hour before a well-aimed grenade had done the trick, silencing the creature's answering fire and bringing the roof of the cave down on top of it. Or so Hung's story went.

Wang Sau-leyan stood there, looking down at the corpse, his eyes taking in everything. Hope warred with cynicism in his face, but when he looked back at his Chancellor, it was with an expression of deep suspicion. 'Are you sure this is it, Hung? The face...'

The face was almost formless. Was the merest suggestion of a face.

'I am told this is how they make some models, *Chieh Hsia*. A certain number are kept for urgent orders, the facial features added at the last moment. I have checked with GenSyn records and discovered that this particular model was made eight years back. It was stolen from their West Asian organzation – from their plant at Karaganda – nearly five years ago.'

Wang looked back at it, then shook his head. 'Even so...'

'Forgive me, *Chieh Hsia*, but we found some other things in the cave.' Hung Mien-lo turned and took a small case from his secretary, then turned back, handing it, opened, to the T'ang. 'This was amongst them.'

Wang Sau-leyan stared down at the face and nodded. It was torn and dirtied and pitted with tiny holes, but it was recognizable all the same. It was his brother's face. Or, at least, a perfect likeness. He set it down on the chest of the corpse.

'So this is how it did it, eh? With a false face and a cold body.'

'Not cold, *Chieh Hsia*. Or not entirely. You see, this model was designed for work in sub-zero temperatures or in the heat of the mines. It has a particularly hard and durable skin that insulates the inner workings of the creature from extremes of heat and cold. That was why it did not register on our cameras. At night they are programmed to respond only to heat patterns, and as this thing did not give off any trace, the cameras were never activated.'

Wang nodded, his mouth gone dry. Even so, he wasn't *quite* convinced. 'And the traces of skin and blood that it left on the stone?'

Hung lowered his head slightly. 'It is our belief, *Chieh Hsia*, that they were put there by the creature. Deliberately, to make us think it really was your brother.'

Wang looked down, then gave a small, sour laugh. 'I would dearly like to think so, Chancellor Hung, but that simply isn't possible. I have checked with GenSyn. They tell me it is impossible to duplicate individual DNA from scratch.'

'From scratch, yes, *Chieh Hsia*. But why should that be the case? All that is needed to duplicate DNA is a single strand of the original. This can even, I am assured, be done from a corpse.'

'And that is what you are suggesting? That someone broke into the tomb before this creature broke out from it again? That they took a piece of my brother's body and used it to duplicate his DNA?'

'That is one possibility, *Chieh Hsia*, but there is another. What if someone close to your brother took a sample of his skin or blood before his death? Took it and kept it?'

Wang shook his head. 'That's absurd. I know my brother was a weakling and a fool, but even he would not sit still and let a servant take a sample of his blood.'

'Again, that is not what I meant, *Chieh Hsia*. What if your brother had a small accident and one of his servants tended to him? And what if that servant kept the materials they used to tend your brother's wound – a piece of bloodied gauze, perhaps, or a bowl with bloodied water?'

'And you think that's what happened?'

Hung nodded. 'That is exactly what happened, *Chieh Hsia*. We have a signed confession.'

'A confession? And how was this confession obtained? By your usual means?'

Hung turned, taking the scroll from his secretary, then handed it across.

'Wu Ming!' Wang laughed with disbelief. 'And is that all the proof you have – Wu Ming's confession?'

Hung Mien-lo shook his head. 'I am afraid not, *Chieh Hsia*. I went back through the household records for details of any small accident to your brother. It seems there were several such incidents over the past five years, but in all but one instance the materials used to tend his wounds were properly incinerated.'

'And that single instance where it was not – that involved Wu Ming, I take it?'

'Yes, *Chieh Hsia*. Wu Ming and one other. The traitor, Sun Li Hua.'

Wang made a noise of surprise. 'This is certain?'

'Absolutely, *Chieh Hsia*. We have a tape of the incident, showing Wu and Sun tending your brother, but no subsequent record of the dressings being destroyed.'

'Ah...' Wang turned, looking down at the corpse again, his fingers reaching out to touch and trace the contours of his brother's face. 'Then it was my cousin's hand behind all this,' he said softly. 'This was Li Yuan's doing.'

'So it seems, *Chieh Hsia*.'

'So it seems...' Yet something still nagged at him. He turned back, facing his Chancellor. 'How long ago did this happen?'

'Two years ago, *Chieh Hsia*.'

'Two years, or almost two years? Be precise, Hung Mien-lo.'

'Twenty-two months, to be exact, *Chieh Hsia*.'

'A month before his death?'

'That is so, *Chieh Hsia*.'

Wang took a deep breath, satisfied. Any earlier and it would have made no sense, for his father would still have been alive, and Li Yuan would have had no motive for his actions. As it was...

He smiled. 'You have done well, Chancellor Hung. You have more than repaid my trust in you. But there are still two things that remain to be answered. First, how did the creature get into the tomb without the cameras seeing it? Second, where is the body of my dead brother?'

Hung Mien-lo bowed low. 'Both questions have troubled me greatly, *Chieh Hsia*, but I think I have the answer.'

Straightening up, he drew something from his pocket and held it out, offering it to his T'ang. It was a small, glassy circle, like the lens cap to a camera.

Wang turned it in his hand, then looked back at his Chancellor. 'What is this?'

'It is an imager, *Chieh Hsia*. Placed over a camera lens, it fixes the image in the camera's eye and maintains it for a predetermined period. After that time, the imager self-destructs – at a molecular level – dispersing in the form of a gas. While it is there, over the lens, you can walk about quite freely before the camera without fear of it registering your presence, and afterwards it leaves no trace.'

'I see. And you think a similar kind of thing – or several of them – were used to mask the cameras about the tomb?'

Hung smiled. 'It would explain how the tomb door was opened without the cameras seeing anything.'

'And my brother's body?'

'Of that there is no sign, *Chieh Hsia*. However, we did find a trace of ashes in a hollow near a stream to the north of the palace. Halfway between here and the foothills.'

'So the creature burned the body?'

Hung gave a slight shrug. 'I am not so sure. If he did, then why did we see no sign of it? It takes a great deal of heat to consume a human body and, from the moment the alarms were sounded, every guard in the palace was on alert for anything suspicious. If the creature *had* burned the body, we would have seen it. So, no, *Chieh Hsia*, I would guess that the ashes were from something else – some small religious ceremony, perhaps. As for the body, I think it is still out there, hidden somewhere.'

Wang considered a moment, then laughed. 'Which is where we shall let it rest, neh? Amongst the rocks and streams, like an exiled Minister.' Again he laughed, fuller, richer laughter now, fed by relief and an ancient, unforgiving malice. He turned, looking down at the corpse and the box holding his brother's face. 'As for these things, have them burned, Chancellor Hung. Outside, before the palace gates, where all can see.'

It was quiet in the lobby of the Medical Centre. As Chen entered, the nurse behind the desk looked up, smiling, but Chen walked straight by, pushing through the gate in the low barrier, heading for where he knew they kept their records.

Someone called out to him as he passed, but Chen ignored them. There was no time for formalities. He wanted to know right now who had killed his child, and why.

Two men looked up from behind their screens as he entered the records room, surprised to see him there. One made to object, then fell silent as he saw the gun.

'I want details of a child mortality,' Chen said, without preamble. 'The name is Kao. K.A.O. A week ago it was. A female child. Newborn. I want the registered time of death, the precise time the call-out enquiry was made at this office, and a duty roster for that evening, complete with duty records for all on the roster.'

The clerks glanced at each other, not sure what to do, but Chen's fierce bark made them jump. He pointed his gun at the most senior of the two.

'Do it. Now! Hard print. And don't even think of fucking me about. If I don't get what I want, I'll put a bullet through your chest.'

Swallowing nervously, the man bowed his head and began to tap details into his comset.

As the printout began to chatter from the machine, there was a noise outside. Chen turned. Three of the orderlies – big, heavily built men – had come to see what was happening. From the way they stood there, blocking the way, it was clear they had no intention of letting him leave.

'Get back to work,' he said quietly. 'This is none of your business.'

He looked back. The younger of the clerks had his fingers on the keys of his machine. Chen shook his head. 'I wouldn't, if I were you...'

The man desisted. A moment later the other machine fell silent.

Chen reached out, taking the printout from the tray. A glance at it confirmed what he had suspected. Jyan had been right. At the time of his daughter's death, no less than four of the medical staff had been free. So why hadn't they answered the emergency call? Or rather, who had instructed them to ignore it?

He would visit Surgeon Fan, the senior consultant of the Centre – the man who should have come at Wang Ti's summons. Would find him and wring a name from him. Then he would kill them. Whoever they were.

Chen turned, facing the orderlies again. 'Did you not hear me, *ch'un tzu*? Go back to work. This does not concern you.'

He could see how edgy they were at the sight of his gun. Edgy but determined. They thought they could jump him. Well, they could try. But they were mistaken if they thought sheer determination would triumph over him.

He tucked the gun into its holster, then reached down, taking the long, sharp-edged knife from his boot.

'You want to stop me, is that it? Well, let's see you try.'

Minutes later he was hammering at the door of Fan Tseng-li's apartment, conscious that a Security alert would have been put out already. He could hear movement inside and the babble of voices. Fearful, panicky voices. He called to them, letting his voice fill out with reassurance.

'Security! Open up! I am Lieutenant Tong and I have been assigned to protect you!'

He saw the door camera swivel round and held his pass card up, his thumb obscuring the name. A moment later the door hissed open and he was ushered inside, the three servants smiling at him gratefully.

The smiles froze as he drew his gun.

'Where is he? Where is the weasel-faced little shit?'

'I don't know who you mean,' the oldest of them, an ancient with the number two on his chest began, but Chen cuffed him into silence.

'You know very well who I mean. Fan. I want to know where he is, and I want to know now, not in two minutes' time. I'll shoot you first, lao tzu, then you, you little fucker.'

The elder – Number Two – looked down, holding his tongue, but beside him the youngest of the three began to babble, fear freeing his tongue wonderfully. Chen listened carefully, noting what he said.

'And he's there now?'

The young man nodded.

'Right.' He looked past them at the house comset, a large, ornate machine embellished with dragons. 'Has anyone spoken to him yet?'

The young man shook his head, ignoring the ancient's glare.

'Good.' Chen stepped past them and fired two shots into the machine. 'That's to stop you being tempted. But let me warn you. If I find that he has been tipped off, I will come back for you. So be good, neh? Be extra-specially good.'

The House Steward smiled, lowering his head. 'If you would wait here, Captain Kao, I shall tell my master...'

A straight-arm to the stomach made the man double up, gasping. Chen stepped over him, heading towards the sound of voices, the clink of tumblers.

A servant came towards him, trying to prevent him from entering the dining room. Chen stiff-fingered him in the throat.

He threw the doors open, looking about him, ignoring the startled faces, then roared ferociously as he spotted Surgeon Fan, there on the far side of the table.

Fan Tseng-li stood, staggering back from his chair, his face white, his eyes wide with fear. Others were shouting now, outraged, looking from

Chen to Fan, trying to make sense of things. For a moment there was hubbub, then a cold, fearful silence fell.

Chen had drawn his knife.

'Ai ya!' Fan cried hoarsely, looking about him anxiously. 'Who is this madman?'

'You know fucking well who I am,' Chen snarled, coming round the table. 'And I know who you are, Fan Tseng-li. You are the evil bastard who let my unborn daughter die.'

Fan's face froze in a rictus of fear. 'You have it wrong. I was detained. A client of mine...'

Fan fell silent. Chen was standing only an arm's length from him now, glaring at him, the look of hatred, of sheer disgust enough to wither the man.

'I know what kind of insect *you* are, Fan. What I need to know is who paid you to let my daughter die.' He reached out savagely, gripping Fan's hair, then pulled him down on to his knees, the big knife held to his throat. 'Who was it, Fan Tseng-li? Tell me.'

There was a murmur of protest from about the table, but Chen ignored it. He was looking down into Fan's face, murderous hatred shaping his lips into a snarl.

'You had better tell me,' he said quietly, tightening his grip on Fan's hair, 'and you had best do it now, Fan Tseng-li. Unless you want a second mouth below your chin.'

Fan grimaced, then met Chen's eyes. 'It was Ts'ui Wei. Ts'ui Wei made me do it.'

'Ts'ui Wei?' Chen frowned, trying to place the name. 'Did he...?'

He stopped, making the connection. *Ts'ui Wei*. Of course! That was the name of the youth's father. The tall, thin man who had threatened him that time, after he'd had the youth demoted. Chen shuddered. So that was it. That was why his child had died.

He sheathed the knife, then turned, looking about him at the faces gathered round the table. 'You heard,' he said defiantly. 'And now you know what kind of creature your friend Fan Tseng-li is.'

Chen looked back down at Fan, then, with a savage grunt, brought his face down on to his knee.

He let Fan roll to the side, then walked back round the table, seeing how they cowered from him. At the doorway the servants parted before him, making no attempt to hinder him. They had seen what had happened and understood. Some even bowed their heads as Chen passed, showing him respect. Back in the dining-room, however, voices were being raised, angry, indignant voices, calling for something to be done.

He stood there, in the darkness on the far side of the restaurant, looking across. There were seven of them in all, five of them seated at one of the tables near the pay desk, their figures back-lit, their faces dark. The other two sat at nearby tables; big men, their watchfulness as much as their size telling Chen what they were. The five were huddled close, talking.

'You should go,' one of them was saying. 'There must be relatives you could stay with for a time, Ts'ui Wei. Until this blows over.'

Ts'ui Wei leaned towards him aggressively. 'I'm not running from that bastard. He had my son sent down. I'll be fucked if he'll threaten me.'

'You do as you feel, Ts'ui Wei, but I've heard that Security have been digging through deck records, putting together a file.'

Ts'ui leaned back arrogantly. 'So? He can't prove anything. All Surgeon Fan has to do is keep his mouth shut.'

The fat man bristled. 'Fan Tseng-li is the model of discretion. He, at least, is taking my advice and going away until this is all sorted out.'

Ts'ui Wei snorted. 'That's typical of that self-serving shit! I should never have listened to your snivelling rubbish. We could have hit him. Hit him hard. And not just a fucking unborn child. We could have hurt him bad. The little girl...'

Chen shivered, his anger refined to a burning point. They were not expecting him. That gave him the element of surprise. But there were still the bodyguards. He would have to deal with them first.

Standing there, listening to them scheme and plot, he had felt his anger turn to deep revulsion. For them, but also for himself – for what had *he* been doing while all this had been happening?

He let out a long, slow breath. No. It could never be the same. For wherever he looked he could see her stumbling towards him like a broken doll, could hear the sound of the detonation...

And the child? He closed his eyes, the pain returning, like an iron band tightening about his chest. It was as if he had killed the child himself. As if he had pressed a tiny button and...

Chen stepped from the darkness. One of the hired men looked up at him as he came closer, then looked away, taking him for what he seemed – a night worker stopped for a bowl of *ch'a* before retiring. It was what Chen had hoped for.

Three paces from the man, he acted, swinging his fist round in a broad arc that brought it crashing into the man's face, breaking his nose. As he fell back, Chen turned and spun, high-kicking, catching the second man in the chest, even as he was getting up from his chair. At once he followed through, two quick punches felling the man.

Chen turned, facing the men at the table. They had moved back, scattering their chairs. Now they stared at him, wide-eyed with fear.

'Tell me,' Chen said quietly, taking a step closer. 'My little girl... What would you have done, Ts'ui Wei? Tell me what you had planned.'

Ashen-faced, Ts'ui Wei tried to back away, but the end wall was directly behind him. He turned his head anxiously, looking for somewhere to run, but his way was blocked on both sides.

Chen lifted the weighted table and threw it aside, then reached down, taking the big hunting knife from his boot.

'I have no stomach for a fight, eh, Ts'ui Wei?' He laughed coldly, all of the hatred and self-disgust he had been feeling suddenly focused in his forearm, making the big knife quiver in the light.

Ts'ui Wei stared at him a moment longer, his mouth working soundlessly, then he fell to his knees, pressing his head to the floor, his body shaking with fear. 'Have mercy,' he pleaded. 'For the gods' sakes, have mercy!'

Chen took a shuddering breath, remembering how Wang Ti had looked, remembering how it had felt, knowing he had not been there for her – and Jyan, poor Jyan... how had it felt for him, knowing he could do nothing? And this... this piece of shit... wanted *mercy*?

He raised the knife, his whole body tensed, prepared to strike...

'No! Please, Daddy!'

He turned. It was his son, Jyan.

The boy ran across, throwing his arms about Chen, embracing him, holding him so tightly that Chen felt something break in him. He began to sob, the words spilling from him. 'Oh, Jyan... I'm so sorry... I didn't know... I didn't know. Was it awful, boy? Was it really awful?'

Jyan clutched his father fiercely, looking up at him, his face wet with tears. 'It's all right, Father... It's all right now. You're back. You're here now.'

Chen lifted him up, hugging him tightly. Yes. But it would never be the same.

He turned, looking back into the shadows. Karr was standing there, a troop of his guards behind him. 'Are you all right, dear friend?'

Chen nodded. 'I...' He laughed strangely. 'I would have killed him.'

'Yes,' Karr said quietly. 'And I would have let you. But Jyan... Well, Jyan knew best, neh? After all, you have a life ahead of you, Kao Chen. A good life.'

Chen shivered, tightening his grip on his son, then nodded. Karr let his hand rest on Chen's shoulder briefly, then moved past him, taking command of the situation. 'All right!' he barked, towering over the frightened men. 'Let's get this sorted out right now! You – all of you! – against the back wall, hands on your heads! You're under arrest, as principals and accessories to the murder of a child and for conspiring to pervert the course of justice.'

Karr sat on the stone ledge, staring across at the floodlit shape of the Memorial Stone. It was after nine and the lotus lake was dark. Elsewhere, beneath the lamps that lined the narrow pathways, lovers walked, talking softly, keeping a proper distance between them. Behind Karr, seated in the shadows of the teahouse, sat Chen, his head fallen forward, his story told.

Karr sat there a moment, motionless, and then he sighed, as if waking from a dark and threatening dream. 'And that's the truth?'

Chen was silent.

Karr closed his eyes, deeply pained. Of course it was the truth. A tale like that – it was not something one made up about oneself. No. But it was not only Chen he felt sorry for. He had liked the woman greatly. If he had known for a moment...

'This is wrong, Kao Chen. Very wrong.' Karr was quiet a moment, fingering the dragon pendant about his neck, then he drew it out, looking down at it. He was *Chia ch'eng*, Honorary Assistant to the Royal Household. By right he could claim audience with his T'ang.

He turned, facing Chen across the table. 'I will go and see Li Yuan. I will tell him everything you told me just now.'

'You think he does not know?'

Karr nodded. 'I am convinced of it. He is a good man. Someone is keeping these things from him. Well, then, we must be his eyes and ears, neh? We must let him know what is being done in his name.'

Chen turned his head. 'And Tolonen? He will have the report of my debriefing by the morning. What if he says you are to do nothing?'

Karr looked down. That was true. He was Tolonen's man, and by rights he should talk to the old man first. But some things were greater than such loyalties.

'Then I must do it now.'

The wall had changed. Had become a view of Tai Shan, the sacred mountain misted in the early morning light, the great temple at the summit a tiny patch of red against the blue of the sky. Within the room a faint breeze blew, spreading the scent of pine and acacia.

Fat Wong turned from the wall, looking back at his guests, then raised his cup. 'Brothers...'

There were five men seated round the low table, each the equal of Wong Yi-sun, each the Big Boss of one of the great Triads that ran the lowest levels of City Europe. It had cost him much to get them here tonight, but here they were. All of them. All that mattered.

They stared back at him, cold-eyed, returning his smile with their mouths alone, like alligators.

'I am glad you could all come. I realize what sacrifices you have made to come here at such short notice, but when you have heard what I have to say, I know you will agree that I was right to convene this meeting of the Council.'

'Where is Iron Mu?'

Wong turned, facing the old man seated at the table's end. 'Forgive me, General Feng, but I will come to that.'

The Big Boss of the 14K stared back at him humourlessly. 'The Council has seven members, Wong Yi-sun, but I see only six about this table.'

'Hear Wong out, Feng Shang-pao,' the short, shaven-headed man seated two along from him said, leaning forward to take a cashew from the bowl. 'I am sure all your questions will be answered.'

Feng sat back, glaring at his interrupter. 'We must have laws amongst us, Li Chin. Ways of conducting ourselves.'

Li Chin – Li the Lidless – turned his bony head and looked at Feng, his over-large eyes fixing on the older man. 'I do not dispute it, Feng Shang-pao. But the Wo Shih Wo would like to know what Fat Wong has to say, and unless you let him say it...'

Feng looked down, his huge chest rising and falling, then he nodded.

'Good,' Wong said. 'Then let me explain. This afternoon, I received a letter.'

Whiskers Lu, Boss of the Kuei Chuan, leaned forward, the melted mask of his face turned towards Wong, his one good eye glittering. 'A letter, Wong Yi-sun?'

'Yes.' Wong took the letter from within his silks and threw it down in front of Lu. 'But before you open it, let me say a few words.'

Wong drew himself up, his eyes moving from face to face. 'We of the *Hung Mun* are proud of our heritage. Rightly so. Since the time of our founding by the five monks of the Fu Chou monastery, we have always settled our disputes amicably. And that is good, neh? After all, it is better to make money than make war.' He smiled, then let the smile fade. 'This once, however, the threat was too great. Iron Mu sought more than simple profit. He sought to build a power base – a base from which to overthrow this Council. To replace it.' He nodded, his face stern. 'Let us not hide behind words any longer. Iron Mu sought to destroy us.'

Dead Man Yun of the Red Gang cleared his throat. 'I hear your words, Wong Yi-sun, but I find them strange. You speak of things we all know, yet you speak of them in the past. Why is this?'

Wong smiled, then turned, going across to the tiny pool. For a moment he stood there, watching the seven golden fish swim lazily in the crystal waters, then, with a quicksilver motion, he scooped one up and turned, holding it up for the others to see. For a moment it flapped in the air, then Wong threw it down on to the dry stone flags.

There was a murmur of understanding from about the table.

'So Iron Mu is dead. But how?' Three Finger Ho asked, eyeing Wong warily.

Wong came closer, a trace of self-satisfaction at the corners of his mouth. 'I will tell you how. All thirty-seven decks of the Big Circle heartland were hit simultaneously, thirty minutes back. A force of one hundred and twenty thousand *Hei* went in, with a back-up of fifteen hundred regular guards.'

Hei... That single word sent a ripple of fear through the seated men. They had seen the *Hei* in action on their screens, the big GenSyn half-men clearing decks of rioters with a ruthlessness even their most fanatical runners could not match. For a moment they were silent, looking amongst themselves, wondering what this meant, then Li the Lidless leaned across Whiskers Lu and took the letter. He unfolded it and began to read aloud, then stopped, his face filled with a sudden understanding.

This letter from Li Yuan – this brief note of agreement – changed everything. Never before had one of their number received such a favour from Above. Never had the *Hung Mun* worked hand in glove with the Seven. Today Fat Wong had gained great face. Had re-established his position as Great Father of the brotherhoods. Li turned his head, looking about him, seeing the look of understanding in every face, then turned back, facing Wong, his head lowered in a gesture of respect.

The tapestries were burning. Flames licked the ancient thread, consuming mountain and forest, turning the huntsmen to ashes in the flicker of an eye. The air was dark with smoke, rent with the cries of dying men. *Hei* ran through the choking darkness, their long swords flashing, their deep set eyes searching out anything that ran or walked or crawled.

The door to Iron Mu's Mansion had been breached ten minutes back, but still a small group of Mu's élite held out. *Hei* swarmed at the final barricade, throwing themselves at the barrier without thought of self-preservation. Facing them, Yao Tzu, Red Pole to the Big Circle, urged his men to one last effort. He was bleeding from wounds to the head and chest, but still he fought on, slashing at whatever appeared above the barricade. For a moment longer the great pile held, then, with a shudder, it began to slide. There was a bellowing, and then the *Hei* broke through. Yao Tzu backed away, his knife gone, three of his men falling in the first charge. As the first of the *Hei* came at him, he leaped forward, screeching shrilly, meeting the brute with a flying kick that shattered the great chestbone of the half-man.

Encouraged, his men attacked in a blur of flying feet and fists, but it was not enough. The first wave of *Hei* went down, but then there was the deafening roar of gunfire as the *Hei* commander opened up with a big automatic from the top of the collapsed barricade.

There was a moment's silence, smoke swirled, and then they moved on, into the inner sanctum.

His wives were dead, his three sons missing. From outside he could hear the screams of his men as they died. It would be only moments before they broke into his rooms. Even so, he could not rush this thing.

Iron Mu had washed and prepared himself. Now he sat, his legs folded under him, his robe open, the ritual knife before him on the mat. Behind him his servant waited, the specially sharpened sword raised, ready for the final stroke.

He leaned forward, taking the knife, then turned it, holding the needle-sharp point towards his naked stomach. His head was strangely clear, his thoughts lucid. It was the merchant Novacek who had done this. It had to be. No one else had known enough. Even so, it did not matter. He would die well. That was all that was important now.

As he tensed, the door shuddered then fell open, the great locks smashed. Two *Hei* stood there, panting, looking in at him. A moment later a man stepped through, wearing the powder-blue uniform and chest patch of a Colonel. A filter-mask covered his lower face.

Iron Mu met the Colonel's eyes, holding them defiantly. In this, his last moment, he felt no fear, no regret, only a clarity of purpose that was close to the sublime.

Nothing, not even the watching *Hei*, could distract him now.

A breath, a second, longer breath, and then...

The Colonel's eyes dilated, his jaw tensed, and then he turned away, letting his *Hei* finish in the room. He shivered, impressed despite himself, feeling new respect for the man. Iron Mu had died well. Very well. Even so, it could not be known how Iron Mu had died. No. The story would be put out that he had cried and begged for mercy, hiding behind his wives. Because that was what the T'ing Wei wanted. And what the T'ing Wei wanted, they got.

Yes, but while he lived, Iron Mu's death would live in his memory. And one day, when the *T'ing Wei* were no more, he would tell his story. Of how one of the great lords of the underworld had died, with dignity, meeting the darkness without fear.

Fat Wong stood by the door, bringing things to a close, thanking his fellow Bosses for coming. And as they left, he made each stoop and kiss the ancient banner.

It should have been enough. Yet when they were gone it was not elation he felt but a sudden sense of hollowness. This victory was not his. Not *really* his. It was like something bought.

He went across and stood there over the tiny pool, staring down into the water, trying to see things clearly. For a moment he was still, as if meditating, then, taking the letter from his pocket, he tore it slowly in half and then in half again, letting it fall. No. He would be beholden to no man, not even a Son of Heaven. He saw it now with opened eyes. Why had Li Yuan agreed to act, if not out of fear? And if that were so...

He took a long, deep breath, then, drawing back his sleeve, reached in, plucking the fish from the water until five of the bloated golden creatures lay there on the ledge, flapping helplessly in the hostile air.

His way was clear. He must unite the underworld. Must destroy his brothers one by one, until only he remained. And then, when that was done, he might lift his head again and stare into the light.

He looked down, watching the dying gasps of the fish, then turned away, smiling. His way was clear. He would not rest now until it was his. Until he had it all.

Li Yuan stood on the terrace, beneath the bright full circle of the moon, looking out across the palace grounds, conscious of how quiet, how empty the palace seemed at this late hour. No gardeners knelt in the dark earth beneath the trellises of the lower garden, no maids walked the dark and narrow path that led to the palace laundry. He turned, looking towards the stables. There, a single lamp threw its pale amber light across the empty exercise circle.

He shivered and looked up at the moon, staring at that great white stone a while, thinking of what Karr had said.

Standing there in the wavering lamplight, listening to the big man's account, he had been deeply moved. He had not known – had genuinely not known – what was being done at Kibwezi, and, touched by the rawness of the man's appeal, had given his promise to close Kibwezi and review the treatment of convicted terrorists.

He had returned to the reception, distracted by Karr's words, disturbed by the questions they raised. And as he went amongst his cousins, smiling, offering bland politenesses, it had seemed suddenly a great pretence, a nothingness, like walking in a hall of holograms. The more he smiled and talked, the more he felt the weight of Karr's words bearing down on him.

But now, at last, he could face the matter squarely, beneath the unseeing eye of the moon.

Until this moment he had denied that there was a moral problem with the Wiring Project. Had argued that it was merely a question of attitude. But there was a problem, for – as Tolonen had argued from the first – freedom was no illusion, and even the freedom to rebel ought – no, *needed* – to be preserved somehow, if only for the sake of balance.

Were it simply a matter of philosophy – of *words* – it might have been all right. But it was not. The population problem was real. It could not be simply wished away.

He looked down, staring at his hands – at the great iron ring on the first finger of his right hand. For men such as Kao Chen, a common phrase like 'We are our masters' hands' had a far greater literal truth than he had ever imagined. And a far greater significance. For what was a man? Was he a choosing being, forging his own destiny, or was he simply a piece on the board, there to be played by another, greater than himself?

And maybe that was what had troubled him, more than the fate of the woman. That deeper question of choice.

He turned, looking back into his room, seeing Minister Heng's report there on the desk where he had left it.

It was a full report on the 'police action' against the Big Circle Triad, a report that differed radically from the T'ing Wei's official account. He sighed, the deep unease he had felt at reading the report returning. The *Hei* riot squads had gone mad down there. More than two hundred thousand had been killed, including many women and children.

Yes, and that was another argument in favour of wiring. If only to prevent such massacres, as 'necessary' as this one might have been.

He turned back, standing there a moment, the night breeze cool on his face.

The moon was high. He looked up at it, surprised, his perception of it suddenly reversed, such that it seemed to burn like a vast shining hole in the blackness of the sky. A big circle of death. He shivered violently and looked down, noting how its light silvered the gardens like a fall of dust.

Before today he had striven always to do the right thing, to be a good man – the benevolent ruler that Confucius bade him be – but now he saw it clearly. In this there was no right course of action, no pure solution, only degrees of wrongness.

And so he would make the hard choice. He would keep his word to Karr, of course. Kibwezi Station would be closed. As for the other thing, he had no choice. No real choice, anyway. The Wiring Project had to continue, and so it would, elsewhere, hidden from prying eyes. Until the job was done, the system perfected.

He sighed, turning his back on the darkness, returning inside. Yes. Because the time was fast coming when it would be needed.

Broken glass littered the terrace outside the guardhouse, glistening like frosted leaves in the moonlight. Nearby, the first of the bodies lay like a discarded doll, its face a pulp, the ragged tunic of its uniform soaked with blood. Through the empty window a second body could be seen, slumped forward in a chair, its head twisted at an unusual angle, the unblemished face staring vacantly at a broken screen.

Behind it, on the far side of the room, a door led through. There, on a bed in the rest room, the last of the bodies lay, naked and broken, its eyes bulging from its face, its tongue poking obscenely from between its teeth.

At the end of the unlit corridor, in the still silence of the signal room, the morph stood at the transmitter, its neutered body naked in the half-light. To one side, a hand lay on the desk like a stranded crab, the fingers upturned.

The morph tensed, the severed wrist of its left hand pressed against the input socket, the delicate wires seeking their counterparts, making their connections to the board, then it relaxed, a soft amber light glowing on the eye-level panel in front of it. There was a moment's stillness and then a faint tremor ran through the creature. At the count of twelve it stopped, as abruptly as it had begun. The message had been sent.

It waited, the minutes passing slowly, its stillness unnatural, like the stillness of a machine, and then the answer came.

It shuddered, then broke connection, drawing its wrist back sharply from the panel, a strange sigh, like the soughing of the wind through trees, escaping its narrow lips.

Reaching across, it took the hand from where it lay and lined it up carefully against the wrist, letting the twelve strong plastic latches – six in the hand, six in the wrist – click into place. The hand twitched, the fingers trembling, then was still again.

It turned, looking out through the dark square of the window. Fifty ch'i away, at the edge of the concrete apron, was a wire fence. Beyond the fence was the forest. For a time it stood there, staring out into the darkness, then it turned, making its way through.

For the past few nights it had dreamed. Dreams of a black wind blowing from beyond; of a dark and silent pressure at the back of it. A dream that was like the rush of knowledge down its spine; that set its nerve ends tingling in a sudden ecstasy. And with the dream had come a vision – a bright, hard vision of a world beneath the surface of this world. Of a world ruled by the game. A game of dark and light. Of suns and moons. Of space and time itself. A game that tore the dark veil from reality, revealing the whiteness of the bone.

On the terrace it paused, considering. From Tao Yuan to Tashkent was six thousand li. If it travelled in the dark it could make eighty, maybe a hundred li a night for the first ten days or so. Later on, crossing the great desert, it could increase that, travelling in the heat of the day, when no patrols flew. With any luck it would be there in fifty days.

It smiled, recalling DeVore's instructions. In Tashkent it would be met and given new papers. From there it would fly west, first to Odessa, then on to Nantes. From Nantes it would take a ship – one of the big ships that serviced the great floating Cities of the Mid-Atlantic. There it would stay a while, biding its time, working for the big ImmVac company of North

America, putting down roots inside that organization, until the call came.

For a moment longer it stood there, like a silvered god, tall, powerful, elegant in the moonlight, then it jumped down, crossing the circle of light quickly, making for the fence and the darkness beyond.

DeVore looked up from the communications panel and stared out into the darkness of the Martian night. It was just after two, local time, and the lights of the distant City were low. Beyond them was a wall of darkness.

He stood, yawning, ready for sleep now that the message had come, then turned, looking across at the sleeping man.

Hans Ebert lay on the camp bed, fully clothed, his kit bag on the floor beside him. He had turned up four days back, scared, desperate for help, and had ended here, 'rescued' by DeVore from the Governor's cells.

DeVore went across and stood there over the sleeping man, looking down at him. Ebert looked ill, haggard from exhaustion. He had lost a lot of weight and – from the smell of him – had had to rough it in ways he had never experienced before. His body had suffered, but his face was still familiar enough to be recognized anywhere in the system.

Well, maybe that was a problem, and maybe it wasn't. A familiar face might prove advantageous in the days to come. Especially when behind that face was a young prince, burning with ambition and eager for revenge. And that was why – despite the obvious dangers – he had taken Ebert in. Knowing that what was discarded now might prove extremely useful later on.

He bent down, drawing the blanket up over Ebert's chest, then turned away, looking outwards, conscious once more of the guards patrolling the frosted perimeter, the great, blue-white circle of Chung Kuo high above them in the Martian sky.

Chen crouched there on the mountainside, looking down the valley to where the dark, steep slopes ended in a flat-topped arrowhead of whiteness. It was like a vast wall, a dam two li in height, plugging the end of the valley, its surface a faintly opalescent pearl, lit from within. Ch'eng it was. City and wall.

The moon was high. Was a perfect circle of whiteness in the velvet dark. Chen stared at it a moment, mesmerized, held by its brilliant, unseeing eye, then looked down, his fingers searching amongst the ashes.

He turned, looking across at Karr, then lifted the shard of broken glass, turning it in his hand, remembering.

'What is this place?' Karr asked, coming closer, his face cloaked in shadow.

Chen stared at him a while, then looked away.

'This is where it began. Here on the mountainside with Kao Jyan. We lit a fire, just there, where you're standing now. And Jyan... Jyan brought a bottle and two glasses. I remember watching him.'

A faint breeze stirred dust and ash about his feet, carrying the scent of the Wilds.

He stood, then turned, looking north. There, not far from where they stood, the City began, filling the great northern plain of Europe. Earlier, flying over it, they had seen the rebuilt Imperial Solarium, which he had helped bomb a dozen years before. Chen took a long breath, then turned back, looking at the big man.

'Did you bring the razor, as I asked?'

Karr stared at him fixedly a moment, then took the fine blade from his tunic. 'What did you want it for?'

Chen met his eyes. 'Nothing stupid, I promise you.'

Karr hesitated a moment longer, then handed him the razor. Chen stared at it a moment, turning it in the moonlight, then tested it with the edge of his thumb. Satisfied, he crouched again, and, taking his queue in the other hand, cut the strong dark hair close to the roots.

'Kao Chen...'

He looked up at the big man, then, saying nothing, continued with the task. Finished, he stood again, offering Karr the blade, his free hand tracing the shape of his skull, feeling the fine stubble there.

Karr took the razor, studying his friend. In the moonlight, Chen's face had the blunt, anonymous look of a thousand generations of Han peasants. The kind of face one saw everywhere below. A simple, nondescript face. Until one met the eyes...

'Why are we here, my friend? What are we looking for?'

Chen turned, looking about him, taking in everything: the mountains; the sky; the great City, stretched out like a vast glacier under the brilliant moon. It was the same. Twelve years had done little to change this scene.

And yet it was quite different. Was, in the way he saw it, utterly transformed. Back then he had known nothing but the Net. Had looked at this scene with eyes that saw only the surfaces of things. But now he could see right through. Through to the bone itself.

He nodded slowly, understanding now why he had had to come here. Why he had asked Karr to divert the craft south and fly into the foothills of the Alps. Sometimes one had to go back – right back – to understand.

He shivered, surprised by the strength of the returning memory. It was strange how clearly he could see it, even now, after almost thirty years. Yes, he could picture quite vividly the old Master who had trained him to be *kwai*; a tall, willowy old Han with a long, expressionless face and a wispy beard who had always worn red. Old Shang, they had called him. Five of them, there had been, from Chi Su, the eldest, a broad-shouldered sixteen-year-old, down to himself, a thin-limbed, ugly little boy of six. An orphan, taken in by Shang.

For the next twelve years Old Shang's apartment had been his home. He had shared the *kang* with two others, his sleeping roll put away at sixth bell and taken out again at midnight. And in between, a long day of work; harder work than he had ever known, before or since. He sighed. It was strange how he had hidden it from himself all these years, as if it had never been. And yet it had formed him, as surely as the tree is formed from the seed. Shang's words, Shang's gestures had become his own. So it was in this world. So it had to be. For without that a man was shapeless, formless, fit only to wallow in the fetid darkness of the Clay.

He turned, meeting Karr's eyes. 'He had clever hands. I watched him from where you're standing now. Saw how he looked into his glass, like this, watching the flames flicker and curl like tiny snakes in the darkness of his wine. At the time I didn't understand what it was he saw there. But now I do.'

Karr looked down. It was Kao Jyan he was talking about. Kao Jyan, his fellow assassin that night twelve years ago.

'A message came,' he offered. 'From Tolonen.'

Chen was still looking back at him, but it was as if he were suddenly somewhere else, as if, for a brief moment, his eyes saw things that Karr was blind to.

'He confirms that Li Yuan has ordered the closure of Kibwezi.'

'Ah...' Chen lowered his eyes.

Karr was silent a moment, watching his friend, trying to understand, to empathize with what he was feeling, but for once it was hard. He crouched, one hand sifting the dust. 'Your friend, Kao Jyan... What did he see?'

Chen gave a small laugh, as if surprised that the big man didn't know, then looked away again, smoothing his hand over the naked shape of his skull.

'Change,' he said softly, a tiny tremor passing through him. 'And flames. Flames dancing in a glass.'

IN TIMES TO COME

I n *Monsters of the Deep*, the ninth volume in the *Chung Kuo* saga, the long-repressed divisions within the Council of the Seven finally come to the surface in a bitter internecine struggle. From the outset, Li Yuan, Tsu Ma and Wu Shih form a secret triumvirate, dedicated to ensuring the survival of Chung Kuo and its traditions and institutions, but, as ever, outside forces conspire against them.

In America, a new breed of young men has risen up, impatient to inherit. The heirs of powerful men, they have recently emerged from imprisonment, determined to grasp political power in the soon-to-be-reopened House of Representatives at Weimar. Chief among these is Michael Lever, heir to ImmVac, the giant pharmaceuticals company of North America. His attempts to revolutionize the politics of his City bring him mixed fortunes as the forces of conservatism, led by his father, Charles, line up against him.

In Europe, Jan Mach's revolutionary party, the *Yu*, continues its campaign against corruption and the decadent excesses of the Above, escalating their Program of Purity until it threatens the Seven themselves. Meanwhile in the very depths of the City, Stefan Lehmann, the albino lieutenant of DeVore, re-enters the fray, his ruthless ambition unbounded as he takes on the six great Triads that run the lawless regions down below.

Across the silent divide of space, on Mars, DeVore is busy reorganizing his forces and preparing the geno-technology by which he will wage the next stage of the great War of the Two Directions. Back on Chung Kuo, however, Li Yuan has instigated changes – radical amendments to the great

Edict of Technology, the cornerstone of Han stasis – which might yet allow him to face and overcome the seemingly inevitable onslaught.

For Li Yuan this is again a time of some contentment. A baby son and three loving wives transform him, but, as ever, he has to learn that love is a frail and fragile thing. Once again his character is put severely to the test, but this time he finds decisions forced upon him as the pace of change accelerates and events outstrip his plans.

In this period of great instability, Li Yuan must rely on his servants heavily, and none more so than Major Karr and his Captain, Kao Chen. To them falls the task of policing the reforms Li Yuan has set under way. But their task is not an easy one as they soon find out. Chung Kuo is rotten to the core and it will take far more than mere persuasion to change the system. Their struggle with the decaying corpse of Chung Kuo's officialdom leads them beyond their given brief and into the greatest danger they have yet faced.

Beyond the City's walls, these prove fruitful years for Ben Shepherd as he begins to create the first of his great works of art, but even in the peaceful setting of the Domain – his idyllic West Country valley – he is unable to escape the dark tide of change and finds himself thrown into conflict; a conflict in which he must succeed or die.

For Kim Ward these are years of promise. Wooed by the Old Men of North America, who want to secure his talents for their great Immortality program, he struggles to set up his own small company, trading upon his unique inventiveness. But things are far from straightforward, neither at work, nor in his relationship with Marshal Tolonen's daughter, Jelka. Kim's experience of the mercantile world – of its deviousness and power games – is a sobering lesson: one that forces him to make a choice. A choice that will ultimately bring him into conflict with the Above.

For thirteen years – since the assassination of Li Shai Tung's Minister, Lwo Kang – the threat of change has hung over the great changeless empire of Chung Kuo, but now, at last, change is set to come. Gone are the golden days of peace and stability. Gone are all hopes that the Seven might rule for ten thousand years. Ahead lies only darkness.

In *Monsters of the Deep* we witness the first cracks in the great edifice as cousin is set against cousin in a war that is as tragic as it has become inevitable.

CHUNG KUO

CHARACTER LISTING

MAJOR CHARACTERS

DeVore, Howard
A one-time Major in the T'ang's Security forces, he had become the leading figure in the struggle against the Seven. A highly intelligent and coldly logical man, he is the puppetmaster behind the scenes as the great 'War of the Two Directions' takes a new turn.

Ebert, Hans
Son of Klaus Ebert and heir to the vast GenSyn Corporation, he has been promoted to Major in the T'ang's Security forces, and is admired and trusted by his superiors. Ebert is a complex young man; a brave and intelligent officer, he also has selfish, dissolute ambition to become not merely a prince among men but a ruler.

Fei Yen
'Flying Swallow', daughter of Yin Tsu, one of the Heads of the 'Twenty-Nine', the minor aristocratic families of Chung Kuo. Once married to Han Ch'in, the murdered son of Li Shai Tung, she subsequently married his brother Li Yuan, nine years her junior. This classically beautiful woman seems fragile in appearance, but is actually strong-willed and fiery, as was proved in her secret affair with Tsu Ma, the T'ang of West Asia.

Kao Chen
Once a *kwai*, a hired knife from the Net, the lowest level of the great City, Chen has raised himself from those humble beginnings and is now a Captain in the T'ang's Security forces. As friend and helper to

Karr and a close associate of Haavikko, Chen is one of the foot soldiers in the war against DeVore.

Karr, Gregor

Major in the T'ang's Security forces, Karr was recruited by Marshal Tolonen from the Net. In his youth, Karr was a 'blood'; a to-the-death combat fighter. A giant of a man, he is the 'hawk' Li Yuan plans to fly against his adversary, DeVore.

Lehmann, Stefan

Albino son of the former Dispersionist leader, Pietr Lehmann, he has become a lieutenant to DeVore. A cold, unnaturally dispassionate men, he seems to be the very archetype of nihilism, his one and only aim to bring down the Seven and their great City.

Li Yuan

Second son of Li Shai Tung, he became heir to City Europe after the assassination of his elder brother. Considered old before his time, his cold outward manner conceals a passionate nature, as expressed in his brief marriage to, and divorce from, the fiery Fei Yen, his dead brother's wife.

Mach, Jan

A maintenance official in the Ministry of Waste Recycling and a part-time member of Li Yuan's Reserve Security Force, Mach has a second identity as one of the Council of Five, the policy formulators of the newly split-off Yu, the revolutionary successors to the Ping Tiao, a new and yet darker force within the depths of City Europe.

Tolonen, Jelka

Daughter of Marshal Tolonen, Jelka has been brought up in a very masculine environment, lacking a mother's feminine influence. However, her genuine interest in martial arts and in weaponry and strategy masks a very different, more feminine side to her nature – a side brought out after the unsuccessful attack on her by Ping Tiao terrorists.

Tolonen, Knut

Marshal of the Council of Generals and one-time General to Li Shai Tung, Tolonen is a big, granite-jawed man and the staunchest supporter of the values and ideals of the Seven. Possessed of a fiery, fearless nature, he will stop at nothing to protect his masters, yet after long years of war even his belief in the necessity of stasis has been shaken.

Tsu Ma

T'ang of West Asia and one of the Seven, the ruling Council of Chung Kuo, Tsu Ma has thrown off his former dissolute past to become one of Li Yuan's strongest supporters in Council. A strong, handsome man in his mid-thirties, he has extricated

	himself from a secret affair with Fei Yen, which – had it become public – might easily have destroyed the Seven.
Wang Sau-leyan	Young T'ang of Africa. Since his father's murder he has thrown off his former ways and become a sharp and cunning adversary to Li Yuan and the old guard among the Seven. An abrasive, calculating figure with sybaritic tastes, he is the harbinger of Change within the Council of Seven.
Ward, Kim	Born in the Clay, that dark wasteland beneath the great City's foundations, Kim has a quick and unusual bent of mind that has marked him from the first as potentially the greatest scientist Chung Kuo has ever seen. His vision of a gigantic star-spanning web – formulated in the darkness of the Clay – has driven him up into the light of the Above. Now, after a long period of personality reconstruction, he has, through Li Yuan's generosity, been given the means to build his own great Company. But there are those who do not wish him success in this venture.
Ywe Hao	Born into the lowest levels of City Europe, Ywe Hao – 'Fine Moon' – joined the Yu, a terrorist organization, after the murder of her elder brother. A strong, idealistic woman, she represents the new tide of indignant rebellion that is stirring in the depths of the great City.

THE SEVEN AND THE FAMILIES

An Liang-chou	Minor Family Prince
An Sheng	Head of the An Family (one of the 'Twenty-Nine' Minor Families)
Chi Hsing	T'ang of the Australias
Chun Wu-chi	Head of the Chun Family (one of the 'Twenty-Nine' Minor Families)
Fu Ti Chang	third Wife of Li Yuan
Hou Tung-po	T'ang of South America
Hsiang K'ai Fan	Minor Family Prince; heir to the Hsiang Family (one of the 'Twenty-Nine' Minor Families)
Hsiang Shao-erh	Head of the Hsiang Family (one of the 'Twenty-Nine' Minor Families)
Hsiang Te-shang	Minor Family Prince and youngest son of Hsiang Shao-erh

Hsiang Wang	Minor Family Prince and second son of Hsiang Shao-erh
Lai Shi	second Wife of Li Yuan
Li Yuan	T'ang of City Europe
Mien Shan	first Wife of Li Yuan
Pei Ro-hen	Head of the Pei Family (one of the 'Twenty-Nine' Minor Families)
Tsu Ma	T'ang of West Asia
Wang Sau-leyan	T'ang of Africa
Wei Chen Yin	Son of Wei Feng; regent for City East Asia
Wei Feng	T'ang of East Asia
Wu Shih	T'ang of North America
Yin Fei Yen	'Flying Swallow' ex-wife of Li Yuan and daughter of Yin Tsu
Yin Han Ch'in	bastard baby son of Yin Fei Yen
Yin Tsu	Head of Yin Family (one of the 'Twenty-Nine' Minor Families)

FRIENDS AND RETAINERS OF THE SEVEN

Chan Teng	Master of the Inner Chambers at Tongjiang
Ebert, Berta	wife of Klaus Ebert
Ebert, Hans	Major in Security and heir to GenSyn
Ebert, Klaus Stefan	Head of GenSyn (Genetic Synthetics) and advisor to Li Yuan
Haavikko, Axel	Lieutenant in Security
Hung Mien-lo	Chancellor of Africa
Kao Chen	Captain in Security
Karr, Gregor	Major in Security
Nan Ho	Master of the Inner Chamber to Li Yuan
Shepherd, Ben	son of Hal Shepherd
Shepherd, Beth	wife of Hal Shepherd
Shepherd, Meg	sister of Ben Shepherd
Shou Chen-hai	*Hsien Ling*, or Chief Magistrate of Hannover *Hsien*
Sun Li Hua	Master of the Royal Household at Alexandria
Tolonen, Helga	wife of Jon Tolonen
Tolonen, Jelka	daughter of Knut Tolonen
Tolonen, Jon	brother of Knut Tolonen
Tolonen, Knut	Marshal of the Council of Generals and father of Jelka Tolonen
Tong Chou	alias of Kao Chen
Viljanen, Per	Lieutenant in Security; assistant to Marshal Tolonen

| Wu Ming | personal assistant to Sun Li Hua |
| Yu | Surgeon to Li Yuan |

THE TRIADS

Feng Shang-pao	'General Feng', Big Boss of the 14K
Ho Chin	'Three-Finger Ho', Big Boss of the Yellow Banners
Hui Tsin	'Red Pole' (the 426,or Executioner) to the United Bamboo
Li Chin	'Li The Lidless', Big Boss of the Wo Shih Wo
Lu Ming Shao	'Whiskers Lu', Big Boss of the Kuei Chuan (Black Dog)
Mu Li	'Iron Mu', Big Boss of the Big Circle
Wong Yi-sun	'Fat Wong', Big Boss of the United Bamboo
Yao Tzu	'Red Pole' (the 426 or Executioner) to the Big Circle
Yun Yueh-hui	'Dead Man Yun', Big Boss of the Red Gang

YU

Chi Li	alias of Ywe Hao
Edel, Klaus	brother of Vasska
Erika	fellow member of Ywe Hao's Yu cell
Hsao Yen	Yu terrorist
Klaus	Yu terrorist
Mach, Jan	Maintenance official for the Ministry of Waste Recycling, ex-*Ping Tiao* and Founder of the split-off Yu faction
Rooke	Yu terrorist
Tu Li-shan	Yu terrorist
Vasska	fellow member of Ywe Hao's Yu cell
Veda	Member of the Yu 'Council of Five'
Ywe Hao	'Fine Moon', female Yu terrorist from the Mid-Levels

OTHER CHARACTERS

Boden, Mikhail	alias used by Stefan Lehmann and Howard DeVore
Cherkassky, Stefan	retired Security special services officer; friend of DeVore
Chi Su	childhood companion to Kao Chen
Curval, Andrew	experimental geneticist, working for ImmVac
Debrenceni, Laslo	acting Administrator at Kibwezi Station
DeVore, Howard	former Major in Li Shai Tung's Security forces

Drake, Michael	supervisor at Kibwezi Station
Enge, Marie	woman server at the Dragon Cloud teahouse
Fan Tseng-li	Mid-levels surgeon
Fang Shuo	underling to Shou Chen-hai
Ganz, Joseph	alias of DeVore
Golden Heart	young prostitute bought by Hans Ebert for his household
Gustaffson	security guard at Kibwezi Station
Kao Ch'iang Hsin	daughter of Kao Chen and Wang Ti
Kao Jyan	eldest son of Kao Chen and Wang Ti
Kao Wu	second son of Kao Chen and Wang Ti
Kung Lao	young boy; friend of Ywe Hao
Kung Yi-lung	young boy; friend of Ywe Hao
Lehmann, Stefan	albino son of former Dispersionist leader Pietr Lehmann and former lieutenant to DeVore
Lever, Charles	'Old Man Lever', Head of the ImmVac pharmaceuticals company of North America; father of Michael Lever
Lever, Michael	American; son of Charles Lever
Leyden, Wolfgang	Security guard at Hannover *Hsien*
Mu Chua	Madam of the House of the Ninth Ecstasy, a singsong house or brothel
Novacek, Lubos	merchant; go-between for Triads
Palmer	security guard at Kibwezi Station
Peng Lu-Hsing	Minister of the T'*ing Wei*; the Superintendency of Trials for City Europe
Reid, Thomas	sergeant in DeVore's forces
Shang	'Old Shang'; *Kwai* and childhood 'Master' to Kao Chen
Sheng	Minister to Wei Feng
Shou He	second wife to Shou Chen-hai
Shou Wen-lo	first wife to Shou Chen-hai
Ts'ui Wei	father of teenage troublemaker
Tuan Wen-ch'ang	alias of 'morph' sent by DeVore from Mars
Wang Mai Yu	uncle to Wang Ti
Wang Ti	wife of Kao Chen
Ward, Kim	'Clayborn' orphan and scientist
Wong Pao-yi	steward to Shou Chen-hai
Wu	surgeon for Security
Yen T'ung	Third Secretary to Minister Peng Lu-Hsing
Yue Mi	young maid in Shou Chen-hai's household
Ywe Chang	uncle to Ywe Hao

Ywe Sha	mother to Ywe Hao
Ywe Su Chen	wife to Ywe Chang

THE DEAD

Aaltonen	Marshal and Head of Security for City Europe
Alex	close friend of Jake Reed and fiancée of Jenny; Security Captain in Special Forces
Anders	a mercenary
Anderson	Director of 'The Project'
Ascher, Mary	mother of Emily Ascher
Ascher, Mikhail	junior credit agent in the *Hu Pu* (the Finance Ministry) and father of Emily Ascher
Ascher, Walter	Account Overseer for Hinton Industries
Bakke	Marshal in Security
Barrow, Chao	member of the House of Representatives Dispersionist
Barycz, Jiri	communications officer for the Wiring Project
Bates, Alan	English actor
Beatrice	daughter of Cathy Hubbard, granddaughter of Mary Reed
Berdichev, Soren	owner of the SimFic Corporation and leading Dispersionist
Big Wen	a landowner
Boss Yang	an exploiter of the people
Branagh, William	King of Wessex
Brogan, Margaret	Old Ma Brogan, resident of Church Knowle
Buck, John	Head of Development at the Ministry of Contracts
Buckland, Eddie	farmer from Corfe
Captain Sensible	English pop musician
Chang Hsuan Han	painter from the eighth century
Chang Lai-hsun	nephew of Chang Yi Wei
Chang Li Chen	Junior Dragon in charge of drafting the Edict of Technological Control
Chang Lui	woman who adopted Pavel
Chang Te	Han soldier member of Jiang Lei's bodyguard
Chang Yan	guard on the Plantations
Chang Yi Wei	senior brother of the Chang clan owners of MicroData
Chang Yu	Tsao Ch'un's new appointment as First Dragon, during the War of Liberation

Chao Ni Tsu	Grand Master of *wei chi* and a computer genius; servant of Tsao Ch'un
Ch'eng I	Minor Family prince and son of Ch'eng So Yuan
Ch'eng So Yuan	Minor Family head
Chen So I	Head of the Ministry of Contracts
Chen Yu	steward to Tsao Ch'un in Pei Ch'ing
Cheng Ro	Song Dynasty painter
Cheng Yu	one of the original Seven, advisor to Tsao Ch'un, subsequently T'ang
Chi Fei Yu	a usurer
Chi Lin Lin	legal assistant to Yang Hong Yu
Chin Shih Huang Ti	the First Emperor
Ching Su	friend of Jiang Lei
Chiu Fa	Media commentator on the Mids news channel
Cho	Han soldier servant to Wang Yu-lai
Cho Yi Yi	Master of the Bedchamber at Tongjiang
Chris	close friend of Jake Reed, gay partner of Hugo and multi-millionaire industrialist
Christie, Julie	English actress
Chung Hsun	'loyalty' a bond servant to Li Shai Tung
Coldplay	an English pop group
Cooke, Dick	farmer from Cerne Abbas
Cooper, Charlie	son of Jed and Judy Cooper
Cooper, Jed	husband of Judy Cooper and father of Charlie and John
Cooper, John	son of Jed and Judy Cooper
Cooper, Judy	wife of Jed Cooper and mother of Charlie and John
Cooper, Will	farmer from Corfe
Croft, Leopold	father of Becky
Croft, Rebecca	'Becky', daughter of Leopold, with the lazy eye
Curtis, Tim	Head of Human Resources, GenSyn
Daas	DAAS4 – the Data Automated Analysis System – an enhanced intelligence unit belonging to Hinton Industries
Dag	a mercenary
Denny, Sandy	English folk singer
Depp, Johnny	American actor
Dick, Philip K.	American science fiction writer
Douglas, John	businessman and Dispersionist
Drake, Nick	English folk singer
Duchek, Albert	Administrator of Lodz and Dispersionist

Ebert, Gustav	genetics genius and co-founder of GenSyn (Genetic Synthetics)
Ebert, Ludovic	son of Gustav Ebert and GenSyn director
Ebert, Wolfgang	financial genius and co-founder of GenSyn (Genetic Synthetics)
Einor	a mercenary
Ellis, Michael	assistant director on the Wiring Project
Endfors, Jenny	wife of Knut Tolonen and mother of Jelka Tolonen
Fan Chang	a member of the original Seven, and advisor to Tsao Ch'un
Fan Cho	son of Fan Chang
Fan Lin	son of Fan Chang
Fan Peng	eldest wife of Fan Chang
Fan Si-pin	Master of *wei chi* from the eighteenth century
Fan Ti Yu	son of Fan Chang
Feng I	Colonel in charge of Tsao Ch'un's elite force
Fest	lieutenant in Security
Fu Jen Maitland	Stefan Lehmann's mother
Gaughan, Dick	Scottish folk singer
Gessell, Bent	leader of the *Ping Tiao*
Gifford, Dick	farmer from Corfe and son of Ted
Gifford, Ted	farmer from Corfe and father of Dick
Goodman, Frank	farmer from Langton Maltravers
Gosse	elite guard at the Domain
Grant, Thomas	Captain in Security
Griffin, James B.	Sixtieth president of the United States of America (the 69 States)
Grove, Dick	resident of Corfe
Gurney, Tom	watchman from Corfe
Haavikko, Knut	major in Security
Haavikko, Vesa	sister to Axel Haavikko
Haines, Billy	landlord of The Wessex Arms in Wool
Hamilton, Jack	landlord of The Quay Inn in Wareham
Hammond, Joel	official on the Wiring Project
Hammond, Matthew	butcher from Church Knowle
Hart, Dr	doctor from Church Knowle
Hendrix, Jimi	American rock guitarist
Heng Chi-po	Li Shai Tung's Minister of Transportation
Henrik	a mercenary
Hewitt	lieutenant to Branagh, leader of a horse patrol
Hinton, Charles	CEO of Hinton Industries
Hinton, George	Senior Executive at Hinton Industries

Hinton, Henry	'Harry', Head of Strategic Planning, Hinton Industries
Ho	Steward Ho, body servant of Jiang Lei when in the field
Ho Ti	ancient Han emperor; conqueror of Europe
Horsfield, Geoff	historian and resident of Corfe
Hou Hsin-Fa	one of the original Seven, advisor to Tsao Chun and subsequently T'ang
Hsieh Ho	art critic and author of *The Six Principles*
Hsu Jung	friend of Jiang Lei
Huang Tzu Kung	Seventh Dragon servant of the 'Ministry', 'the Thousand Eyes'
Hubbard, Beth	second daughter of Tom and Mary Hubbard
Hubbard, Cathy	eldest daughter of Tom and Mary Hubbard
Hubbard, Mary	wife of Tom Hubbard and mother of Cathy, Meg and Beth; second wife of Jake Reed
Hubbard, Meg	youngest daughter of Tom and Mary Hubbard and girlfriend of Peter Reed
Hubbard, Tom	farmer, resident of Church Knowle, husband of Mary and father of Beth, Meg and Cathy; best friend of Jake Reed
Hugo	close friend of Jake Reed and gay partner of Chris, acclaimed classical composer
Hui	receptionist for GenSyn
Hui Chang Ye	Senior Legal Advocate for the Chang clan
Hung	Tsao Ch'un's spy in Jiang Lei's camp
Hung Feng-chan	Chief Groom, Tongjiang
Hwa	a master 'blood', or to-the-death fighter from below the Net
Jenny	a close friend of Jake Reed and fiancé of Alex
Jiang Ch'iao-chieh	eldest daughter of Jiang Lei
Jiang Chun Hua	wife of Jiang Lei
Jiang Lei	general of Tsao Chun's Eighteenth Banner Army, also known as Nai Liu
Jiang San-chieh	youngest daughter of Jiang Lei
Joel	senior engineer in the datscape for Hinton Industries
Jones, Micky	lead guitarist of Man, a Welsh rock band
Jung	steward to Tobias Lamme
Kan Ying	the Roman Emperor, Domitian
Kao Jyan	assassin
Kao Tzu	ancient Chinese philosopher
Karl	a mercenary

Ku	Marshal of the Fourth Banner Army
Kurt	Chief Technician at GenSyn
Kustow, Bryn	American, friend of Michael Lever
Lahm, Tobias	Eighth Dragon at the 'Ministry', 'the Thousand Eyes'
Lampton, Sir Henry	Head of Security, Hinton Industries
Lao Jen	Junior Minister to Li Shai Tung
Leggat, Brian	farmer from Abbotsbury
Lehmann, Pietr	Under Secretary of the House of Representatives, father of Stefan Lehmann and leader of the Dispersionists
Li Han	soldier, servant to Wang Yui-lai
Li Chang So	sixth son of Li Chao Ch'in
Li Chao Ch'in	one of the original Seven, advisor to Tsao Ch'un and subsequently T'ang
Li Fa Han	soldier and technician, working for Jiang Lei
Li Fu Jen	third son of Li Chao Ch'in
Li Hang Ch'i	great-great-grandfather to Li Shai Tung
Li Han Ch'in	first son of Li Shai Tung and heir to City Europe
Li Kuang	fifth son of Li Cao Ch'in
Li Peng	eldest son of Li Chao Ch'in
Li Po	T'ang Dynasty poet
Li Shai Tung	T'ang of City Europe and father of Li Yuan
Li Shen	second son of Li Chao Ch'in
Li Weng	fourth son of Li Chao Ch'in
Lin Yua	first wife of Li Shai Tung
Ling	steward at the Black Tower
Little Bee	maid to Wang Hsien
Liu Ke	Han soldier; member of Jiang Lei's bodyguard; an adept at the pi-p'a or Chinese lute
Lo Wen	granddaughter of Jiang Lei
Lovegrove, John	farmer from Purbeck
Lu Tung	merchant; third cousin to Lu Wang-pei
Lu Wang-pei	third cousin of Lu Tung
Ludd, Drew	biggest grossing actor in Hollywood and star of Ubik
Lung Ti	secretary to Edmund Wyatt
Lwo Kang	son of Lwo Chun-yi and Li Shai Tung's Minister of the Edict of Technological Control
McKenzie, Liam	owner of The Stables in Dorchester
Ma Feng	Han soldier; member of Jiang Lei's bodyguard
Mao Shao Tu	senior servant to Li Chao Ch'in
Man	Welsh rock band

Mao Liang	Minor Family princess and member of the *Ping Tiao* Council of Five
Mao Tse T'ung	first *Ko Ming* emperor of China (ruled AD 1948–76)
Mason, Harry	landlord of the Thomas Hardy inn in Dorchester
Melfi, Charles	father of Alexandra Shepherd
Meng Tzu	Chinese philosopher, better known as Mencius, third century BC
Mi Feng	'Little Bee'; maidservant to Wang Hsien
Ming Hsin-Fa	senior advocate for GenSyn
Ming Huang	T'ang dynasty emperor; the Purple Emperor
Nai Liu	'Enduring Willow', pen name of Jiang Lei and the most popular Han poet of his age
Nicolson, Jack	American actor
Nietzsche, Friedrich	German nineteenth-century philosopher
Nocenzi, Vittorio	General to Li Shai Tung
Oatley, Jennifer	young Englishwoman 'processed' by Jiang Lei
Padgett	retired doctor from Wool
Palmer, Joshua	'Old Josh', father of Will and an avid record collector
Palmer, Will	landlord of the Banks Arms Hotel, Corfe and son of Josh
Pan Chao	the great 'hero' of Chung Kuo, who conquered Asia in the first century AD
Pan Tsung-yen	friend of Jiang Lei
Pavel	young worker on the Plantations, with a crooked back
Pei Ko	one of the original Seven, advisor to Tsao Ch'un and subsequently T'ang
Pei Lin-Yi	eldest son of Pei Ko
P'eng Chuan	Sixth Dragon at the Ministry, 'the Thousand Eyes'
P'eng K'ai-chi	nephew of P'eng Chuan
Presley, Elvis	American rock and roll singer
Ragnar	a mercenary
Raikkonen	Marshal in Security
Randall, Jack	farmer from Church Knowle and husband of Jenny
Randall, Jenny	wife of Jack
Reed, Annie	first wife of Jake Reed; mother of Peter Reed and sister of Mary Hubbard (Jake's second wife)
Reed, Jake	'Login' or 'webdancer' for Hinton Industries; father of Peter Reed
Reed, Mary	second wife of Peter Reed
Reed, May	sister of Jake Reed
Reed, Peter	son of Jake and Annie Reed; GenSyn executive

Reed, Tom	son of Jake and Mary Reed
Rheinhardt	Media Liaison for GenSyn
Rory	Music store holder in Dorchester; owner of Rory's Record Shack, father of Roxanne
Sam	'Hopper' pilot, working for Hinton Industries
Sanders	Captain in Security
Schwarz	aide to Marshal Tolonen
Shan	Han soldier; Captain and one of Jiang Lei's men
Shao Shu	First Steward at Chun Hua's mansion
Shao Yen	Major in Security; friend of Ming Hsin-fa
Shen	Han soldier; bodyguard to Jiang Lei
Shen Chen	son of Shen Fu
Shen Fu	First Dragon, Head of the Ministry, 'the Thousand Eyes'
Shen Lu Chua	computer expert and member of the Ping Tiao 'Council of Five'
Shepherd, Alexandra	wife of Amos Shepherd and daughter of Charles Melfi
Shepherd, Amos	great-great-grandfather of Hal Shepherd; chief advisor to Tsao Ch'un and architect of City Earth
Shepherd, Augustus	great-grandfather of Hal Shepherd Raedwald
Shepherd, Beth	daughter of Amos Shepherd
Shepherd, Hal	chief advisor to Li Shai Tung and Head of the Shepherd family; father of Ben and Meg Shepherd
Shu Liang	Senior Legal Advocate
Shuh San	Junior Minister to Lwo Kang
Si Wu Ya	'Silk Raven', wife of Supervisor Sung
Spatz, Gustav	Director of the Wiring Project
Spirit	Californian rock band
Su Ting-an	eighteenth-century Master of wei chi
Ssu Lu Shan	official of the Ministry, 'the Thousand Eyes'
Stamp, Terence	English actor
Su Ting-an	Master of wei chi from the eighteenth century
Su Tung-p'o	Han official and poet of the eleventh century
Sung	supervisor on the Plantations
Svensson	Marshal in Security
Sweet Rain	maid to Wang Hsien
Tai Yu	'Moonflower', maid to Augustus Ebert, a GenSyn clone
Tarrant	lieutenant to DeVore
Tender Willow	maid to Wang Hsien

Teng	'Master Teng', a '*shou*' (literally 'a hand'); a servant of the First Dragon, the first lord of the Ministry or 'Thousand Eyes'
Teng Fu	guard on the Plantations
Teng Liang	Minor Family princess betrothed to Prince Ch'eng I
Trish	artificial intelligence 'filter avatar' for Jake Reed's penthouse apartment
Ts'ao P'I	'Number Three', steward at Tsao Ch'un's court in Pei Ch'ing
Tsao Ch'i Yuan	youngest son of Tsao Ch'un
Tsao Ch'un	ex-member of the standing committee of the Communist Party politburo and architect of 'The Collapse'; mass murderer and tyrant; 'creator' of the world state of Chung Kuo
Tsao Heng	second son of Tsao Ch'un
Tsao Hsiao	Tsao Ch'un's elder brother
Tsao Wang-po	eldest son of Tsao Ch'un
Tsu Chen	one of the original Seven, advisor to Tsao Ch'un and subsequently T'ang
Tsu Lin	eldest son of Tsu Chen
Tsu Shi	steward to Gustav Ebert; a GenSyn clone
Tsu Tiao	T'ang of West Asia
Tu Mu	assistant to Alison Winter at GenSyn
Tung Ch'i-ch'ang	Ming dynasty *shanshui* artist
Tung Men-tiao	artist of the original *Chou* (or 'State') cards
The Verve	English pop group
Waite, Charlie	landlord of The New Inn, Church Knowle
Wang An-Shih	Han official and poet from the eleventh century
Wang Chang Ye	eldest son of Wang Hsien, heir to City Africa
Wang Hsien	T'ang of Africa
Wang Hui So	one of the original Seven, advisor to Tsao Ch'un and subsequently T'ang
Wang Lieh Tsu	second son of Wang Hsien
Wang Lung	eldest son of Wang Hui So
Wang Ta-hung	third son of Wang Hsien
Wang Yu-lai	'cadre'; servant of the Ministry, 'the Thousand Eyes', instructed to report back on Jiang Lei
Webber, Sam	youth from Corfe
Wei	a judge
Wei Shao	Chancellor to Tsao Ch'un
Weis, Anton	banker and Dispersionist
Wen	Captain in Security on Mars

Wen P'ing	close acquaintance and body servant of Tsao Ch'un; a man of great power
Wiegand, Max	lieutenant to DeVore
Williams, Charles	husband of Margaret and father of Kate; retired head of a stockbroking company
Williams, Kate	fiancée of Jake Reed and daughter of Charles and Margaret
Williams, Margaret	wife of Charles and mother of Kate
Wilson, Dougie	farmer from Kimmeridge
Winter, Alison	ex-fiancée of Jake Reed; head of Evaluation at GenSyn; mother of Jake Winter
Winter, Jake	only son of Alison
Wolf	elite guard on The Domain
Wu Chi	AI (Artificial Intelligence) for Tobias Lahm
Wu Hsien	one of the original Seven, advisor to Tsao Ch'un and, subsequently, T'ang
Wyatt, Edmund	Company head, Dispersionist and (unknown to him) father of Kim Ward
Yang Hong Yu	legal advocate
Yang Kuei Fei	the famous concubine of T'ang emperor Ming Huang
Yates, Andrew Isiah	Prime Minister of the UK in 2043
Ying Chai	assistant to Sun Li Hua, brother to Ying Fu
Ying Fu	assistant to Sun Li Hua, brother to Ying Chai
Yo Jou Hsi	a judge
Young, Neil	Canadian singer-songwriter
Yu Ch'o	family retainer to Wang Hui So
Ywe Kai-chang	father of Ywe Hao

GLOSSARY OF MANDARIN TERMS

I t is not intended to belabour the reader with a whole mass of arcane Han expressions here. Some – usually the more specific – are explained in context. However, as a number of Mandarin terms are used naturally in the text, I've thought it best to provide a brief explanation of those terms.

aiya!	a common expression of surprise or dismay
amah	a domestic maidservant
Amo Li Jia	the Chinese gave this name to North America when they first arrived in the 1840s. Its literal meaning is 'The Land Without Ghosts'
an	a saddle. This has the same sound as the word for peace, and thus is associated in the Chinese mind with peace
catty	the colloquial term for a unit of measure formally called a *jin*. One catty – as used here – equals roughly 1.1. pounds (avoirdupois), or (exactly) 500 gm. Before 1949 and the standardization of Chinese measures to a metric standard, this measure varied district by district, but was generally regarded as equalling about 1.33 pounds (avoirdupois)
ch'a	tea; it might be noted that *ch'a shu*, the Chinese art of tea, is an ancient forebear of the Japanese tea ceremony *chanoyu*. *Hsiang p'ien* are flower teas, *Ch'ing ch'a* are green, unfermented teas
ch'a hao t'ai	literally, a 'directory'
ch'a shu	the art of tea, adopted later by the Japanese in their tea ceremony. The *ch'a* god is Lu Yu and his

	image can be seen on banners outside teahouses throughout Chung Kuo
chan shih	a 'fighter', here denoting a *tong* soldier
chang	ten *ch'i*, thus about 12 feet (Western)
Chang-e	the goddess of the Moon, and younger sister of the Spirit of the Waters. The moon represents the very essence of the female principle, *Yin*, in opposition to the Sun, which is *Yang*. Legend has it that Chang-e stole the elixir of immortality from her husband, the great archer Shen I, then fled to the Moon for safety, where she was transformed into a toad, which, so it is said, can still be seen against the whiteness of the moon's surface
chang shan	literally 'long dress', which fastens to the right. Worn by both sexes. The woman's version is a fitted, calf-length dress similar to the *chi pao*. A south China fashion, it is also known as a *cheung sam*
chao tai hui	an 'entertainment', usually, within *Chung Kuo*, of an expensive and sophisticated kind
chen yen	true words; the Chinese equivalent of a mantra
ch'eng	The word means both 'City' and 'Wall'
Ch'eng Ou Chou	City Europe
Ch'eng Hsiang	'Chancellor', a post first established in the Ch'in court more than two thousand years ago
ch'i	a Chinese 'foot'; approximately 14.4 inches
ch'i	'inner strength'; one of the two fundamental 'entities' from which everything is composed. Li is the 'form' or 'law', or (to cite Joseph Needham) the 'principle of organization' behind things, whereas *ch'i* is the 'matter-energy' or 'spirit' within material things, equating loosely to the *Pneuma* of the Greeks and the *prana* of the ancient Hindus. As the sage Chu Hsi (AD 1130–1200) said, 'The li is the *Tao* that pertains to "what is above shapes" and is the source from which all things are produced. The *ch'i* is the material [literally instrument] that pertains to "what is within shapes", and is the means whereby things are produced... Throughout the universe there is no *ch'i* without li. Or li without *ch'i*.'
chi ch'i	common workers, but used here mainly to denote the ant-like employees of the Ministry of Distribution
Chia Ch'eng	Honorary Assistant to the Royal Household

chi'an	a general term for money
chiao tzu	a traditional North Chinese meal of meat-filled dumplings eaten with a hot spicy sauce
Chieh Hsia	term meaning 'Your Majesty', derived from the expression 'Below the Steps'. It was the formal way of addressing the Emperor, through his Ministers, who stood 'below the steps'
chi pao	literally 'banner gown', a one-piece gown of Manchu origin, usually sleeveless, worn by women
chih chu	a spider
ch'in	a long (120 cm), narrow, lacquered zither with a smooth top surface and sound holes beneath, seven silk strings and thirteen studs marking the harmonic positions on the strings. Early examples have been unearthed from fifth century BC tombs, but it probably evolved in the fourteenth or thirteenth century BC. It is the most honoured of Chinese instruments and has a lovely mellow tone
Chin P'ing Mei	The Golden Lotus, an erotic novel, written by an unknown scholar – possibly anonymously by the writer Wang Shih-chen – at the beginning of the seventeenth century as a continuation of the Shui Hui Chuan, or 'Warriors of the Marsh', expanding chapters 23 to 25 of the Shan Hui, which relate the story of how Wu Sung became a bandit. Extending the story beyond this point, The Golden Lotus has been accused of being China's great licentious (even, perhaps, pornographic) novel. But as C.P. Fitzgerald says, 'If this book is indecent in parts, it is only because, telling a story of domestic life, it leaves out nothing.' It is available in a three-volume English-language translation
ch'ing	pure
ching	literally 'mirror', here used also to denote a perfect GenSyn copy of a man. Under the Edict of Technological Control, these are limited to copies of the ruling T'ang and their closest relatives. However, mirrors were also popularly believed to have certain strange properties, one of which was to make spirits visible. Buddhist priests used special 'magic mirrors' to show believers the form into which they would be reborn. Moreover, if a man looks into one of these mirrors and fails to recognize his own face,

	it is a sign that his own death is not far off. [See also *hu hsin chung*.]
ch'ing ch'a	green, unfermented teas
Ch'ing Ming	the Festival of Brightness and Purity, when the graves are swept and offerings made to the deceased. Also known as the Festival of Tombs, it occurs at the end of the second moon and is used for the purpose of celebrating the spring, a time for rekindling the cooking fires after a three-day period in which the fires were extinguished and only cold food eaten
Chou	literally, 'State', but here used as the name of a card game based on the politics of Chung Kuo
chow mein	this, like chop suey, is neither a Chinese nor a Western dish, but a special meal created by the Chinese in North America for the Western palate. A transliteration of *chao mian* (fried noodles), it is a distant relation of the *liang mian huang* served in Suchow
ch'u	the west
chun hua	literally, 'Spring Pictures'. These are, in fact, pornographic 'pillow books', meant for the instruction of newly-weds
ch'un tzu	an ancient Chinese term from the Warring States period, describing a certain class of noblemen, controlled by a code of chivalry and morality known as the *li*, or rites. Here the term is roughly, and sometimes ironically, translated as 'gentlemen'. The *ch'un tzu* is as much an ideal state of behaviour – as specified by Confucius in the *Analects* – as an actual class in Chung Kuo, though a degree of financial independence and a high standard of education are assumed a prerequisite
chung	a lidded ceramic serving bowl for *ch'a*
chung hsin	loyalty
E hsing hsun huan	a saying: 'Bad nature follows a cycle'
er	two
erh tzu	son
erhu	a traditional Chinese instrument
fa	punishment
fen	a unit of currency; see *yuan*. It has another meaning, that of a 'minute' of clock time, but that usage is avoided here to prevent any confusion

feng yu	a 'phoenix chair', canopied and decorated with silver birds. Coloured scarlet and gold, this is the traditional carriage for a bride as she is carried to her wedding ceremony
fu jen	'Madam', used here as opposed to *t'ai t'ai*, 'Mrs'
fu sang	the hollow mulberry tree; according to ancient Chinese cosmology this tree stands where the sun rises and is the dwelling place of rulers. *Sang* (mulberry), however, has the same sound as *sang* (sorrow) in Chinese
Han	term used by the Chinese to describe their own race, the 'black-haired people', dating back to the Han dynasty (210 BC–AD 220). It is estimated that some ninety-four per cent of modern China's population are Han racially
Hei	literally 'black'. The Chinese pictogram for this represents a man wearing war paint and tattoos. Here it refers specifically to the genetically manufactured half-men, made by GenSyn and used as riot police to quell uprisings in the lower levels of the City
ho yeh	*Nelumbo Nucifera*, or lotus, the seeds of which are used in Chinese medicine to cure insomnia
Hoi Po	the corrupt officials who dealt with the European traders in the nineteenth century, more commonly known as 'hoppos'
Hsia	a crab
hsiang p'en	flower *ch'a*
hsiao	filial piety. The character for *hsiao* is comprised of two parts, the upper part meaning 'old', the lower meaning 'son' or 'child'. This dutiful submission of the young to the old is at the heart of Confucianism and Chinese culture generally
Hsiao chieh	'Miss', or an unmarried woman. An alternative to *nu shi*
hsiao jen	'little man/men'. In the *Analects*, Book XIV, Confucius writes, 'The gentleman gets through to what is up above; the small man gets through to what is down below.' This distinction between 'gentlemen' (*ch'un tzu*) and 'little men' (*hsiao jen*), false even in Confucius's time, is no less a matter of social perspective in Chung Kuo

hsien	historically an administrative district of variable size. Here the term is used to denote a very specific administrative area, one of ten stacks – each stack composed of thirty decks. Each deck is a hexagonal living unit of ten levels, two li, or approximately one kilometre, in diameter. A stack can be imagined as one honeycomb in the great hive that is the City. Each hsien of the city elects one Representative to sit in the House at Weimar
Hsien Ling	Chief Magistrate, in charge of a Hsien. In Chung Kuo these officials are the T'ang's representatives and law enforcers for the individual hsien. In times of peace each hsien would also elect one Representative to sit in the House at Weimar
hsueh pai	'snow white', a derogatory term here for Hung Mao women
Hu pu	the T'ang's Finance Ministry
hu hsin chung	see ching, re Buddhist magic mirrors, for which this was the name. The power of such mirrors was said to protect the owner from evil. It was also said that one might see the secrets of futurity in such a mirror. See the chapter 'Mirrors' in The Broken Wheel for further information
hu t'ieh	a butterfly. Anyone wishing to follow up on this tale of Chuang Tzu's might look to the sage's writings and specifically the chapter 'Discussion on Making All Things Equal'
hua pen	literally 'story roots', these were précis guidebooks used by the street-corner storytellers in China for the past two thousand years. The main events of the story were written down in the hua pen for the benefit of those storytellers who had not yet mastered their art. During the Yuan or Mongol dynasty (AD 1280–1368) these hua pen developed into plays, and, later on – during the Ming dynasty (AD 1368–1644) – into the form of popular novels, of which the Shui Hu Chuan, or 'Outlaws of the Marsh', remains one of the most popular. Any reader interested in following this up might purchase Pearl Buck's translation, rendered as All Men Are Brothers and first published in 1933
Huang Ti	originally Huang Ti was the last of the 'Three Sovereigns' and the first of the 'Five Emperors' of ancient Chinese tradition. Huang Ti, the Yellow

Emperor, was the earliest ruler recognized by the historian Ssu-ma Ch'ien (136–85 BC) in his great historical work, the *Shih Chi*. Traditionally, all subsequent rulers (and would-be rulers) of China have claimed descent from the Yellow Emperor, the 'Son of Heaven' himself, who first brought civilization to the black-haired people. His name is now synonymous with the term 'emperor'

hun — the higher soul or 'spirit soul', which, the Chinese believe, ascends to Heaven at death, joins Shang Ti, the Supreme Ancestor, and lives in his court for ever more. The *hun* is believed to come into existence at the moment of conception (see also *p'o*)

hun tun — 'the Chou believed that Heaven and Earth were once inextricably mixed together in a state of undifferentiated chaos, like a chicken's egg. Hun Tun they called that state' (*The Broken Wheel*, Chapter 37). It is also the name of a meal of tiny sack-like dumplings

Hung Lou Meng — *The Dream of Red Mansions*, also known as *The Story of the Stone*, a lengthy novel written in the middle of the eighteenth century. Like the *Chin Ping Mei*, it deals with the affairs of a single Chinese family. According to experts the first eighty chapters are the work of Ts'ao Hsueh-ch'in, and the last forty belong to Kao Ou. It is, without doubt, the masterpiece of Chinese literature, and is available from Penguin in the UK in a five-volume edition

Hung Mao — literally 'redheads', the name the Chinese gave to the Dutch (and later English) seafarers who attempted to trade with China in the seventeenth century. Because of the piratical nature of their endeavours (which often meant plundering Chinese shipping and ports) the name continues to retain connotations of piracy

Hung Mun — the Secret Societies or, more specifically, the Triads

huo jen — literally, 'fire men'

I Lung — the 'First Dragon', Senior Minister and Great Lord of the 'Ministry', also known as 'the Thousand Eyes'

jou tung wu — literally 'meat animal': 'It was a huge mountain of flesh, a hundred *ch'i* to a side and almost twenty *ch'i* in height. Along one side of it, like the teats of a giant pig, three dozen heads jutted from the flesh,

	long, eyeless snouts with shovel jaws that snuffled and gobbled in the conveyor-belt trough...'
kai t'ou	a thin cloth of red and gold that veils a new bride's face. Worn by the Ch'ing empresses for almost three centuries
kan pei!	'good health!' or 'cheers!' – a drinking toast
kang	the Chinese hearth, serving also as oven and, in the cold of winter, as a sleeping platform
k'ang hsi	a Ch'ing (or Manchu) emperor whose long reign (AD 1662–1722) is considered a golden age for the art of porcelain-making. The lavender-glazed bowl in 'The Sound Of Jade' is, however, not kang-hsi but Chun chou ware from the Sung period (960–1127) and considered amongst the most beautiful (and rare) wares in Chinese pottery
kao liang	a strong Chinese liquor
Ko Ming	'revolutionary'. The Tien Ming is the Mandate of Heaven, supposedly handed down from Shang Ti, the Supreme Ancestor, to his earthly counterpart, the Emperor (Huang Ti). This Mandate could be enjoyed only so long as the Emperor was worthy of it, and rebellion against a tyrant – who broke the Mandate through his lack of justice, benevolence and sincerity – was deemed not criminal but a rightful expression of Heaven's anger
k'ou t'ou	the fifth stage of respect, according to the 'Book of Ceremonies', involves kneeling and striking the head against the floor. This ritual has become more commonly known in the West as kowtow
ku li	'bitter strength'. These two words, used to describe the condition of farm labourers who, after severe droughts or catastrophic floods, moved off their land and into the towns to look for work of any kind – however hard and onerous – spawned the word 'coolie' by which the West more commonly knows the Chinese labourer. Such men were described as 'men of bitter strength', or simply 'ku li'
Kuan Hua	Mandarin, the language spoken in mainland China. Also known as kuo yu and pai hua
Kuan Yin	the Goddess of Mercy. Originally the Buddhist male bodhisattva, Avalokitsevara (translated into Han as 'He who listens to the sounds of the world', or 'Kuan Yin'), the Han mistook the well-developed breasts of

the saint for a woman's and, since the ninth century, have worshipped Kuan Yin as such. Effigies of Kuan Yin will show her usually as the Eastern Madonna, cradling a child in her arms. She is also sometimes seen as the wife of *Kuan Kung*, the Chinese God of War

Kuei Chuan	'Running Dog', here the name of a Triad
kuo yu	Mandarin, the language spoken in most of Mainland China. Also rendered here as *kuan hua* and *pai hua*
kwai	an abbreviation of *kwai tao*, a 'sharp knife' or 'fast knife'. It can also mean to be sharp or fast (as a knife). An associated meaning is that of a 'clod' or 'lump of earth'. Here it is used to denote a class of fighters from below the Net, whose ability and self-discipline separate them from the usual run of hired knives
Lan Tian	'Blue Sky'
Lang	a covered walkway
lao chu	singsong girls, slightly more respectable than the common *men hu*
lao jen	'old man' (also *weng*); used normally as a term of respect
lao kuan	a 'Great Official', often used ironically
lao shih	term that denotes a genuine and straightforward man – bluff and honest
lao wai	an outsider
li	a Chinese 'mile', approximating to half a kilometre or one third of a mile. Until 1949, when metric measures were adopted in China, the *li* could vary from place to place
Li	'propriety'. See the *Li Ching* or 'Book Of Rites' for the fullest definition
Li Ching	'The Book Of Rites', one of the five ancient classics
liang	a Chinese ounce of roughly 32gm. Sixteen *liang* form a *catty*
liu k'ou	the seventh stage of respect, according to the 'Book of Ceremonies'. Two stages above the more familiarly known 'k'ou t'ou' (kowtow) it involves kneeling and striking the forehead three times against the floor, rising to one's feet again, then kneeling and repeating the prostration with three touches of the forehead to the ground. Only the *san*

	kuei chiu k'ou – involving three prostrations – was more elaborate and was reserved for Heaven and its son, the Emperor (see also *san k'ou*)
liumang	punks
lu nan jen	literally 'oven man', title of the official who is responsible for cremating all of the dead bodies
lueh	'that invaluable quality of producing a piece of art casually, almost uncaringly'
lung t'ing	'dragon pavilions', small sedan chairs carried by servants and containing a pile of dowry gifts
Luoshu	the Chinese legend relates that in ancient times a turtle crawled from a river in Luoshu province, the patterns on its shell forming a three by three grid of numeric pictograms, the numbers of which – both down and across – equalled the same total of fifteen. Since the time of the Shang (three thousand-plus years ago) tortoise shells were used in divination, and the Luoshu diagram is considered magic and is often used as a charm for easing childbirth
ma kua	a waist-length ceremonial jacket
mah jong	whilst, in its modern form, the 'game of the four winds' was introduced towards the end of the nineteenth century to Westerners trading in the thriving city of Shanghai, it was developed from a card game that existed as long ago as AD 960. Using 144 tiles, it is generally played by four players. The tiles have numbers and also suits – winds, dragons, bamboos and circles
mao	a unit of currency. See *yuan*
mao tai	a strong, sorghum-based liquor
mei fa tzu	common saying, 'It is fate!'
mei hua	'plum blossom'
mei mei	sister
mei yu jen wen	'subhumans'. Used in *Chung Kuo* by those in the City's uppermost levels to denote anyone living in the lower hundred
men hu	literally, 'the one standing in the door'. The most common (and cheapest) of prostitutes
min	literally 'the people'; used (as here) by the Minor Families in a pejorative sense, as an equivalent to 'plebeian'

Ming	the dynasty that ruled China from 1368 to 1644. Literally, the name means 'Bright' or 'Clear' or 'Brilliant'. It carries connotations of cleansing
mou	a Chinese 'acre' of approximately 7,260 square feet. There are roughly six *mou* to a Western acre, and a 10,000-*mou* field would approximate to 1,666 acres, or just over two and a half square miles
Mu Ch'in	'Mother', a general term commonly addressed to any older woman
mui tsai	rendered in Cantonese as 'mooi-jai'. Colloquially, it means either 'little sister' or 'slave girl', though generally, as here, the latter. Other Mandarin terms used for the same status are *pei-nu* and *yatou*. Technically, guardianship of the girl involved is legally signed over in return for money
nan jen	common term for 'Man'
Ni Hao?	'How are you?'
niao	literally 'bird', but here, as often, it is used euphemistically as a term for the penis, often as an expletive
nu er	daughter
nu shi	an unmarried woman, a term equating to 'Miss'
Pa shi yi	literally 'Eighty-One', here referring specifically to the Central Council of the New Confucian officialdom
pai nan jen	literally 'white man'
pai pi	'hundred pens', term used for the artificial reality experiments renamed 'Shells' by Ben Shepherd
pan chang	supervisor
pao yun	a 'jewelled cloud' *ch'a*
pau	a simple long garment worn by men
pau shuai ch'i	the technical scientific term for 'half-life'
pi-p'a	a four-stringed lute used in traditional Chinese music
Pien Hua!	Change!
p'ing	an apple, symbol of peace
ping	the east
Ping Fa	Sun Tzu's *The Art of War*, written over two thousand years ago. The best English translation is probably Samuel B. Griffith's 1963 edition. It was a book Chairman Mao frequently referred to

Ping Tiao	levelling. To bring down or make flat. Here, in Chung Kuo, it is also a terrorist organization.
p'o	The 'animal soul' which, at death, remains in the tomb with the corpse and takes its nourishment from the grave offerings. The *p'o* decays with the corpse, sinking down into the underworld (beneath the Yellow Springs) where – as a shadow – it continues an existence of a kind. The *p'o* is believed to come into existence at the moment of birth (see also *hun*)
sam fu	an upper garment (part shirt, part jacket) worn originally by both males and females, in imitation of Manchu styles; later on a wide-sleeved, calf-length version was worn by women alone
san	three
San chang	the three palaces
san kuei chiu k'ou	the eighth and final stage of respect, according to the 'Book of Ceremonies', it involves kneeling three times, each time striking the forehead three times against the ground before rising from one's knees (in *k'ou t'ou* one strikes the forehead but once). This most elaborate form of ritual was reserved for Heaven and its son, the Emperor. See also *liu k'ou*
san k'ou	abbreviated form of *san kuei chiu k'ou*
San Kuo Yan Yi	*The Romance of the Three Kingdoms*, also known as the *San Kuo Chih Yen I*. China's great historical novel, running to 120 chapters, it covers the period from AD 168 to 265. Written by Lo Kuan-chung in the early Ming dynasty, its heroes, Liu Pei, Kuan Chung and Chang Fei, together with its villain, Ts'ao Ts'ao, are all historical personages. It is still one of the most popular stories in modern China
sao mu	the 'Feast of the Dead'
shang	the south
shan shui	the literal meaning is 'mountains and water', but the term is normally associated with a style of landscape painting that depicts rugged mountain scenery with river valleys in the foreground. It is a highly popular form, first established in the T'ang dynasty, back in the seventh to ninth centuries AD
shao lin	specially trained assassins, named after the monks of the *shao lin* monastery

shao nai nai	literally, 'little grandmother'. A young girl who has been given the responsibility of looking after her siblings
she t'ou	a 'tongue' or taster, whose task is to safeguard his master from poisoning
shen chung	'caution'
shen mu	'she who stands in the door': a common prostitute
shen nu	'god girls': superior prostitutes
shen t'se	special elite force, named after the 'palace armies' of the late T'ang dynasty
Shih	'Master'. Here used as a term of respect somewhat equivalent to our use of 'Mister'. The term was originally used for the lowest level of civil servants, to distinguish them socially from the run-of-the-mill 'Misters' (*hsian sheng*) below them and the gentlemen (*ch'un tzu*) above
shou hsing	a peach brandy
Shui Hu Chuan	*Outlaws of the Marsh*, a long historical novel attributed to Lo Kuan-chung but re-cast in the early sixteenth century by 'Shih Nai-an', a scholar. Set in the eleventh century, it is a saga of bandits, warlords and heroes. Written in pure *pai hua* – colloquial Chinese – it is the tale of how its heroes became bandits. Its revolutionary nature made it deeply unpopular with both the Ming and Manchu dynasties, but it remains one of the most popular adventures among the Chinese populace
siang chi	Chinese chess, a very different game from its Western counterpart
Ta	'Beat', here a heavily amplified form of Chinese folk music, popular amongst the young
ta lien	an elaborate girdle pouch
Ta Ssu Nung	the Superintendency of Agriculture
tai	literally 'pockets' but here denoting Representatives in the House at Weimar. 'Owned' financially by the Seven, historically such *tai* have served a double function in the House, counterbalancing the strong mercantile tendencies of the House and serving as a conduit for the views of the Seven. Traditionally they had been elderly, well-respected men, but more recently their replacements were young, brash and

	very corrupt, more like the hoppoes of the Opium Wars period
t'ai chi	the Original, or One, from which the duality of all things (*yin* and *yang*) developed, according to Chinese cosmology. We generally associate the *t'ai chi* with the Taoist symbol, that swirling circle of dark and light supposedly representing an egg (perhaps the *Hun Tun*), the yolk and the white differentiated
tai hsiao	a white wool flower, worn in the hair
Tai Huo	'Great Fire'
T'ai Shan	Mount T'ai, the highest and most sacred of China's mountains, located in Shantung province. A stone pathway of 6,293 steps leads to the summit and for thousands of years the ruling emperor has made ritual sacrifices at its foot, accompanied by his full retinue, presenting evidence of his virtue. T'ai Shan is one of the five Taoist holy mountains, and symbolizes the very centre of China. It is the mountain of the sun, symbolizing the bright male force (*yang*). 'As safe as T'ai Shan' is a popular saying, denoting the ultimate in solidity and certainty
Tai Shih Lung	Court Astrologer, a title that goes back to the Han dynasty
T'ang	literally, 'beautiful and imposing'. It is the title chosen by the Seven, who were originally the chief advisors to Tsao Ch'un, the tyrant. Since overthrowing Tsao Ch'un, it has effectively had the meaning of 'emperor'
Ta Ts'in	the Chinese name for the Roman Empire. They also knew Rome as Li Chien and as 'the land West of the Sea'. The Romans themselves they termed the 'Big Ts'in' – the Ts'in being the name the Chinese gave themselves during the Ts'in dynasty (AD 265–316)
te	'spiritual power', 'true virtue' or 'virtuality', defined by Alan Watts as 'the realization or expression of the Tao in actual living'
t'e an tsan	'innocent westerners'. For 'innocent' perhaps read naive
ti tsu	a bamboo flute, used both as a solo instrument and as part of an ensemble, playing traditional Chinese music

ti yu	the 'earth prison' or underworld of Chinese legend. There are ten main Chinese Hells, the first being the courtroom in which the sinner is sentenced and the last being that place where they are reborn as human beings. In between are a vast number of sub-Hells, each with its own Judge and staff of cruel warders. In Hell, it is always dark, with no differentiation between night and day
Tian	'Heaven', also, 'the dome of the sky'
tian-fang	literally 'to fill the place of the dead wife'; used to signify the upgrading of a concubine to the more respectable position of wife
tiao tuo	bracelets of gold and jade
T'ieh Lo-han	'Iron Goddess of Mercy', a ch'a
T'ieh Pi Pu Kai	literally, 'the iron pen changes not', this is the final phrase used at the end of all Chinese government proclamations for the last three thousand years
ting	an open-sided pavilion in a Chinese garden. Designed as a focal point in a garden, it is said to symbolize man's essential place in the natural order of things
T'ing Wei	the Superintendency of Trials, an institution that dates back to the T'ang dynasty. See Book Eight, *The White Mountain*, for an instance of how this department of government – responsible for black propaganda – functions
T'o	'camel-backed', a Chinese term for 'hunch-backed'
tong	a gang. In China and Europe these are usually smaller and thus subsidiary to the Triads, but in North America the term has generally taken the place of Triad
tou chi	Glycine Max, or the black soybean, used in Chinese herbal medicine to cure insomnia
Tsai Chien!	'Until we meet again!'
Tsou Tsai Hei	'the Walker in the Darkness'
tsu	the north
tsu kuo	the motherland
ts'un	a Chinese 'inch' of approximately 1.4 Western inches. Ten ts'un form one ch'i
Tu	Earth
tzu	'Elder Sister'

wan wu	literally 'the ten thousand things'; used generally to include everything in creation, or, as the Chinese say, 'all things in Heaven and Earth'
Wei	Commandant of Security
wei chi	'the surrounding game', known more commonly in the West by its Japanese name of Go. It is said that the game was invented by the legendary Chinese Emperor Yao in the year 2350 BC to train the mind of his son, Tan Chu, and teach him to think like an emperor
wen ming	a term used to denote civilization, or written culture
wen ren	the scholar-artist; very much an ideal state, striven for by all creative Chinese
weng	'Old man'. Usually a term of respect
Wu	a diviner; traditionally, these were 'mediums' who claimed to have special psychic powers. *Wu* could be either male or female
Wu	'non-being'. As Lao Tzu says: 'Once the block is carved, there are names.' But the Tao is unnameable (*wu-ming*) and before Being (*yu*) is Non-Being (*wu*). Not to have existence, or form, or a name, that is *wu*
Wu ching	the 'Five Classics' studied by all Confucian scholars, comprising the *Shu Ching* (Book of History), the *Shih Ching* (Book of Songs), the *I Ching* (Book of Changes), the *Li Ching* (Book of Rites, actually three books in all), and the *Ch'un Chui* (The Spring and Autumn Annals of the State of Lu)
wu fu	the five gods of good luck
wu tu	the 'five noxious creatures' – which are toad, scorpion, snake, centipede and gecko (wall lizard)
Wushu	the Chinese word for Martial Arts. It refers to any of several hundred schools. *Kung fu* is a school within this, meaning 'skill that transcends mere surface beauty'
wuwei	non-action, an old Taoist concept. It means keeping harmony with the flow of things – doing nothing to break the flow
ya	homosexual. Sometimes the term 'a yellow eel' is used
yamen	the official building in a Chinese community
yang	the 'male principle' of Chinese cosmology, which, with its complementary opposite, the female *yin*,

	forms the *t'ai ch'i*, derived from the Primeval One. From the union of *yin* and *yang* arise the 'five elements' (water, fire, earth, metal, wood) from which the 'ten thousand things' (the *wan wu*) are generated. Yang signifies Heaven and the South, the Sun and Warmth, Light, Vigor, Maleness, Penetration, odd numbers and the Dragon. Mountains are *yang*
yang kuei tzu	Chinese name for foreigners, 'Ocean Devils'. It is also synonymous with 'Barbarians'
yang mei ping	'willow plum sickness', the Chinese term for syphilis, provides an apt description of the male sexual organ in the extreme of this sickness
yi	the number one
yin	the 'female principle' of Chinese cosmology (see *yang*). Yin signifies Earth and the North, the Moon and Cold, Darkness, Quiescence, Femaleness, Absorption, even numbers and the Tiger. The *yin* lies in the shadow of the mountain
yin mao	pubic hair
Ying kuo	English, the language
ying tao	'baby peach', a term of endearment here
ying tzu	'shadows' – trained specialists of various kinds, contracted out to gangland bosses
yu	literally 'fish', but, because of its phonetic equivalence to the word for 'abundance', the fish symbolizes wealth. Yet there is also a saying that when the fish swim upriver it is a portent of social unrest and rebellion
yu ko	a 'Jade Barge', here a type of luxury sedan
Yu Kung	'Foolish Old Man!'
yu ya	deep elegance
yuan	the basic currency of Chung Kuo (and modern-day China). Colloquially (though not here) it can also be termed *kuai* – 'piece' or 'lump'. Ten *mao* (or, formally, *jiao*) make up one *yuan*, while 100 *fen* (or 'cents') comprise one *yuan*
yueh ch'in	a Chinese dulcimer, one of the principal instruments of the Chinese orchestra
Ywe Lung	literally 'The Moon Dragon', the wheel of seven dragons that is the symbol of the ruling Seven throughout Chung Kuo: 'At its centre the snouts

of the regal beasts met, forming a rose-like hub,
huge rubies burning fiercely in each eye. Their
lithe, powerful bodies curved outward like the
spokes of a giant wheel while at the edge their tails
were intertwined to form the rim.' (Chapter 29 of
The Middle Kingdom)

CHUNG KUO

AUTHOR'S NOTE AND ACKNOWLEDGMENTS

The translation of Li Ho's 'On The Frontier' is by A. C. Graham from his excellent *Poems Of The Late T'ang*, published by Penguin Books, London, 1965, and used with their kind permission.

The translation of Li Shangyin's 'Fallen Flowers' is by Tao Jie and is taken from *300 T'ang Poems, A New Translation*, Commercial Press, Hong Kong. The passage from *On Protracted War* is from Mao Tse-tung's *Selected Works*, II, Peking Press.

The passages quoted from Book One [XI] and [XXXVII] of Lao Tzu's *Tao Te Ching* are from the D. C. Lau translation, published by Penguin Books, London, 1963, and used with their kind permission. The quotation from Confucius' *The Analects* [Book XII] is once again from a D. C. Lau translation, published by Penguin Books, 1979, and used with their permission.

The passage from Sun Tzu's classic *The Art of War* is from the Samuel B. Griffith translation, published by Oxford University Press, 1963.

Thanks must go to the following for their help. To my editors – Nick Sayers, Brian DeFiore, John Pearce and Alyssa Diamond – for their sheer niceness and (of course) for their continuing enthusiasm, and to Carolyn Caughey, fan turned editor, for seeing where to cut the cake.

To Mike Cobley, thanks not merely for the encouragement but for Advanced Cheerfulness in the face of Adversity. May both your patience and your talent be rewarded. And to Andy Sawyer, for a thoughtful reading of the text. I hope I can reciprocate one of these days.

To my first-line critic and safety-net, the stalwart Brian Griffin, may I say yet again how much it's all appreciated. The notes you've done will make a fine book one day!

To family and friends – particularly to my girls, Susan, Jessica, Amy, Georgia and Francesca – go the usual thanks in the face of my at times monomaniacal neglect. And especial thanks to everyone I've met on my travels – in Leeds, Manchester, Oxford, Cambridge, Southampton, Brighton, Canterbury, Dublin and Glasgow. To all... *Slainte Mhath!*

David Wingrove

Spring 1991, Autumn 2013